WISHFUL THINKING

"*Kethili-cha,*" Molly said quietly, not fully understanding why.

Wade stared at her like she had unexpectedly removed the top of her head and poured her coffee inside. "*Kethili-anh.*"

Electricity flowed between them. The fine hairs on her arms and neck stood on end. Every pore in her body tingled with anticipation, with power. A point had been reached, she understood, a turning point from which there would be no going back.

Dump your coffee on the floor, Wade.

His lips curled in a faint, uncertain smile. He caught her eye and gave the slightest shrug, raising his eyebrow just a fraction of an inch.

Then he leaned forward, took his mug in his right hand, held it out, poured the coffee. It hit the ground, splashed, puddled.

"God," Wade said, blushing. "What a klutz, huh? Sorry. I didn't get you, did I?"

"Don't worry about it, Wade," she said. She kept her voice calm, but inside her emotions raced.

She had made him do that. Ordered him to, with her mind. And he had done it.

She *controlled* him.

It felt right, somehow. Natural. The way it should be, should always have been.

She had been waiting for this, she realized. Waiting for a very, very, very long time . . .

RIVER
RUNS RED

JEFFREY J.
MARIOTTE

JOVE BOOKS, NEW YORK

THE BERKLEY PUBLISHING GROUP
Published by the Penguin Group
Penguin Group (USA) Inc.
375 Hudson Street, New York, New York 10014, USA

Penguin Group (Canada), 90 Eglinton Avenue East, Suite 700, Toronto, Ontario M4P 2Y3, Canada
(a division of Pearson Penguin Canada Inc.)
Penguin Books Ltd., 80 Strand, London WC2R 0RL, England
Penguin Group Ireland, 25 St. Stephen's Green, Dublin 2, Ireland (a division of Penguin Books Ltd.)
Penguin Group (Australia), 250 Camberwell Road, Camberwell, Victoria 3124, Australia
(a division of Pearson Australia Group Pty. Ltd.)
Penguin Books India Pvt. Ltd., 11 Community Centre, Panchsheel Park, New Delhi—110 017, India
Penguin Group (NZ), 67 Apollo Drive, Rosedale, North Shore 0632, New Zealand
(a division of Pearson New Zealand Ltd.)
Penguin Books (South Africa) (Pty.) Ltd., 24 Sturdee Avenue, Rosebank, Johannesburg 2196, South Africa

Penguin Books Ltd., Registered Offices: 80 Strand, London WC2R 0RL, England

RIVER RUNS RED

A Jove Book / published by arrangement with the author

PRINTING HISTORY
Jove mass-market edition / October 2008

Copyright © 2008 by Jeffrey J. Mariotte.
Text design by Laura K. Corless.

ISBN: 978-0-515-14477-2

JOVE®
Jove Books are published by The Berkley Publishing Group,
a division of Penguin Group (USA) Inc.,
375 Hudson Street, New York, New York 10014.
JOVE® is a registered trademark of Penguin Group (USA) Inc.
The "J" design is a trademark belonging to Penguin Group (USA) Inc.

PRINTED IN THE UNITED STATES OF AMERICA

10   9   8   7   6   5   4   3   2   1

For Maryelizabeth, who took me to Texas

ACKNOWLEDGMENTS

For their contributions to my understanding of El Paso and west Texas, I would like to thank Cindy Chapman, Charles Bowden, Elmer Kelton, Clay Reynolds, the *El Paso Times*, the *Desert Candle*, the El Paso Museum of History, the Hueco Tanks State Historic Site, the Museum and Missile Park at White Sands Missile Range, and many more, particularly the good residents of El Paso themselves. Courageous reporters whose personal accounts of Iraq proved extremely helpful include (but are by no means limited to) Jill Carroll and Richard Engel. To these people and others, including Howard Morhaim, Katie Menick, and Ginjer Buchanan, I offer my greatest appreciation.

The past is never dead; it's not even past.

WILLIAM FAULKNER, *REQUIEM FOR A NUN*

None of them would ever know when it all began. Human memory doesn't reach that far back. Recorded history has its limits. Time is a veil not easily pierced.

Where it began? That's another story. It began on the river, always on the river. This, everyone could see. Rivers take the long view, and the signs they carve into the earth survive the ages.

Every ripple, every riffle, every eddy, each rush of wild whitewater over rocks or between towering limestone walls, every still-seeming pool hiding quick currents—all these aspects of the river exist in the now but hold the memory of eons gone by, and at night the river whispers or roars or babbles its secret memories to those who know how to listen.

The river is at fault, yet blameless. The river doesn't choose sides or hold grudges.

But the river remembers. . . .

PART ONE

EL PASO

The river's tent is broken; the last fingers of leaf
Clutch and sink into the wet bank.

> T. S. ELIOT, "THE WASTE LAND"

And listen again to its sounds; get far enough away so that the noise of falling tons of water does not stun the ears, and hear how much is going on underneath—a whole symphony of smaller sounds, hiss and splash and gurgle, the small talk of side channels, the whisper of blown and scattered spray gathering itself and beginning to flow again, secret and irresistible, among the wet rocks.

> WALLACE STEGNER, "OVERTURE,"
> IN *THE SOUND OF MOUNTAIN WATER*

Lawrence Ingersoll intended to take the night off from death.

The fact that it didn't turn out that way was no fault of his. He got caught up in events. Best laid plans and all that. A man who took his gaming seriously, he might have said that he played the cards he was dealt. But when the red king calls, somebody has to answer.

All day long, bitterly cold rain had fallen from skies as gray as a stretch of old road; after the November evening enveloped the San Juans, it turned into a gentle, persistent snowfall. Ingersoll had no appointments, and no client would make the trip up the mountain—not until the snowplows went through—so he looked forward to a rare quiet night. In his lodge-style home outside Creede, he stirred the embers of a fire with an iron poker, jabbing the poker into a piñon log and releasing swirling nebulae of sparks that wafted up the chimney and away. He liked the warmth against his nose and cheeks, enjoyed watching the orange clouds he agitated, and when his phone made an obnoxious chirping noise that could in no way be described as ringing, he swore, closed the wire mesh curtain, and set the poker down on the stone hearth.

The bearskin rug he crossed on his way to the phone had once been a mature black bear; Ingersoll had bought it from the neighbor who had killed it a couple of miles from the house. Life was that way in the mountains; more to the point, so was death.

Ingersoll cared about the natural world. He chose to live in rural Colorado, far from big cities, because he wanted to feel connected to nature, but he was no stranger to death and he had no problem with those who hunted for sport. His occult studies taught him that death was a transition, not an ending.

Although he could no more know if wild creatures had an after-life than he could know their hearts and minds while they lived, he had no reason to think they didn't. He was, further-more, pretty sure they didn't spend their lives afraid of death, as so many people did.

But then, most people didn't share his profound understand-ing of it. Death was as much a part of Ingersoll's daily life (or nightly, since he met most of his clients after dark) as numbers were a part of an accountant's or whips a dominatrix's. He made his living—a very comfortable one—communicating with the dead on behalf of the living. When not working, he was usually in his study reading rare, often forbidden texts, try-ing to increase his understanding of the various worlds outside the one most people knew, which he had always referred to as the straight world.

He had his fears, of course, as did everyone. Ingersoll's in-cluded high ledges and cliffs (roof edges and the like), public speaking, incapacitating injury, and the idea that restaurant chefs might spit disease-ridden saliva into his food.

Not death, though. Never that.

". . . the seventeenth day of apparent captivity in Iraq for CNN reporter Wade Scheiner," his plasma TV blared. "Last seen in a video released more than a week ago, bruised and gaunt but—"

Ingersoll snatched the remote off the arm of a sofa, punched MUTE, then grabbed up the phone.

"Ingersoll," he said. A bad habit, he knew, left over from corporate days when he and the other guys in his technical writing office had pretended that first names didn't exist.

"Lawrence." A female voice, throaty and velvet, with a Chi-nese accent evident in the single word.

"Millicent," he answered. Millicent Wong of Hong Kong, whose identity, so like a child's rhyme, disguised the fact that she was a mature, graceful, accomplished woman, far from childlike in every way but physical appearance. "What a plea-sure to hear from you."

"You won't think so in a moment, Lawrence."

"Something's wrong?" He had already noticed an unfamil-iar tightness in her voice. She was worried. "What is it?"

"I'm not certain," she said. "There's a problem of some

kind. It's disrupting the ley lines. I've been trying to perform a reading and nothing's working as it should. I am very concerned, Lawrence. Frightened, a little."

"I'm no expert at that sort of thing, Millicent," Ingersoll said. Ley lines directed mystical energies around the world, and to points beyond, worlds beyond. Like electricity or the Internet, he could use them but that didn't mean he could fix them when they were broken. "Why call me?"

"As well as I can determine from here, you're the nearest of my acquaintances, physically, to the disruption's focal point. I hoped that perhaps you could learn something from there."

His mind buzzing with possibilities, Ingersoll quickly agreed. As he had warned her, this sort of thing was far from his realm of expertise. He considered himself a novice compared to an old hand like her, a mere dabbler in the petrifyingly deep waters of the occult. No way to learn like on-the-job training, though. Anything that scared Millicent had to be significant, and therefore something from which he might gain wisdom.

On the other hand, if Millicent, with her wealth of experience, was afraid, it had to be pretty damn scary. Treading carefully would be a good idea.

He exchanged a few more terse words with her—the usual *how're you doing, what's new, how about them Broncos* pleasantries didn't seem appropriate—and ended the call, anxious to get started. A cup of tea he had brewed earlier was abandoned in the living room along with the muted TV.

Ingersoll's study was the sort of "masculine" room that model home designers built and magazine editors loved. The lifeless, unblinking eyes of mounted elk and bobcat heads gazed down at his rough-hewn wooden desk from high on knotty pine walls. Indian rugs covered part of the polished plank floor. Other artifacts, mostly mystical objects he had collected around the world, crowded onto bookshelves and a wide burl coffee table set in front of a pair of low-slung brown leather chairs. The bookshelves would have looked wrong in a magazine layout, because they were stuffed with books, mostly old, thick, bound in leather, and well used.

He used the study to sit and read when he needed a large desk surface, and he interviewed prospective clients there, but it was primarily a showplace. For his real work, he left the study through a doorway almost hidden between two of the massive bookcases. As a private joke, he called the next room his inner sanctum, aware of its pretentiousness and also of the old radio show with the same name.

The room itself was no place for jokes. The study was meant to impress, while the inner sanctum was purely functional. Its hardwood floor was painted a dull battleship gray. Dark purple curtains draped every wall, to muffle sound. The room was wired for electricity, but Ingersoll preferred to light the candles scattered on top of antique wooden tables and chests. He lit one now, placing it on a small table in the exact center of the room, then pulled up a shabby but comfortable chair and sat down.

Gazing into the nascent flame, he worked on blanking everything else from his mind—the cup of tea that had seemed so important a short time before, the television news, the snow outside, the checks for his mortgage and the payment on the Escalade that had to be mailed before the end of the week, even the greasy scent of the thick black candle. Mentally taking each topic and closing it into a black box, he folded down the flaps and stacked those boxes neatly on a shelf. His greatest gift was the ability to slip quickly and easily into a trance state, in which he could commune with any of several spirit guides with whom he had developed relationships.

Ingersoll stroked his mustache a couple of times, the few white whiskers thrusting through the darker ones notable for a little extra wiriness. He had been forty pounds heavier when he worked in the tech industry (and living in a second-floor apartment in Cupertino, California, overlooking a sea of carports, instead of a six-bedroom lodge with its own sauna and a stunning view of Uncompahgre Peak). He had cultivated a new image to meet the expectations his clients brought with them: a drooping, Fu Manchu–style mustache, a thick head of curly hair that required a curling iron to get just right, a sturdy but not intimidating physique. He wore dark pants and a fitted dark shirt or V-neck sweater with a couple of esoteric-looking but purely decorative medallions on thin gold chains around his neck. He had patterned the look, basically, on Dr. Strange from the Marvel comic books—although he didn't think he could pull off the voluminous red cloak—and once he adopted it, the difference in attitude on the part of potential clients had persuaded him that he had nailed it.

More meaningful than any physical changes, though, was the change in how he felt about what he did. He helped people now. In his previous career, he had written technical documents read by precisely no one. Engineers thought they already understood everything, and laypeople didn't believe they ever could. Now people left his home with deeper comprehension of their own lives and acceptance of the things they couldn't change. He had never felt so rewarded as a technical writer, not in any emotional sense.

He appreciated the rewards of his new life, his new career, both tangible and not. Better the rustle of wind in the firs than the rush of freeway traffic, the glow of stars at night than the flash and tawdry glitter of city lights. Better a sense of real satisfaction than a steady but inadequate paycheck.

Dropping his hand to his lap, Ingersoll stared into the candle's flame, which grew and flickered and reached ceilingward like a mutilated paw. He let the fire fill his vision. The silence was broken only by the hiss and spit of the candle. He willed his breathing and heartbeat to slow.

The flame was everything.

The world fell away; in its place, a universe of yellow-white light embraced him.

After several seconds of nothing but that light, he saw himself walking through an indistinct glow. He looked down on that other Lawrence Ingersoll, as if watching from a height of twenty-five or thirty feet. His dark clothing had turned to white, his hair gone as thick and snowy as Mark Twain's. He walked on cobblestones made of pure light.

He knew this way well. The cobblestone road led toward a gleaming city, its spires and minarets jabbing at a golden sky. One of his spirit guides would meet him outside its gates. He hoped it would be Alicia, which would save time. Alicia was well versed in ley lines, arcane energies, and the like; a noted spiritualist in her day, even before death she had been extremely knowledgeable about the occult.

Along the way, though, an unexpected sense of unease—bordering on panic—clutched at his chest. The road twisted where it should not have, leading toward a bridge arching over a dry, reed-choked riverbed into what looked like dense forest. Ingersoll took a few steps back, trying to return to the spot from which he had been able to see down the straight, glowing road all the way to the city, but that view was gone.

Inside the riverbed, something rattled, like the river's bones under a loose coat of skin.

The Ingersoll sitting safely in Colorado felt the other one's growing dread, but at the same time part of him remained detached. *This must,* he told himself, *be what Millicent Wong was talking about.* Something was screwing with the other worlds, near enough to the straight world to threaten it, too.

Time to pull out of the trance, before something terrible happened to the astral Ingersoll, defenseless on that road of light. As if reeling in a fish, he psychically tugged at his other self.

Instead, his physical self was yanked forward, like someone had jerked him from his chair. He flew through the ether and slammed into his astral self with enough force to make him sway unsteadily.

For the first time in his life, Ingersoll was totally inside his astral self, with no consciousness remaining behind in his inner sanctum.

And his astral self quaked with terror.

That rattling noise came from the river again, a dry, somehow covetous sound. Then a shape reared up from the riverbed, a shape Ingersoll thought he could make out until it flared into dazzling light. He blinked and threw his hands up protectively, but could still hear it coming at him. Behind his hands, his eyes burned, as if the brilliant flame were cooking them, and they ran down his cheeks like hot wax. The top of his head smoldered from the inside, as if he held a candle in his mouth.

For an instant, he saw himself sitting in his inner sanctum, through the eyes of his astral body. That wasn't supposed to be possible. The head of his physical body was thrown back, smoke wafting from beneath his hair, from empty eye sockets, from his mouth and nose and ears. His hands clutched at empty air. The desiccated rattling noise came from *him*, he realized, as the heat sapped all the moisture from his body.

The image flashed out of existence almost before it had time to register, then the heat grew even more intense and the rattling thing from the river reached him and white heat overwhelmed his consciousness. He was back in his inner sanctum just long enough to know two things: the heat radiating from his body had set the drapes on fire, and his fear of death was actually much, much stronger than he had ever realized.

2

When James Livingston Truly raised his blinds and pressed his
brow against the window of his small office on the third floor
of the CIA's New Headquarters Building, he could see a sad,
scrawny tree—a sapling eighteen months ago when he'd been
assigned this office and this posting (dead-end in every sense
of the phrase)—waving crimson leaves like an underfed street-
walker trying to draw attention to her wares with a flashy red
skirt.

Watching the bright leaves flutter in the morning breeze was
preferable to sitting at his desk, because at least by the window,
its glass cold against his palms and forehead, he was less likely
to fall asleep. If last night hadn't been the worst night of his
life, it was only because the competition for that honor was so
steep.

Around two thirty, while he slept in his Georgetown brown-
stone, a hammering noise had drilled into his skull. Truly
dragged himself from bed, cursing the cold that seeped through
the walls at night, and managed to stumble to the front door
without falling down the stairs. The pounding continued until he
opened the door. On his front stoop stood a mountain of a man
dressed only in a long-sleeved T-shirt, jeans, and work boots. He
should have been an icicle, but he looked ready to kill.

Truly recognized the guy immediately, from pictures in his
girlfriend Bethany Gardner's house and wallet. The aggrieved
husband. His short blond hair, squared-off jaw and chin, and
slightly hooded blue eyes all looked like they did in Bethany's
pictures, although in none of those had he been wearing an expression of barely restrained fury.

He wore one now.

At five ten and one eighty-five, Truly was in reasonable

shape. He knew he didn't *look* like much of a threat, with his neat brown hair, round-cheeked baby face, and wide, liquid blue eyes. Especially dressed in green plaid cotton pajamas. At least it was winter, so he wasn't wearing his summer-weight silk Bugs Bunny boxers. Bethany's husband edged two fifteen and six four, with reach to match, and none of it appeared to be the kind of useless weight that Truly wished, especially at this moment, had been hidden in the photographs.

That and the tenor of the pounding—not a polite knock but an insistent barrage—made Truly believe that Bethany's husband (Perry, he remembered, a name he had always associated with wimpy little stamp collector types, a prejudice he would have to revisit) had come with a different sort of pounding in mind. Truly backed away from the door a couple of steps and threw the big man a friendly, confused grin. "Help you?"

"You're Truly."

"That's right. And you are . . . ?" He didn't want to let on that he had already figured it out. He'd take any advantage he could get, however slight.

"I would think you'd want to know what the husband of the chick you're fucking looks like, if only so you could avoid me at the supermarket."

"Look, it's late," Truly said, trying to sound gracious but a little peeved. That last part, at least, was real. "Maybe you had a little too much to drink or something, made a mistake, but I don't know what you're—"

"Don't bullshit me, Truly, because it won't work. Bethany told me everything. How else would I have found you?"

Which was, Truly had to admit, an excellent question. If he hadn't just been snatched from a sound sleep (and a moderately satisfying dream that had vanished like a soap bubble in the wind when he'd tried to capture it), he might have thought of it himself. How had Perry Gardner found him? Only Bethany's betrayal could explain it. He made a halfhearted beckoning gesture. "All right," he said. "Come on in and we'll see if we can't straighten this out."

Somehow Perry squeezed through the doorway, banging the door shut behind him. He smelled like he had opened a whiskey barrel with his teeth. "There's nothing to straighten out except you," he said, advancing on Truly with his massive hands bunched into fists. "You don't fucking fuck other men's wives."

"I know that," Truly said, "believe me." At some point he'd have to stop playing innocent and focus on defending himself. He was awake now, and he could take the guy. Bethany had said Perry was a sports nut and a college jock, but he worked in an office at the Treasury Department. He was a middle management type, not a man who found himself in physical altercations very often. Besides, the booze that had jacked up his nerve enough to approach Truly would also hamper his reflexes.

Then again, it had been years since Truly had been in a real fight. He was trained, and he kept fit, running a couple of miles a week, working out in the Langley gym. But he wasn't a big man or an especially strong one. And his training was largely of the lethal variety. If Perry didn't back off, Truly might not be able to stop the bigger man without killing him.

"Look, you want some coffee or something?" Truly asked, still hoping to defuse Perry's anger. "I think we should sit down and talk about this." He started for the couch.

Perry surprised him by throwing a punch instead of another threat. Truly tried to dodge it, but he was hemmed in between the couch and a coffee table. The big fist caught him in the ribs. The breath huffed out of him and he staggered back, raising an arm to block the next punch. He took this one on his left forearm and tried to catch Perry's arm, missed. Another idea coming to mind, Truly feigned a stumble that landed him on top of the couch.

"Get up, you punk-ass motherfucker," Perry said. He waited at a reasonable distance, apparently willing to give Truly a chance to gain his feet before continuing to pummel him.

But instead of rising, Truly reached under the couch and drew out an M9 Beretta pistol he'd cached there. He thumbed off the safety, pointed it at Perry, and made a "back up" motion. Perry's eyes went wide when he saw the weapon. Truly had no idea if Perry knew he was an operations officer at the CIA—the guy might think he was a cop or a criminal or just a well-armed citizen. "Dude . . ."

"I don't want any trouble, Perry," Truly said. "Which is what I've been trying to tell you since you showed up."

"Then put away that gun," Perry suggested. Truly gave that idea exactly a half second of consideration before deciding against it.

"I don't think so. Seems like the first time you've been willing to listen to reason."

"I don't want to get shot," Perry said. "But you're fucking my Bethany."

"You don't think I'm going to admit to that, do you?" Truly settled back on the couch, a brown and gold monstrosity that he'd been meaning to throw out or donate for about a dozen years now. He kept the 9mm aimed at Perry. "But just to be conversational, let's say I was. Hypothetically, of course. Two points come to mind. First, she must have wanted me to, so the discussion you really should be having is with her. And second, now that I've met you, surely you don't think I'm stupid enough to ever do it again. You're a walking tank, pal, and I won't always have this nine on me." He was dissembling—he was usually armed, just not with the gun he kept hidden under his couch. Then again, in his trade dissembling was a way of life.

"I guess that's true."

"I know it's got to hurt, Perry. Trust me, I never would have intentionally done anything to cause you pain. I'm still not saying it's true—that's something you're going to have to work out with Bethany—but if it is, it was intended to be something you would never know about."

Perry nodded, understanding that Truly's was, in the proper spirit of Washington, D.C., a non-confessional confession. He looked like he wanted to go a few more rounds, but the barrel of a gun resembled a gaping tunnel when it was pointed right at you. "Maybe you're right," Perry said after several long moments. "I guess we have some stuff to work out. Me and Bethany, I mean."

"I guess you do."

After a couple more minutes, during which Perry fumbled about like a naked man who had unexpectedly found himself inside a convent with no knowledge of how he had come to be there, lost, embarrassed, and deeply troubled, he went back out into the cold night. Truly stayed on the couch, his weapon in his hands, not trusting that Perry was really gone until he heard a car start up and drive away. He sat for another ten minutes or so, wondering why Bethany would have told Perry anything about their affair, much less given her husband his name and home address. Things had seemed to be fine between them, or so he had believed.

There were two points of view to any relationship, of course. And when one person thought everything was jim-dandy because he was able to see his girlfriend a couple of evenings a week, getting laid, and enjoying nice but not painfully long dinners; once every month or two even spending the night together in a hotel someplace like Front Royal or Lexington or Baltimore's harbor area—maybe the other was tired of lying to her spouse, or wanted to be able to spend holidays with him without thinking of the lover left behind, or to hold her man's hand in public without worrying about who might see them. Bethany had seemed subdued on their last couple of evenings together, reticent, which she had attributed to pressures at work, but which might also have been a sign, if only Truly had been able to read it, of growing discontent.

Their last really good date, he realized, had been to see Shawn Colvin at Wolf Trap Farm Park, at the end of summer. They had arrived before sunset, and sat on the lawn with a picnic basket and a nice Merlot. The sky had turned gold and then indigo, stars popping out one by one like musicians walking onstage, then flooding into the sky. Colvin's voice had washed across them like honey, singing about joy and heartbreak, triumph and despair, and he and Bethany had snuggled close together against the cooling night air.

Every date after that had been marred by something—a pointless fight, Bethany's unknowable sadness. He should have recognized it, should have pressed her on it more thoroughly. Maybe he could have headed this off in some way. As it was, the changing tide of her heart had carved a hole in his.

The hell with it, he decided at last. It was almost three in the morning. He had to go to work in a few hours, fighting Key Bridge traffic to get to McLean. If he was going to get any sleep, it had to be now. He tucked the Beretta back into its hidey-hole under the couch and headed upstairs.

His cell phone beeped when he was halfway up. By the time he reached it, on his nightstand next to an empty cup of water and a T. Jefferson Parker paperback thriller, it had stopped. He looked at the screen and saw that he had received a new text message.

Terrific. He sat down hard on the bed, shoulders slumping. This could only be more shitty news. Nobody texted at three a.m. to tell you that you had been promoted or won a trip to Tahiti.

His sigh was melodramatic, but he allowed himself that small theatrical touch as he read the screen. "Perry will be over to see you, if he hasn't already been there. I'm so sorry, James. Honestly. I know you won't think so, and I won't blame you if you hate me for it. I had to tell him, had to be truthful with him so we can fix our marriage before its too late. Its over between us, James, and I'm sorry and I wish I was brave enough to tell you in person, but I'm not. Please don't contact me."

At least Bethany had written the message herself. She refused to use modern text-speak, which would have been more like "I no u wont think so" and, "b4 its 2 late." Besides, although she was an educated woman, she had never been able to get the hang of which "it's" was which, so this note was right in character.

But the whole idea of breaking up via text message seemed more appropriate for a seventeen-year-old than for a professional woman closing in on thirty-five. Truly was just four years older, and it never would have occurred to him as an acceptable method. He guessed Bethany was more high-tech savvy than he would ever be.

Truly was distracting himself with nonsensical details in order to avoid dwelling on the real hurt that waited on the other side of them. He possessed enough self-awareness to understand that it was a survival mechanism he needed right now. He felt like he had been hit by an eighteen-wheeler that was backing up in order to squash him again.

He put the phone down, climbed back under his covers, and sat there with the light off, willing sleep to take him. It hadn't then, and so he fought it now, in his office after lunch, feeling the cold smoothness of the window and watching the flutter of red leaves and wishing that his life belonged to someone else.

The phone on his desk startled him—he had actually drifted off for a moment, his face against the glass—and he lunged for it. Bethany! She knew the direct number to his desk, and not many other people did. He snatched up the receiver. "This is James Truly," he said.

"James, it's Millicent. Millicent Wong."

His heart sank. "Hello, Millicent."

"I detect a distinct drop in your level of enthusiasm," she said. "I've disappointed you in some way?"

"I . . . I was expecting another call," Truly said. "It has nothing to do with you, Millicent. I'm always happy to talk to you."

"People keep saying that, and then I keep sharing bad news and changing their minds."

"Maybe it's time to try a new approach."

"I would love to, James. But at the moment, I'm afraid, bad news is the only kind I have. Something has happened to Lawrence."

He had been picturing Millicent—petite, with a luxurious head of rich black hair that, capping her slender body, almost made her look top-heavy. She was no taller than five two, not counting the hair, which added another three or four inches. She often wore spike heels and gained another couple of inches that way. Still, she'd have to hold on to a couple of five-pound bags of sugar to push the scale over a hundred.

Now that mental image shifted. "Lawrence Ingersoll?" he asked, envisioning the curly haired, dour-faced man in his typical dark clothing.

"Yes, Lawrence Ingersoll," Millicent said.

"What happened to him?"

"I'm hoping you can find out. Last night—your time—I detected a serious occult anomaly. Disruptions of the ley lines—"

"Spare me the details, please," Truly interrupted, knowing that she could go on about them at some length, but that she would lose him by the end of the first sentence. The fact that he had been put in charge of Moon Flash, the CIA's officially non-existent continuation of psychic research programs Grill Flame, Sun Streak, and Star Gate—discontinued in 1996, as far as anyone outside the building (with a very few exceptions) knew—didn't mean he understood such things. "What about Ingersoll?"

"Well, the disruption seemed to be centered not far from his home, so I asked him if he might be able to look into it. I never heard back from him, and when I tried to call him again I got no response. Concerned, I went online and checked the *Mineral County Miner*, the newspaper in his town in Colorado. It said that there was a fire at his house last night, and although he isn't mentioned by name, it reported that no one survived."

"Christ," Truly said. His bad day was getting worse. He could almost hear the air brakes of that metaphorical semi as it slowed for another run at him.

"Exactly," Millicent said. "So I hoped you could investigate, see if he really died in the fire, and find out just what is going on there."

"I'll check it out," Truly said. "Thanks for the tip."

"One thing I'd like to make clear, James. To we practitioners of the occult arts, the immediate consequences of this sort of thing are inconvenient—and, obviously, sometimes dangerous. But the mystical energies around us can't be divorced from the rest of life—there are vast areas of convergence, for instance, between ley lines and string theories of physics. Over the long term, this sort of disruption could affect—well, we just don't know. Time? Weather? The very nature of reality as we understand it? If it continues, I fear that we'll find out. But I'd really rather not."

Truly didn't know what to say. Doomsday scenarios were common enough in the intelligence game, but they were usually attached to the threat of Commies or Islamic fundamentalists or some other group with access to nuclear weapons. A mystical version was beyond his imagining.

Millicent seemed to grasp that, and kept her sigh brief and subdued. "Please let me know what you find out, James. Lawrence and I weren't particularly close, but I like him. I would hate to not know."

"I will," Truly promised.

"At the same time, I shall be exploring some alternative angles on my end."

He knew she meant paranormal angles, and didn't pursue it. Those were the kind she was qualified at, while he decidedly was not.

But he wouldn't turn down the help.

* * *

In the next twenty-five minutes, Truly made four phone calls. The last one was to his boss, Ronald Loesser, whom he met shortly after in the atrium of the New Headquarters Building (called that to distinguish it from the Old Headquarters Building that had once been the main structure at the Langley campus—a compound Truly still had a hard time thinking of as the George Bush Center for Intelligence, named in 1999 for the former president and director of Central Intelligence), beneath the suspended U-2 plane model. Loesser hated to let Truly come to his office almost as much as he hated going into the nearly empty suite of offices dedicated to the Moon Flash project, so they usually met on neutral ground.

Truly wore a navy blue pea coat over his suit, and when he spotted Loesser, the older man not only had a leather barn coat on but was clutching a foam cup of coffee and letting steam wash over his mouth and chin. He barely glanced Truly's way, then ticked his gaze outside and started walking. Truly adjusted his course and caught up with Loesser in the courtyard, where the man had taken a seat on a bench near the main section of the Kryptos sculpture. During warmer weather, there might be Agency employees standing around the sculpture—a blue green oxidized copper wall shaped like a piece of paper scrolling out of a printer, with a sequence of letters punched into it—trying to decipher the code it carried. This time of year, Truly and Loesser were alone, and the babbling fountain running beside the sculpture would help keep their conversation private from anyone who might wander by.

"What is it, Jim?" Loesser asked without preamble. He knew Truly never went by Jim, but he regularly pretended to forget. Just one more illustration of the way he felt about Truly. Loesser was an assistant to the director of the National Clandestine Service—or an assistant to that assistant, Truly could never be certain how many levels from the top his supervisor really was. Loesser would fire Truly in a hot minute if he thought he could, but he believed Truly to be protected—a belief Truly didn't share—by his father, former United States senator Willard Carsten Truly. Instead, he had arranged for Truly to be given ownership of the Moon Flash project, which was as close to fired as one could get while remaining on the Agency's payroll.

"One of our people has been killed."

"An Agency employee?"

"One of *my* people," Truly amended. "A contract operative. Lawrence Ingersoll. Winston brought him in, after the first World Trade Center bombing." Barry Winston had been Truly's immediate predecessor in this post, until the day he ran a hose from his exhaust pipe into his car window and sat in his sealed garage listening to Sidney Bechet CDs until the car ran out of gas. His housekeeper found him two days later.

"One of Winston's charlatans, then." Loesser sipped his coffee, his hard gray eyes appraising Truly over the cup's rim. His hair was short and silver, neatly combed, and he affected the air of an old-time parson who disapproved of virtually everything and everyone created since the end of World War II.

"They're not all charlatans," Truly began. At Loesser's disapproving frown he stopped. "I don't necessarily have a lot more faith in them than you do, Ron," Truly said. In fact, although he hadn't when he had accepted the job, he had since grown to respect their abilities more than he'd ever expected. He would never admit that to Ron Loesser, though. "But you've assigned me to deal with them, and I'm doing that. Now one of them is dead. And it's not just that. Another one told me she called him last night, to ask him to look into—I know what you're going to say—a disruption in the ley lines. He agreed to check it out, and the next thing anybody knew his house burned down with him inside. He didn't even try to get out, and the arson investigator's initial conclusion is that the fire began where he was sitting, although they couldn't find any source of ignition or fuel there. It all sounds suspect to me."

"He's a U.S. citizen?" Loesser asked.

"Yes."

"And there's no definitive evidence of foul play? Have the locals completed their investigation? Probably not, if it all happened last night."

"Of course they haven't. I don't know how big Creede, Colorado, is, but it's no major metropolis. It's going to take them a while."

"Then let them do what they have to do," Loesser said. "No

sense in you running off to Colorado now. You'd just be in the way, and we don't have any indication that this is any of the Agency's business. We don't mess around with American citizens inside the U.S."

He said that last part as if he were explaining something that Truly had never heard before. "But he works for us."

"Part-time. He works for others, too, right? Or for himself? What's to say this is at all related to what he does for us?"

"What Millicent Wong told me, for starters." He left out her warnings of global catastrophe—that would just muddy the water even more.

"Unless Millicent Wong pays your salary, Jim, you ought to give more credence to what I tell you." He crushed the empty cup and looked about for someplace to toss it. "Just wait and see."

Ron Loesser rose from the bench and walked toward a free-standing trashcan. He tossed his cup at it. The cup hit the rim and bounced away, but Loesser was already taking rapid strides toward the building. He didn't look back, at his cup or at Truly.

Truly picked up the cup and dunked it into the can. He felt an obligation toward those who had worked for the Agency, even if it wasn't their primary occupation, even if no practical application had been found for their abilities. But given the way his day had begun, he didn't mind being told not to put any effort into finding out what had happened to Lawrence Inger-soll. Just staying alert and coherent would take all the energy he had to offer.

Walking back toward his office he realized some of Loesser's coffee had leaked onto his fingers. He shook a drop away, then sniffed his hand. Loesser took his coffee black, strong and rich. Suddenly a cup seemed like a good idea. Truly couldn't drown himself in booze at work—and he wasn't a hard-drinking guy under any circumstances—but a good jolt of caffeine might keep him going until it was time to head back to his empty home, and his now equally empty life, on the other side of the Potomac.

3

The Colorado River. The Conchos. The Crooked. The Cannonball.
The Missouri, the Musselshell, the Madison. The Snake, Salt,
Salmon, Secesh, St. Mary. The Canadian River. The Russian
River. The American, the Frenchman, the Republican. Sho-
shone, Sheyenne, Gila, Mohawk, Flathead, Klamath, Koote-
nai, Pawnee. Eel, Snake, Swan, Bear, Beaverhead.

In his cell—a cave, really, with a triple-locked solid steel
door over the opening—Wade Scheiner tried to make the hours
pass by remembering the names of as many western rivers as
he could. He had visited many of those rivers. Some he had run
in rubber rafts or wooden dories or canoes made of steel or fi-
berglass. He had gone swimming in some, wearing trunks or
not, most often in the company of Byrd McCall, his best friend
during those carefree summer days of youth when hurtling
headlong into the greenish-brown waters of the Guadalupe or
the ever-present Rio Grande seemed like the ultimate expression of sweet freedom.

Outside his prison, he was certain, the war raged on, Iraqis
killing Iraqis, with Americans caught in the middle. Before his
abduction, he had covered it for CNN. Now he was part of the
story.

Tongue, Milk, Knife, Kettle, Boulder, Sun, Powder, En-
campment, Big Hole. The Green, the White, the Red, the Ruby,
Big Blue, Little Blue, the Greys, the Vermilion, the Verdigris,
the Yellowstone. Neosho, Niobrara, Little Nemaha, Wy-
noochee, Owyhee, Coweeman, Humptulips.

Wade had attempted to keep track of the days of his imprisonment by scratching out hash marks on the cave wall with a
bit of stone. Without windows, though, with captors who fed
him when they wanted to and woke him at will and allowed

him to bathe (using lukewarm water in a metal pail) only sporadically, he had no way to accurately gauge the passage of time. At least ten days had passed, he believed, but maybe it had been two weeks or a little more. Seemed like forever.

His dark blond hair was matted, his normally clean-shaven cheeks and chin thick with whiskers. He itched all over, but when he scratched he worried that he was rubbing the stench of this place into his pores. His jeans and long-sleeved dress shirt were torn and filthy, and they had taken his belt, his wallet, his ID, had thrown his cell phone out the car window as soon as they had shot his driver and squeezed inside around him. He was glad he'd left his iPod and his satellite phone and his video equipment in the hotel room, along with backup identification and most of his cash reserves. He just hoped it would all still be there whenever he was freed. The cave's temperature was steady, humid, and not too cold, and he had been taking off his shirt and wadding it up as a pillow when he slept.

All he knew about the time now was that he had slept for a longer period than usual, and he was hungry. No, starving. No one had come with food. His captors had left nothing in his cell to occupy his attention; once the crude steel bunk and toilet had lost their entertainment value, all he had were occasional meals and even more occasional conversation. Lacking both left him with only his rivers, in whose waters he could feel untethered, adrift. There he could stave off the terror that threatened to drown him when he considered his lonely plight.

The San Joaquin, he remembered, the San Jacinto, San Pedro, St. Joe, St. Regis, St. Maries.

And that dream! He inspected the rugged rock wall next to his cot, where during the night he had believed that he saw several glowing shapes. They had reminded him of some of the Indian rock art he had seen at Smuggler's Canyon and Hueco Tanks close to home, and scattered elsewhere throughout the West. A jagged line, a double arch, an openmouthed face with looping ears. He remembered seeing them, an unexpected source of light in the dark cave—which never happened, since the weak steel-caged incandescent bulb in his cell stayed on all the time—and getting up for a closer look, feeling faint heat reflecting off them. At the time he would have sworn he was awake.

But that wasn't possible, he realized now. None of it. He had dreamed the whole thing. Not the first bizarre dream he'd had in captivity; they were quickly becoming the norm, nightmares of being cornered and shot, or beaten to death, or having his limbs sawed off one by one. He bolted awake from one of those at least once during every period of deep sleep, and then, not knowing how long he had been asleep or if he would soon be visited, he would have difficulty going back to sleep, and he would lie back on the hard cot willing the panicked drumming of his heart to slow, the surge of adrenaline coursing through him to taper off. Few of those dreams had seemed so real, though. He tucked the memory away, returned to countering fear and hunger with his beloved rivers.

Rio Costilla, Rio Paraje, Rio Chama, Rio Penasco, Rio Puerco. The Rio Grande, on whose banks he had grown up, and where he would rather be, at this moment, than somewhere near the Tigris. McKenzie, James, Dolores, Gunnison, Owens, Solomon, Reese, Quinn, Madison.

The names were coming more slowly as the protestations of Wade's stomach grew more insistent. His last meal had consisted of stale bread and cheese, which he'd been given with a cup of water before he had gone to sleep. Fear trumped hunger in the short term, Wade figured, but over the long run, a man had to have something in his belly if he was going to put any energy into being afraid. He hadn't seen anyone since Ali (he just assumed all the names he'd been given were phony, but having nothing else to go by he used them just the same) had come to collect his dishes. That had been many hours ago. By now someone should have come in to shout abuses at him, to accuse him of being a spy, to hit him with sticks, or else to engage him in what seemed like a serious discussion of the Koran and the advantages of the Muslim faith over the Christian—"seemed," because while Wade was no religious zealot, nor did he have any problem with Islam except when it was used as an excuse for murder, the few arguments he tried to make in favor of Christianity's precepts as he understood them were shouted down instead of given a legitimate hearing.

But they were in charge, so he listened when they talked and he didn't try to convert them. He wanted them to see him as a person and not an object, certainly not a soldier for Christ.

They called American soldiers "crusaders" and "occupiers," and he tried to impress upon them that he was a journalist without a horse in the race except for the truth.

Had they forgotten about him? He didn't see how that was possible, unless perhaps they had captured someone else with a higher profile. He was sure U.S. media were covering his disappearance, which probably meant that Al Jazeera and Al Arabiya were as well. Still, he was just a TV reporter, and the city teemed with better captive material than that.

He had tried not to call undue attention to himself. He didn't want to be the kind of problem that was most easily solved by putting a couple of bullets in his skull and dumping him in the reeds beside a road. Now, though, his stomach felt like it was twisting in on itself. Even last night's stale bread would taste like a slice of heaven on a plate. He steeled himself for the worst and pounded on the steel door with both fists. "Hey!" he shouted. "I'm hungry!" He repeated the appeal in his functional Arabic.

He didn't hear any response. He waited several seconds and banged again, getting a steady drum riff going. *The Max Weinberg of the cell block,* he thought, before realizing that while his own Germanic name had set off some alarms for his captors, the name of the E Street Band's drummer would have been even worse to have in this situation. Not much was less palatable to the Sunni fundamentalists who had captured him than an agnostic journalist, but a Jewish rock musician would easily top that on the hate parade.

I could sure go for a rocking version of "Rosalita" or "Badlands" or "Adam Raised a Cain" right now, though, he thought. He'd heard the expression "I'd give my left nut," but never before in life had the likelihood of needing that body part again seemed so remote, and the desire to hear some flat-out rock and roll so strong, that he would have considered it.

Even more than music, though, he needed food. His anger growing along with his hunger, he grabbed at the door handle and pounded again.

The handle turned easily in his grasp.

Wade pulled. The door creaked and swung open.

A trap? It almost had to be. He couldn't see any other reason his captors would have left him in his cell with all three locks on the door unlocked. Still, they weren't the kind of people who would need the "prisoner trying to escape" excuse if they wanted to snuff him. The Sunni insurgency had made no secret of its willingness to kill for their cause, with little provocation or none at all. Journalists were not exempt from that; they seemed a favorite target, as somewhere around eighty of them had been murdered so far during this war. If they wanted to kill him, they would do it, excuse or no.

Still, he looked both ways, up and down a dimly lit tunnel, before he stepped through the door. When no one shot at him, he kept going.

He had been brought in with a canvas bag over his head, his hands zip-tied behind him, insurgents hauling him along by the arms. Now he wasn't sure which way to go. He stood in the hallway, the hairs on the back of his neck tickling as if some-one stared down a gun sight at him, and tried to hear anything except the beating of his own heart.

He couldn't. Total silence. As if the world had gone away.

Wade didn't know if he should call out, or keep his trap shut and thank whatever god was looking out for him. If he did en-counter his captors, surprising them might guarantee taking a bullet. And really, what were the chances that he could get all the way outside—with no clue what the layout was, how far underground he had been held, or anything else about his prison?

He walked a dozen steps to his right and stopped. The air tasted stale. He turned and went the other way. Fresher. Fresh enough, anyway, to make him aware of his own brutal stink.

The arching cave roof brought back horrific memories, as had being beaten up, memories that threatened to . . . He shook his head to halt that train of thought, back-burnered both topics and kept going. Ahead, the strand of wires connecting caged lightbulbs took a sharp right. Wade followed. Now he could feel an actual draft, faint but unmistakable.

With every step, he expected to hear the click of a weapon being readied, the banging of a door or the scuff of anxious shoes on the tunnel floor. None of that happened. He reached a staircase that wound up, the steps shallow and worn smooth by what must have been centuries of use. As Wade climbed, a smell insinuated itself into his consciousness, overpowering his body odor.

He allowed himself a fleeting grin.

A river.

An urban river, with water and fish and organic wastes—feces and corpses—and spilled diesel fuel mixed into it in more or less equal proportions. It *had* to be the Tigris. Wade hurried his ascent, his right hand brushing against the rough rock inner wall of the tightly curving staircase. Here and there wooden timbers shored up the roof.

He reached a level where another rock-walled tunnel led away from the stairs. Lights led down this tunnel as well, but the staircase continued to wind up, and it seemed like the river smell wafted down from above. Wade skipped the side tunnel and kept climbing.

Finally, he came around a curve and saw a door at the top of the staircase. End of the line? He thought he might just sit down and weep if that door was locked, after all this. Maybe the whole thing was some new form of torture. Maybe he was being videotaped right now, his captors watching a monitor and laughing at the distraught expression on his face. "Stupid American spy journalist actually thought he could walk out of here," one would say, and the rest would just crack up.

Whatever. He wasn't turning around now, not without at least trying the door. He climbed to the top and listened, pressing his palms against the door's bare wooden planks. He couldn't hear a thing on the other side.

He pushed against the door. The wood was old and weak, spongy. Locked or not, he could smash through it without much trouble. Not without noise, of course. If insurgents were on the other side, they'd hear him coming. At this point, he no longer cared. He had come this far and he would keep going if the slightest hope of freedom remained.

As it happened, he didn't need to break the door down. A rusted bolt held it closed, and that snapped easily. He passed into what seemed like a vast chamber, although the light from the bulbs in the staircase below didn't penetrate far and there was no light source inside. The river smell was overlaid here with something sour, like garbage.

This looked like a storeroom, although not one that had seen use in the last century or so. Wooden shelving had collapsed near one wall, with what appeared to be many layers of dust coating the debris. Wade oriented himself and let the door close long enough to scramble to the pile and snatch up one of the larger pieces. Retracing his steps, he found the door and propped it open with the hunk of wood.

He still hadn't heard a sound made by anything but his own progress. Twenty minutes must have passed since he had left his cell, but no audible alarm had been raised. Something didn't add up. *Not that I'm complaining.* It was strange enough to keep him on edge, expecting an ugly surprise at any moment.

The big room contained trunks and crates, all of which, like the shelves, looked ancient and seldom visited. Wade had no idea what might wait beyond where the faint light fell. He couldn't imagine that the door he had come through was the only entrance, though. Why put a storeroom at the top of a high staircase, when there seemed to be plenty of space in the tunnels below?

So there had to be another way in. Wade walked across the floor—ceramic tile, not rock like the cavern floors—into the darkness beyond the light's reach. He barked his shin on something hard and round and muttered a soft curse. Feeling his way around it (some kind of urn, he thought), he kept working his way toward where the far wall should be.

After two more bruises on his legs and a growing ache in his lower back from bending forward to grope for obstacles in the dark, he found another wall. It felt dry and dusty, but relatively smooth beneath the layer of dust. Plaster maybe, instead of bare stone. Solid, too. Tapping on it, Wade felt no give beneath his knuckles.

He kept one hand on the wall and started working his way left. After a couple dozen steps, the wall vanished. He probed with his foot and found a stair. He crouched beside it. Wood, not stone or plaster. The staircase was at least eight feet wide, leading up into impenetrable darkness.

Anything could be up there. He wouldn't be able to see a snake, a tiger, an entire Sunni militia. Or a Shia one—they were no better.

Biting back his fears, Wade climbed again.

This had all taken too long. By now they knew he was out. They had to. Maybe it was a trap all along, and maybe not, but they would certainly have the exits covered—if this indeed led to an exit, and wasn't just a long, exhausting journey toward ultimate disappointment. Hopelessness filled him and he almost sat down where he was, to wait in the dark until they found him with their flashlights and their guns.

But then he smelled the river again, and he climbed.

At the ninth stair Wade had to push through a spiderweb that wrapped around him like a shroud. He pawed it from his eyes and mouth and kept going. A dozen stairs, fourteen, and then he came to another wooden door. A double door this time, latched from the other side. Pressing his eye to the minute gap between the two doors, he saw natural light.

This door was at the top of the stairs, with no level space to get a running start. In the darkness he felt unbalanced, so he didn't want to rear back and kick at it. If he fell down those stairs, he could easily break a leg—or his neck. Surviving the fall might be his worst option; if no one found him he would stay there until he died of thirst. Everybody had to die sometime, but not that way, he hoped. Wade loved the water; he wanted to die beneath it, leaving behind only a splintered boat washed up on a sandy spit in some river, not craving a drink in a dark hole beneath Baghdad.

He pressed against the door. Something snapped and it started to give way at the hinges. He pushed harder, putting all of his weight against it. Wood splintered, the hinge pulled free, and Wade tumbled into a lighted space, landing on his hands and knees on top of most of the door.

The racket he made was ferocious.

And yet no one came running, no gunshots echoed though the space, no bullets *spanged* into the tiled walls around him.

Gaining his feet, he saw that he had fallen into a mosque— old, no longer used, but a mosque just the same. It had probably been hit in the early bombing, the days of "shock and awe," he guessed, but on further reflection he thought the damage might predate even that assault. Massive holes Swiss-cheesed the walls and an intricately filigreed blue roof dome, letting daylight in. The back wall—the one through which he had come— was pockmarked with bullet holes. Wooden benches had been reduced to rubble, and trash—including newspapers (Wade recognized several of the papers that had sprung up out of nowhere in the weeks following Saddam's fall: *The Dawn of Baghdad*, *A New Day*, and *Those Who Have Been Freed*, mixed in with older, pre-invasion copies of *Babel* and the *Iraq Daily*, the official English-language paper of Saddam's government), glass and plastic bottles, greasy food wrappers, flattened shipping cartons with Arabic writing on the sides—covered the floor. This was where the garbage smell originated. For all he knew there might be bodies beneath the detritus. Wade didn't think his captors had taken this route into the tunnels, because it didn't look like anyone had passed through here in months.

He didn't stand around wondering for long. Across the big room a doorway gaped, sunlight streaming through it. Wade pushed through the debris and outside. He found himself on a city street lined with low, mud-walled buildings and courtyards. Peering over the top of a low wall, he saw a quiet, shaded yard, and beyond that, the Tigris itself tossed shards of sunlight back at him. The sparkle was all show—since the war had started, the Tigris had become ever more polluted. It was not a river he would choose to swim in, but at this distance it looked inviting.

From the position of the sun, he knew that if he followed the river to his left—to the west—it would eventually lead him to the Green Zone. There he would find Americans, soldiers and diplomats. Until then, he could only hope to encounter a U.S. or Iraqi patrol, and pray that no militia soldiers or insurgents spotted him. Or anyone else. Americans were about as popular in Iraq as avian flu was in the States.

He started walking, keeping the river on his right. The streets were strangely empty, as were the skies. He heard no screaming F-16s, no big lumbering transports, no helicopters buzzing overhead. He didn't even hear any birds. It was as if a nuclear bomb had gone off while he'd been underground, wiping out all life in the city. He hadn't been that far underground, though. He would have felt the blast. If they had survived, his captors would have brought him up, forced him to bear witness to yet another American atrocity.

Except for the silence, it was a typical Baghdad residential street. Power and phone wires crisscrossed overhead, and here and there obviously illegal splices directed pirated electricity into homes. Buff-colored buildings, some with balconies, faced onto the street. Their yards were hidden behind walls. A few spindly palms brushed the sky.

Cars and trucks had been parked haphazardly along the sides of the road. Wade kept an eye out for any with keys inside, since hot-wiring wasn't in his skill set but wheels might make the trip to the Green Zone quicker. On the streets, the smell of shit competed with the river's odor, because trucks hosed down the dust with untreated sewer water. The aromas of sewage and death had become inescapable inside the city.

At the end of a city block, someone had hauled together the carcasses of three burned-out cars as a barricade. This was the dividing line between neighborhoods, between Sunni and Shiite. Ordinarily men would be gathered here with guns, but there weren't any now. Wade passed through the narrow space left for foot traffic. *So much for stealing a car,* he told himself. *That might just complicate things.*

The next block was rubble, burned-down buildings, chunks of stone and concrete, twisted steel, flame-blackened timbers. Both sides of the street had been destroyed, the debris almost meeting in the middle. He picked his way gingerly down the narrow aisle. At the beginning of the next block was another barricade, this one made with materials salvaged from the rubble. Still no guards.

After ten minutes or so, he finally saw a sign of life.

A pig, a scrawny sow with ribs showing through her flesh, trotted across the street ahead of him and disappeared into an alley. When Wade reached the alley, he paused, looked around the corner cautiously, in case someone waited there who had released the pig, or whom she had been running from. But the alley was as empty as the rest of the streets. He looked the other way, but the pig was gone.

The emptiness of the tunnels beneath the mosque had been unexpected, but this was just too weird. People had been fleeing the city—hell, the whole country—by the hundreds of thousands. An Iraqi with a toothache had to go to Jordan, because all the dentists already had. But there were still plenty of people around.

So where could they be? What had happened to everyone?

Wade hated questions that didn't have answers. He tried to block them out with his rivers, running through their names as he walked, his own private rosary. Belle Fourche, Marais des Cygnes, Coeur D'Alene, Loup, Gros Ventre, Touchet, Sevier, Deschutes, Payette. Arikaree, Apishapa, Chikaskia, Yampa, Yaak.

After another few minutes wondering why there had been no boat traffic on the river, he heard a vehicle. At last! *Someone* was alive.

The sound came from the direction Wade was headed anyway, toward the Green Zone. With each passing second, though, his heart hammered in his chest harder and harder. To have come all this way just to be shot down by militia soldiers, or worse, by Americans who didn't realize who he was. . . .

He crouched down between a white Toyota and a Mercedes panel truck and watched, ready to dive beneath the truck if necessary. When he saw a small convoy of Humvees flying United States colors, he thought he might burst out crying. He had to take the chance. He wiped away a single tear, sniffed, and stepped into the middle of the street, waving his hands.

The front Humvee braked to a stop, road dust billowing around it like smoke. Long moments passed. Wade couldn't see them from here, but he could envision the barrels of dozens of weapons all leveling on him. One guy with a nervous twitch and it was all over.

Finally, a soldier, a jug-eared, gap-toothed black kid who looked fresh off the family farm, climbed down from the passenger side of the front Humvee. "Wade Scheiner?" the kid asked. "Sir, are you Wade Scheiner, with CNN?"

Then the tears did come, and Wade couldn't stop them, and when the soldiers spilled from their vehicles, shouting his name, recognizing him, he couldn't even make out their features through the salt water in his eyes. *Saved,* he kept thinking, *I've been saved, I've been motherfucking saved at last and I don't even know how or why.*

4

᛭

Although the tiny kitchen inside the offices of the *Voice of the Borderlands* newspaper smelled like coffee, only about a teaspoon of black sludge coated the bottom of the pot. Molly McCall sighed and set her mug on the counter with a heavy *clack*. Monday morning and she by god needed some caffeine in her system before she could face her desk and the story waiting there.

The story's intent was serious enough. The American Southwest had been racked by a decade-long drought, and a couple of rainy years had done little to tip the balance back. Rather than one more sober-minded, drowse-inducing investigation of that, however, managing editor Franklin Carrier had instructed Molly to work a local angle. With Halloween behind them, Thanksgiving and the holiday season would rush in soon enough, so Molly had been talking to growers, florists, and party planners about how the drought and the reprieve of the past summer's rains would affect what plants and flowers would grace El Paso's holiday tables this year.

It seemed like a strange take, focusing on those affluent enough to purchase plants for centerpieces. Generally the *Voice*'s concern was for the less fortunate, those who might pluck some greenery from their own yards (if they had yards) to place on their tables (if they also had tables). She had diligently called on a wide variety of farmers, flower shop owners, even some of the people who set up pumpkin and Christmas tree or chili *ristra* stands on street corners. Today she planned to work on beating those random bits of conversation into a shape that readers would recognize as a newspaper story.

She rinsed out the coffeepot, stuck a new filter pack in the holder, filled the pot from the tap, and poured the water into the coffeemaker's receptacle. Whoever took the last cup was supposed to start a new pot. That was the rule. The office was never empty; any time of the day or night somebody might need a cup.

When the coffee finished brewing, she filled her mug, tossed in a dash of cream, and started toward her desk. The message light on her phone had been blinking when she came in, but she hadn't wanted to deal with voice mail until she was fortified.

She had almost reached her desk when Frank's voice boomed from the doorway of his private office. "McCall!"

Molly turned mid-stride, diverting around Suzi McKellar's desk toward Frank's office. He stood in the doorway, his right hand on the jamb over his head, left leaning casually against his hip. Almost everything about Frank Carrier was casual. He wore a tie to the office, but no jacket, and most of the time his tie was tugged away from his throat, collar button open, shirt-sleeves rolled back over muscular forearms. He was a tall man, solidly built, with skin darker than Molly's coffee since she'd added the cream but not as dark as it had been straight from the pot. His hair had begun turning gray in the last couple of years. He smiled as Molly approached, and his soft brown eyes seemed to illuminate from within. While he was no candidate for sainthood, at times Molly thought he could groom himself for that role, given the right incentive.

"What's up, Chief?" she asked when she neared him. Her brother Byrd had bought her the DVD set of the 1950s *Superman* TV show for Christmas two years ago because, he had said, "If you're going to be Lois Lane, you need to learn from a pro." They were both far too young to have caught the show on its original run—she was thirty-three, Byrd four years older—but he had been into comics throughout his teens and had seen episodes here and there. Watching the surprisingly entertaining, if cheesy, series, she had decided that her favorite aspect was the chagrin with which Perry White responded to Jimmy Olsen calling him "Chief," and ever since she had done the same to Frank.

"Inside," he said, suddenly serious. He met her questioning gaze, but his eyes revealed nothing. Still holding her mug, she squeezed past him. He came in behind her, closing the door.

In addition to Frank's cluttered desk, a couple of filing cabinets, a bookcase, and a long wooden credenza, the office held a ratty old couch and two visitor chairs. Oscar Reyes, the *Voice*'s owner, sat on the couch with his hands folded over his soccer ball of a stomach and a dour look on his face. His hair, pure silver, was combed away from that face, which was creased and lined enough to suggest a lifetime of hard labor in the sun.

"Oh, hi, Oscar," Molly said. "I didn't realize you were in here. How are you?"

Oscar had an office of his own, but some days he didn't come in at all. Lately he'd been around a lot, closed up in his office, sometimes calling Frank in for private meetings. None of it boded well, she had thought. Neither did this. Were they firing her?

Oscar smiled, a sincere grin that radiated warmth. "Tired as hell," he said. "And sore. I spent all weekend working on the lawn and the garden. Edging, trimming, weeding, all that stuff. I told my wife it's almost winter, why bother, and I thought she was going to tear me a new one."

"You should get yourself a Mexican for that kind of thing," Frank said, settling behind his desk. The curtains were drawn across his window, as they usually were since it just looked out on a little paved parking area in back. On his walls he had hung framed front pages of the *Voice*. The very first issue occupied the place of honor behind his desk. Over the couch where Oscar sat was one with a headline that blared "LOCAL ELEMENTARY SCHOOLS FAIL AIDS TEST."

It was supposed to be "AIMS" test. Frank kept the page where he could see it, as a reminder that it never hurt to read over every page at least one more time than seemed necessary.

"I got a Mexican for that," Oscar replied, chuckling. "You're looking at him."

The two men were old friends, and they teased each other mercilessly. Sometimes Oscar retaliated with attacks on Frank's homosexuality, which was no secret. Both took the barbs as good-natured harassment. Molly suspected they found it hilarious that a Latino and a gay African-American ran the only real alternative newspaper in El Paso. The *Voice* stuck it to what they called the "lily-white *El Paso Times*"—even though its editor was also Hispanic—as often as they could.

"Sit, Molly," Frank urged.

Molly sat in one of the visitor's chairs, angling it so she could see Frank and Oscar. She let the mug heat the palms of her hands. "What's up?"

"Your brother is about to have a visitor," Frank said.

"A very famous visitor," Oscar added.

"Byrd is?"

"You got any other brothers?" Frank asked.

"Just the one." Byrd had been in the oncology ward at Providence Memorial Hospital for several weeks. His leukemia had degraded to the point that he needed constant supervision and full-time medical care. He was convinced that he wouldn't be coming out again, and his doctors were beginning to agree. "What visitor?"

"Wade Scheiner's on his way to El Paso," Frank said. "He said he wants to spend time with Byrd while he still can. He's been in Germany, getting checked out in a military hospital there and being debriefed. A friend at CNN tipped me that he's headed here."

"That's great! Byrd will be thrilled." So was she, really. She hadn't been in touch with Wade much these last few years, but he had been a huge part of her life as well as Byrd's for the last two decades or more. She had always believed that his example had set her on course for a career in journalism.

"CNN hasn't announced where he's going, just that he's taking a leave of absence," Frank went on. "They don't want him swamped with well-wishers or job offers or any of the fruitcakes who come out of the woodwork after a story like his. So it's kind of hush-hush. I thought you'd want to know."

"Thanks, Frank." She took a sip of the coffee, waiting for the rest of the story. There was another shoe floating somewhere over her head, and she wasn't going anywhere until it dropped.

"One more thing," Oscar said. *And here it comes.* She wondered if she should duck. "Scheiner hasn't told anyone—on the record, anyway—what happened to him in Baghdad. The whole story of his kidnapping, how he escaped, all that. It's a huge story, and he's keeping it to himself."

"Maybe he'll do a special report for CNN," Molly speculated. "Or write a book."

"Maybe so," Oscar said. "And then again, maybe he just needs some time to process everything he went through before he talks about it."

"Could be."

"The thing is, getting an exclusive on a story like that would be good for the *Voice*," Oscar said. The corners of his lips turned up in a kind of dreamy smile of which he was probably unaware. "Really good. The kind of good that boosts circulation, which makes advertisers happy, which allows us to increase ad rates. That kind of good."

Things clarified for Molly. "So you want me to work him."

"Everyone in America wants to know what happened to him and how he got away. He's your friend," Frank said. "And your brother's. Right?"

"Yes."

"So presumably you'll be seeing him, spending time together, anyway. We're not asking you to do anything underhanded. Just try to make sure that if he wants to talk about it, you—and by extension, the readers of the *Voice*—are the who that he wants to talk to."

"You are a newspaper editor, right?" Molly asked. "Because that was one hell of a terrible sentence."

Frank nodded, his gaze downcast. "You're right, it was. I even offended myself with that one. But I think you get my point."

"I think so. You want me to prey on my friend's misfortunes to hike our ad rates."

"That's a cynical view of it, Molly," Oscar said.

"I'm a girl reporter for a big city newspaper. Cynical is what I do best."

"And we wouldn't want you any other way, Molly."

"I can guarantee you one thing," she said, knowing it would be important to both men. "He won't give his story to the *Times*."

"Why not?"

"He hates that paper. To begin with, he thinks their editorial page is somewhere to the right of Attila the Hun."

"Was Attila conservative?" Oscar asked, his right eyebrow arching up his forehead.

"Oh yeah," Frank said. "One of the first neocons. He was sure the Romans would greet him as a liberator."

"Right, I almost forgot. And he hated the gays, too. Or was that the Gauls?"

"So that's something, right?" She started to raise her mug to her lips.

"Don't do that," Frank said sharply.

She paused with the cup at chin level. "Do what?"

"You know the swill we buy for the kitchen isn't real coffee. Let's go out for a while. You can hold down the fort, right, Oscar?"

Oscar gave his workingman's smile. His left canine was gold. "Consider it held, Frank."

Although it pained her to admit it, when she had heard about Wade's kidnapping, her first thought had been of herself and Byrd. Especially Byrd. Her big brother had saved her life— emotionally, and in actual, literal fact. He had done the same for Wade. For years, Byrd and Wade had been inseparable, joined at whatever bone or nerve ending made people want to risk their lives in tiny boats on roaring rivers. She had been part of the group in their earlier days, before the boys started leaving Palo Duro to live their adventures on a bigger canvas.

Molly had been a gangly kid in those days, when Wade first moved into their little ranching town on the Rio Grande. Since then she had blossomed into a woman. Now, in her early thirties, she had continued blossoming, to the point that she was glad that J Lo had popularized a little extra mass in the ass. Her phrase—the more common vernacular was "junk in the trunk," but Molly was precise when it came to words, and to her a person's trunk was her midsection, not her behind. Molly had dark brown hair that she kept shoulder-length, and bright green eyes and perfect lips, she thought, just full enough and heart-shaped; not much of a chest but, on the bright side, not much of a gut either. She was five seven, no model, but not ashamed to catch her own reflection in a shop window. Not at all the little girl she had been when they had met Wade.

It tore at her heart that now that Byrd was in need, she

couldn't save his life in return. Neither could Wade. But she had been afraid, in those first moments and through the days since then, that Byrd would die without ever seeing Wade again—or worse, that news of Wade's death would trigger Byrd's final spiral.

Her joy at Frank and Oscar's information was tempered by a gut reaction to their full-court press on her. She wanted Wade to spend time with Byrd. She didn't want that time to be soured by her squeezing him for a story. She especially didn't want to piss him off, make him sorry he had ever come to town.

Frank and Oscar were both reasonable men, and they'd understand if she refused to exploit her connection. They would understand, but they would be disappointed. They might begin to doubt her reporter's instincts, her willingness to chase a story. Maybe a refusal here would put the brakes on her advancement prospects.

She had studied journalism at the University of Texas, El Paso, encouraged by Wade's early success. She had worked hard as a freelancer, selling articles to the *Times* and *Texas Monthly* and other markets. Then a staff job had opened up at the alternative weekly, and she had pushed and cajoled, managing to win the position. She would hate to see an attack of conscience impair that job, not to mention chances of moving up to more interesting and meaningful stories. An editorship one day, even publisher. Molly was ambitious, and she had an abiding respect for the journalistic predecessors that she hoped to emulate. The names of H. L. Mencken and Nellie Bly, Edward R. Murrow, Woodward and Bernstein, even the recent stars Keith Olbermann and Christiane Amanpour, were a personal pantheon to her. Since Thomas Paine, the dream of America had been tied to the written word, and the more powerful government became, the more good journalists were required to keep it honest. In her wildest fantasies, she leveraged a significant career at the *Voice* to one of more nationwide prominence, where she could have an impact on the nation similar to that of her heroes.

If it happened, it happened, and she would keep working toward that goal. But she hoped her job wouldn't threaten her relationship with her brother's best friend.

When she had learned of Wade's escape (coincidentally

from Byrd, who, stuck in the hospital and in a world of pain, couldn't do much except watch TV), once again her first thought had been of her brother. *Thank God he won't die knowing that Wade went first,* she had thought. Concern for Byrd's emotional health outweighed her worry about their friend's life.

She would have thought that made her a shitheel, except that if she did then a voice inside her head (a voice that, when it came from outside her head, belonged to Byrd) would tell her to *knock it off, swearing's not ladylike, and besides you don't fucking do it well enough.* To which she would respond, if talking to the real, outside Byrd, *Yeah? Up yours, bro.*

Thereby proving his point.

The Byrd inside her head couldn't be effectively silenced, so she tried to keep the reins on her own language, on his behalf.

The day was coming when that would be the only Byrd left.

She could hardly bear to imagine it.

5

ㅡ〓ㄷ

Frank drove his Volvo station wagon, which he'd had for decades
and which had come in handy in the newspaper's earliest days,
according to the legends that had grown up around the *Voice*,
when he'd stuffed the back full of papers at the printers and
delivered them to street boxes and markets around town. As
soon as he had the engine started, he turned up the radio, letting
the blaring Eagle 99.1 make it clear that he didn't want to talk
until they got where they were going.

That was okay. He had stirred up the old memory river (a
swimming spot Molly didn't dip her feet into when she could
help it), and the sediment hadn't all settled yet. Molly folded
her hands in her lap and listened to Bad Company and thought
about her tenth summer.

I saw him first.

That was the thing about Wade that always stood between
Molly and Byrd, although it had gone unspoken since the very
beginning. If she had given voice to it, Byrd would have pooh-
poohed it anyway. *What about it?* he would have asked. *What
does that matter? Okay, you saw him first, big deal. I saw Mom
and Dad first. I saw you before you saw me. So what?*

And he would have been right. She wouldn't have had an
answer for that.

Still, it meant something to her, even if she couldn't explain
it. She had seen Wade first, but he had become Byrd's best friend.
Her friend, too, but primarily by default because she was Byrd's
sister. Which made sense in the ways that really mattered. He
and Byrd were boys, and young ones when they met, Byrd just
fourteen, Wade a year younger. Just beginning to be interested in

girls, she remembered, and then only in girls their own age or slightly older, the ones who were blossoming into unattainable young women. At ten, Molly wouldn't have counted.

Still, although she understood all the reasons, she had never completely shaken that little hint of resentment. It had itched at her over the years, like a too-stiff tag on a T-shirt.

The day it happened had been one of the worst days of her life to that point—which, given that she had only seen ten years' worth of days, in retrospect couldn't have been all that terrible. It was an August day, when the days were long and hot, and the summer had been long, too, so that school—which she had been only too glad to be finished with in June—had started to look appealing again. Byrd and their father had gone into town, which in this case meant El Paso, fifty-some miles up the Rio Grande from their ranch outside Palo Duro. She was alone with Mom, and bored. It wasn't long, therefore, before she and Mom started getting on each other's nerves, the way daughters and mothers do.

Chafing had turned to sniping, which had led inexorably (as Molly had known it surely would, ever since she had heard Byrd say it on the bus one afternoon near the end of the school year) to Molly shouting, "Blow me, Mom!"

She hadn't known what it meant, then, only that it sounded angry and had elicited a loud reaction from the other kids on the bus when Byrd had used it. It elicited a reaction from Molly's mother, too. She had thrown her laundry basket down on the floor, her face instantly turning purple. She was a lanky woman, hair bleached and skin browned by the west Texas sun until they were almost the same color. That same sun had dried her skin until it was deeply lined, aging her before her time.

Just at this moment, she reminded Molly of a harpy from a mythology book she had checked out of the school library that spring. She lunged toward Molly, her mouth ratcheting open, her limbs all choppy angles, her hands grasping like claws. Molly evaded her with a swift dodge, knowing she had strayed over a line. "Where did you hear somethin' like that?" Mom shouted, still trying to catch her.

"At school!" Molly cried. "I'm sorry!" They were both in the kitchen, where the washing machine was (that was the year before they got a dryer, when wash was still hung on the clothesline outside), and Molly banged her elbow against the kitchen table as she scrambled to evade her mother's reach. "Oww!"

"Serves you right," Mom said. "Come here, Molly McCall. I mean it."

Her mother wasn't likely to actually strike her—at least she hadn't for several years, and even then nothing worse than the very occasional swat on the butt—so Molly didn't quite understand why she was so afraid of the woman. But she kept the table between them just the same. "I didn't mean it, Mom," she said, sniffling after she got the words out. Tears welled in her eyes. She sniffed again and wiped her fingers across them. They came away damp. "I don't even know what it means, I just heard it and thought it sounded funny."

"Well, there's nothin' funny about it, young lady."

"I know. I mean, I do now."

"I don't ever want to hear that from you again."

"You won't, Mom, I swear."

"I'd better not. As it is, you've lost TV privileges for a week."

God. Endless summer days without TV to fall back on? Molly didn't know how she would survive.

"And right now I think you'd best get out of the house, before I think of something else to take away."

Molly didn't wait around for a second invitation. As Mom picked up her discarded laundry basket, Molly high-tailed it outside where she'd be safe from further retribution. Safer, anyway.

The day wasn't just hot, it was scorching. The kind of day when she would have given anything for a trip to Balmorhea State Park and a dip in the cold, spring-fed pool there, where you could swim with turtles and feel tiny fish nibbling at your toes. Since that was out of the question, she went into the barn instead, to share her gloom with Freckles, her Appaloosa gelding. The air in the barn was warm and musky, not as hot as outside, and the sweet smell of the horses was as welcome as the aroma of fresh-baked cookies.

Freckles nickered softly when she entered his stall, swinging his head around to greet her. The big horse let Molly stroke the gray pink mottled skin of his nose, and she drew his muzzle against her own cheek, feeling his hot breath down her neck. The horse listened without judging while she explained what had happened. As she talked, an idea started to dawn on her, a way guaranteed to shake off the sadness that felt like it would crush her into the ground. She wore shorts and sneakers, not the jeans and boots she ordinarily would, but she was still feeling rebellious.

She hadn't ridden bareback very often. Always, when she had, someone had been around to help, even if it was just Byrd. But she was alone now, so she opened the stall door into the barn and led Freckles to a stool from which she could climb onto his back. Freckles was as easygoing as an animal could be, totally relaxed around Molly. He let Molly slide onto him, hugging him with bare legs, rubbing his neck. Then she nudged him toward the big open front door and gave his ribs a light kick.

"Come on, Freckles," she urged. "Hah!"

Freckles had grown up with Molly and understood her intent. If he thought it strange that she would ride without saddle or tack, he didn't express that, but he set his own limits. Out in the pasture, he hesitated when she wanted him to trot, and he downright refused to gallop.

That didn't matter. Molly drew pleasure from the great muscles working beneath her, from the way he tossed his head, shaking his mane, from the breeze that his motion accentuated as he cut through the still summer air. She rode across the pasture, to the far fence, and was starting to turn Freckles around when everything went wrong.

First she caught a glimpse of Wade, although at the time she didn't know who he was, just knew that he was a boy on a bicycle starting across the road toward her. More of her attention was fixed on the eighteen-wheeler laden with hay barreling down the same road. She thought the boy would surely brake and wait on the far side until the truck had passed. Instead, he leaned into his handlebars and pumped on the pedals and tried to dart across the street ahead of the truck.

The truck driver hit his air brakes and his horn at the same time, a deafening bleat that mixed with the scream of rubber on pavement. So near, so unexpected—even if he could have braced himself, Freckles was already turning, looking toward where he was going instead of where he had been—the startled horse reared up. As if remembering too late that Molly rode on his back, he cut the motion short, trying awkwardly to return to earth.

But Molly had already lost her grip, and the horse's aborted move bucked her the rest of the way off. With a screech, she sailed through the air, landing on her back in tall summer grass.

When she opened her eyes again, she saw blue, cloudless sky, a white disk of sun, and then, between the sun and her, a boy's blond head haloed from behind. "Are you okay?" he asked.

"I think . . . I'm fine," she said. Winded, but not injured. She started to sit up and he came around in front of her, offering a hand. Molly took it and he hoisted her to her feet, his grip strong. He wore a blue and white Joe Jackson T-shirt and blue jeans, and while he couldn't have been more than a couple of years older than her—no older than Byrd, certainly—his muscles seemed more developed than her big brother's. His face was handsome, sunny and blue-eyed, with a spray of freckles dusting his cheeks like spilled cinnamon and a lopsided smile that reminded her of Elvis Presley in those movies her Mom watched on her VCR.

"Good, because that was impressive," he said. "I've never seen a girl fly before. You aren't Supergirl, are you? Or Wasp?"

More angry and embarrassed than hurt, she snapped at him. "If I was, I wouldn't have landed on my back." Molly dusted grass off the bottom of her shorts. "Anyway, I don't think I've ever seen a boy stupid enough to try to race a truck."

"I won, didn't I?"

The truck was gone, the roar of its engine receding. Freckles was gone, too, halfway back to the barn. "You were lucky."

"Maybe. Or maybe I just know what I can do."

"I don't think that truck driver trusted you as much as you do."

"He doesn't know me," the boy said.

"Neither do I. And you're standing in my pasture, and I'm not sure I want to know such a stupid boy."

"I'm not stupid. Anyway, I'm not the one who went riding bareback."

"What do you know about riding?"

"I've ridden horses before."

"I hope you ride them better than you do that bike." She eyed him suspiciously, as if maybe the whole thing had been one of her brother's pranks. "I've never seen you before."

"We just moved here." He pointed back across the road,

where cotton fields hemmed in the road. "Couple of miles that way, I guess."

"Where the Merricks used to live?"

"I don't know. Maybe."

"Do you have any sisters?"

"No, it's just me and my mom and dad."

"I have a brother. Byrd. He's fourteen."

"I'm thirteen. My name's Wade."

"I'm Molly." She shoved her hands deep into her pockets in case he wanted to shake. He had already held on to hers long enough, when he helped her up, and she had felt a certain unexpected, unwelcome thrill from it. She pointed at his shirt. "My big brother likes his video."

"*Steppin' Out*?" Wade asked. "It's rad."

"I like Duran Duran better. And Bananarama."

"Is your brother home?"

"No, he's in El Paso."

"Well, maybe I'll come back some other time, then."

"If you don't get hit by a truck first, I guess that would be okay."

"If I do get hit by a truck, I won't bother coming over, how's that?"

"That's a good idea." Molly shrugged. "I have to get Freckles. My horse."

"Okay," Wade said. "I should probably get home, too."

Molly started toward the barn and house. She looked back to see him hop the barbed wire fence at the pasture's edge and pick up his bike from where he had ditched it in the high grass by the road. Part of the frame was bent, and the front wheel wouldn't quite straighten out. He must have jumped off it in a hurry when he saw that she had fallen.

He didn't look her way again, just walked the bike across the street and toward home. She was too young to feel that the encounter had been momentous in any way, didn't yet have a sense that her own life would have a history worth recounting, or turning points that couldn't be backed away from.

But it was both of those, and more. She would come to find that out, soon enough.

Once Wade Scheiner had crashed into her life, nothing would ever be the same.

* * *

Good Coffee Mexican Restaurant was on Piedras, not far from the *Voice*'s office in a strip mall storefront on Montana. As the name suggested, the coffee was indeed good, hot and rich and strong enough to defend itself in a brawl. The food was good, too, but it was a little early in the day for lunch.

Now that they were seated at a table in the nearly empty establishment and Molly finally had a cup of java she could concentrate on, Frank caught her gaze and held it for a long moment. Serious chat coming, she knew.

"How's the story, Molly?"

"The flower thing?" Not what she had expected. "I'm having a hard time getting a handle on it. It seems like a society page story to me, and we don't have a society page."

"It wouldn't hurt us to have some more affluent readers," Frank said. "But I don't think that's really the route you want to take into the story."

"The route into it?"

"You know this instinctively. I've seen you do it a thousand times." He exaggerated; she hadn't written a thousand pieces for the paper, and he hadn't seen more than a handful of her student work or her earlier freelance stuff, just enough to offer her the gig. "You can always start a story any old way. The five Ws work as well as anything else. Who what when where why. But half the time—two-thirds, more like—your reader won't follow you beyond those five Ws. That's the whole point of them, isn't it? To convey the bare facts to the reader in the shortest space so he can move on to the next piece that starts off the exact same way.

"But a good writer—and Molly, you are a good writer—can find a path into a story that isn't the expected way, that takes the reader by the hand and leads him along, feeding bits of story like bread crumbs, until he's begging to be allowed to go all the way to the end. It's not just in how the printed story begins, although that's part of it. It's how you, the writer, approach the telling of the story. You can go for the obvious way in, or you can find the road less traveled, the way that makes your reader know you're taking him—or her, no need to be sexist here—on a trip that she or he is going to appreciate."

"Okay," she said, for lack of any more coherent response.

"Talking about the rich folks and how they'll decorate their holiday tables is one path into this story, but it's not the only one."

"And you have a better idea."

"You've mostly been talking to growers and sellers, right? Not the ultimate customers. That's where you need to stay, with the people whose lives are affected by how many plants they can sell to the wealthy, and for how much. People who need some rain this winter or they might not have a holiday at all, much less a big table laden with flowers."

She thought about what he was saying. Really, he was confirming her gut instinct, but she had been trying to deny that instinct, trying to find her way to those big tables. "Thanks," she said. "I needed to hear that, I think."

"Then I'm glad I said it, Molly. But that's not why we got out of the office."

"I figured that."

"I wanted to get you away from Oscar," he said. "Because he wouldn't want me to tell you what I'm going to tell you."

"Okaaay," Molly answered. Wherever this was headed, it didn't sound good. It no longer sounded like she was being fired. That didn't mean it couldn't be something worse.

"We really didn't intend to get your hackles up about Wade Scheiner, and I hope we didn't," he said. "I know he's a family friend. I also know that your brother's medical condition has to be your first priority. Oscar and I didn't want to put you in an uncomfortable position, we just figured that if you were going to be spending time with Scheiner anyway, maybe he'd feel kindly disposed toward the *Voice*. Or maybe the subject would come up, and you could drop a hint or two. The intent wasn't to pressure you."

"I respect that," Molly said. "Thanks." Certainly Oscar wouldn't have a problem with that, so she waited for the real reason for this little junket to emerge.

It didn't take long.

"You've been to Oscar's house, right?"

"Sure," she said. There had been a couple of staff Christmas parties there. It was a tidy brick house, up Piedras, hard by the foot of the Franklin Mountains. "It's nice."

"Yeah, it is. I don't want him to lose it."

Oscar had made his early money in manufacturing, down in Mexico, then more in real estate on this side of the border. He had become a naturalized citizen thirty years before. He had funded the *Voice* almost single-handedly, and had made that funding conditional on the paper's also covering news from Juárez and operating a website with a Spanish language version of the print edition. He called his baby the *Voice of the Borderlands* because he believed the border was virtually a separate nation unto itself, neither fully of the United States or Mexico, and Juárez and El Paso had more in common with each other than El Paso had with Chicago, say, or New York or San Francisco.

She knew the history. Obviously there were aspects of the present she didn't know anything about. "Lose it?"

"He's put everything he has into this paper," Frank said. "For better or worse, at a time when a lot of indy papers are struggling and the Internet is sucking up readers, he risked it all to provide an alternative for El Paso. His house is mortgaged to the hilt. I'm sure he has a little money left in the bank for he and Sofia to live on, but I'm also sure it's not much."

"That's awful." Her retort didn't seem to carry the weight she wanted it to, but she didn't know what else to add.

"If he runs out of dough," Frank continued, "the *Voice* goes away. We all lose our jobs. I could maybe go back to the *Times*. You could probably get hired there, too. Some of the others. But I put in twenty-two years at the *Times*, and I don't really want to go back. I'm not sure you'd love it there either."

"Not from what I hear."

"Right. I'm not trying to put it all on you, Molly. We're doing whatever we can think of to get the paper in the black. Everything's on the table. I've renegotiated our printing costs, and I'm considering different paper stocks and inks right now. We're looking into increasing the cover price. We're looking at cutting staff compensation. There's no golden bullet that'll take care of things, but we have to hope that the right combination of bullets will put us on the right track."

"Which is where I come in," Molly said. The big picture was becoming clearer.

"Right," Frank said again. "Wade Scheiner's exclusive story

isn't going to save the paper all on its own, no matter how great it is. But it could help. It might generate some national attention. Maybe even Pulitzer consideration. That kind of thing bumps circulation, and it sounds good when the ad reps go out to the clients. Not to mention that with Scheiner's mug on TV every day for the last three weeks or so, the story itself would generate business on the street. Which, again, makes a better story for the sales reps."

Molly was still stuck a few sentences behind him. "Pulitzer? You think?"

"It depends on what the story is, and how he tells it. If he tells it to you, or if he wants to write it up himself for us, Molly, I don't care which, the news world will notice. If your byline ends up on the story, of course, it's better for you. You'd be able to write your own ticket at the *Voice*, and if it gets enough attention you could probably go to Los Angeles or New York or wherever else you'd like."

She had never lived outside west Texas. Palo Duro and El Paso, those were home. She had visited other cities, L.A. and New York and even London once. She didn't know if she would want to move to any of them, though. As awful and polluted and congested as El Paso could be, it could also be beautiful and warm and colorful, and she had a sneaking suspicion that if she let herself examine her feelings, she would discover that she was in love with the place.

But her ambition wouldn't allow her to stay there if those other cities beckoned. New York and Washington, those were where real journalism came from. If she had a shot, she'd have to take it.

And saving the paper and her job all at once? That had a certain appeal, too.

"I'll try, Frank," she said finally. "I'll see what I can do, all right? No promises beyond that."

"I wouldn't ask for any, kid. That's all I want."

His smile was genuine, and she lost herself in it for a moment, enjoying its glow. Sainthood. If he ever really campaigned for it, he was a lock.

6

Lawrence Ingersoll had lived in a big house. James Livingston
Truly, no stranger to big houses, was impressed. Truly's father
had been wealthy even before he'd been a senator, and his father before him, and as far back down the Truly line as anyone
cared to trace. There were investments, there were family businesses, there were extensive real estate holdings. Other things.
One didn't talk too much about it, except during a political
campaign when every effort was made to pretend that they
weren't really that rich after all, and even if they were it didn't
mean they were unlike everyone else. It was almost funny to
see the old man, patrician to the core, acting like a regular joe, a
man of the people.

Big houses had changed in these past couple of decades,
though. The Truly homes, for the most part, had been older.
Palatial for their times, perhaps, but except for the one they
called the Lake House, his father's primary residence now, they
seemed modest. Today it seemed like everyone with some
stock market success built a McMansion. Ingersoll's place
couldn't have been more than five years old or less than seven
thousand square feet.

It was, almost literally, toast.

Truly stood on the driveway, bundled against the cold, gazing at the remains of the once-grand mountain lodge. The heat
of the fire had melted the snow around the house, but the ground
had frozen again, hard and slick, around the building's enormous footprint. Charred logs were strewn about like a giant
child's Lincoln Logs shaken from the box into a campfire.
Thick pines surrounding the house were browned on their near
sides. A couple of outbuildings stood among the trees: a barn
big enough to park a school bus in, and what must have been a

storage shed, both constructed in the same log cabin style, both coated with ash. Yellow CAUTION tape had been wrapped around some of the pines and surrounded the entire scene. It fluttered in a stray breeze with a noise like a small fan. The acrid smell of ashes lay thick in the air.

After Ronald Loesser had told him to leave the Ingersoll case alone, Millicent Wong had called back. This time she had been insistent. "If you don't do something, James, you'll lose us. You don't pay us, but you've always sworn that you would take care of us."

It had been Truly's predecessor, or the ones before him, who had made those promises. He understood that his assignment had been meant as punishment. During the days before the Iraq War, when the administration had made claims about intelligence indicating weapons of mass destruction in that country, Truly had argued that the intelligence was being massaged, manipulated. He had told his superiors that they had to speak out, in public, to prevent the country from going to war on the basis of information they knew to be incorrect. When they wouldn't, he talked to a reporter—off the record, as deep cover, but still in violation of orders.

He would have been fired the day the story broke, if not for Senator Willard Carsten Truly. The old man still had some influence on Capitol Hill, all these years after giving up politics. Influence on the Hill, apparently, translated into job security for his son. Truly had been marginalized, though, and then some evil genius had hit on the idea of marginalizing him entirely by putting him in charge of a program that barely existed, that was a secret to most of the world, and that had no hope of ever entering the mainstream.

Truly had accepted the position, since his only other option was to quit the Agency. His first weeks there, he had spent reading every file he could lay hands on, all the way back to the 1950s and Grill Flame, which had been started as a response to Soviet psychic experimentation. There had been months and months of ESP testing—"reading" the symbols on cards held by the researchers, "seeing" the suits and numbers of playing cards, and the like. Eventually they had moved on to remote viewing tests, where the psychics were given coordinates and drew pictures of what they "saw" in those faraway spots.

Even though he'd been put in charge of Moon Flash, Truly had to dig a bit to find the records of the more controversial tests. Telekinesis, pyrokinesis, spiritualism, ritual magic, the summoning of demons—if it existed in the imagination, it had been tried, and the records were buried in CIA files.

Many of the tests, most even, had been failures. Of course.

What astonished Truly were how many had not.

He had come into the job a confirmed skeptic. Reading some of the reports—and watching video of some of the tests—had shaken that skepticism. He didn't have any way to confirm that the events described in the files had happened the way they were written down, and even video could be faked. But seeing a demonic visage appear in a puff of smoke above a pentangle marked on the floor of a test room right there at Langley made an impact that couldn't easily be denied. Looking at drawings of a power plant in Irkutsk and seeing photographs of the same plant taken *after* the remote viewing that had generated the drawings was also convincing. He had listened to a tape of a test subject who demonstrated such thorough knowledge of the tester's private thoughts that the interview was cut short, the tester's discomfort evident on audio twenty-seven years later. He had heard recordings of mind control experiments in which test subjects really did seem to have their consciousness taken over by someone sitting in a different room.

These things couldn't easily be explained away.

So when Millicent hinted that the psychics and occultists he had inherited from Barry Winston might feel betrayed, he worried. He had come into the job thinking it was a joke, that he would put in his time until he either retired or was forgiven. Neither would happen any time soon. Not yet convinced, he was at least willing to explore further now, and he didn't want to have his network torn apart before he really learned what his people might be capable of.

"Millicent, I'm not sure what I can do," he had argued. "The Agency has strict rules about what we can look into, domestically, and what has to be left up to local law enforcement or some other agency. I'm afraid this case is one that's not in my jurisdiction."

"I hope you're not telling me that you refuse to look into it, even informally, James. Because we would take that as an indication that you are not serious about working with us. That— how did Robb Ivey put it? That it's a one-way street for you—we help you but you don't help us. We're still getting to know you, James. This would be a bad signal to send."

Ultimately, he'd had to agree. She had forced him into a corner, and he couldn't get out of it without sending exactly the signal she had described.

He had gone back to Loesser and told him that he was going to Colorado even if he had to pay for it himself. Money wasn't a problem for him, what with the family wealth, but without Loesser's approval, the whole situation could get ugly. After a testy exchange, Loesser had finally agreed that Truly could go, but only for the reason that Millicent had laid out. He should avoid taking any action, Loesser said, and should be there only as an interested observer. Local law had to take the lead on the investigation. Truly's purpose was smoothing relations with his "psychic friends network," nothing more.

That was fine with Truly. He didn't want to get that involved anyway. Ingersoll was one of the few members of the network he had met face-to-face, and he hadn't particularly liked the man. And he didn't intend to go too far out on a limb anyway for people who would never be allowed to participate meaningfully in any real intelligence work—people he would doubtless abandon whenever he was transferred again. Even if he believed Millicent's doomsday warnings, he wasn't sure there was anything he could do to set things right.

But it would get him out of Washington for a couple of days, give him something to think about besides missing Bethany (he had dialed her number at least twenty times, always managing to hang up before the call went through). He had thought he was keeping her at an emotional arm's length, since she was, after all, married and had never given any indication that she might want to change that status. The breakup had hit him harder than he'd expected, causing him to believe that he had misread his own investment in the affair. It would not have been the first time. He tried to keep tabs on his emotional state, but there had been occasions—and this seemed to be one of them—when he realized that while he was pretty good at reading other people, when it came to his own feelings he was functionally illiterate.

In Colorado, he had stopped at the Mineral County Sheriff's Department, since they had jurisdiction over the fire scene. There a deputy told him that Ingersoll's death had already been ruled accidental. "No sign of foul play," the man said, running a finger across his thick white brush of a mustache. "We figure he fell asleep in a chair, knocked over a candle, and never woke up. There was candles all over the room, looked like. An accident waiting to happen."

The deputy let Truly read the file, which confirmed what he had already said. Arson investigators had concluded that the blaze began in a sealed interior room, spreading rapidly throughout the log structure. The sheriff had signed off on the report just that morning.

That seemingly settled, Truly drove his rented car up to the Arbor House Inn in nearby South Fork. He didn't think there was much more he could learn on his own, but Millicent's plea had given him an idea. She had mentioned Robb Ivey, a psychic who ran an occult bookshop in San Francisco. Truly hadn't even bothered asking Ron for permission, had used his own money for Robb's expenses and fee. Robb had agreed to come out and take a look at the house, check the ley lines or whatever it was psychics did at this kind of scene. He picked Robb up at the hotel where he'd left him before visiting the sheriff's office, and they drove to the house together, letting the car's GPS navigation unit tell Truly the turns.

An hour later, he watched Robb pick his way carefully through the rubble, in which seemingly random objects (a stainless steel refrigerator and matching stove, a plasma screen TV, a single section of wall with a bookcase in front of it) still stood, buried in ash but intact. The psychic was a tall man, skeletally thin and with a shaven head. He looked unhealthy, but up close he had an inner glow that showed itself in his deep-set blue eyes and beneath his pale skin. In Washington, Truly didn't seem to meet many people who were utterly centered and at peace, but that was the impression he got from Robb the moment he shook the psychic's hand in the terminal of the San Luis Valley Regional Airport in Alamosa.

As Robb emerged from the wreckage, he offered a loose-limbed shrug. "I get a sense of fear, right?" he said, his breath steaming in the chill air of late afternoon. "That may be too weak a word. More like terror." He gestured back over his shoulder. "It's especially strong back where you said the room the fire started in was, right? I'm assuming it's a trace emotion Ingersoll left behind, and if that's correct, then just before he died he was freaking petrified of something."

"The knowledge that he was about to burn to death might do that to a guy," Truly observed. "What about what Millicent said she asked him to look into in the first place? The disruption of the ley lines?"

Another shrug. "That's been an ongoing issue since that night. It might be why I can't pick up anything more concrete than that generalized sensation of terror here. But it seems to be easing up a bit now, right, like maybe it was an anomaly caused by a specific incident, and it's normalizing again."

Truly tucked his gloved hands under his arms. The temperature seemed to be dropping by the minute. "That's something to be thankful for, I guess."

Robb glanced over his shoulder, as if worried that something might have followed him from the house. "Depends on what caused the disruption in the first place. If it was something really bad that decided to stick around for a while, it might have only affected the ley lines when it originally passed through. Metaphorically, of course—this might not have been an actual passage but simply a change in status."

"Sounds like you're almost describing something physical, like an object entering our atmosphere."

"Not physical per se, but otherwise the analogy isn't bad."

"Like a wave of . . . what? Power?" Truly genuinely wanted to understand what the man was saying. "Passing through the energy fields?"

"More or less." Robb drew a series of roughly parallel vertical slashes in the air with both hands, then turned them and did the same horizontally. "Think of the ley lines as a grid, like longitude and latitude lines on a globe, right? Except they have no known beginning or end point, they just continue infinitely throughout space. Through our universe and however many other universes there are. Anything that moves has to move through those lines, but most things—you, me, an airplane, a cricket—don't disturb them, because although we generate psychic waves, they're so minute as not to matter. Something that would disturb them—especially to the extent that they seem to have been disrupted the other day—would have to carry major occult weight. And once something that significant passed through, then it would have caused a ripple effect. To mix my metaphors, imagine that the lines are a body of water that envelops the Earth; then whatever passed through would have caused wavelets that ran all the way around, eventually slapping against each other and generating mini-wavelets that started back. Finally things would calm down again, but it would take a while. And whatever the original force was, it wouldn't necessarily be gone now—just not moving around anymore."

"You're not making me feel any better here, Robb."

"I tell all my clients that they may not like what I tell them. Same goes for you."

"How bad could it get? If you're wrong, and things don't go back to normal?"

Robb shrugged. "That's impossible to say. How bad would it get if, say, gravity stopped working? Or the oceans all dried up overnight? Depending on the severity of the disruption, we could be looking at that kind of scale. As I said, I think it's getting better, that the disruption was temporary. But I don't know that for sure, nor do I know how long the ripple effects might last."

Robb rubbed his slender, ungloved hands together to warm them. Truly watched him, then looked back at the burned rubble. He couldn't find a diplomatic way to phrase his next question, so he just asked it. "So you picked up a sensation of fear from a spot where a man burned to death. That it?"

Robb blinked, blew into his clasped hands. "One other thing, but I don't know what it means. A vague sense of a river. Is there a river around here?"

Truly had studied a map of the area on the plane out. "The headwaters of the Rio Grande are nearby. They're not that significant this high up, but that's the biggest. Plenty of other rivers and creeks in the area though."

"Maybe that's what it is, then. I don't know . . . it's just this feeling. Flowing water. A river. Could mean anything, or nothing at all."

Truly stamped his feet. The ground was hard, the cold shooting up through his shoes.

"You know what I would do? In your place?" Robb asked.

"What?"

"Bring Millicent over here."

"Millicent Wong?"

"Nobody's more sensitive than her. If there's anything here—and I think there is—she'll be able to grab hold of it. I wish I could, but it's defeating me. And it sounds like she's upset enough by the whole thing that she might be willing to make the trip."

Which Truly knew he'd be paying for. In more ways than one, he had no doubt. It would entail another argument with Ronald Loesser, for starters. When he came back empty-handed from this trip, after a brief command appearance at his father's home in Michigan, Loesser's limited patience would have run out. Truly would have to be very convincing, or he'd have to lie about where he was going and why.

And if Millicent came up blank, then what? With the official report calling Ingersoll's death an accident, Truly was running out of options fast.

On the bright side, he didn't really need to solve this thing. Maybe asking Millicent to come to Colorado would be good enough to convince her and the others that he was serious about looking after them.

That, after all, was what this had been about from the beginning. The appearance of competence, not the real thing.

His masters in Washington would be proud.

᛫᛫᛫

7

Truly dropped Robb Ivey off at the airport in Alamosa after dark.
From there Robb would catch a United Express flight to Denver, then fly home to San Francisco. He hated flying, had ever
since 9/11, when it had changed from being an occasional treat
to an annoyance. At least he had no luggage to deal with. It had
been a long day, but Sandra was home with the twins, two boys,
eight years old, and they were a handful and a half. Then there
were the dogs, two Italian greyhounds, and they demanded attention as well. So he had made the journey a one-day turn-
around, scheduling the first flight that would get him into
Alamosa and the last one that would take him away.

When he was younger, his older sister had played Donovan
albums until her record player wore out, and he had grown up
hearing the warbling Welshman. Now he wished Donovan's
Trans-love Airways was an actual option, because at least they
would probably serve vegan food and spiritual enlightenment,
and he was pretty certain that neither was part of United Express's customer service regime.

Plus, Donovan promised that Trans-love would get you
there on time, and that also seemed a thing of the past when it
came to air travel.

Alamosa's tiny airport was far from crowded, but even here
he saw people standing at the security checkpoint holding their
liquids in zippered plastic bags. The whole idea was absurd. It
was like the whole country, maybe the whole world, had gone
nuts.

And Agent Truly, of course, worked for one of the nuttier
organizations around. Robb had agreed to perform some tests
for them, because he had wanted to test his skills in a rigidly

controlled environment where, he suspected, no one would expect him to actually succeed. Besides, he loved his country, and if the CIA could use him for some productive purpose he would happily do as he was asked.

So far, with this one exception, it had been a lot of testing and re-testing but without much in the way of positive contributions. For that matter, this one hadn't worked out the way anyone would have preferred. But at least it *resembled* useful, even if it hadn't really proved to be.

Truly was an odd duck, too. His wide blue eyes seemed to take up a full third of his face, like he was some cartoon icon designed for maximum cuteness. Hard to take seriously as a CIA agent, though, with that face. He projected an absolute lack of guile, which might come in handy as long as it was only an illusion.

He had seemed distracted, too. His body was in Colorado but his mind was elsewhere. Robb had sensed that a woman was involved. Maybe he had broken up with someone recently, or maybe the trip had brought back strong memories of someone he had been to Colorado with in the past. Robb had tried not to pry, but some things just forced themselves on him, if the emotions were strong enough. In Truly's case, they had been raw and powerful.

With thirty-five minutes before his flight, he decided to go into the restroom. He'd been holding his bladder since halfway down the mountain from Ingersoll's place, and he felt ready to burst. A few minutes in there, then he'd go through security and wait at the gate.

"Fly Trans-love Airways" repeated over and over in his head.

Thanks, Sis.

Captain Vance Brewer had been debating whether or not to kill both men since they had arrived at the psychic's house up in the San Juans. He had reached the scene before them and had hunkered down in the trees about six hundred yards away. By the time the two men showed up, he had assembled a parabolic microphone, set it up on a tripod, and pointed it toward the wreckage. When they got there (as the old man's drawings had predicted they would), he could hear every word as easily as if he'd been standing right next to them.

In the end he had decided to let them go. The guy who drove—the baby-faced man with the wide blue eyes—didn't seem to know anything about anything. And the other one, the one who was clued in, was clearly working for him. He was a psychic, apparently, but maybe not a very good one, since he had drawn a blank here, not even sensing an onlooker.

Brewer followed them to the airport and parked at the curb with a Homeland Security placard on his dashboard when Baby-Face let the tall, bald psychic out.

The guy had just gone into the men's room, which meant Brewer had to make a final decision now. Restrooms were an ideal killing ground—almost no business or institution had put surveillance cameras in them yet, although cameras were commonplace almost everywhere else. And you could lock the body up in a stall, so by the time anyone found it (even janitors weren't inclined to disturb a man in a locked stall) you could be long gone. He had gone inside the terminal after the psychic on the off chance that he'd been lying to Baby-Face, that he really had learned something he hadn't shared with his boss.

Brewer watched the men's room door for thirty seconds, forty. Finally, he went inside. The tall man was at a sink, washing his hands. Brewer stopped in front of the mirror and ran water into his own hands. He dashed some into his face, wiped it off the bridge of his flat, prominent nose, and smoothed down the short, once-black hair (*more gray in it every week,* he mused) that he combed back off his forehead. He pretended to examine the bags that had formed under his eyes these last few years, the lines at the corners of those eyes, the creases around his mouth, while he watched the psychic wash up. At fifty-two he had a physique that men in their early thirties envied—a few pounds not precisely where he'd like them, maybe, but solid and muscular, flat-stomached, with broad, sloping shoulders and a thick neck and powerful arms that ended in hands that looked big enough to choke a lion.

"Getting old sucks," he said after a few moments.

"Tell me about it," the psychic replied. He gave Brewer a long, curious look in the mirror, then turned away, shook water from his hands, turned to the automated paper towel machine, waved in front of it. A towel was dispensed and the psychic tore it off, wiped his hands dry. It wasn't until he was tossing the wadded-up towel into the trash that Brewer decided to let him live.

Your lucky day, pal. Good thing for you I don't think you know anything.

By the time he was out of the restroom, the psychic was passing through the security checkpoint. Brewer watched his back until he was out of sight, then went back to his car. He had a long drive ahead of him, through the night. He hated to be away from the old man for too long.

Who knew what the man might draw next?

8

From the air, El Paso and Ciudad Juárez looked like a single city bisected by the Rio Grande. Like Paris and the Seine, or London and the Thames, Wade thought. From the low point of the river's concrete channel, buildings spread across the hills, reaching farther every time he flew in or out, it seemed, a quickly metastasizing cancer of urban sprawl.

Which, given that his main reason for coming was to see Byrd before the leukemia took him, might not have been the best analogy. Fortunately, he hadn't spoken it out loud, and he could chastise himself mentally for it without embarrassing himself.

CNN had kicked in for a first class seat home, and as much downtime as he needed. Wade understood the unspoken warning that he'd better not need more than a month or six weeks, including the holidays, since twenty-four-hour cable news waited for no man or woman, however damaged.

He could always find another job, though. He'd never find another Byrd McCall. Which meant he would stay right here as long as it took. It would be just fine with him if the war ended while he sat beside Byrd's hospital bed. The days of captivity had been a bitch, no denying that, but over the long haul he thought the days of reporting on mass deaths—forty in a marketplace on one day, seventy at a police station the next, then thirty-four job seekers killed by a car bomb, American troops slaughtered by IEDs, and more, and more—wore on him even harder.

It was all part of the job. Adding to the stress, stateside politicians blamed the media for not reporting the good things that were happening, the schools being opened and the electricity being restored. That wasn't the case—Wade longed for positive stories, if only to clear his palate of the shitstorm that was his daily life, and the daily life of virtually everyone else in Iraq.

As the plane dropped toward El Paso International Airport, he felt the weight of war lift off his shoulders, as surely as if he was leaving it behind at thirty thousand feet. Another weight— the fear of facing a dying friend—was replacing it, but that weight he was willing to bear.

These last few days had been strange ones, almost as bizarre as the captivity itself. After being checked out at Ibn Sina Hospital in Baghdad (some cracked ribs, two teeth gone, various bruises and lacerations), he had spent a day being debriefed by military intelligence officers. Based on his description, they had backtracked and found the bombed-out mosque, but the tunnels beneath were empty, a colonel told him unhappily, with no indication that they had been occupied anytime in the recent past. Wade wasn't trying to keep any secrets, although he had glossed over the more unbelievable aspects of his escape, wanting more time to think over what had happened—and to convince himself that it wasn't all in his head—before discussing those. Colonel Cox said that the neighborhood had been populated when the troops went in, which didn't square with Wade's experience. He suffered the colonel's thinly veiled implications that he was hiding something, but he was glad to get on a plane.

His next stop was the American military hospital in Landstuhl, Germany, where his injuries were looked at once more and a new batch of intelligence officers took a shot at his story. He told it the same way, glossing over the weirdness. He spent a night there, then got on yet another airplane, bound for Atlanta and CNN headquarters.

At CNN, he received a hero's welcome, with cameras rolling the whole time. The footage must have aired fifty times in the next twenty-four hours; every time he caught the channel, on a hotel set or in an airport, it seemed to come up again, like coleslaw that had sat in the sun too long at a Fourth of July picnic.

After dinner with some of the network's top brass and a night in Atlanta, he finally got onto a flight for El Paso. He had taken several long, hot showers in the interim, but he hadn't shaved; he wouldn't be on camera for a good while, and it seemed like a good time to regrow the beard he'd had to hack off for his first television gig so long ago.

Because it promised decent gas mileage, Wade drove a rented Ford Focus straight from the airport to Providence Memorial Hospital, on Oregon Street. The hospital was a collection of yellowish tan buildings, several stories tall, just up the hill from UTEP. The neighborhood was full of medical facilities, so many that it seemed everyone on the streets must be a sickie or a student.

Unlike the hospital in Germany, which had stunk of disinfectant, or Baghdad's, which reeked of blood and decay, Providence's scent was clean and fresh. Even here, he was recognized and fussed over. While he hoped it wouldn't be a regular occurrence, it did help him cut through the red tape and find out where Byrd's private room was, in the Young Tower.

Byrd looked awful.

He smiled when Wade entered the room, but his gums were pink and raw, his face gaunt, as if it had begun to collapse in on itself, the skin bruised and covered with sores. His formerly thick brown hair was gone, stolen away by chemotherapy. The scar across his left eyebrow stood out more than it used to, the damaged tissue there slick and white. He sat up in the bed, bracing himself on a right arm from which the muscle tone had gone, along with most of the fat, leaving behind loose, damaged skin.

"I look swell, huh?" he said as Wade regarded him. "You look good, though, under those bruises." He stroked his chin. "Beard, too. I like."

"Thanks. You've looked better, dude," Wade admitted.

"I know. You want to see my peri-rectal abscess? I can't get a good view of it, myself, but I'm told it's a beaut."

"I'll pass on that particular pleasure." Wade crossed the room and leaned over the bed to embrace his friend. Byrd seemed almost weightless in his arms, as if he held a bundle of dry sticks instead of a man. "How're you feeling?"

"You know how I look?"

"Yeah?" Wade released him and backed away a couple of steps. Byrd waved him toward a guest chair.

"That's about how I feel. Pretty shitty, most of the time. The doctors do what they can, and the nurses. There's this one nurse, a little Latina, yum. If you can stick around until shift change, I think you can meet her. Single, too."

Wade lowered himself into the chair by feel, unable to tear his gaze from Byrd. "God, man, this is so . . . I can't believe it. I just can't."

"Believe it, bro. Acute myelocytic leukemia, they call it. Came up out of nowhere, and the docs were amazed at how fast it progressed. Not exactly my definition of progress, but you know what I mean."

"Right. You always were an odd one."

"I am this time. A regular showpiece. They've had all sorts of visitors, doctors from all over the place, comin' in to look at me. It's comforting to be a visual aid for disease studies, let me tell you."

Wade wasn't sure how to approach his next question, so he just stepped right up to it. Journalistic instincts kicking in. "Do they know . . . ?"

He couldn't finish, but Byrd took it from there. "How much longer? No. Could be months or years, under normal conditions. But I, of course, haven't presented them with normal conditions yet, and they don't expect me to start any time soon. In technical terms, my monocytes and granulocytes are fucked. They're not maturing properly—"

"Well, that's in character, at least."

"Thanks. Pick on the sick guy. Anyway, my immature cells—they like to call them blasts, maybe so they'll sound like they're watchin' an action flick instead of a bunch of microscopic gunk—affect my ability to create red blood cells and platelets, and interfere with . . . well, just about everything else my body has to do to keep going. It's been a real learnin' experience, bud. And a treat. Blood in my urine, shortness of breath, weight loss. What they call 'abdominal fullness.' Bone marrow transplants, now there's a joyful time. Thank God for Molly; I'm sure being a donor was no picnic either. And then there's the chemo. And buying clothes in the boy's department because they don't come skinny enough in men's. You've really been missin' out on the good stuff." Byrd smiled again, a death's head grin that chilled Wade to the core. "But you didn't come here to talk about my illness."

"Actually, I did."

"I heard you were missing in Iraq, though. That must have been interesting, at least. What happened?"

"I got kidnapped by insurgents, they smacked me around for a while, then I got away. No big."

"That's not what CNN says." Byrd indicated the TV mounted high on the wall. "You've been all over it. I told the nurses I knew you. Thought it might get me a hand job, but you know, no luck yet."

"Juárez isn't far away," Wade said. "Can't you take field trips?"

"I don't know how much good it'd do, but I can go anywhere I want. It's just a matter of staying awake, out of pain—and in Juárez, I guess, of gettin' it up."

"You're not taking my brother to some Mexican whorehouse, Scheiner." Wade glanced up to see Molly walking in carrying a brown paper bag with the top folded over several times. "You want him to get syphilis or something?"

"Like that's my biggest worry right now," Byrd said with a dry chuckle.

Wade hadn't seen Byrd in a couple of years, but it must have been eight or nine since he'd seen Molly. He had met Byrd for runs on various rivers, and a couple times Byrd had flown out to Atlanta or Washington, when he'd been living there. Escaping west Texas had, for Wade, been like escaping from the cell beneath the mosque, on a far grander scale. He had been in no hurry to return.

And Molly, who had been a lovely, grown-up college graduate the last time he had been to town, had matured even more in the intervening years. Her face had filled out a little, and a minute tracery of lines around her eyes and the corners of her mouth hinted at plenty of laughter, and maybe some worry—living, anyway—in that time. Her hair was almost black, lustrous even this late in the day.

She dropped the sack onto the bed and opened her arms as Wade thrust himself out of the chair toward her. After Byrd, he was glad to hug someone he wasn't worried about breaking in his arms. Plus, she smelled better than her brother. Wade breathed in the aromas of shampoo and soap, lotion and sweat, all helping to dull the bitter, sharp stink of Byrd's encroaching death. "I'm so glad you're here," she said, her face pressed against his collarbone.

"Me too," he replied. The words almost caught in his throat and for a moment he was afraid he would burst into tears. "I've missed you guys so much."

"Enough of that mushy shit," Byrd interrupted. "What'd you bring me?"

Molly disengaged from Wade and shoved the paper bag to where Byrd could reach it. He pawed at it eagerly, unrolling the top and shaking a couple of magazines onto the bed.

"Porn?" Wade asked.

Byrd held them up so Wade could see. *Outside*, *National Geographic Adventure*, and *Outdoor Explorer*. "Nature porn," Byrd announced. "The only thing that gets me off these days."

"Why the brown paper bag treatment?" Wade asked.

"He has a reputation to uphold," Molly said. "The nurses would be horribly disappointed if they thought I wasn't sneaking titty mags in for him."

"That's right," Byrd said. "I'm the ward perv."

"Didn't Elena divorce you because she didn't think you'd ever grow up?"

"I still can't decide if she was a bitch, or just prescient," Molly said. "Can't argue with her conclusion, though."

"If it hasn't caught up with me yet, it's not goin' to," Byrd said. "How's she doing, anyway?" Wade asked. "She been around to see you much?"

"She's living in Indiana, for fuck's sake," Byrd answered. "With her new husband, who's a dentist or something like that. Orthodontist. Somethin' serious and grown-up and boring. They have a munchkin, too."

"And you sold the store, right?" McCall Adventure Gear, Byrd's attempt to extend his river rat lifestyle into something that the former Elena Oliveros would have considered a respectable trade. Most days Byrd had spent behind the counter trading lies about river runs with the customers, in between selling maps, guidebooks, backpacks, GPS units, and bags of gorp. The only indication of his passion in the room, besides the magazines Molly had brought and a stack of similar ones on a bedside table, was the handle half of a broken wooden oar leaning in one corner.

"What do you think's paying for a private room?" Byrd said. "The McCalls are nothing if not bad with money."

"Financial incompetence was our only inheritance from our folks," Molly added. She sat on the edge of Byrd's bed, and Wade took his seat in the guest chair again. The room had seemed to brighten when she came in, its peach-colored walls lighter by a shade or two, the dying sunlight leaking through closed blinds more golden than before.

"How long"—Byrd stifled a yawn—"are you stayin', Wade?"

Wade had hoped the question would not be put to him in quite that way. The visit would be finite, but he didn't want to talk about its ending. "As long as you want me to."

"Shit, buy a house then," Byrd said. "Settle in." He yawned again.

"We should let you get some rest, Byrd," Molly said.

Wade expected Byrd to argue (the old Byrd would have, and he would have won the battle), but he simply nodded. "Come back in the mornin'?" he said.

"I'm here for you," Wade assured his friend. "If you want me here, I'll be here."

"Oh, I want you, baby," Byrd said. He laughed, a ghastly, weary sound. "So bad."

"I'll be here whenever they open the doors," Wade promised. He and Molly started toward the door.

"Wait, listen up, y'all!" Byrd called. "How's this? 'That guy has to stop. He'll see us.'" He grinned fiercely at them.

"What's that from?" Wade asked.

Molly gave a dramatic sigh. "He's been studying up on famous last words."

"Got to be ready," Byrd said. "That was James Dean, right before someone smashed into his Porsche Spyder. 1955. What do you think?"

"Doesn't apply," Molly said. "Keep hunting."

"Don't worry," Byrd said. "I got a million of 'em."

Molly led Wade from the room, shaking her head. "He does, too. Whole books of them."

"At least he thinks ahead," Wade said. "I didn't think he ever did that unless he was planning a river trip."

"He's matured in some ways. Obviously not completely. If

he lived another forty years, maybe. . . ." She swallowed hard, pressed her knuckles against her lips so hard the color vanished from them. "Where are you staying, Wade?"

"I don't know yet. I'll get a hotel, I guess, somewhere close by."

"The Hilton Garden Inn is just down the street," Molly said. "You can walk here from there. But you might want to think about something longer-term. It could be days, Wade, but it could be weeks, too. Or longer. Nobody knows because nobody's seen a case move as fast as his. The doctors think he's had chronic leukemia, maybe since childhood, that never exhibited any symptoms, was never caught. When it turned acute and he started to fall apart, they were amazed by how quickly it spread." She had stemmed the tears, but her green eyes glistened in the overhead light of the hospital corridor. Ahead, someone pushed a patient in a wheelchair through an intersection. "What I'm saying is you should think about an apartment, maybe one of those short-term places that come furnished. You could be here awhile."

"I hope I am," Wade said. "There's a lot of lost time to make up for."

"It wasn't lost if you were doing something with it."

"You know what I mean. Time I wasn't with Byrd, when I would rather have been."

"He's thrilled you're here now. You don't know what he's been like. I mean, he'll always be Byrd, you know, funny and goofy and profane. But it's been an effort for him. It's taken a toll. With you here, though, it comes more easily, more naturally. So thanks for that." She started walking again, reached an elevator and pushed the down button. The elevator dinged and the door opened immediately. "I'll try to find you a place," she said. "After all, I'm the star reporter for the fastest-growing independent weekly newspaper in El Paso County. What good is all my power if I can't sneak an advance peek at this week's classifieds?"

9

⊐╫⊏

Molly took Wade to dinner at the Greenery Restaurant in the Sun-land Park Mall, which she said had become one of her favorites in town. He couldn't fault the choice. After his time in captivity, followed by hospital food and the ceremonial fare he was fed by CNN, he was happy to order a hamburger, happier still to find it big and delicious. He had checked into the hotel she recommended, and decided to stay there for a while, to see what the future would bring.

While they dined, they talked about things other than Byrd's condition. She told him about the *Voice of the Borderlands* and her work there, and threatened to pick his brain for tips on career advancement. "I don't think you'd want to listen to my advice," he said. "I wanted to be an environmental reporter. If I knew how to manage my career, that's what I'd be—Byrd would be reading my stuff in *Outside*, maybe. But someone thought I'd look good in front of a camera, and the money was better, and the next thing I knew I was anchoring in San Francisco, then a network reporter in D.C., and then CNN came calling with buckets of cash."

"There are worse things than buckets of cash," Molly said.

"Sure there are. No buckets, for one. Or empty buckets. But the point is, I didn't guide my career in any direction at all. I just took the cash, let it lead me around like it had my nose in a death grip." Bad word choice, but it was already out so he left it there. "I went where the money was instead of planning my moves."

"Well, that's a problem I don't have," Molly said. "The *Voice* is definitely not where the money is. But I like it there. It's a good fit, at least right now."

"That's the important thing," Wade said. "If you're making

enough to live on and you love what you're doing, that's great."

"I think there's an inalienable law of physics. Only one superstar can come from a place like Palo Duro, and you're it."

"Malo Duro, you mean."

Molly genuinely laughed for the first time since he had seen her in her brother's hospital doorway. "Malo Duro."

"I'm glad you've kept some of your accent," Wade said. When she said "Malo Duro," she stretched out the *a* in *Malo* and almost turned *Duro* into two words: *Doo Row*. Of the three of them, though, Byrd had the strongest Texas accent by far.

"I cain't even hear y'all's," Molly said, intentionally exaggerating hers. People from east Texas were Southerners, but in west Texas, they were Westerners, and the accent differed accordingly. "A body'd think you'd never even set foot in Texas."

"You can thank my voice coach for that. She worked me over good."

He took another bite of burger and the conversation faded. Palo Duro meant "hard wood" in Spanish—literally, "wood hard." The town had been named after a peculiarly hardy stand of mesquite trees near the river. As bored teenagers in their small rural town, they had christened it Malo Duro, which meant "bad hard," or idiomatically, "long-lasting bad." Although Wade could no longer recall the new name's precise origin, that had to have been Byrd's idea. He had always been the cleverest of them. The biggest and oldest, too, the natural leader.

It just wasn't right that he should die first. He was the best of them, and always had been.

And this, Wade reflected, was why he had stayed away from west Texas for so long. All coming back did was dredge up the past, and the past was something that he would rather leave undisturbed. In his job he could focus his attention on the present—what happened today, not what happened twenty years ago.

That was exactly how he liked it.

"How's that burger?" Molly asked, dragging him back into the now. "You're eating it with a great deal of relish."

"No, just—" he started, then he caught the narrowing of her eyes and the crinkling around her nose that had always meant she was teasing, all the way back to when she was ten. "Okay, you got me. Sorry I was kind of drifting there."

"I've been kind of drifty myself today."

"So how's your love life?" he asked, completing his return to the present. "I'm surprised you're not married. If, y'know, marriage is your thing these days. Or women, or whatever."

"Oh, I'm straight, for what that's worth. Not really looking too hard at the moment. There was a guy, but . . . I'll come off as some kind of a man-hater or something, and that's totally not me. I understand that some guys are nice and some guys are jerks, and I just don't get why some women decide that it's better to be with the jerks and hate it and complain incessantly about it, rather than being alone and maybe waiting for one of the nice ones to show up. I was with a guy, and we were starting to talk about moving in together, maybe getting married."

"And he turned out to be one of the jerks?" Wade asked.

"Bingo." She punctuated that by pointing a French fry at Wade. "I found out before we took the next step, which was lucky. Turned out he liked booze more than women, and he thought a wife might make a handy designated driver. It wasn't just that, either. He was sincerely convinced that he was surrounded by what he called 'haters.' He thought everyone was lying to him all the time, even me. I eventually figured out he was paranoid, suspecting everyone of some ulterior, sinister motive."

"Did he run for political office? Sounds like a natural."

"For all I know, he could be in Congress by now. When I broke it off with him, he made it abundantly clear that he didn't want me in his life at all. He was such an asshole about the breakup that I was happy to oblige. I haven't even Googled him since then, and I'm not curious in the least."

"Sounds like you're better off without him," Wade said. He rubbed the palm of his left hand. The skin there was dry, itchy. He'd need to put some lotion on before bed.

"No doubt."

"And you're happy?" He hoped she said yes. One troubled McCall at a time was plenty.

She hesitated for a long time, dabbing a couple of fries into ketchup and eating them as she considered his question. He had anticipated a quick response, even if it was a facile one, but she had obviously decided to take the question seriously. "I guess I've mostly put my life on hold while I worry about Byrd," she said finally. "That takes over everything else. But except for that, you know, there are some pressures on the job but I basically love that. Would I like to get laid more often? Who wouldn't? I don't mind waking up in the morning and I'm not afraid of going to bed at night, so I guess I'd have to say that makes me pretty happy. Happy with reservations."

"That's not a bad summation," Wade said. "A lot of people couldn't say that." Himself included, although he left that bit of fluff in his pocket. He couldn't point to a time that he had believed himself to be genuinely happy—content, sure, satisfied, but not happy in the word's truest sense—in the last decade or so. Longer, really, when he pushed it. The last truly happy times he remembered were days and night on rivers, with Byrd; floating or paddling to keep the bow headed down the chute, or driving Byrd's clattering old pickup hundreds of miles to or from a river, spinning the radio dial at night to pick up distant AM stations at night when their signals bounced around the atmosphere, or simply lying at night on a sand spit looking at whatever stars could be seen between tall sandstone walls while a small fire burned, smoke and sparks rising into the darkness as meager offerings from the river rats to the river gods.

He thought there had been happy times back in Malo Duro, but those days were so inextricably wound up with the awful ones that it was hard to know for sure.

He did know that he felt *alive* now, in a way that he hadn't for many years. The renewed sense of freedom that came from having survived his Iraqi ordeal and the contrast with Byrd's precarious state both reinforced that. He had been granted a rare second chance, the opportunity to back away from false steps, to build his own future starting now.

It was more than that, though. Something else, too, some unknown, unanticipated vitality, seemed to bubble just under the surface of his consciousness, where he couldn't quite get a handle on it. It was like that hated sensation of knowing the right word but not being able to seize it, when you were live on camera and you couldn't stop to consult a thesaurus.

But oh, did it bubble and churn. When he got his hands on it, he would be a new (*Kethili*) man. That he knew with absolute certainty.

"Sorry?" Molly asked.

"What?"

She speared an asparagus stalk with her fork. "I thought you said something, but I didn't catch it."

Had he? In retrospect he thought that perhaps *she* had said something under *her* breath, an unfamiliar word. He was pretty sure *he* hadn't, although he might have subvocalized something without realizing it. "No, I don't think so."

She shrugged and returned to her meal.

And he picked up where his train of thought had left off. Old Wade Scheiner, Wade the golden boy, the star reporter, news anchor, river rat, was becoming something else. Turning a page.

A new man.

10

Gretchen Fuchs—and yes, she'd heard all the jokes, most of them about a thousand times each—bustled around her little house near Sunland Park, on the west side of El Paso. Her friends, Lucy, Carole, and Trish, had left about ten minutes before, after asking twice if she wanted help with the dinner dishes. Of course she did, but she had done the polite thing and refused, hoping they would just get off their asses and start washing.

For a second, it looked like Trish would, and her ass was the skinniest, most barely there of the lot, thanks to all the running she did. To hear her talk about it, running was not only her favorite activity, it was almost the only activity she allowed herself. The conversation had, as always, ranged far and wide, but also as always, given that they were four single, heterosexual, relatively sane and balanced women in their thirties, often veered back toward men and sex and how much they were or were not getting. Lucy, whose standards were a little more flexible than the rest (Gretchen didn't want to apply judgmental terms like "morals" to the equation), got the most of all of them, and Trish, thin and muscular as a racing greyhound, had been on an unfortunately long dry streak.

They talked about other things, too—about the state of the world, the political situation, the seemingly interminable war, traffic on Interstate 10 and in downtown El Paso, and how with the price of gas what it was, stretching a paycheck all the way to the end of the month was harder than ever.

Gretchen kicked off her shoes and washed the dishes. She had a window above the sink, but at the moment, she couldn't see into the dark backyard (small, mostly paved with cracked concrete, through which weeds were starting to sprout—she'd have to get out there and pull them soon), so she settled for glances at her ghostly reflection in the glass. Not as skinny as Trish or as voluptuous as Lucy, she felt okay about her body. While she could stand to lose a few pounds, she was healthy, and the fullness actually helped keep her face from being too long and gaunt. Her blond hair had been contained before the dinner, but had since slipped loose of its moorings, strands of it floating around her face like satellite appendages.

She had scraped all the bones—she'd served Cornish game hens, with green beans and a nice salad and French fingerling potatoes roasted in loads of garlic and rosemary—off the plates and into the kitchen wastebasket. The bag would have to go out tonight, with bones and meat scraps in it, or her kitchen would stink to high heaven by morning. And that was assuming Briscoe, the Persian who had disappeared into the house's nether regions as soon as the first doorbell rang that evening, would leave it alone.

When the last of the dishes were either arranged in the dishwasher or put away in her cabinets, she pulled the plastic bag from the wastebasket, twirled it around a couple of times to close the neck, and tied it off. It felt heavy at the bottom, as if fats and grease from the little birds had already sunk through the other trash.

She carried it to the back door, half-expecting to see Briscoe emerge from some closet or hallway now that the strange voices had been gone for a while. At the door, she paused and flicked the switch to turn on the backyard light. Her garbage cans were kept back there, tucked behind a little half fence beside her air-conditioning unit.

The light didn't come on.

Something else to add to her chores list. Without a ladder she couldn't reach the bulb, mounted high up on the back wall, so she wasn't about to mess with it tonight. She knew her way to the garbage cans, after all. She closed the door behind herself—Briscoe was strictly an indoors kitty—and descended the four concrete steps, holding the bag at arm's length. Somebody on the street had a fire going, and the smoke lent a comfortable fragrance to the night air.

Her yard was about twenty feet square and partially enclosed by high concrete block walls. In addition to the AC unit and garbage cans, it contained a rarely used charcoal grill, an

eight-foot-long wooden planter box in which she grew herbs
and strawberries, and a bicycle she rode even less often than
she barbecued. The last couple of feet of the yard weren't paved,
and the developer had planted trees there that still hadn't matured into anything impressive. Of course, she also hadn't
watered them much, since in west Texas desert landscaping was
more appropriate than whatever kind of trees they were. It
was obvious that a wooden fence had, at one time, connected
the two straight walls, probably with a gate, and the trees would
have stood up against that fence, but at some point before
Gretchen bought the place the wooden fence had been torn
down, leaving just those spurs of concrete block and those
spindly trees to seal off the yard.

Beyond the trees, the yard opened onto a gravel-covered alleyway (where she would drag the garbage cans, come Tues-
day night). She didn't like having the alley back there, although
it did come in handy at times. People who hung out in alleys
weren't the kind of people she wanted skulking around the back
of her house. And Briscoe wasn't much of a watchcat.

In the dark—really dark tonight, the moon having ducked
behind a cloud, and the neighbors' lights, which usually
flooded directly at her rear wall, turned off for a change—
Gretchen felt her way to the garbage cans. She tugged off the
plastic lid of the nearest and dropped her bag in. It hit the bottom with a wet thump that made her think of a dead thing, as if
it were Briscoe and not just dinner scraps being thrown away.

When she had put the lid back on, snapping it into place,
she started back toward the house.

Then a sound from the alleyway froze her in place.

She couldn't identify it. Maybe a raccoon or a javelina or
something walking around out there. It had definitely sounded
like something moving deliberately, not just a bit of debris skit-
tering along on the wind. Anyway, there was no wind; the night
was as still as any she could remember.

Still, and dark.

For God's sake, she thought, smiling in the darkness, y*ou'll
give yourself a heart attack.* Whatever made the noise had
stopped. Probably a stray cat, ordinarily silent, who had
stepped in something sticky.

It wasn't someone sneaking around the alley looking for a

victim, which had been her first thought. *That's just stupid, Gretch. Paranoid.*

Still, stupid or not, she picked up her pace a little, hurrying back to the stairs so fast that she stubbed her big toe on the bottom one. "Ow!" she said. "Shit!" She bent over to inspect the toe in the light that came through the kitchen window, afraid she had torn off the nail.

And it was while she stood there, bent almost double, right hand clutching her foot, that Gretchen heard another noise, louder this time, closer. She released her foot and scrambled up the stairs and closed her fist around the doorknob, but it had locked itself. Sometimes the thumb latch did that if she wasn't careful when she closed it, and this must have been one of those times.

By the time it occurred to her to scream, it was too late. A bulky, shadowed form closed on her, a hand clapped over her mouth, and as her attacker wrenched at her neck she could smell rank sweat and something else, maybe steak sauce on his hands.

You weren't paranoid after all, Gretch, she thought at the end. *There really was someone in the alley.*

11

Ginny Tupper watched a hawk wheel through the blue Texas sky
until she lost it in the bright burn of the morning sun. She
thought it was a Harris's hawk, but birds weren't her specialty
by any means, just a pleasant occasional fringe benefit of her
specialty. Anthropology kept her outdoors more often than not,
which she appreciated. Her trade also, by necessity, sent her to
places where she could be alone, or with a few chosen companions, away from the crowded cities she had lived in until these
past couple of years, with college behind her at last and her
life's real task ahead.

She had awakened around dawn in the Palo Duro Motel, an
establishment with absolutely nothing to recommend it except
its proximity to the little-explored rock art at Smuggler's Canyon on the Rio Grande. Its walls were brick and did little to keep
out November's chill, and the heater under the window roared
like a wounded water buffalo when it was turned on. After a
tepid shower she tromped across the gravel parking lot to the
adjacent Café (that was its whole name, as far as she could tell),
set up in a similar brick building except that it was painted yellow instead of adobe buff. She caught a few of the diners eyeing
her out the window, looking away quickly when she met their
stares, and she could guess what they were seeing and saying.
Wonder if she plays basketball was the top choice. A modern
classic was *Did you know Janet Reno had a daughter?*

Ginny was accustomed to the stares and the comments. You
didn't grow up as the most noticeable person on your block
without either developing a thick skin and a sense of humor or
throwing yourself under a bus. The people in the café saw a
tall, sturdy woman, a hairsbreadth shy of six one, with a shock
of frizzy red curls and fair skin on which her frequent exposure

to the sun had raised vast fields of freckles. She was dressed in jeans and a hooded blue sweatshirt, with a red windbreaker pulled over that, and hiking boots with fluorescent pink laces.

She had, in fact, played basketball in school, but she was no relation to the former attorney general. The topic of her parentage was what had brought her to Palo Duro, though, and it was at Smuggler's Canyon (an hour later, the hawk having disappeared in the sun, Ginny beginning her anxious scramble up into the rocks) that she hoped to finally find out what had happened to her father more than twenty years earlier.

She had spent the previous two days at the Canyon, climbing and crawling, bellying beneath overhangs and inching into narrow slots, looking at the ancient rock art her father had sketched and studied. Somewhere around thirty million years ago, give or take a millennium or two, molten magma had bubbled up from beneath the earth's crust here, forcing limestone formations through the surface, then cooling and weathering into a massive jumble of granite-like boulders that soared a couple hundred feet into the air. The Rio Grande had sliced a channel right through the formation, leaving most of it on the U.S. side but a separate, smaller chunk in Mexico. According to the stories, its network of caves and canyons had made it ideal for smuggling going both ways across the border for at least the last hundred years.

Before that, however, Smuggler's Canyon had been sacred to dozens of different First Americans, from Paleo-Indians of twelve thousand years ago, through Archaic, Mogollon, Comanche, Apache, and no doubt others who had lived in the area or simply passed through. Hollis Tupper had taken minute samples of some of the pictographs he had recorded and had them dated in labs, and the pigments (made from local berries, insects, mud, minerals, animal fats, even urine, in an astonishing variety of colors) had been almost ten thousand years old. Petroglyphs, art etched or pecked on the surface of the rocks, were likely older but couldn't always be dated as precisely.

Even more diverse and surprising than the materials and workmanship was the sheer number of individual rock drawings. Ginny's father had recorded 243 of them, and had hinted that he believed there were more he had not yet been able to get good looks at. There were dozens of face masks, many animal portraits, hunting and war scenes, pictures representing the seasons, the sun and the moon, and abstract images that had yet to be identified.

Studying the records he had sent home, Ginny was surprised by how fascinating she found it all, and an adolescent obsession turned into a degree and a career. Always, though, she had kept her main goal in mind: getting to Smuggler's Canyon, which was the last place she was certain her father had been, and figuring out what had happened to him when she was six years old, a little girl who couldn't understand why Daddy went on one of his trips and never came home again.

Her favorite childhood memory—one that had sustained her through hard times during the years of his absence—was from a family trip to the Grand Canyon when she was eight. They had spent a few days on the South Rim, admiring the expansive views, changing minute by minute and hour by hour as the sun slipped through cloudless blue skies. Then they had driven to Lees Ferry and taken a raft into the canyon, stopping at different points along the Colorado so her father could show his family traces of the prehistoric occupation of the area. His enthusiasm for the Anasazi people had been evident, and when he had taken them up to ancient storage bins in Nankoweap Canyon, it had been contagious. To this day, she remembered her childish amazement at the way stones had been fitted together so carefully that they remained in place thousands of years later. Hollis Tupper had taken a few sticks and twisted them into the shape of a deer, demonstrating how the Anasazi people had made toys for their own children centuries before. She still had one of those twig animals in her room at her mother's house. Holding it in her hands invariably summoned memories of her father's warm hands and scratchy cheeks and the dry summer air that had surrounded them that day.

This morning, for the first time, she had company at Smuggler's Canyon. When she arrived, a blue van was parked in the little dirt circle where she had been leaving her Kia Sportage. She parked some distance from the van and climbed out, looking at the other vehicle like it was an unwanted intruder, a burlesque dancer in church. What was someone doing here, among *her* rocks? The license plate was from Nebraska (although her own SUV had California plates, so she couldn't buck much about that) and the van screamed "tourist" to her. It even had one of those plastic shells on the luggage rack for carrying yet more luggage.

She scouted around for discarded water bottles or candy wrappers, certain that these interlopers couldn't care as much for the canyon as she did. Seeing no immediate despoiling of the landscape, she opened her passenger door, pulled out a worn leather backpack, containing some of her father's note-books as well as her own, a camera, binoculars, water, and a first aid kit, and slung it over one shoulder.

The lack of visible trash encouraged her a little, but she still worried about tourists up in the rocks. Nothing protected the rock art except the site's remoteness and some state laws posted on a sign near the parking area that most people probably didn't bother to read. She had seen names spray-painted over some of the ancient markings. People going back to the 1840s had added their own identities to these walls, with chisels or paint or fire, and each one obscured some of the original art found here.

They wouldn't do it while she was around to stop them.

She stalked into the rocks, her sunny mood fouled by the appearance of the van. If she came across some idiot smearing graffiti on this sacred place, she would—well, she didn't know, but the object of her wrath would wish she hadn't come along.

The most obvious trail led from the parking area into a natu-ral gully between two huge jumbles of rock. About a quarter mile in, the rocks sloped away from the trail at a gentle enough angle that people could easily climb up and find the first batch of masks. Most tourists never went any farther into the rocks than that, judging by the sudden drop-off in the amount of litter Ginny had found strewn about.

Ginny followed this trail first, guessing the tourists had come this way. Hiking boot prints marked the dirt path, scuff-ing over the tracks of lizards, snakes, and birds. Mesquite and creosote and amaranth grown tall from late summer rains scented the still morning air with a faint dry, peppery aroma. From somewhere up ahead, Ginny caught the sound of laugh-ter on the air. She set her jaw and clenched her fists, anticipat-ing a confrontation with a rowdy bunch of defilers. They had to be at the first section of masks, just around a sharp bend, her

view of them blocked by a pile of massive boulders that stacked
thirty feet high.

Before she reached the bend, she heard what sounded like a
cry of alarm, with lesser shouts following in its wake. She
rounded the curve at a sprint. On the slope up toward the flat
wall where the masks were painted, she saw them. Four people
stood near the wall, looking down the rock slope with varying
expressions of shock. A fifth scrambled down at a half-crouch,
hurrying toward the last, who was about twenty yards away
from the others, trying to sit up. The one on the ground was a
woman, and she looked unsteady. Her nylon jacket was torn,
her dark hair tugged from its ponytail. Blood smeared both her
palms.

With a leap, Ginny made the slope and started up toward the
sitting woman. Her long strides covered ground faster than
the guy, probably in his fifties, who was trying to descend
to the woman without falling himself, and when Ginny was a
dozen feet or so away, the woman heard her and turned.

"Are you okay?" Ginny asked. "Did you fall?"

The woman looked at Ginny with eyes wide, as if Ginny
were an apparition of some sort, and not a particularly welcome one. *Maybe she hit her head,* Ginny thought. *Suffering
from shock.*

"Can you call for an ambulance?" the man called. He had
almost reached the woman, who was trying to regain her feet
but looked as if the rock slope might be spinning beneath her.
"She fell quite a ways."

Ginny pulled her cell from her backpack and glanced at the
screen, but as usual, she had no service. "Sorry," she said. "I
can drive into Palo Duro, but we're too far out here."

"I'm all right," the woman insisted. "Never mind an ambulance, I'll be fine." Other members of the group came down the
slope and surrounded her, helping her to her feet. If she was in
shock, that might be a bad idea, but after a couple of minutes
they let go of her and she seemed able to keep her balance.
Color had started to return to her cheeks. She was probably a
couple years younger than Ginny, maybe twenty-five. She kept
shooting Ginny uncertain sideways glances, as if she was not at
all comfortable having her around.

Relieved, Ginny put the phone away and caught the eye of

the older man in the group, the one who had hurried down after the woman (the only other man was a short, pudgy guy who had been the last to reach her). "Thanks anyway," the man said. "Damnedest thing."

"What happened?"

The man had the look of a Midwestern merchant, a grocer or a hardware store owner, with an open, friendly face, short hair the color of dry straw, and a smile that flashed even when it wasn't necessarily appropriate. White, like his companions. He grinned as he began to answer, then seemed to think better of it and showed a more solemn face halfway through. "We were all up looking at those faces," he said. "We read about 'em on the Internet when we were plannin' our trip. We're headed to the Alamo, down there in San Antonio. Anyway, Juliet there was lookin' at that one on the end, kind of angry lookin' with a mask over the eyes. She was by herself at the end and all of a sudden she screamed. When I looked up, she was airborne, like she'd been hit with an electric shock. She hit the ground and rolled down to where you saw here when you showed up."

"Electric shock? From the rocks?"

"I guess she was touchin' it. I don't know if there's some kind of security deal or whatnot, but—"

Ginny couldn't believe what she was hearing. She worked to keep the incredulity from her voice. "There's no security system here, and the rocks aren't electrified."

"Well, I don't know what did it, then. Juliet says that face glowed when she touched it, like it was white-hot. Then she got that shock and it just blew her right down the hill."

Ginny didn't know how to respond to that. None of these people looked like they'd been drinking or using hallucinogens. But glowing pictographs?

"Mandy went over and touched it after," he said, nodding toward a white-haired woman who could have been Juliet's mother. "She said it was still warm then."

"I've been around these for days, and hundreds of others at different sites," Ginny said. "And I've never heard of anything like that."

"Well, we by God hadn't or we wouldn't even have come."

"I'm sure. I'll just take a look, if that's okay."

"Just be careful, miss."

"I will." Ginny climbed the rest of the way up the slope, to the wall where the masks had been painted. There were nine of them here, grouped in threes. The "angry" one was on the far left. An overhanging boulder that had fallen from above slanted near it, and if you ducked beneath that overhang you entered a little sheltered area where there were more drawings, including some that seemed to represent a river, clouds, some warriors, and a huge, vaguely threatening being. Most visitors never made it that far.

Ginny touched the image that had supposedly shocked Juliet, pressing her palm against rock smoothed by centuries of wind and rain and other people doing this exact same thing. There might have been some trace warmth coming off it. She touched bare rock nearby, to see if the mask was just radiating sunlight, but that surface was cool against her hand.

On the off chance, she crouched and crab-walked under the overhanging slab. The images there were just three feet off the ground, but the ceiling was low, too. On her knees, Ginny pressed her hands to the river and the warriors.

Also warm. Direct sunlight hadn't fallen on these paintings for hundreds of years, if not thousands, depending on when that slab had fallen and blocked in this little depression. She moved her hands over the unpainted rock, over the clouds and the unknown creature looming over the scene. Cold rock, maybe a degree or two warmer where the paint had stained the wall.

Could it be a chemical difference, the virgin rock and the painted rock radiating at different temperatures? She'd have to do some research. It had to be something like that, some obscure bit of geological trivia she had never encountered, because any other explanation was too bizarre to consider.

Suddenly Smuggler's Canyon had added a new mystery to the one that overarched her life. In the cool shade of the overhanging slab, Ginny shivered.

12

It had taken Simon Winslade decades to acquire his property in Bath, close to the hot springs dedicated by the Celts to the goddess Sulis. Once he bought several old houses and tore out the walls between them, renovating the interiors into big living and ritual spaces, he decided the wait had been worth it. Years of pagan worship had permeated the place with occult power, and he made the most of it. Within a year, he discovered that his powers and abilities had expanded geometrically as a result of his proximity to such a special place.

He lived in the house alone, although at any given time one of a number of girl- or boyfriends might be spending the night. None had stayed over the night before, and none were expected today. Simon's libido was the source of considerable gossip and speculation throughout the city, but at the moment he had other things on his mind.

Today he wasn't actively trying to summon a demon or perform a particular spell. Instead, he was casting about for information. He wanted to know what had caused the disturbance in the ley lines the night that Lawrence Ingersoll died in the U.S. He had been in touch with Millicent Wong and knew that Robb Ivey had met with an American intelligence agent at Ingersoll's place but had been unable to reach any solid conclusions.

Instead of relying on his specialty, which was ritual magic, Simon had spent the day in quiet meditation, secluded in an inner chamber with a few candles lit. This was, from all reports, similar to what Ingersoll had been doing when he'd died. That fact caused Simon a certain trepidation, but he went ahead with the meditation just the same. Any information he could glean would help the entire community, and was worth whatever risk might be involved.

He cleared his mind of extraneous clutter and tried to open

it to the forces that swirled around the universe, out of sight
and awareness for most people. After some time had passed, he
began to hear the soft tinkling of distant bells. A spicy aroma,
like mulled cider, wafted to his nostrils. He couldn't see anything but color—now a wash of peach, which changed to egg-
shell, which was suddenly flooded with scarlet.

As the red darkened toward purple and then black, the ringing sound raced faster and faster, as if a strong wind whipped
the bells around. Simon felt cold, too, a bitter chill that seeped
into his bones, as if he were outside the house naked and not
snugly ensconced within its reinforced, insulated walls.

The cold, the dark, the raucous din of the once-soothing
bells . . . it all combined to make Simon too uncomfortable
to continue. He opened his eyes and snapped his consciousness back to the present, to the house in Bath with its views
over the tops of the houses and old Roman ruins out toward
the Cotswolds. His heart hammered like it wanted to break
free of its fleshy cage. Blood trickled from his right ear and
nostril.

There at the last, just before his panic got the better of him,
he had . . . no, not seen, but *sensed*, something awful, terrifying
even to a man who had faced Asmodeus and foul-breathed
Ashtaroth, crouching Nergal, Balam with his three heads riding the back of a bear, and more.

It had only been a sensation, he realized, nothing he could
see with his eyes or hear or smell or taste.

He left the ritual space at once, passing through a silent, book-
walled library and into his living space. He kept these rooms
modern, and as he entered he clicked on some lights, grabbed the
remote control for a state-of-the-art stereo system, and turned on
the radio. An advert for laundry soap came on, bringing with it a
feeling that the world continued to spin in its place, inhabited by
people who could never begin to understand—or survive—what
he had just experienced.

When the White Stripes started playing, Simon picked up
his phone, dialed a number he knew by heart. The telephone
rang three times, clicked, then Robb Ivey's voice came on the
line. "Ivey's," he said, as Simon had dialed the shop.

"Robb, it's Simon."

"Is everything okay? You sound—"

"Everything is bloody well not okay. Everything is bollocks up, it seems to me."

"What?" Robb asked. "What's the matter?"

"I just spent the worst few moments of my life meditating. Hoping that I could ascertain just what the hell went on the other night."

Robb, he was certain, knew what "other night" was under discussion—everyone in the community had taken to calling it that. "What happened?"

"Fuck if I know. Nothing good, though."

"Simon . . ."

"I can't describe it, Robb. It was just this horrible feeling, like when you're watching election returns and the wrong damn bloke is pulling ahead. Only a thousand times worse. Fraught with cosmic significance, and just unbearable fucking dread. My ear and nose were literally bleeding when I was finished, and I was afraid I'd shat myself, too."

"That might be a little too much information, Simon."

"Like I fucking care, Robb. I'm the one who went through it. I'm just telling you—"

"I was at his house, Simon. Ingersoll's house. I felt it, too, or something very much like it. And I don't mind telling you it scared me."

"I'm not scared, mate, I'm fucking terrified."

"What do you want to do about it, then? Anything?"

"Not sure yet. Something, though. I'm thinking maybe I'll summon someone who can tell us what's going on."

"Someone? Like a demon?"

"That's what I do, right?" Simon asked. "And yes, at this point I think a demon might just be the thing. You don't have a problem with that, do you?"

"Simon, if you can do something about whatever it is out there, I don't care if you call up Satan himself."

"Right, then."

"As long as you keep him on a tight leash."

"No worries, Robb. I'll let you know what happens." Simon put the phone down, and when he did the sensation of dread returned, almost as if the simple act of speaking to another human being had held it at bay for those few moments.

He needed to get some sleep. Preparing for a ritual summoning was a long, hard slog, and the ritual itself would be wearying and difficult. He couldn't go into it rushed or tired—not if he hoped to survive it.

And survival, really, was the whole point.

13

⌗

"Molly." Frank Carrier beckoned from his office. *"Pronto, por favor."*

Molly put her purse and laptop down on her desk and hurried to Frank's office, raising her eyebrows at Suzi McKellar on the way. Suzi gave a tiny shrug in return. By the time she reached the office, Frank had settled in behind his desk, perusing a printout of some kind. "Yes, Chief?"

"What kind of newspaper are we, Molly?" he asked. He didn't suggest that she sit, so she stayed where she was.

A trick question? "Umm . . . independent? Honest? Struggling?"

"All of the above. What we aren't is the kind of paper that jumps on sensationalistic stories for no reason. We leave that to the *Times*. By the time we hit the streets, the real juicy stuff isn't even news anymore."

"Right." She began to wonder if she had lost the ability to understand him—more and more, everything he said seemed to be couched in riddles.

"You want to know why I'm telling you things you already know."

"Pretty much."

"I'm telling you this so you know that when I ask you to cover a murder story, you'll know it's an anomaly."

"A murder?"

"That's right."

"Why would we cover a murder? What's special about it?"

"In a lot of ways, it's not special at all. A thirty-four-year-old white woman was killed near Sunland Park last night. Strangled and brutalized. TV's been all over it this morning, and I'm sure the *Times* will be, too."

"Then why us?"

"I guess just a hunch. From what I've seen on TV, and what I believe about the *Times*, I think they'll focus on the brutality and the whodunit aspect and ignore the question of who this woman is. Was. Her name was Gretchen Fuchs. She worked at a travel agency, and she didn't have a lot of money. Middle-class all the way. El Paso is one of the safest big cities in the country, so why did violent death choose this person? I think maybe this is an opportunity for us to show how real journalists can approach a story like this and make it mean something, by exploring the victim. Maybe when, or if, there's a suspect, we can get deeper into his story, too."

"I'm still on that flower thing, Frank."

"I know. Back-burner that."

"Why not give this to Bill?" Bill Dallek covered El Paso politics for the *Voice*, but his burning interest was crime, particularly those shady areas where crime and politics came together.

"Bill's busy. Anyway, it's not his kind of caper."

"And what about Wade's story?"

"Did he spill anything earth-shattering last night?"

"No."

Frank handed her the printout he'd been looking at. "Then you don't have anything in the way today. Here are the details. Tell me who this woman was and why she died. If you can tell me what the rest of us can learn from her story, so much the better."

"I've never covered a murder, Frank." Amado Suárez Cardona and Jaime Espino covered the Juárez beat and had reported on plenty of murders, but she couldn't suggest bringing one of them across the line for this. She was on her own.

"Then you don't have any bad habits to overcome," Frank said.

Molly started for the door, but he stopped her with a word, a look. "So. How was it, anyway? Seeing Wade?"

"It was . . . It was fine." It had been fine. Comfortable. Surprisingly so, she had thought in retrospect, because it had been so long and the circumstances of their reunion were so trying. "Good. We didn't talk about . . . you know, what happened to him."

"I'm sure he's talked about that plenty in the last few days. He was probably relieved to have some normal interaction with friends without thinking about it."

"That's how it seemed to me."

"And your brother? Byrd?"

The answer to that one didn't come as easily. "Still dying," she said at last, and then she hurried from his office, nearly forgetting to stop at her desk to pick up her purse.

Thirty minutes later Molly parked in front of a red brick ranch house on the west side of El Paso, about a mile from the Sunland Park Mall, where she'd had dinner with Wade the night before. Sunland Park was a New Mexico community that jutted underneath El Paso, straddling the Rio Grande before the river became the international boundary line, and the Sunland Park Mall was up the road from that, on the Texas side.

The house was on Palo Alto, between Cabrillo and San Saba. The front yard wasn't quite xeriscaped, but the lawn sloping toward the street hadn't been watered in so long it might as well have been. Yellow police tape had been strung across the door and the driveway, and a bored-looking cop sat in a cruiser on the street. When Molly parked and approached the house, he perked up fast, practically springing from the car and intercepting her.

"You can't go in there," he said. "This is a crime scene."

She showed him the plastic press pass that she wore on a lanyard around her neck. "I'm with the *Voice*," she said, aware of its redundancy as he studied the card.

"Didn't recognize you, ma'am," he said. He was a beefy guy, practically still a boy, with a baby face and short dark hair. He looked like he'd been shaving for about three weeks and still had problems with it.

"I'm not usually on this beat," Molly admitted. "So that's probably why. Can I take a look inside?"

"If you want to, I guess," he said. His name badge read "Kozlowski." "But the murder happened in back."

"Can you tell me what happened?" She flipped open a spiral notebook so she could jot down anything that hadn't been in the police report Frank had given her.

"She was in her backyard. Someone must have come in through the alley. There was a gate there once, but not anymore, so whoever it was had no problem getting into the yard. The suspect choked her, bashed her head against some concrete steps several times, cracked open her skull. Blood and brains everywhere. The suspect left her there, didn't go into the house that we can see. No sign of robbery, sexual assault, or anything else."

"You keep saying 'the suspect.' Is there a suspect?"

He twitched a bushy eyebrow. "Nobody in particular yet. But when there is, he'll be the suspect until he's convicted."

"Cop talk."

"That's right, ma'am."

Molly suddenly felt old, hearing this baby cop calling her "ma'am." At thirty-three, she couldn't have been that much older than him—he had to have graduated from high school, at least, and then the police academy or whatever they called cop school (she didn't know if the term "police academy" was used outside of the comedy movies she had loved as a teen, but figured if Frank was going to assign her to a lot of crime stories, she'd have to learn).

"Can you show me where it happened?" She wasn't sure she really wanted to look. From his description, it sounded awful, and chances were it hadn't been cleaned up yet. She didn't think she could count on a neat chalk outline, like in the old movies. More likely, from the sound of things, a bloody gorefest, like in the new movies. And no doubt accompanied by smells that moviegoers never had to deal with.

"I just need you to sign in," he said. "Wait right here."

He went back to his patrol car and returned a moment later carrying a clipboard. Molly signed with trembling hands. She was surprised by how nervous she felt about this—nervous, and at the same time, she couldn't deny that a thrill of anticipation coursed through her. There might have been some twisted excitement about the fact that she had been less than a mile away, sometime around the hour of the murder. Wade, who hadn't been to the mall in years, had parked on the wrong side. After dinner at the Greenery she had helped Wade buy a few groceries at the upscale market attached to the restaurant. They had carried them to Molly's car (really Byrd's Nissan Xterra, which he hadn't been able to bring himself to sell even though he couldn't drive it), parked by the Macy's that had been a JCPenney the last time Wade had been there, and she had driven Wade around the mall to his rental. He had parked at the northeast corner of the mall, the end closest to where Gretchen Fuchs had been murdered. For all they knew, the killer might have been stalking her while they chatted in the SUV.

After she signed his list, Officer Kozlowski escorted her under the tape and up the driveway. A narrow gate opened into the backyard. He hung back a little here and let her go in first.

The backyard was even less impressive than the front. Gretchen worked in a travel agency, and apparently didn't include yard work high on her list of priorities. The back didn't have grass she could kill, although she had been doing a pretty good job of destroying a row of saplings at the back that partially blocked the view of an unpaved alleyway. Mostly, it was concrete, cracked and dry. *Like the skin on my legs this morning,* Molly thought, remembering how they had itched.

She was stalling, inspecting the yard like she was house hunting instead of looking at the actual crime scene. She made herself face it. Four concrete steps led up to a solid back door. Blood coated the lower two steps, as thick as paint in places. More had spattered the upper steps and even the bottom half of the door. Embedded in the blood, in spots, were chunks of some thicker, meatier material. Molly's stomach lurched when she realized they were probably pieces of brain and bone.

"That's it?" she asked after regarding it for a minute or two. "Nothing inside?"

"Like I said, there's no evidence that the suspect ever went in. We believe he came and left through the alley."

"Do you mind if I look around some? My editor wants me to try to find out who Gretchen really was, and I can't get much sense of her from out here."

"I'll have to accompany you."

She had watched enough *CSI* on TV to know that she was ignoring all kinds of things that the police had probably spent hours poring over. That didn't matter—she wasn't here to find a killer, but to know the victim. She had needed to see the actual murder scene, but what was more important was what she could find inside, where Gretchen had lived.

They went around to the front of the house and Koslowski peeled back the tape over the door, letting her in. She had never before, to her knowledge, walked into the home of a murder victim. She took a deep breath before the door closed, as if the air inside might be toxic in some way, and went to work trying to get a feeling for the life of the newly dead Gretchen Fuchs.

14

⨆⊞⊏

Water.

Not very helpful, Truly thought. He stood in the formal dining room of his father's house in northern Michigan, looking out a massive picture window. Snow covered the property, right to the edge of Lake St. Clair (iced over at the shore, but still liquid farther out). The snow was essentially water, the ice was water, the water was . . . well, that was water, too.

So for Robb Ivey, in mountainous Colorado, to say that he felt a sensation of water at Lawrence Ingersoll's house was essentially saying nothing at all. Water was everywhere.

Truly had flown from Colorado to Michigan because it was his mother's birthday, and the fact that she had been dead for more than fifteen years didn't stop his father from wanting his only son there to mark it with him. The house was a virtual shrine to Barbara Livingston, former Hollywood starlet and political wife. Truly thought his dad would have run for president, and might have won, if she hadn't become ill—if not for himself, just so that the country could have his beloved wife as a first lady.

Turning away from the window, Truly came face-to-face with his mother, immortalized in oils at the height of her career and her nearly legendary beauty. The painting was almost life-sized, surrounded by an ornate gold frame that added another six inches on every side. She wore a satiny blue dress with an off-center V-neck, trimmed with black velvet. Her honey blond hair was freshly coiffed and curled, her blue eyes glittering, her lips bright red, her teeth white and straight. She was trim and lovely and she carried a hint of mystery, an almost *Mona Lisa*–like enigmatic quality to her smile and the way her eyelids were partially lowered, her gaze drifting off to her right.

The painting was mounted over a white marble fireplace. On the mantel (to the painting's right, not blocking an inch of it) was her Emmy Award for a TV movie she'd appeared in— her last role, as it turned out. She had been in her early forties by then, too old for the ingenue roles that had made her famous, but in the drama *Across Town*, she had played against type, as a shrewish Southern wife and mother, and had been rewarded with the statuette.

To the left of the painting, as if to balance out the mantel, two silver candlesticks held tall white candles, never lit.

Framed stills from Barbara Livingston's movies and TV appearances were scattered around the walls. A glass-fronted cabinet contained other souvenirs of her Hollywood career. Signed scripts, props (a brush and mirror from *Across Town* on the top shelf, a gold cigarette lighter from her first feature, *Island Girl*, even the cowboy hat she had worn on an episode of *The Big Valley*), a warm note from John Huston, and more. The household staff kept the glass case and the big window equally spotless. Truly didn't think his father hosted a lot of dinner parties anymore, but this room was always ready for one.

Tonight it would be just the two of them, Senator Willard Carsten Truly and James Livingston Truly, dining in awkward solitude, served by white-coated African-American waiters, occasionally lifting a glass toward the portrait above the fireplace. The younger Truly returned to the window and gazed out at the dock jutting into the lake. For just a second, he remembered long summer twilights when his mother would stand out there, one hand touching the pilings, or sometimes sit on the dock's end, smoking cigarettes and watching the sun's last rays caught and fragmented by the water. She had seemed impossibly glamorous, as if the sun hoped to bask in her glory and not the other way around. When she came inside for the evening, the sun, its dreams dashed, hid its disappointment behind the horizon.

"Dinner won't be for hours yet."

Truly hadn't even heard his father come in, but there he was, standing just inside the double doors. He had a mane the MGM lion would envy, pure white now but impressive just the same. He still commanded the attention of any room he was in. His shoulders were stooped these days, his back hunched a little, and his face sagged at the jowls, the flesh spotted and tinged with red from a network of capillaries just beneath the skin.

When he looked at his father's face, Truly felt sure he was looking into his own future. He'd never have that hair or the regal bearing, and he wouldn't wear, as his father did now, a blue pin-striped dress shirt with white collar and cuffs, suspenders, navy blue dress pants, and an Italian silk tie in his own house in the middle of the day. But his face owed much more to his father than his mother—the same roundness, the same big blue eyes and soft lips, lacking only some indefinable quality that in the older man suggested strength. He would look baby-faced until he was in his sixties or seventies, he guessed, and then, overnight, he would look like his father did now.

"I know," he said, aware that his father still waited for an answer. "I was just looking at the view."

"It never stops being impressive, does it?"

"No, it doesn't."

"Your mother loved it."

Truly had known that was coming. He brought up Truly's mother frequently, especially when they were together for her birthday commemoration. Usually on occasions like that one, when there wasn't much of a response possible.

"I wish your lady friend had been able to join you, James."

"So do I." Truly's father had expected Bethany to come along, and when Truly showed up alone he pressed for an explanation. Truly hadn't wanted to tell him that he was seeing a married woman—not because he was necessarily ashamed or embarrassed, but because until falling in love with Barbara Livingston, that had been his father's habit, too. Admitting that he was fooling around with a married woman was like saying he was more like his father than he felt comfortable with.

"You could have shown better judgment, James. You're lucky it hasn't become public knowledge."

"Who would care? I'm not really in the public eye."

"Your father is. You could be. And with you in the CIA, you could be compromised. Of course, I suppose someone would have to care about your branch to go to the effort."

"That's true." Truly's father spared no opportunity to take potshots at his son's Agency posting. He had made his reputation as a hardheaded realist, and if the press got wind that his son, as he put it, "chased ghosts" for the Agency, he feared they would somehow use that knowledge to attack him—never mind that he'd been out of the Senate for years.

"Then be more careful. If you should take my advice and run for office someday, you won't want something like this in your closet. These days the press will use any kind of dirt they can dig up."

"Not like in your day, right?"

"They were a bit more circumspect then. Imagine what today's press corps would do to Jack Kennedy if he tried to run now."

"A frightening thought." Truly had no intention of running for office, ever. His father had idolized Kennedy, and remained convinced that an unholy collaboration of CIA agents, mobsters, and anti-Castro activists had assassinated him—one more reason he despised his son's job.

"It really wouldn't be a bad idea to try something else." This was a familiar refrain around the Truly house. "I know we could turn something up with a phone call or two."

His father was certainly right. He was still connected to enough important people that he could unearth a job offer without breaking a sweat. The idea of it, though, made Truly's heart race. He had to do something worthwhile on his own, had to climb out from under his father's long shadow, or he would never feel like his own man. Breaking up with Bethany had already left an empty space in his life—a space he realized had been only partially filled by his affair with someone else's wife. If he couldn't make his own way in the world, what good was he?

Suddenly the urgency of the Ingersoll situation weighed on him. "Listen, Pop, speaking of phone calls, I need to make a few."

"You can use my study, James. And there's a phone in your room, too."

"I have my cell, but thanks."

"Is that secure?"

"Someone would have to care enough about me to listen in, right?"

Willard Carsten Truly peered at him, as if trying to tell by sight if he was mocking his father.

Which he was. He left the senator to wonder and went to his room to make the calls.

"Yes, Monsieur Truly, of course." Bernard Frontenac's French accent was so thick it was hard to understand him over the phone. His English was much better than Truly's French, but that didn't always help. "I know the night you mention."

"The night Ingersoll died."

"Yes, of course. The night of the disturbance."

"Right. Did you notice anything unusual that night?"

"It was terrible! All that day, I could accomplish nothing." Frontenac was a world-class remote viewer whose file had chilled Truly's blood. According to CIA records, he had been able to see into places he'd never been, with remarkable accuracy.

Truly looked around at his room, which had been his room when he was a boy (his room *here*—the family had always maintained residences in Washington, New York, and Los Angeles as well), which was mostly unchanged since then, and hoped the Frenchman would explain what he meant. When Frontenac's silence stretched on, he probed. "What do you mean, Bernard? What happened?"

"It was . . . I do not have the words to explain. Everything I tried to do gave me a sense of impending disaster, some doom that could not be escaped."

"What did you do?"

"I gave up and had a glass of good French wine. Then I had another, and then several more. By the next afternoon, when I felt well enough to continue, everything seemed to be back to normal."

"I see." So he drank himself into oblivion. Not very helpful. "Well, thanks, Bernard. I'll let you know if I learn anything more."

"Be well, my friend."

The line went dead. Truly pushed the END button. He had been sitting on his bed—the one he had slept on for years, although the mattress had been replaced—but now he got up and went to the desk, which sat in front of a window overlooking the front yard. More snow out there, flocking the trees and fill-

ing the spaces between them. Somewhere beyond his sight was
a tall iron fence, but from here the view might have been of a
park or a sparse forest.

He hadn't learned much from Frontenac, from Johnny
Crow, a telekinetic in Las Vegas, or from Robb Ivey, that he
hadn't already known. Which wasn't much to begin with. All
he really had was the fact that something bad had happened,
but not what it was or if he could do anything about it. Or even
if he should try. He needed better data if he was going to make
a decision, much less convince Ron Loesser that it was the
right decision.

Time to try Millicent Wong again.

He sat down at the desk chair and dialed, gazing out the
window the whole time.

Twenty minutes later, he put the phone down and took a deep
breath. She had agreed to meet him in Colorado, but the price
would be high. Millicent's passion was ballroom dancing. He
had to agree to find someplace in Colorado where she could
dance and to escort her there. His offer to hire a hall, a band,
and willing partners was rebuffed; it had to be the real deal or
she wasn't interested.

Truly was no dancer. The idea filled him with the same sort
of indescribable dread Frontenac talked about having felt on
the night of the disturbance.

He would do what he had to. *Doesn't mean I have to like it.*

15

Pencil clutched, the old man's hand flew so quickly, so surely across
the paper that an observer would never have known he was
blind. With a few sure strokes he finished the sketch, then he
shoved the paper off the table and started a new one. The sheet
fluttered to the uneven wooden floor, joining a dozen or so that
had already fallen there.

Back from his brief Colorado junket, Captain Vance Brewer
crossed the tiny room, moving quietly—out of habit; the artist
wouldn't have noticed if he stomped or danced around in tap
shoes—and picked up the sketches. They were all of the same
general subject: a woman dancing. Her skirt swirled around
her, her arms variously raised over her head or bowing out
away from her body or holding on to a partner who was never
pictured.

Brewer wished he could ask the old man what the pictures meant. Their subject matter was obvious, but there
had to be something behind it, some meaning to the dancing
woman. That meaning was locked in the old man's head, and
try as he might, Brewer would never persuade the man to
reveal it.

He looked over the man's shoulder at the next work in progress. A woman, the same or another he couldn't tell, still dancing. The old man would keep drawing, sitting in that chair, and
then at some point he would stop, and then he would start again.
The room didn't contain a bed or a toilet or much of anything
else, just the chair and the drawing board, a supply of paper
and dozens of pencils.

No reason to mess with a good thing.

Brewer left the room, locking it from the outside with a

case-hardened padlock. He had the only key, on a key chain with nine other keys, and he kept it in his right front pocket at all times. If anything ever happened to him, someone would have to break the door down to get to the old man.

It could be years before anyone bothered.

16

ਸਮੀਟ

Outside, a fierce wind blew sand against the walls and windows.
Maha Yamani lived in Riyadh, in the old Al-Bathaa district
near the center of the city, but still, when it blew hard enough
the Saudi Arabian desert seemed to rise up from its bed and
blanket the entire city, from the newest high-rise buildings to
the ancient mud-brick structures.

She had been scrying—or trying to, at any rate—hoping to
determine which of two possible courses of action a client was
considering might prove more favorable to his business. Her
specialty was hydromancy—it seeming particularly ironic, in
the midst of one of the world's great desert regions, to use water as a means of divination. Her copper basin was full. She
meditated to the point of trance, staring into the water, waiting
for the spirits to use it to send their messages.

After a time, the water started to churn, as if it was beginning to boil. Maha peered into it, willing it to reveal something,
to settle into images or impressions of some kind. Instead of
settling, though, the water merely bubbled more ferociously.

Something wasn't right. The water had no heat source beneath it, so there was no reason for it to boil. She came out of
the trance state, held her palm out over the basin. Water spat
against it, scalding her. When she snatched her hand away, the
water seemed to leap at her face, and she felt it hit, like tiny hot
pokers stabbing her skin. She bit her lower lip and jumped from
her chair, backed away from the table. Still, the water churned
and roiled.

On the other side of the room, away from the plain table and
chair at which she did her divination, Maha had a modern,
Western-style living room set up, with leather couches and a
steel-and-glass coffee table and, most important at the mo-

ment, a cordless phone. She snatched it from its cradle and hit a speed-dial button, then listened as it beeped through all the digits necessary for an international call.

Eduardo Pinedo answered on the third ring. He was tele-kinetic, not clairvoyant, so she supposed he had caller ID. "Hello, Maha," he said.

"Eduardo." Neither knowing the other's native tongue, they conversed in English. He lived in Ipala, Guatemala, and spoke Spanish. "Are you well?"

"As well as can be," he replied. He was ordinarily effusive, and such a noncommittal answer was unlike him. It was a dodge, a transparent one at that.

"I wish I could say the same." She had called him, so she didn't plan to be similarly evasive. "I've had a problem."

"What is it? Something I can help with?"

"I don't know if anyone can help, Eduardo."

"What is it?" he asked again.

"I . . . I have been trying to do some scrying, and something is . . . blocking me. It attacked me just now."

He was silent for so long she began to wonder if she had been disconnected. Just before she said his name again, Eduardo spoke. "Ever since that night, Maha, my talents are virtually useless. I believe the ley lines are still in some sort of disarray. The frequencies that our powers utilize are off, some-how. It's like I'm trying to operate a gas oven on an electric line. Is that how it's been for you?"

"I worry that it might be more than that, Eduardo. More serious."

"What, then?"

"Eleven years ago, I had a client who I could not help. I tried all my scrying techniques, but nothing worked at all. Finally, she left, furious, calling me a cheat and a fraud. In the street outside, still angry, she didn't pay attention. She walked in front of a truck. It dragged her nearly a block before it was able to stop. The street looked like someone had painted a wide red stripe down it."

Eduardo was silent.

"What if the reason I cannot divine the future," she asked, straining to find the words, "is because there *is* no future? What do we do then?"

⊐⊫⊏

17

Wade set the digital clock for seven thirty. He hoped to wake up early, grab some breakfast in the hotel, then get over to the hospital to see Byrd. Molly was taking good care of him, but that didn't mean there weren't errands he could run. He wanted to do whatever he could for his friend while there was still time.

When the alarm buzzed, he slapped it into silence. His eyeballs felt heavy, like lead fishing weights in his skull. His eyelids were sandpaper. He pulled a pillow over his head, shielding it from the faint light leaking in around the curtains.

By the time he looked at the clock again, its display showed 12:35. Only the daylight limning the curtain convinced him that it was still daytime. "Jesus," he said softly. "Guess I was more tired than I thought."

He clicked on the hotel's TV, switching to CNN out of habit. War news still dominated the headlines, then politics, then celebrity nonsense. He left it on while he showered, rubbed lotion into skin that seemed to be drying out more every day, and dressed. The news had been a constant in his life, the stories changing, the graphics growing more sophisticated, the business models shifting to include online dissemination. But it was still people, mostly white, mostly men, sitting in front of a camera reading, without passion or nuance, whatever scrolled in front of them on the teleprompter. Cynical, maybe, but he had earned his cynicism in those same trenches and considered it his due.

He had lunch, not breakfast, in the restaurant, because that's what they were serving when he finally got there. After that, he went back to the room and called Molly at the *Voice*. Her recommendation sent him all the way to the west edge of town, almost to New Mexico.

When he finally saw Byrd that afternoon, he was startled all over again by how much his friend had shrunk. He wasn't quite someone you could carry away in a shoebox, but he looked like he was headed in that direction. The cookies Wade brought from Cookies in Bloom, to which Molly had directed him, were chocolate chip, Byrd's traditional favorites. Byrd just nibbled at his, holding it with both hands at his mouth, like a squirrel, like one cookie was too heavy to lift.

Byrd had laughed when Wade handed over the bag, though, which made it worth it. "Contraband!" he said. "I love it!" After a few minutes of casual back-and-forth, the conversation turned, as it always did, to rivers.

"Sometimes when I'm lyin' here and light reflects on the ceiling, like from cars in the parking lot or whatever, I feel like I'm out there. Like it's noon and I've stopped beside the river for lunch, and the sunlight shafts down into the canyon and you can see the river movin' in the reflection on the wall, remember?"

"Yeah," Wade said. He sat in a guest chair and absently started turning his yellow rubber bracelet around on his wrist. "I know that feeling."

"And then I'll start to think my bed is moving. Like I'm lying in it and starting to drift away from the bank, then picking up speed. The foot of the bed starts dipping and rising, and there's a little side-to-side motion, and I can see the walls of the room rushin' past, and smell that dry-dusty river smell. You think I'm nuts, right? Hallucinatin'."

"Dude, with as many drugs as you've had pumped into you lately, I'd be shocked if you weren't."

"The thing is, those are the times I sleep the best. I drift off to sleep as my bed drifts into the river. I don't have any hospital dreams then, no sick dreams, just peaceful ones, river ones. Outdoors with maybe a coyote pack yipping or an owl's call. Stars overhead, and mirrored in the river. Times like that, I'm just about ready to go, you know? Just let go."

"Byrd . . ."

"What, Wade? I should hang on? Why? What's my future?"

Wade bit back the simplistic answer he started to give. Byrd was his best friend. He didn't want to start lying to him now. Byrd's future was probably limited to staying in a hospital bed until the end. The fact that he was ready to die was most likely healthier than fighting it or pretending it wasn't happening.

At least Byrd was more awake now. He sat up in bed, eyes bright. "Right," he said. "That's the correct answer. Silence."

"Byrd, I'm not saying that there are any good options. It's just an instinctive reaction. You know. Until things are hopeless, there's always hope, right? No matter how fast the rapids, there's always an eddy up ahead somewhere. You just have to get there."

"I think this is my last class four, pal. It's all whitewater from here. I don't think I can bail the boat out anymore, either. All I can do is hang on to the gunwales and ride it out."

Wade offered a smile. "You always were good at that."

"Fuck you, too," Byrd said. Wade was glad to hear it—when Byrd turned profane it meant he was feeling better.

They were both silent for a few moments. Byrd stared at the ceiling. Wade watched Byrd stare. "You remember the mountain lions?" Byrd asked after a while.

Wade remembered. "In Cataract Canyon," he said. They had just come out of the double whammy of Little Niagara and Satan's Gut, fighting all the way down, and were exhausted. It had just been the two of them in a twelve-foot Vanguard inflatable, and they had both stretched out, limp and soaked, and let the easy current carry them downriver. After the pounding roar of the big water, the quiet stream seemed virtually silent. They were silent, too, oars in the boat, just drifting.

Both knew that Lake Powell waited ahead, and they shared the river rat's disdain for that artificial lake, knowing it had drowned Glen Canyon, one of the Colorado River's most beautiful natural wonders—and given that the Colorado also cut through the Grand Canyon, that was high praise indeed. The river had been dammed in 1963, before Wade and Byrd were born, but they had seen pictures, even old 16mm movies, and it was one of those things the old-timers talked about around campfires at night. Not so much on commercial river trips, although some guides still bemoaned the loss of the Glen, but for the most part they were intent on making sure the paying customers had a good, safe ride, and complaining about times past wasn't the best tactic. But when Wade and Byrd met up with longtime river rats—once, for one night, even sharing space around a fire with Ed Abbey, toward the end of his life—Glen

Canyon almost invariably came up, and glowing descriptions of its attributes would follow.

Like most river rats, Wade and Byrd looked upon dams in general with contempt, but shared a special, burning hatred for the Glen Canyon dam.

The Abbey meeting had been one of the high points of Wade's young life. They were near Mexican Hat, Utah, and had fallen in with some people who knew Abbey. Wade had just sold a story to *High Country News*, his first professional sale since graduating from UTEP, and as soon as the check had come in the mail, he had taken it—and thirty bucks of his savings—and purchased a first edition of Abbey's classic book *Desert Solitaire*, from an antiquarian bookseller in El Paso. When he told Abbey that he'd bought it, the aging curmudgeon had chuckled. "I'll never understand those prices," Abbey said. "Most of my friends can't afford 'em—present company excluded, of course—and my enemies wouldn't pay a nickel for 'em."

He had agreed to sign the book, the next time they met up. But he had died a couple of years later, and Wade never saw him again. It hardly mattered to Wade, who still had the book at his apartment in Atlanta, because the memory of Edward Abbey calling him a friend made it a prized possession, signature or no.

Abbey spoke of Glen Canyon, too. Even the names of the canyon's wonders were magical, Wade always thought. Cathedral in the Desert, Hidden Passage, Aztec Creek, Little Eden, Coyote Bridge, Music Temple. All of it lost, buried under the floodwaters backed up behind Glen Canyon Dam. The old-timers still called the Reclamation Bureau the Wreck-the-Nation Bureau in the dam's honor, and still dreamed of ways to destroy the dam and free the Canyon. A few years back, drought had exposed parts of Glen Canyon that hadn't been seen for decades, and Wade hadn't been able to get away from work. Byrd had made a quick run, and never stopped bragging about it.

They had come across the mountain lions as they drifted, silent as sycamore leaves on the current, around a sharp bend. A mother and her cub were standing on a sandy bank, sipping from a shallow pool. As soon as she saw the raft, the mother's ears twitched; she opened her mouth in quiet protest, and then she turned and bounded onto a flat boulder, then up the slender side canyon they must have come down through. The cub followed, and within seconds, both were out of sight, leaving behind no indication that they had ever been there.

The boys—Wade had been twenty at the time, Byrd twenty-one—sat in the raft, stunned by the sight, until the raft had drifted around another bend. Then, as if released by the fact that they could no longer see where the lions had been, both began whooping with the sheer joy of what they had experienced.

"They were beautiful," Byrd said. "Just amazing."

"They were," Wade agreed.

"See, here's the thing, Wade," Byrd said. "I had that moment. We had it. And a hundred more like it. Shit, a thousand. Not with lions, but the things we've seen? There aren't two luckier fuckers in the world, Wade. Think of all those people in New York and L.A. and Cleveland and everywhere else who've never even seen a tenth of what we have. Not to mention people in the rest of the world. I can go easy, Wade. Anytime. It don't get better than we've had it."

"You're right, Byrd." Wade was nodding his head, convinced. Nothing he had experienced in these last ten years of his life had come close to the things he and Byrd had done together. He could have happily skipped the whole Iraq trip. Maybe Byrd made sense after all . . . maybe they would both have been better off if they'd simply aimed their boat into a wall inside some canyon or other, or flipped it in a rapids. *Would have spared Byrd a lot of pain, anyway.*

"We've seen some special things," Wade added. "No doubt about that."

"Some pretty fucked-up ones, too," Byrd said.

Wade waved his hand dismissively. He knew what Byrd meant. He didn't want to talk about Smuggler's Canyon, and he didn't think Byrd really did either. If he wasn't half-stoned on painkillers, he never would have brought it up. Painkillers and chocolate chip cookies.

"How about this one, Wade? 'Am I dying or is this my birthday?' Lady Astor when she woke up on her deathbed to find that she was surrounded by her family."

"If it was your birthday, there'd be cake."

"Yeah, you're right. No cake here."

After a slightly awkward silence, Wade excused himself

and went down the hall to the men's room, hoping to bring his raging sorrow back under control. He stood in the bathroom (it smelled like bubble gum, which was an improvement over the smell in Byrd's room), gazing at the mirror and listening to the buzz of the lights. He wasn't surprised to hear a pattern in the seemingly random noise. He'd noticed a lot of patterns lately—in the hum of the air conditioner at the Hilton, the rush of traffic on the roads, the trilling of crickets outside at night. It had begun—although he hadn't become aware of it until just this morning—on the flight from Baghdad to Frankfurt, listening to the rumble of the jet engines.

Earlier this afternoon, he had been in the shower when he realized that the whole time he'd been listening to these patterns, hidden just beneath the hums and buzzes and roars and clicks, a voice had been speaking some secret language, trying to communicate with him. He had almost said something about it just now, to Byrd, but stopped himself just in time. If he tried to explain, he'd just sound like a head case. So he kept quiet and listened. He hadn't yet reached the point that he could understand what they were saying to him, but he would soon be able to. Already he had figured out that—although he couldn't understand the language, had never heard it in his life—it was an ancient tongue, not spoken in centuries. But he recognized it. Its name was on the proverbial tip of his tongue, or stuck in his brain someplace he couldn't quite dislodge it.

Even the night before, at dinner with Molly, he had thought she'd said something in that language. What was the word? *Kethili*, or something like that. And she had thought that he'd said it. What did that mean?

Returning to Byrd's room, he watched his friend sleep, fully aware that it didn't just *sound* crazy, it *was*—someone speaking to him in a dead language, hidden behind, or layered into, everyday noises. Why him? Why now? None of it made sense.

And yet . . . and yet he couldn't deny the truth of it, either. He could almost grasp what the fluorescents were getting at. If he could just listen better, clear his mind of distractions, he could rein it in and bring it home.

While his friend slept, he sat in the visitor chair and listened, straining to make sense of it. He scratched his dry forearms.

And the lights in the hallway jabbered on. . . .

18

⊐Hｺ

Outside Ginny Tupper's room at the Palo Duro Motel, an orange
cat—not feral, he acted perfectly tame, maybe abandoned by
travelers passing through—rubbed up against her door. Sometimes he jumped up on the brick ledge and tapped on her window with his paws. Once she had made the mistake of inviting
him in, thinking a little feline company might be entertaining,
but he had made himself at home, stalking across the bed where
she had been trying to organize her father's papers. He tram-
pled and strewed and mixed up until Ginny was able to catch
him and haul him back outside.

That was all it took, though, as far as the cat was concerned.
They were friends for life, and he seemed to wait around the
parking lot until she returned to the room at night. Then he
raced toward her, trying to intercept her between her car and
the room. She usually stopped and scratched him for a couple
of minutes, glad *someone* was there to greet her, before she
went inside and closed him out.

He was out there now, bumping against the window, letting
her know he wanted attention. She was intent, however, on trying to find any references in her father's writings to pictographs
that glowed or gave off heat or electrical charges. She didn't remember any, but there were boxes and boxes of his work—some
contained in notebooks, some in letters or notes scrawled on
whatever he had available. She had tried to cross-reference it,
but that seemed an endless task, and given the chaos of all the
individual sheets of paper, hard to achieve with any finality.

He had always sent his papers home to Mission Viejo from
whatever site he'd been working at, for Marguerite, Ginny's
mother, to transcribe and file. Her mother had done so willingly, if without a lot of enthusiasm. When Ginny was four-

teen, years after her father's disappearance, someone had broken into the house and stolen some of his original notebooks but missed the transcriptions. Now she went back and forth between originals and transcriptions, trying to interpret his scratchy handwriting and Marguerite's frequently misspelled renditions of the same.

Making things more challenging, she thought that her father might have been going mad toward the end of his life. It had started after a trip to South America, where he had experimented with some of the local hallucinogens. The things he wrote about stopped making sense, as if instead of reporting his own observations, he had started writing down his nightmares. Some of the craziest stuff she had practically committed to memory, having studied it again and again, trying to understand.

"Raven kept me up all night again, dancing and clattering beads on the cliff. Three nights in a row now. The only thing that quiets him is if I chant with him, and then only for a while."

"Masks that aren't masks, eyes that see, lips that tell stories of ancient days, nights of fire, the desecrated temples of warring gods."

"Kethili ra, kethri chil chilitonate, kethoon ke kelindiri."

"Today I flew. Into the air, a foot, two, a dozen. Then more, higher, until the canyons spread out before me like a map, the river only a line. I stayed up for a couple of hours, then lowered gently to the ground, and drifting leaf and went to sleep for three days and nights."

Entries like that, frequent in the last year or so before he vanished, were hard for Ginny to read. For most of his life, Hollis Tupper had been a respected anthropologist. He hadn't written a lot of books, but he published monographs and often spoke at universities and professional gatherings. He had married late in life, wanting to get his career solidly established before he did. When Ginny came along, the whole parenthood thing seemed to take him by surprise, according to stories her mother told. He had stayed close to home during the pregnancy, but after trying his hand at fatherhood for a few months, he began going back into the field much more often. When he finally disappeared, Marguerite assumed that he had simply decided he couldn't handle it anymore, and chose not to come home.

Even as a child, Ginny couldn't buy that explanation. She remembered her father being awkward with her, but loving. He hadn't been the world's greatest dad—no one would have bought him the mug or the plastic trophy—but he wouldn't have abandoned his only daughter.

Which meant his disappearance was a mystery.

Anthropology was all about mystery, about using clues to reconstruct what must have been. Even cultural anthropology involved people going into societies that weren't their own and trying to understand them. The kind Hollis Tupper had excelled at—the field Virginia Tupper had followed her father into, earning a doctorate because no one would offer meaningful grants to anyone with a lesser degree, and she had her own agenda, studying the pictographs of Smuggler's Canyon in order to find clues to her father's disappearance—was the other kind, physical anthropology. Physical anthropologists tried to understand societies that had long since disappeared, to reconstruct their beliefs and the way they lived by studying the minute bits of evidence left behind: skeletons and structures, shards of pottery, scratchings on walls of rock.

Hollis Tupper had only vanished two decades ago, and he had left a voluminous paper trail before he went. If she couldn't figure out what happened to him, she needed to find a new line of work.

Then again, when the organization that had provided her grant found out that she was at Smuggler's Canyon for personal, not scientific, research, she might have to do so anyway.

She was deep into a paper that she had read before but felt she needed a refresher on, when a loud thump from the window startled her. She dropped the paper onto the bed and jerked her head around. Through a gap in the curtains she saw the familiar orange cat pressed up against the window, mouth wide, looking as startled as she felt—as if someone had thrown him against the glass.

Well, maybe she needed a break. And that cat obviously needed comforting. She didn't know how he had hit the window—maybe jumping at a bird or a cricket or something. However it had happened, he remained on the brick ledge outside, yowling and looking completely freaked out.

Ginny went to the door, opened it, and stuck a hand out

toward the beast. The parking lot was empty. Out on the interstate, a truck growled through its gears, its array of lights streaking against the night sky.

"Are you okay, kitty?" she asked. "What happened?"

The cat meowed, backing away from her hand instead of coming toward it.

"It's okay, kitty. Whatever happened, I'm not going to hurt you." She took another step closer, reaching to scoop him up.

Ordinarily the cat would have jumped into her hands.

Instead, he hissed and lashed out with his right front paw, claws bared. Ginny barely snatched her hand away in time. An inch closer and her flesh would have been lacerated. "Jesus!" she said. "What was that?"

The cat didn't answer. He jumped down off the window ledge and stalked away, back to Ginny, tail switching defiantly in the air.

Like he's just vanquished an enemy, Ginny thought.

An enemy who thought she was a friend.

19

Gilbert Ramirez was the oldest of them, at twenty-three, and he had crossed over many times before, so he knew the tricks. Where it was easiest to cross, how to dodge *la migra*, where to look for work—all of these things he had learned and he was willing to share that knowledge with his friends from Taxco, Guillermo Romo (who had gone by the name Billy since he was nine) and Carlos Quintano.

This trip wasn't even for real. Gilbert had a job in Ciudad Juárez, washing cars for a used car dealer. It wasn't the best job he'd ever had, but it paid okay, and he had met a local girl who liked him, and life was good. He had no particular interest, just now, in working on the other side of the line, dealing with all the crap that was going on these days, the anti-migrant forces, the vigilantes and the politicians who called it a crisis when a man wanted to pick vegetables or paint houses to earn a few American dollars.

But he and Billy and Carlos had been drinking cervezas they bought at Bip Bip, downing bottles and talking about the land they could see from the dirt embankment they sat on. Across the street, across the river that they called Rio Bravo and Americans called Rio Grande, across the canal and the fences and the barriers of the law, that was *los Estados Unidos*, *Gringolandia*, the promised land, or that's how some described it. Gilbert knew that wasn't quite the case. There was work there, and money to be made, and places to spend it—he had been inside a mall in Houston that literally made him gasp with wonder at the sheer variety of merchandise one could buy, and the money it would require to truly take advantage of it.

But Mexico wasn't so bad when a man had a job and a girl. Teresa was slender and pretty and earned good tips from *gringos* who thought they'd be able to get with her, so that helped, too. A person could keep away from the gangsters and the government and the cops, could mind his own business and have a decent life.

So they were drinking, he and Billy and Carlos, and talking, and drinking some more, and Gilbert got to telling them stories about how many times he had crossed over, how he knew El Paso like it was sleepy little Taxco, and he could show them where the strippers from the clubs along the interstate drank when they weren't working.

Billy was the one who challenged him first. "If it's so easy, then show us," he'd said. "Take us over there. Teach us how the master crosses the line." Billy had always taunted Gilbert about being the "lucky one" of the three friends, and the fact that Gilbert had spent time in the north just added to his case. One glimpse of Teresa had fueled the fire even more. "You're the lucky one, Gilbert," he said now. "Show us how you get your luck."

Carlos took up the appeal then, and after a couple more drinks, Gilbert agreed. The two younger men had come up from Taxco intending to cross, to go looking for work in the north, and if he could help them, he had to do it. Recognizing that crossing drunk wasn't the best idea—on the concrete banks of the river, he kept slipping, falling on his ass, scraping his palms, and laughing out loud—he ignored his condition and went ahead with the plan they had discussed sitting outside Bip Bip, sometimes shouting to be heard over the loud *corridos* coming from a truck parked nearby.

There was hardly any water in the river, just a muddy stream, then a kind of island choked with tall, stiff grass, mud-caked around the bottom, and some other bushes, then a second muddy stream. Both streams were narrow enough to jump over if you were sober, which they weren't, and Billy, trying to clear the second, hit the bank on the other side and fell backward, landing on his hands and ass in the muddy water with a shout.

"Shut up!" Gilbert said in a loud whisper. "*Silencio*, dude! You want BP to hear you?" He had lived on the border so long that he spoke half English, half Spanish, switching back and forth between them without even thinking about it.

Billy sat in the thick stream for a few seconds, wide-eyed in

the darkness, then stood up and tried to wipe his jeans off.
"Forget about that," Gilbert urged, knowing what came next.
Carlos rolled on the cement bank, arms wrapped around his
sides, trying to laugh silently. Gilbert envisioned Border Patrol
agents at the fence, ready to beam those bright lights right
down at them, blinding them as they climbed the bank.

But maybe there was no *migra* out tonight, because no
shouts came, no piercing beams of light. Billy and Carlos
calmed down, and Gilbert led them up the bank, down into the
Franklin Canal (this one had water they had to wade through,
up to their chests, cold and swiftly flowing; this water, unlike
the Rio Grande, would be confined to the U.S. side), through a
gap clipped in the chain link fence by some other crossers, earlier that night or the night before, and they were there. American soil.

They passed through a thick growth of tall, stiff weeds that
reminded Gilbert of corn, and found themselves in a small,
grassy park. It was some sort of historical site from the early
days of American control—that part was all explained on a
plaque standing with some other monuments and a grave site
near the parking area. The funny part, to him, was that the historic American site was now a Mexican restaurant. One of Teresa's older brothers worked there.

Silently—Gilbert because he wanted to be careful, that dip
in the cold canal having sobered him right up, Billy and Carlos
presumably because they were in awe that they had finally
reached *El Norte*, so far from Taxco in every way—they
crossed the grassy field. Gilbert led them between the various
monuments, pausing to check the name on a gravestone. MAJ.
SIMEON HART, it read, and the place had once been called Hart's
Mill, but no longer. Before Maj. Simeon Hart, *El Camino Real*
had cut across this land, connecting Mexico City with San
Francisco, all Mexican territory in those days. El Paso's name
had come from the Mexicans, as another plaque pointed out:
Don Juan de Oñate had called the place *El Paso Del Rio Del
Norte* back in 1598.

These days the Americans wanted to keep the Mexicans off
land that had formerly been theirs, and not that long ago. A
Mexican had to steal across the line in the night, like a criminal. It was insanity.

Past the little gravel parking lot were a highway and a railroad track. El Paso waited for them on the other side. But Billy and Carlos hadn't been intending to make the crossing tonight; all their stuff was back in Gilbert's apartment.

"We should go back over," he whispered. "Before someone sees us." He didn't want them caught when they were just here on a lark.

"No, *ese*," Billy said. "What about those strippers you told us about? What about the stores full of everything a person could ever want? Didn't you say there were swimming pools filled with champagne in El Paso?"

Gilbert didn't think he had ever mentioned any such thing, although in the grip of cerveza or tequila he sometimes said things that weren't strictly true, things he forgot by morning.

But before he could say anything at all, Carlos clutched his arm in a painful grip. "Gilbert!"

Gilbert saw what Carlos did—a man coming out of the trees toward them. He was in the shadows, but he walked with purpose, and Gilbert had a bad feeling about him. A Border Patrol officer would have announced himself by now, might even have had a gun in his hand. This man appeared empty-handed at first, but then he passed through the beam cast by a pole-mounted floodlight and Gilbert saw that he had something in his right hand after all, and it gleamed, metallic, in the light.

"*Vamonos!*" Gilbert shouted, remembering to use Spanish so his friends would understand. He tried to break into a run, but when he swiveled to head back to the fence, his wet shoes slid on the damp grass and he flew facefirst in the little circle where the monuments and plaques were.

He tried to rise, but all the strength seemed to have fled from his arms and legs. He raised his head enough to see the man reach Billy. The man's arm slashed out and then Billy crumpled to the ground, blood shooting from his neck and pattering on the grass like rain.

That restored Gilbert's strength, and he pushed off the ground, regaining his footing. He started for the fence again. Carlos reached the tall plants before he did, and when they both tried to shove through at once, sharp leaves sliced Gilbert's skin. The two friends got tangled together and Gilbert fell again. This time he caught himself on the tall plants and didn't go all the way down. Before he could free himself, however, he felt a powerful hand gripping his collar, wrenching him back to his feet. Not Carlos, who was several inches shorter than him and had never been so strong.

The man's blade flashed again. For a moment, Gilbert couldn't feel anything. Had he missed? Or was it so sharp, the slice it must have made so fine, that air had not yet penetrated the cut, blood not yet found passage to the outside?

It was, he realized, the latter. The pain came all at once, searing, as if he had leaned into a white-hot wire, and when blood began to spray from his throat the world seemed to go dark, as if the Border Patrol had decided to shut off all the floodlights after all, and every other light, too.

The light didn't fade away fast enough, though, to keep Gilbert from seeing the man catch up to Carlos at the fence. Down in the wet grass again, feeling his life slip away a little more with every pulse of blood that burbled through his throat, Gilbert heard Carlos's long, last screams, and he decided that Billy, who hadn't even seen what was coming, had been the lucky one after all.

20

Molly had spent the day before sweating the Gretchen Fuchs story. Murder wasn't her usual beat by a long shot, and the more she worked on it, studying what little she'd been able to get from the cops—which, perhaps unfortunately, included crime scene photos—the more it disturbed her. She understood that tackling new things was the key to growing as a reporter, and that if she wanted to make her bones she'd have to prove herself in a variety of ways. So she did what she was told, and tried to think of it as a resume builder.

Gretchen Fuchs had been a single woman, like her. Was that what made it so awful? Or was it backlash from Byrd's prolonged death, making her more attuned to the mortality of every human being?

Gretchen had entertained some friends at her home, something Molly had also done. Her guests left and Gretchen started the after-dinner cleanup, another familiar activity. Then something horrible happened. Was it just the wrong person happening by at the wrong time? Or had Gretchen been stalked, followed, observed by someone waiting for just that moment to strike?

Molly hadn't been able to figure that out. She wasn't Brenda Starr or Lois Lane, and she couldn't solve, through a simple examination of the dry facts of murder, a mystery the police hadn't.

Today her plan was to call some of Gretchen's friends—in the house she had managed to copy numbers out of Gretchen's address book, when Officer Kozlowski had left her alone for a few minutes—to try to get more information about who Gretchen had been in life. That, as Frank had suggested, would be the focus of her piece.

Gretchen had worked in a small travel agency, which was

getting smaller as the Internet replaced travel agents. Besides the owner, only Gretchen and two other employees had kept their jobs through the most recent downsizing. Molly would be calling them today, too.

She had swung by Providence Memorial on her way in this morning. For most of her life, she had never imagined that the nursing staff of a hospital's oncology unit would know her by name, but as she walked down the halls (marveling, as she always did, at how squeaky the floors were under rubber-soled shoes, and didn't most people who worked here wear rubber soles?), several of them greeted her cheerfully.

Wade was already there. She had known because she'd parked next to his rented Ford Focus, which she recognized by the books and magazines he had already strewn on the passenger seat, in the parking lot behind the Hilton Tower, one of the hospital's three main buildings. Mud caked the car's lower side, around the bottom of the driver's door, and she wondered briefly how that had happened on the short trip between the hotel and the hospital. By the time she got upstairs and found the two of them engaged in a loud and obscene recollection of women they'd known over the years, she had forgotten all about the mud. Deciding that discretion was, after all, the better part of valor, Molly simply stopped in for a quick hello before leaving the boys to their memories.

The abbreviated visit allowed her to get to her desk early—the downside being that Gretchen Fuchs, who had haunted her dreams, making for a restless night, waited at that desk. In spirit, if not in fact. She seemed to be hunched over Molly's computer, waiting for Molly to reach conclusions about why she couldn't be there in the flesh.

Molly was immersed in Google listings, having entered Gretchen's name just to see what turned up, when Frank startled her by touching the back of her chair.

"Sorry," he said when she wheeled around. She figured she looked like she'd been kicked. "I didn't mean to frighten you."

"It's okay," she said. "Maybe I just scare easily when I'm digging around in the pasts of murder victims." She hadn't quite forgiven Frank for assigning her to this story.

At the same time, she couldn't deny that a certain fascination with it was setting in.

"Funny you should mention murder."

"Oh God, Frank, what now?"

He pulled a chair over from an unoccupied desk and rolled it close. He smelled like coffee and a hint of some citrus shampoo or soap. "There were three men killed, late last night or this morning. Two of them had their throats cut. The third . . . well, it sounds like the killer tried to push him through a chain link fence. Not through a hole in the fence, *through* the fence."

Molly wasn't able to quite picture it, but the image she got was bad enough. "Oh my God. Who were they?"

"Migrants, it looks like. They were still wet from swimming across. You ever been to La Hacienda, that Mexican restaurant by the river, just west of downtown?"

"Off Highway 85. Sure."

"Apparently they were killed in that little park there."

She pictured a grassy swath with a few mesquite trees around it, the little circle of plaques that she had read once and then completely forgotten the contents of, the mud and gravel parking lot—mostly mud, during the summer storms and this time of year. Then she envisioned the fence at the back, through which Mexico was just a stone's throw, and seeing that fence in her mind allowed her to get a better sense of what someone might look like after having been pushed through it. Kind of like garlic going through a press, she imagined, only with blood and organs and lots and lots of pain.

"Last night?" she asked, although she already knew the answer.

"Border Patrol found them a little before midnight."

"You don't want me to work this into my story about Gretchen Fuchs, do you? Because I'm sure these aren't related. I don't see how they could be, anyway."

"No, Molly. This is a separate story. At least, I hope it is, and the cops don't seem to believe there's a link. But it's one I'd like you to think about, when you're finished with the Fuchs piece and while you're not otherwise pumping your friend Wade for his life story."

"Fine," she said, suppressing a sigh. Boosting circulation was fine, but she had never been, or wanted to become, a crime reporter.

Molly wore a pink "*Ni Una Vida*" pin sometimes. "Not One

Life" referred to the unexplained murders of hundreds of women in Juárez over the span of a decade or so. More than four hundred bodies had been found, and hundreds of other women were still missing. The killings had tapered off—some people claimed they had stopped altogether, that the killer had died or been imprisoned on some other charge—but that presumed that there was only one killer for all those women, which seemed impossible. Every now and then, yet another body turned up, sexually assaulted and brutalized.

Everyone who had lived in El Paso during the worst of it knew that only a thin strip of water and a tall fence stood between the killers and them. Some even speculated that the killers were Americans, crossing the border to satisfy their psychotic urges.

Gretchen Fuchs hadn't been raped, and the three migrants had been men, so the murders didn't match the Juárez killings. Still, the idea that four people had been murdered in the space of twenty-four hours disturbed Molly.

She thought about the little park again, the lights of Mexico across the way. The men must have stood on that side, looking at the lights of the United States, and hoped to come here in search of a better life.

And then she remembered the muddy parking lot, how when she had eaten at La Hacienda she'd had to wash her car the next day because she'd got mud halfway up her door.

And that reminded her of Wade's rental car, and the mud she had seen on it at the hospital.

Mud he couldn't have picked up between the Hilton Garden Inn and the hospital, all of two or three blocks apart on paved roads.

Frank stared at her. "What?" he asked.

"Nothing," she said, shaking her head. "Just . . . nothing. I need to make some calls, that's all, so I can get moving on this story."

"Make the magic happen, Molly," he said as he wheeled the borrowed chair back to its original home. "That's what you do best."

21

⌐▯═

Millicent Wong was, in fact, full of demands.

The worst was the ballroom dancing, and that was the one that had nearly made Truly rescind his plea for her help. Having agreed to it, though, the others seemed minor in comparison.

The next most egregious was that she would only fly as far as Denver. Truly understood why—the flight from Hong Kong was plenty long enough, and the last thing she would want at the end of it was to climb onto a puddle jumper down to Alamosa. It meant driving her halfway across the state, but he could manage. And the ballroom dancing options were more numerous in the Denver area than elsewhere in Colorado. That night, she would dance, and the next day they'd drive to what remained of Lawrence Ingersoll's house.

In Michigan, Truly arranged a quick lesson. He would be no Fred Astaire, but if he was forced to dance he might be able to avoid crushing Millicent's tiny feet. When she deplaned in Denver, resplendent in a red outfit—all red; hat, coat, dress, shoes, purse—he realized that the pictures he'd seen in her files, and the statistics he'd read, didn't quite do her doll-like appearance justice. She was just over five feet tall. She might weigh ninety pounds, attired as she was at the moment. Her features were delicate, her hands miniature. She could have been anywhere from thirty to sixty, but her file said she had been born in 1922.

He took her directly to the Hotel Monaco, where he reserved rooms for both of them, and she had a bath and a couple hours' sleep. Truly was sure she would rather not dance immediately after flying, but they didn't have a choice. The next night they would spend in a decidedly less luxurious motel in Alamosa, and the day after that he had to get her to Denver International by noon for a two o'clock flight home.

He'd promised her dancing, and that's what she'd get. Not his problem if she was too worn out to enjoy it.

When it was time, he called her room and told her he would meet her in the lobby, which had the feel of a Turkish mosque designed by someone who'd spent a little too much time with the hookah. He was staying in the Grace Slick Suite, all stripes and modernity, while she had opted for a Mediterranean Suite, perhaps out of a general distaste for rock (and jazz, another option was the Miles Davis Suite).

She stepped into the lobby and he found himself astonished all over again. She looked radiant. She had exchanged the red traveling clothes for a red silk dress cut snugly over a body that was petite but surprisingly curvy. Her dress flared just below her knees. Her red coat was draped over one arm. Truly didn't know how she would be able to dance in her spike heels, but she walked with confidence. She had bathed and made up her ageless face, and he couldn't see a hint of weariness in her.

"James," she said, taking one of his hands in both of hers. She seemed as light as a bird, hollow-boned and about to take flight. Looking into his eyes, she added, "You don't have to dance, you know."

"No, it's fine, Millicent," he said.

"Remember who I am."

Who she was was the most powerful sensitive the CIA had ever turned up. Calling her a mind reader wouldn't have been too far off the mark, except that it understated her gifts. "You're right," he said. "I kind of wish you wouldn't do that, but it's true, I'm not really much of a dancer, I'm afraid."

"I'm sorry," she said, "but you're virtually screaming it. One wouldn't have to be sensitive to know that you don't want to dance with me."

"I guess that's probably true, too."

"You're an open book, Mr. Truly."

"So I've been told. Shall we go?"

"By all means." Grinning, she hooked her arm beneath his and let him lead her to the rented Escalade waiting in front of the building.

The dance was held in the second-floor ballroom of a Lakewood hotel. The place was on the seedy side, making Truly glad he had chosen the luxurious Monaco to stay in. But nicely dressed couples, and some singles, headed into it from the parking lot and milled around the lobby. Truly and Millicent climbed a wide, carpeted staircase with inexplicable sticky black spots on it, emerging onto a mezzanine full of people who had come for the dance. In the ballroom a small orchestra played. Truly didn't recognize the song, but doubted he would know many of the songs he heard tonight. Everyone seemed to be in high spirits, and he hoped his own lack of enthusiasm didn't bring anyone down.

He needn't have worried.

During their first two hours in the ballroom, Millicent probably spent about forty seconds without a dance partner. Those were the first forty seconds, when she walked in behind Truly and he hadn't yet moved out of her way. Once she became visible to the room, the men seemed to sniff out a superb dancer and pleasurable companion. They flocked to her, and she disappeared into someone's arms.

Truly sought out the bar.

A couple of times, as he observed from the sidelines, women approached him and asked him to dance. He declined all invitations. He hadn't come to dance, or to meet anyone, although from the vibe in the room he doubted that it was much of a pickup spot. He made an effort to keep an eye on Millicent, while trying not to stare at his wristwatch. They'd have to get an early start in the morning, and he hoped, without actually believing, that she would get bored quickly and they could return to the hotel.

For the second hour, most of her time was dominated by one man. He had a stern face with a flat nose, a jutting chin, and short salt-and-pepper hair. His jaw was firm, his build solid, and he danced with an economical grace that made Truly think he was a powerful man. He wore a black suit that strained at the shoulders, with a narrow tie and plain black shoes that reminded Truly of military dress shoes.

At the bar again (he was drinking slowly, interspersing glasses of club soda between the alcohol), he had to wait while a young woman ordered a vodka and Coke, which sounded repulsive to him. Truly went with club soda again—he'd been drinking a nice fourteen-year-old Scotch when he was drinking at all—and wondered how people mixed colas with clear alcohol, or Red Bull with anything.

While he was at the bar, a couple had taken over the table he'd been hogging most of the evening. The man had his shoes off and was massaging his feet. Truly decided not to sit there again, at least not right away.

That was when he realized he hadn't seen Millicent in quite a while. Holding his drink, he cruised the floor, trying to feign gracefulness and not spill on anyone. He couldn't find Millicent anywhere.

"You looking for that Asian lady?" a man asked him as he stood by himself on the dance floor, no doubt appearing hopelessly lost.

Truly focused on the man. He was short and would have been called portly once. Truly didn't know if that word was still in common use, but it described this guy perfectly. "Yes, have you seen her?"

"I saw you come in with her. She's a hell of a dancer, I gotta say. Hell of a dancer. We don't get her kind in here very often."

"Have you seen her?" Truly asked again.

"Few minutes ago." The man jerked his thumb over his shoulder toward a balcony overlooking the parking lot. Truly had gone out there once, for a minute, found it mostly full of smokers willing to risk the cold for their nicotine fix, and hadn't given it another thought.

Millicent didn't smoke, but that didn't mean she hadn't accompanied someone who did.

"She was with some guy," the man continued. "Big bruiser, not someone I've seen here before. Anyhow, I was thinking about asking her to dance again, but she hasn't come back in."

"Thanks," Truly said, already moving away from the man. He burst through the glass door and out onto the balcony. As before, a handful of dedicated smokers huddled near the door. Millicent wasn't among them, and neither was the man in the dress shoes.

Truly pushed through the smokers. The night was bitterly cold, the kind of cold that makes you think your lungs will freeze and crack open if you breathe deeply. But the balcony angled around the building, and he had to check the area he couldn't see in case the couple had gone in search of privacy.

Around the corner, he found Millicent.

She was crumpled against the solid wall of the building.

Her head lolled at an unnatural angle. Her unseeing eyes were open, blood trickled from her mouth and ran, due to the angle, into her left nostril.

His lungs hadn't frozen, but Truly thought maybe his heart had.

She had been as nice as anyone he'd ever met—dedicated to her passions, but so what? She had been willing to fly all the way from Hong Kong to help him. She was, it seemed, one of the most popular players in the subculture of the occult, and with good reason.

And she'd been able to read minds.

Still, someone—the guy in the dark suit and shiny shoes, Truly was certain—had been able to lure her outside, where he snapped her neck like an iced-over branch.

Truly was supposed to work with these people, and, to the best of his abilities, to take care of them. Now he'd lost two, in less than a week.

Lawrence Ingersoll hadn't been his fault.

Millicent Wong was. No question about that.

He would be in the shit over this, and it would fly from every direction. And he would deserve it. Not only had he failed to make his own mark, he'd been responsible for the death of a good woman.

He went back inside to find the club's manager. On the way he stopped by a table where Millicent and the big man had sat and talked between dances. There were still two glasses on it, one with Millicent's crimson lipstick staining the top. Truly lifted the other one with a cocktail napkin and dropped it into his jacket pocket.

He hadn't been fully invested in this whole business before. It had been a distraction from his personal issues, something to break up the boredom of his nowhere job.

Whoever the big man was, he had changed that by killing Millicent Wong. Now Truly was on board. He would find out who the gray-haired man was, and that man would pay. Truly owed his network at least that much.

And he owed himself, too.

22

Molly knew it was stupid.

It was stupid because she knew Wade. Had known him since they were kids.

At the same time, she hadn't seen much of him for the last ten years or so. And he'd been through a traumatic experience recently, held captive by Iraqi insurgents. Who knew what that could do to a person? How could he come out of it *not* messed up even a little?

Still, it was stupid.

It was all circumstantial evidence. That's what they would have called it on a TV lawyer show, right? She had no physical evidence, nothing the *CSI* crew could stick under a microscope, unless they could match the mud on Wade's rented Ford to that from the parking lot outside La Hacienda. And from the other killing, Gretchen Fuchs, she didn't even have mud. Just the knowledge that Wade, who hadn't spent much time in El Paso over the last decade or so, hadn't known where to park at the mall, and Gretchen's home had been near where he had parked. Out the mall exit, left at the light, and you were practically to her house.

Molly had spent all day on the phone and at the computer, and what she had come up with was this: nobody on Earth had any reason to kill Gretchen.

She was universally liked. Even the people who had been laid off from the travel agency, where she had kept her job, hadn't blamed her, and they'd all said they would miss working with her. Gretchen didn't have the greatest luck with men, and she was not, at the moment, dating anyone seriously (or even frivolously, that Molly could determine), but the men she had dated still liked her. Nobody had anything to gain from her death. Nobody profited. Nobody wanted to see her dead.

Which made the murder a crime of opportunity. She had been killed because she had been there, outside in the backyard at the time the murderer happened to be there. He hadn't been stalking her, had just seen her and taken his shot. The police, utterly without clues, agreed.

Wade had just flown into town. He would have had no opportunity to stalk anyone.

Could he, in the intervening decade, have become some sort of psycho killer? Wouldn't there have been signs in his youth?

Well, there were, of course. She didn't know much about killers, but if genetics was a component, he'd be a natural. She'd never known Wade to kill anything bigger than a trout, but maybe that didn't mean anything.

Thinking about it, about sitting across from him at The Greenery, about him spending time in Byrd's room, made her stomach churn and ache.

She had thought there was something strange going on when he had said that unfamiliar word, then denied saying it. *Kethili*? Or had she been the one who said it? She couldn't remember anymore. They had both needed rest, no doubt.

Still, she had to know for certain.

After work, instead of going home, she drove to Oregon Street and managed, with patience and some aggressive driving, to get a parking spot on the street from which she could see the exit for the hospital's public lot. When Wade left Byrd's room—even if he had walked over, because the route from Providence Memorial to his hotel would also take him down Oregon—she would see him.

She had a green iced tea and a PowerBar in the car with her. The hard part would be if she had to pee—the nearest place would be inside the hospital, and if she went in there she had a remote chance of running into Wade. It wouldn't be hard to explain her presence there, but it would be awkward to turn around and follow him if he was on his way out. She sat in the car and watched, worrying at her dry skin and wishing he'd hurry up.

She saw his rented Focus pull out of the lot around seven

thirty. Darkness had fallen while she waited, but headlights from an oncoming car illuminated Wade. A steady flow of traffic blocked his left turn, so he made a right. Molly started Byrd's Xterra and followed. He worked his way down a few blocks, made a left, then another left. She stayed about a dozen car lengths behind, able to keep him in sight because she sat much higher than he did, until he parked in the Hilton's lot.

Walking from the car to the hotel, he looked tired, his head drooping, shoulders slumped, dragged down by his captivity and escape, his whirlwind tour of hospitals and debriefing rooms, and the emotional journey to El Paso. She hadn't been through nearly that kind of hellacious experience and she felt exhausted, too.

After waiting outside the hotel for an hour, Molly decided he was probably in for the night. She risked entering the lobby and using the women's room, then dashed back to the SUV. Wade's car sat where he'd left it. She settled back in. A wind blew up out of nowhere, buffeting the car, and later a light rain fell, *tap-tap-tap*ping on the roof.

She didn't realize she was dozing off until the sound of a car engine close by brought her around. She sat upright, eyes wide open, and tried to shake off the slumber that had enveloped her. Seconds ticked by while she realized what she had seen— Wade's rental car, driving out of the hotel's lot. A quick glance at the empty space it had occupied confirmed it.

Now adrenaline raced through her, waking her all the way. The Ford was already out of sight, somewhere up Oregon Street. She turned the key and started the Xterra, checked for traffic, and pulled into the street. The hospital loomed at the top of the hill, but when she passed it and got a good look down Oregon, Wade's car was nowhere in sight. Just in case, she drove down the street, peering up every side street she passed, watching the cars parked along the way.

No sign of him.

He had wasted no time getting lost. Had he seen her, snoozing in her brother's SUV? Had he just been in a hurry to get somewhere? It was almost ten o'clock at night, late for an appointment.

Molly drove around the neighborhood for another twenty

minutes, searching fruitlessly. Finally, exhausted, she drove home.

On a hunch, when she woke up in the morning, she grabbed the TV remote from her bedside table and turned on the morning news.

Sure enough, the anchors were talking about a double homicide during the night. Two young Latinas had been headed to their home at the South Chihuahua Apartments, just blocks from the border, after drinking in a downtown bar. An unknown assailant had used something like a pipe or a bat to beat them to death, in a manner so gruesome the local network affiliate wouldn't show the crime scene. Their reporter did a stand-up on the other side of Montestruc, with a mural behind him (Molly thought there was blood on the mural, but couldn't be certain), only hinting at the carnage he saw across the street.

Molly suspected Frank would have all the gory details ready for her when she reached the *Voice* offices.

Wade had left his hotel room, late, seemingly in a hurry. Twenty minutes later, he hadn't returned. Two women were killed at some uncertain point during the night. That still didn't necessarily mean it was Wade who killed them.

But it sure as hell didn't rule him out.

PART TWO

MALO DURO

I am fulfilling at last a dream of childhood and one as powerful as the erotic dreams of adolescence—*floating down the river.* Mark Twain, Major Powell, every human who has ever put forth on flowing water knows what I mean.

    EDWARD ABBEY, *DESERT SOLITAIRE*

The River, spreading, flows—and spends your dream.
What are you, lost within this tideless spell?

    HART CRANE, "THE BRIDGE"

We have seen the devil and he is
a cartographer—rivers as wells, the Styx
wrapped seven times around his realm

    CHRISTOPHER CESSAC,
    "RIO GRANDE AT NOON, RIO GRANDE AT MIDNIGHT"

23

⊐ЖЕ

Molly drove.

Wade sat beside her, in the passenger seat. Byrd rode in the back of his own SUV.

She tried to ignore her growing suspicion of Wade. Byrd wanted his best friend along, and the whole trip had been Wade's idea anyway.

She had stopped in at the hospital after a rough morning at the office—Frank had, indeed, hoarded all the gruesome details of last night's double murder for her—and found Byrd and Wade sitting in what she could only describe as morose silence.

"What's up?" she had asked.

"I'm gettin' transferred," Byrd said.

"Transferred where?"

"La Mariposa."

"Which is . . . ?" She sat down heavily in the guest chair Wade didn't already occupy and stared past Byrd at his broken oar.

"Sierra Providence's La Mariposa Hospice."

"Hospice." The word was so close to "hospital," but the meaning was so different.

A hospital was where you went to be fixed. You went to a hospice to die.

"Byrd, no . . ."

"Byrd, yes," Wade said, pointing to each of them in turn. After years of watching him on TV, it was still a shock to see him with his beard growing back in. "Wade yes. Molly yes." A small joke, accompanied by the trembling ghost of a smile.

Molly couldn't return it. Tears forced themselves from her eyes, despite her best efforts to hold them back. She went to her brother, put her arms around him. His thin arms encircled her neck like a bony collar.

This is ridiculous, she thought. *He's the one who's dying, and he's comforting me.*

"Wade had a great idea," he said. Subtly but unmistakably, he pushed her away. Having learned to read his cues, she took her seat again, biting back the sobs she wanted to release.

"What is it?"

"We're going to Malo Duro," Wade said.

"You are?" She looked from Wade to Byrd. "*You're* going?"

"All of us," Byrd said. "You too."

"When? Byrd, I'm swamped—" She cut herself off midsentence. She still had to get Wade's story, despite her growing suspicions. Going on a nostalgic trip to their old hometown might loosen his tongue just enough. And without real evidence, although she had every reason to be cautious, she couldn't spend her life worrying about what he might do. Besides, Byrd would be with them—Byrd, who had always been her protector. He couldn't fight now, couldn't stand up to danger the way he once had, but Wade wouldn't try anything in front of Byrd, no matter how far over the deep end he may have gone.

"Tomorrow's Sunday," Byrd pointed out. "You have Sundays off anyway."

She scraped hair away from her eyes and nodded her assent. "You're right, Byrd. I'm in."

"Excellent," Wade said. "Bright and early in the morning."

"You're sure you feel good enough?" Molly asked her brother.

"I'm not likely to get another chance," Byrd said. He betrayed no emotion as he said it. Just a fact, like any other. *I'm warm. I'm hungry. I'm dying.* All the same.

So here they were, making what amounted to a holy pilgrimage. Back to Palo Duro, the town of Byrd's birth, and hers. The place where they met Wade. Molly drove east through El Paso, on the freeway that sliced through the city, parallel to the Rio Grande. They passed fast-food joints and cowboy boot outlet stores, strip malls and porn shops. Mexico climbed the hills to their right, always a presence. Then they left the city behind and struck southeast, still parallel to the river, slicing through open country now, ranch country, hills and valleys and mesas defining the skyline. The air outside the city turned from brownish gray to blue and stopped smelling like baked sewage.

When they passed a restaurant with a huge sign offering roasted chicken, Byrd broke out in laughter that quickly became a hacking cough. "What is it, Byrd?" Molly asked.

"That restaurant. It reminded me of one of my favorite exit lines this week."

"Oh, God."

"No, listen. Saint Lawrence, a Roman martyr, was being burned to death over hot coals. His last words were, 'Turn me. I am roasted on one side.' I'm just not sure how applicable it is to me."

The exit for Palo Duro appeared about an hour outside of El Paso. The Palo Duro Motel stood beside the interstate, its three signposts stark against the cloudless sky. The tallest of the signs had blown out altogether and its frame stood there empty, surrounding a patch of blue. The next was weather-faded but still legible when you got close. The shortest, still thirty feet tall, was an illuminated sign in which most of the plastic was intact, and Molly suspected that at night it was visible from a great distance.

She peeled off the freeway and onto Palo Duro Road. The motel was on the right as they exited, Café on the left. It was almost noon, and a couple of pickup trucks were parked outside Café. The motel had parking in front and back, but the front part that they could see was deserted.

"Well, this hasn't changed a bit," Wade said. "It's like I never left."

"Did you think it would?" Byrd asked. "What would change it? The motel never relied on business from town. I'm sure it's strictly a stopover for people who can't make it to El Paso coming from the east, or who want to get past it headed that way."

"You're probably right, Byrd," Wade said.

"Anyone hungry?"

"Byrd?" Wade asked.

"Not yet."

"Let's keep exploring," Wade suggested. He caught Molly's gaze with eyes as blue as a mountain lake. He still had the beard, coming in fuller as the days passed, and somehow it made him look young again.

Molly drove past Café and on down the long two-lane that led into town. Some of the farmland they passed was in use, mostly growing cotton, as the McCall family had done for years. This time of year, the fields were brown and white, with cotton strewn along their edges and beside the road like snow. So much cotton, it was hard to imagine anyone going bankrupt. Molly knew it happened all the time, though, just as it had to their parents. Debts grew unmanageable, crops failed, prices fluctuated. Sometimes people just got old, and their children didn't want to stay on the farm.

Other properties were abandoned, their fields fallow, nothing now but vast stretches of bare earth. Some were thick with weeds; others had been so farmed out, toasted with chemicals and overuse, that nothing at all would grow anymore.

"God," Byrd said when they reached Palo Duro's "downtown" at the intersection of Palo Duro Road and River Road. A few buildings flanked the corner in every direction. Most stood empty: the bank, the barbershop (supports for its once cheerful red, white, and blue pole holding nothing but a couple of blown leaves now), Betty's Night Owl Saloon, Irene's Cantina. Two adobe walls of Lou's Hardware had crumbled under the weight of weather and time, although the painted sign could still be read through a patina of rust and dirt above what remained of the door.

Weeds choked the sidewalk around these buildings, even threatening to overrun the businesses that were still operating. The post office was open, and a car was parked in front of it. Next door was the firehouse, its big door open and the single fire engine visible in the gloom. Willie's Laundromat was empty but obviously remained a going concern. Across the street from it was Jo's Burgers Pizza Ribs. "Didn't that used to be something else?" Molly asked. The sign was newer than most of the others in town, the paint job fresher, glass intact in the windows.

"It was that liquor store. The Bottle Shop," Byrd said.

"That's right!" Wade said. "My dad used to spend more money there than we did on groceries."

Molly turned left onto River Road, called that because it ran parallel to the river. From the road, one could get occasional glimpses of the river, fringed with trees in spots, beyond the farms and ranches. Mexico lay on the other side, but Palo Duro had never had a legal port of entry. Fort Hancock's was the nearest.

A rangy, dun-colored coyote stood in the middle of the street, its ribs clearly showing through short fur, staring them down for a moment before darting between two buildings and out of sight.

To the right they saw more shut-down, crumbling businesses. The route took them past the Palo Duro Mercantile, which looked like it had closed its doors a hundred years ago. But when she was growing up, Molly had loved wandering its aisles, looking at toys and housewares, clothing and household appliances. Byrd had worked there a couple of summers. Through the Mercantile, her dad had even bought a tractor once. Now it was gone, blown away by the west Texas wind, apparently like most of the town.

She opened her window and took a deep breath. The town's odor was different than what she remembered. The Mercantile had had a bakery attached, so especially on still winter mornings the fragrance of fresh breads and doughnuts and cakes had hung heavily on the air. The humidity of the Laundromat had leaked out into the street back in those days, but today it was cool and odorless.

Beside the Mercantile was the BBQ Shack, also closed, its big, screened porch covered with sheets of plywood, those covered with graffiti and pocked by bullet holes. That place had always smelled like cooking fires and burning meat and spilled beer, and on warm autumn nights you could usually find much of the town sitting at the rough wooden picnic tables on the porch listening to Hank Jr. or Waylon or George Strait on the jukebox in the corner. Colored Christmas lights hung on the inside walls all year long. Bugs dashed themselves against the screens, moths fluttered unsteadily against the lights, and cool breezes wafted the aromas of ribs and chicken and corn and burgers out to the gravel parking lot. The teenagers usually sat at a table of their own, laughing and swearing, sneaking out for smokes now and again, while their parents did more or less the same thing. The Mercantile and the BBQ Shack had been the town's social centers, and now both were history.

After that, they hit empty farmland again. The houses they

could see from the road were wrecks, tumbling back into the land. The scene wrenched Molly's heart. She had known families who lived in these houses, had gone to school with their children. She remembered riding her bike along this street, maybe headed to the Mercantile for some candy or a soda, maybe to the post office to pick up mail, and waving to people working their fields or sitting on front porches. Now they were gone. Palo Duro had become a ghost town.

When they reached the school complex, tears stung her eyes and she pulled the SUV off the road. Both school buildings, elementary and high school, were boarded up. Their brick walls looked as substantial as ever, but the covered windows (and those without covers, glass smashed out of them) destroyed that impression, leaving instead a sense of promises unfulfilled and dreams dashed. The lawns, athletic fields, and playgrounds were overgrown, the absence of children's cries of joy, of tennis shoes on the grass, of backpacks and lunchboxes thrown aside for playtime, palpable.

"Fuck, look at that," Byrd said quietly. "It's just . . . it's a shell."

"There's hardly any population left to sustain it," Wade said. "All those empty houses we've seen? I wonder where the kids go to school, though. The ones that are left. Fort Hancock? Sierra Blanca, maybe?"

"Either one's a long haul," Molly said. "It's just . . . it's hard to imagine how it got this bad. I mean, I know, I know how these things go. But this was a real town once, you know?"

"I seem to have a vague memory of that," Byrd said.

Molly put the vehicle in gear again. "I hope coming here wasn't a bad idea," she said.

"It's not that awful, Moll," Byrd said, using a nickname for her that he had rarely employed in recent years. "It's not like it's a surprise or anything. Rural flight and all. For the first time in history, more human beings live in cities than in rural areas."

"I *get* that, Byrd," Molly snapped. "I'm just articulating an emotional response, not writing a fucking thesis." As soon as the words escaped her lips, she regretted them. Byrd would be the first to insist that people treat him like anyone else, not to handle him with kid gloves. Although she had tried to live up to his wishes, guilt still wracked her when she lost her patience with him. "Sorry," she said. She pulled the Xterra back onto the road. Not a single vehicle had passed while they'd sat outside the school.

"Next stop, Downerville, USA," Byrd said.

He was right. Molly and Byrd had lived on a farm property adjacent to the school. No matter what shape it was in (but she could see it already, the fields as vacant as the school buildings, pushing up no vegetation to block the view), it wouldn't be what it once was. It wouldn't be the happy home where she had grown up.

Byrd had been away at UTEP when the foreclosure happened. The cotton crop had been bad for three years running—drought, insects, you name it. Her folks had borrowed to the hilt, and then those grim days came when they couldn't buy food and pay the bills. Then they couldn't do either one. Finally, they had to pack up both pickup trucks and leave behind everything they couldn't carry. The bank had already staked AUCTION signs around the property. Molly cried for three days before they moved, visiting her friends (those who hadn't already been foreclosed themselves), choosing what she could take and what had to be abandoned.

Byrd drove down from El Paso to help with the move, but he had been away during what she considered the worst of it, the months of uncertainty, the constant phone calls from creditors, the mailbox full of dunning notices, the questions her classmates asked about rumors they'd heard.

Within a year after winding up in a mobile home park on the northeast side of El Paso, their father was dead. Two years later—Molly had just started at UTEP, living at "home," in the double-wide, to save dorm money—their mother followed him. Byrd had always been Molly's rock; now he was all she had in the world. She couldn't imagine the shape of a life without him in it.

She turned down the long dirt driveway that had led to their house. From the gate, she could already see that it hadn't fared well in the intervening years. The adobe walls surrounding the yard had fallen over, the windows broken out, the bricks faded and chipped. A hole in the green, pitched roof might have been made by a meteorite or a small explosion or simple neglect.

She stopped the car. "I don't want to see any more, Byrd. Do you?"

"I don't think so," he said. "Not here. You're right, it's just too fuckin' sad."

Without another word, she turned around on the dirt lane and headed back to River Road. Their day of touring wasn't over, not by a long shot. They had more important places to visit, and only one day in which to see them.

⊐╫╪⊏

24

After they left the old McCall farm, the place where Wade had met
Molly and, shortly thereafter, Byrd—the two people who
would become his lifelong best friends—they drove out of
town, still heading south on River Road, the Rio Grande always there to the west.

They passed the site of the carnival where Wade had spent a
summer evening with Jenna Blair, the year both were fifteen.
He had won her three stuffed animals and been rewarded with
his first French kiss and his first bare breast (under the blouse
and bra, but flesh against his hand anyway, her nipple spiking
against his palm). Earlier, they'd eaten enough corn dogs and
pizza, cotton candy and churros to revolt a legion of vegans.
When they found a quiet place behind some of the carnies'
trailers and the kissing had started, everything else was forgotten. They made out for an hour before Jenna's older sister
found them and told them Jenna was in trouble for breaking
curfew. Wade had gone to bed that night but had been unable to
sleep for hours, his head spinning, his lips and tongue and teeth
and hands tingling with the memories of all they had done.

Two months later, Byrd had gone to the Permian Basin Fair
in Odessa with Jenna, won six prizes, and had even been invited
to put his hand inside Jenna's unsnapped jeans. Byrd, a year
older than Wade, had been experienced enough to know he'd
better not take advantage of the opportunity until Jenna was of
legal age because, as he explained to Wade the next day, once he
revved up her engines there wouldn't be any stopping her.

That had been the summer before, though. . . .

"Do you want to swing by your old place, Wade?" Molly
asked. They were approaching the McHenry Road turnoff,
which would take them directly to the old frame house he'd

lived in, hard by the river, a few miles away from the McCall farm.

"No thanks." He didn't have to think about that one. He never wanted to see that house again. Nothing happy had started there, nothing good. Not like Byrd and Molly's place, where he'd spotted Molly from his secondhand Stingray bike with its raised handlebars and banana seat.

Anyway, he understood where they were really headed. They all did, even though none of them had spoken it aloud. They'd agreed to go to Malo Duro, or Palo Duro, but what they meant was they were going to Smuggler's Canyon. That had been the centerpiece of their lives, hadn't it? Not school, not the Mercantile or the BBQ Shack. It had always been Smuggler's Canyon that mattered.

Soon, he could see it ahead, a buff rock outcropping that stood out against the sturdy, tall mesquite trees lining the riverbank there, still mostly green although beginning to lose their leaves for the winter. Those particular trees, almost impossible to cut down in the days before chainsaws, had given Palo Duro its name. Smuggler's Canyon had damn near snatched away its respectability.

There was no legal border crossing for miles around, but that didn't mean the border wasn't crossed. At Smuggler's Canyon, the river had been a passageway for longer than the international border had existed. The Treaty of Guadalupe Hidalgo in 1848 and the Gadsden Purchase of 1852 had officially determined the border between the U.S. and Mexico—before that, this had all been Mexico—but to those who crossed at the canyon, those treaties were pieces of paper with little significance. The river was narrow there, the channel closed in by the granite outcroppings thrust up through the limestone beds. The mesquite trees were convenient to tie boats to. And the limestone formations on what became the U.S. side offered ideal hiding places, caves and cliffs and hidey-holes that a smuggler or two or ten could duck into until the law lost interest.

Every parent in Palo Duro told his or her kids to keep away from Smuggler's Canyon. There were illegals there all the time, they said. Drug smugglers. Criminals.

Of course, that just spurred every kid in Palo Duro to get over there at the first possible opportunity. Most quickly lost interest, since the threat of visits by Border Patrol or the county sheriff made it a bad place for beer parties, and there were thousands of square miles of west Texas more welcoming.

Wade, Byrd, and Molly had fallen in love with the place. They'd been fascinated by its whispered history, tales of smugglers and thieves, the fact that raiding Apache warriors had hid out in the canyon, and been chased there not only by white soldiers but by Comanche war parties. The rock art had gripped their imaginations and they'd spent hour after hour studying it, imagining what it might have meant.

They had explored many of its caves, and made one, with a natural chimney for campfire smoke, into a kind of secret clubhouse. They'd stashed snacks in surplus-store ammo cans, comics, books and magazines (Wade and Byrd even burying, in a side cavern, *Playboy*s and *Penthouse*s that they only looked at when Molly wasn't along). They'd meet there on summer mornings and spend the whole day in the canyon, exploring, talking, reading, swimming in the river. On a portable boom box they played cassette tapes: Pink Floyd, Peter Gabriel, Springsteen, Joe Jackson, John Cougar, U2, The Clash, The Police, Elvis Costello. At dusk on summer evenings, bats flowed from the upper reaches like smoke from a campfire, and one year a pair of bald eagles built a nest in the rocks overhead and fished in the river in the late afternoons.

Occasionally they did see illegal immigrants swim across (the river, shallow for much of its length, was relatively deep here because the canyon walls forced it into such a narrow channel). At those times, they ducked into their cave and stayed quiet until the groups had moved on.

Wade watched now as Molly turned onto the dirt track that led to the rocky outcropping. Everything in Palo Duro had changed; this looked just the same. On the way, some of the open land had been carved into farms since the old days, and irrigation canals drew more of the water and majesty from the river. But when they passed over the last of those, all was as it had ever been. Nature had weathered these rocks, but not visibly in Wade's lifetime. Wind and rain and sun sculpted them, and like all sculpture, they experienced minute changes over the years that made each moment spent with them all the more valuable. He had been a kid among these rocks, and in many ways he had become a man among them. They would always, always hold a special place in his heart.

Wade's father had been a cruel man. Like all abusers, Brent Scheiner beat his wife and son at the slightest provocation—a bad grade, a dropped fly ball in a Little League game, an icebox without beer in it, or a table without dinner on it when he was hungry. Excuses, justifications, not reasons—Wade had understood, even as a young boy and the frequent victim of his rages, that there were never reasons for such abuse.

Dad convinced himself that he had reasons aplenty. His wife was no good—she kept a filthy house and she slept around with other men and she couldn't cook worth a damn—and he had only married her because he felt sorry for her in the first place. Then she up and got pregnant, just to trap him into staying, no doubt. So he stayed. "He don't know no better" was her attempt at explanation, the few times Wade had pressed for one. "It's how he was brought up, and how he's lived all his whole life. He don't mean nothing by it, it's just his way." Wade's paternal grandparents had both died before he was born, so he had no way of knowing how likely her story was.

They had lived in Dripping Springs, then. Gateway to the Hill Country, according to the big sign at the edge of town. Dad had worked as a ranch hand and then, after he almost cut his knee off (and oh, yes, that gave him plenty of excuses to throw punches, because it hurt when the weather changed or when it was humid or when he bumped it, for the rest of his life, and if you got in his way then, God help you), at Dripping Springs Feed & Seed, which was where he met nineteen-year-old Gloria Parton.

She'd been a cute blonde, in the pictures Wade had seen of his mother in her younger days, but slender, without the breasts of Dolly Parton, to whom she was not even distantly related. That had been another topic of occasional disagreement between his parents, usually after Brent had downed a few and maybe flipped through a stroke book—he had a stash of them in his workroom, which was where Wade got the ones he took to the cave. He would start to grope and pinch his wife, and if Gloria Parton Scheiner dared complain, because, for instance, she was making dinner or because Wade was standing right there, Dad would start in on the fact that he had expected her breasts to keep growing, so she wouldn't embarrass the Parton name. Wade had never been certain if Dolly Parton's had been natural, or surgically augmented, but he wasn't about to suggest to his mother that she consider surgery anyway, because the expenditure of that kind of money would have resulted in just as many beatings as were incited by the relative flatness of her chest.

Wade grew to hate the tenor of their voices as they rose toward inevitable violence, the flat sound of his father's first slap against his mother's cheek and her sharp intake of breath, then her almost silent weeping as the beating continued. He hated her for letting it continue almost as much as he hated the old man for starting it in the first place.

Once Wade reached adolescence, he became an acceptable alternate target, and childhood spankings and slaps had graduated, by the time he was thirteen, into brawls. Dad was muscular and wiry, all torso and huge arms and shoulders on bandy little legs, and it was easy for him to beat the crap out of a frightened kid.

They had to move from Dripping Springs during his thirteenth year. Dad won the town's annual Knights of Columbus Big Gun Raffle, buying a dozen chances for two bucks each and collecting, at the end of it, a Remington bolt action "Varmint Special" rifle. He'd owned guns his whole life, of course, but never a brand-new one. He took to shooting it from the front porch of their house outside of town, aiming at anything that moved and a few things that didn't. One neighbor complained when two of his dogs went missing, shot, he believed, by Brent Scheiner. Then the milkman complained about the bullet hole in his milk truck. That had brought the law to the Scheiner home, and when Dad pulled a gun on a sheriff's deputy, he earned himself a couple months in lockup.

Those two months, Wade remembered as the best of his early life. It was just him and his mom, and both were more relaxed and happy than they'd ever been. They toured around the region doing things Dad had never wanted to, heading into Austin and San Antonio, swimming in the Guadalupe River, dining in Fredericksburg and Kerrville and Bandera.

But the county let Wade's father go soon enough. When he got home, he was even meaner than before. Mean and scared at the same time. He began to insist that people were out to get him, and he never left the house without a gun or two. When he went into town, people crossed the street to avoid him. He lost his job at the Feed & Seed. Wade's teachers started calling the house to ask about Wade's frequent black eyes and broken bones, which increased his dad's paranoia.

Unable to get hired on anywhere, believing (not without merit) that everyone in town hated him, Brent Scheiner packed up his frightened family and all their belongings and moved out of Dripping Springs. A guy he had once worked with as a ranch hand told him about an opportunity in Palo Duro, working on a cotton farm, and Dad got the job.

Wade met Molly, then Byrd, which was good.

But his father dropped deeper down the spiral of drink and fear and self-loathing that made him abusive. He kept his guns out of sight, passing as a regular guy at work, for a while, but when he came home he needed someone to pound on. More and more often, as the years went by and he got bigger, that was Wade.

Only that all came to an end the year that Byrd turned seventeen and filled out. He worked out with weights at school, joined the varsity football team (which didn't last; Byrd was never a guy who participated well in team sports), and although he was never tall, he was built, cut and strong.

"We're here." Molly said, bringing the SUV to a sliding stop on the gravel lot at the rocks that served as parking for Smuggler's Canyon. There was another vehicle, a maroon Kia Sportage, parked there, with a foil windshield screen up, but its occupants were nowhere in sight. As always, a single plastic outhouse stood at the edge of the parking area with a rock-based trash can beside it.

"Smuggler's Canyon," Byrd said. "Who's got the titty mags?"

"I thought you didn't do those anymore," Wade said.

"I thought maybe I'd get wood for nostalgia's sake."

"Byrd," Molly said. "That's something I really don't need to hear."

"Just cover your ears and pretend you never knew," Byrd said.

"I might just do that."

They opened their doors at the same time. Byrd was a little slower getting out than the others; then they all stood on the gravel and breathed in the smell of the river, wet and dry at the same time, and the peppery aroma of the dusty rock. "That smell," Wade said.

"Takes you back," Byrd said.

"That it does, brother," Wade said. "Way, way back."

25

For all Wade knew, his mom really did sleep around. Gloria Parton
Scheiner never worked more than part-time (at a grocery store
in Dripping Springs, and as a cashier at Lou's Hardware two
afternoons a week in Palo Duro). But she always seemed to
have a few bucks in her purse, despite her husband's efforts to
keep her utterly dependent on him. And there were times she
went out during the day to "run errands" and came home with
no bags or evident purchases, but a smile on her face. As a kid,
Wade didn't think much of it. As an adult, he suspected she was
seeking comfort in the arms of others because her husband was
such an asshole.

If so, he could hardly blame her.

The events that changed Wade's life really began, he remembered, during the summer vacation of his sixteenth year.

The day was hot, the kind of dripping hot it can get sometimes when the humidity builds but the summer storm season
hasn't set in yet. He had been to El Paso with his mom, where
she let him buy a bunch of new comics, the cyberpunk science
fiction novel *Neuromancer*, by William Gibson, and the new
Joe Jackson album. He bought the album on vinyl, and would
record it on a cassette tape later to take to the Canyon. As soon
as he got home, he called Byrd and invited him over to check
out his haul.

Twenty minutes later, Byrd was there and they were in his
room—really, the garage of their small house, converted into a
bedroom—drinking Cokes and listening to side one of the record. Byrd lay on the shag carpeting (gold, brown, and black
threads creating a color that revealed almost no stains) en-
grossed in a *Conan* comic. Byrd's dark brown hair was long in

those days, always hanging down in his eyes, and he tossed his head to move it. Wade's hair, blond and thick, was kept in a shorter cut, because the old man didn't like it in his face and to Wade it wasn't worth getting beat up over.

Byrd put the comic down and rummaged through the rest of the stack. "How come there are women in the *X-Men*?" he asked. "That don't make any sense. Shouldn't it be *X-People* or somethin'?"

Wade was about to respond when the front door banged open and slammed shut, causing a vibration that could be felt throughout the house. "Crap," Wade said. "The old man's home early."

Byrd just shrugged. It took a lot to make him nervous, Wade had noticed. Especially since he'd made the football team. He seemed to take life in stride, no matter what it threw at him. His new status at school hadn't turned him into some kind of jerk, which Wade had briefly feared it might. Byrd still liked comics and fantasy and hanging with Wade and sometimes Molly down at the Canyon, just as he always had.

Wade had his license already, but no working vehicle. He was rebuilding a 1968 Camaro his mom's brother had left him in his will, a document that otherwise detailed only debts unpaid and promises unkept. It would be a sweet ride when it was done, but that summer it was a long way from done. Byrd had a '77 Chevy pickup, but its engine had seized up toward the end of the school year, and he hadn't raised enough money to replace it yet. So while Byrd was seventeen and Wade sixteen, they were both on bikes again for the duration of the summer. The shared hardship kept them close during a time when their lives were changing in other, significant ways.

"Yeah, only he sounds pissed," Wade said. "He's not usually home this early, so something must've happened."

"Whatever."

"Maybe we should get out of here. Go down to the cave, or maybe your place."

"Okay," Byrd said. He had already started reading about the mutant superheroes.

Wade knew that Byrd knew his dad beat him up. It wasn't something they talked about, although they had danced around it a few times. Wade just didn't see the point of involving his friends in what was strictly a family problem.

Besides, if the old man discovered that he'd told outsiders, the next beating would be worse than the last.

They had to go through the house to get out, since the big garage door had been sealed shut in the room conversion. By then, Dad and Mom were engaged in a screaming match. He was interrogating her about their shopping expedition, which he characterized as "throwin' my fuckin' money away on fuckin' bullshit!"

But when he saw Wade with his comics and the album he'd taken off the turntable to play at Byrd's place—never mind that Byrd was right behind him—his demeanor changed.

For the worse.

"How much did y'all spend on that shit?" he shouted. His face was almost the color of an eggplant and his hands were bunched into fists.

Wade had spent exactly twenty-seven dollars and nineteen cents. Not a fortune, considering he only made it into El Paso a few times a year, but not an insignificant sum, either. "Not that much," he said. He had only been in his father's presence for seconds and he was already on the defensive.

"Looks like plenty from here."

"Dad . . ."

"Don't 'Dad' me." The old man stalked toward him. He snarled—literally pulling his lips back, baring teeth, and making a growling noise. His eyes burned with liquid fire. He stank like a used washcloth soaked in cheap alcohol. Wade recognized the symptoms—something had pissed him off, he'd gone out drinking when he should have been working, got in trouble, and he would take it out on whomever he could. Wade hated that Byrd was there to see the pummeling he'd get.

"Dad, listen, not right now. Byrd and me, we're going—"

"You're going fuckin' nowhere till I'm done with you," his father said. He took another step toward Wade.

And then Wade felt a bump against his shoulder as Byrd pushed past him, stepping between him and the old man.

"Mr. Scheiner," Byrd said. Wade caught a hint of a tremor in his voice. So he was afraid of some things after all. "Mr. Scheiner, I know you've been beating up Wade for pretty much as long as I've known him. But it's got to stop. Now. If you ever touch him again, then we'll have a problem."

Dad's eyes went huge with surprise, and the snarl on his lips turned into a wet, menacing grin. "You callin' me out, boy?"

"I didn't want it to go that far, but I guess so. Yeah."

Byrd was strong, but he was still a kid. As far as Wade knew—and Wade knew him very well—he'd only been in a couple of fights. The last one, with Sidney Hughes, a notoriously vicious redneck at school, had happened in the locker room after Byrd's gym class a couple of months before. Wade had seen Byrd afterward, and he'd suffered a black eye and a bloody nose. He claimed Sidney had fared worse, and in fact Sidney had stopped tormenting people for the rest of the school year.

But Brent Scheiner had been fighting his whole life, to hear him tell it. Against adults, some of them armed with knives and clubs and other weapons. If Byrd went up against him, he'd be slaughtered.

Wade grabbed his friend's arm. "Byrd."

Byrd shook off the restraining hand.

"Better listen to the boy," the old man said. "He knows what you're up ag'in'."

"I don't care," Byrd declared, his voice steadier now, firmer. "You've been hittin' him for too long. If you promise to knock it off, I'll leave you alone."

"We go'n do this in the house, or outside?"

"Don't matter to me," Byrd said.

Wade fought back tears that threatened to blind him. "Byrd, no," he pleaded. "Just go home. I'll be okay. I'll see you later on."

"Not happening, Wade."

"Byrd, for fuck's sake, leave it be!"

Byrd turned his head just enough to fix Wade with a glare every bit as frightening as the old man's.

And the old man used the opportunity to charge.

Wade's mother screamed. Wade joined her.

Wade's father threw a punch at Byrd's jaw. Wade had only been on the receiving end of that one a couple of times—usually his father used open hands to pummel him, and body blows—but he had felt the power behind it, the right shoulder pistoning forward, driving the fist. This could end the fight before it really began.

Byrd dodged the punch. It glanced off his left shoulder, and Dad's momentum carried him forward, off balance, into the fist that Byrd drove up at his gut. Dad folded over the fist and gave an *ooof!* sound as the wind went out of him and the color vanished from his face.

Byrd was far from done. He followed that with a couple more quick, sharp jabs to the solar plexus, staggering Dad. Then Byrd threw a combination, right-left-right. The first two snagged the old man's chin, and the last missed it but clipped his ear.

Dad retreated to catch his breath. Oddly, the smile he showed appeared genuine.

"Y'all're fixin' to make this fun," he said. He spat a thick gob of blood on the linoleum tile floor. "Okay. That's okay with me."

Byrd didn't respond. Wade watched his back and shoulders rise and fall with his deep breaths. He kept his fists up, guarding his face, elbows close to his trunk. Maybe he'd only watched boxing on TV—Wade didn't think he'd ever had lessons—but except for the fact that his feet were planted on the floor, and he didn't have much room to move anyway, he seemed to know what he was doing.

Dad walked back and forth in front of him, an arm's length away, throwing easy jabs. His arms were longer than Byrd's, and his fists connected now and again. Byrd tried to bat them away, the blows only landing on his shoulders and arms. Dad was smiling, toying with Byrd, testing his reflexes and his reach.

Wade was glad that Byrd seemed to understand that and didn't let himself get drawn into a close-in slugfest.

After a couple minutes, Dad changed tactics. He lunged in close, threw his long arms out, and wrapped them around the teenager, pinning Byrd's arms to his sides. Then he jerked his head forward, slamming it into Byrd's teeth. Byrd's head snapped back, blood spraying from his mouth. Dad released him and started in with a series of body blows, alternating right and left fists, making a sound like someone hitting a side of beef with a baseball bat. Byrd groaned, tried to cover himself, tried to strike back, but he had been shaken by the head-butt and had lost whatever control of the situation he'd once had.

"Dad!" Wade shrieked. "Leave him be!"

Dad took a couple of steps back and laughed. "He wanted it."

"Brent, really," Wade's mom said. Her complaint was as ineffectual as ever.

Dad raised the back of his hand toward her. "Don't you fuckin' start in."

She cowered away from his threatened blow. Byrd was bent over, breathing hard, wiping blood away from his mouth on the side of his hand and flinging it to the floor. Wade looked for a weapon he could use, a club or a knife. The big knives were in the kitchen, and Byrd and the old man blocked his way, plus his mom was there and she would object. He had a baseball bat in his room, though.

He took a stealthy step backward, then another. His dad caught his gaze and he halted, meeting his father's eyes with what he hoped was a look of intense, searing hatred. The old man just showed his teeth in a malicious grin. Pink-tinged spittle gathered in the corners of his mouth. The fight had turned in his favor, and he liked things to go his way.

"You want to keep going, boy? You decide not to, that's okay with me. I'm just gettin' warmed up, but there's others here I can spar with."

"No," Byrd said, straightening to his full height. He sucked in a deep breath. To Wade, it looked as if he had grown an inch taller and a couple inches broader in the last twenty seconds. "You keep your hands off them."

"This is my house, boy. I do what I want here."

"Not anymore."

Dad touched his lower lip, cut and already swelling, with his knuckles and spat again. "Fuck that. Let's go."

Byrd shrugged and danced toward him, fists probing. Dad laughed at his footwork. "Fuckin' Muhammad Ali here." But when he tried to swing at Byrd, his fist sailed past because Byrd, on his toes now, moving instead of planted, hopped out of range.

Dad took another shot. This time, Byrd grabbed his arm in both hands, threw his weight back, and wrenched Wade's father's arm. He pulled the old man off balance again. This time, instead of punching him, he snapped a fierce kick right into Brent Scheiner's genitals.

The old man turned bright purple, doubling over, throwing his hands down to cover his crotch. The expression on his face was an ugly cross between hatred and agony. Byrd took advantage; his fists shot out, trying to wipe the expression from his face altogether. He landed blows to Dad's jaw, chin, cheek, nose, and eye. Dad's head rocked and shook like a bobblehead doll's. Byrd kept up the assault, raining punches.

Blood flew in the air between them every time Byrd drew back for another shot. Dad's face had turned into a bloody mask, his cheek and brow and lips all opened up. The blood clung to Byrd's fists, and he no doubt contributed some of his own. But he moved with absolute confidence now. He controlled the fight, and it was clear that Dad would go down. Probably soon.

Then one of Dad's feet gave out beneath him, his knee buckling. He had to catch himself on a kitchen counter. The yellow linoleum was slick with blood, the metallic tang of it almost as strong now as sweat and fear and the booze seeping from the old man's pores.

Wade's mom's face was curiously detached, as if she was watching a movie instead of her son's best friend beating the crap out of her husband. Wade wondered if the marriage would survive this day. He hoped not.

Dad kept his balance, barely, and forced himself back onto two feet. He swayed like the drunken man he was. He shook his head, trying to clear his vision, but blood from the cut over his eye and the swelling of his brow had half-blinded him. When he spat again, a tooth hit the floor with a soft clatter. He slurred his words when he spoke, as if his tongue had become too heavy for him. "Amon fuckin' kill you," he said. The redneck in him came to the fore when he was seriously drunk or seriously pissed, and it had done so now. "Amon" meant "I'm going to," a verbal habit he had mostly put aside since his own rural childhood. "C'mere, boy, amon tear your fuckin' fairy head off."

Byrd laughed. Wade was astonished that he felt comfortable enough to find humor in anything. "Fairy?" Byrd repeated.

"*I'm* a fairy? What's that say about you, a fairy kickin' your ass?"

Dad lurched forward in a barely controlled attack, his hands grasping for purchase. Byrd sidestepped the attempt easily, and as he did he swung his right hand sideways, driving its solid edge into the old man's throat. Wade's father gave a choked wheezing sound and crumpled to the blood-soaked kitchen floor in a heap.

"Call 911!" Wade's mom screamed. "Wade, call 911!" She knelt by her husband's side, shaking him gently. He was breathing, but with difficulty, making noises like someone trying to jam a sheep through a bellows.

Wade shoved past Byrd, snatched the phone off the wall, and dialed. An operator answered almost immediately, and he told her that his father was injured, that he'd hurt his throat, and someone had to come quick. She took down some information. Twenty minutes later, they heard sirens. By then, Dad was able to move a little, and he sat up, one hand over his throat, his back against the counter. The spark had gone from his eyes, and he wouldn't look at anyone even when they spoke to him.

"You better get out of here," Wade told Byrd.

"Come with me."

"I should stay."

"Fuck him," Byrd said. "He's been whalin' on you and your mom for as long as I've known you. So he got a little taste of it himself. What's the big deal?"

"I don't know if anyone's ever beat him," Wade said. "I don't know what he'll do. He's got guns. He might call the police or he might decide to just fucking kill you. Just go on. I'll see you later."

Byrd rubbed the bruised knuckles of his right fist against his T-shirt. "Yeah, okay." Before he left, though, he went down on one knee in front of Brent Scheiner, putting his face very close to the old man's. "That's a sample," he said. "You ever lay a hand on Wade or his mom again, I'll know. And what I do to you that time won't be something you'll get back up from."

26

By the time the fire department arrived, Wade's father was up and
breathing on his own. But something had gone out of him. He
wouldn't meet anyone's eye. Wade's mother was on her hands
and knees trying to sponge up blood, and his father patiently let
a paramedic examine him and patch him up. They told him he
didn't absolutely need to go to the medical center, which was
all the way in Sierra Blanca, unless he had trouble breathing or
felt nauseous later that night.

Once they had gone, he took a can of beer from the refrigerator and went into the living room and sat in his chair with
the lights out and the TV on. Wade didn't hear him change the
channel once. He sat in front of the set and let the sounds and
images wash over him like a soothing balm.

He didn't go back to work for a week. During that time, he
mostly stayed at home, sitting in the living room watching TV
or busying himself in his workroom. He didn't attack Wade or
Wade's mother. He barely spoke to them, and when he did it
was in a soft, gentle manner. He was polite, even deferential,
saying "please" when he wanted the mashed potatoes passed,
and "thank you" when they were. If he encountered Wade in
the hall, he stepped aside to let his son pass. He apologized
when he accidentally got in someone's way.

It was as if someone had taken his body, shaken out the insides, and replaced them with those of an entirely different person. Wade couldn't quite believe the difference in him. Not that
he objected—it was a relief not to have to worry about being
assaulted, maybe even killed one of these days, by his own
flesh and blood. But it was strange, too, and a more than a little
worrying. Was Dad just letting the anger build inside him, disguised by this meek new surface? Would he explode one of

these days? Wade had heard about people who slaughtered their families and themselves, and he couldn't help wondering if that's what his dad would do.

But he went back to work, and seemed to get a little of his old spirit back. He was still courteous, even deferential, but Wade stopped thinking he was sucking it all in. Sometimes he complained about work, or shouted at the idiots on TV, and he sounded like the old Brent Scheiner, only without the beatings.

After a few more weeks, he even started going out at night again. Drinking with his buddies, Wade guessed. He came home late, but not as late as he had before. And he didn't come home angry. All in all, Wade considered it a vast improvement.

Wade had started dating Angela Mills, after running into her swimming in the river one day and admiring the way she filled out her bikini. She had red hair the color of sunset and green eyes set into a face that he hadn't realized was so pretty until he saw her pop out of the water, mouth open, gasping for air. He began to think his life had turned around, that he no longer had to be afraid of his father, that he was attractive to girls, and that good things were heading his way. Most days he spent time with Byrd and Molly, with Angela often joining them. Evenings were reserved for Angela and some spirited making out wherever they could find privacy. Nights he slept better than he had in years.

It was on July 19, he remembered, that he lost his virginity. He had taken Angela to the cave, where she'd been several times before, but always during the day with Molly and Byrd around. This night, they were inside with a lantern glowing, fooling around some and talking some, and she got to exploring. Wade barely remembered the nudie magazines he and Byrd had cached a couple of years earlier, but she found them and started flipping the pages, looking at the naked women.

"Are my boobs as big as hers?" she asked, letting a center-fold flop open.

Wade wasn't sure how to answer. Was this one of those "does this dress make me look fat?" questions? You didn't need to watch a lot of relationship sitcoms on TV to know there was no safe answer to that one.

He tried to dodge. "It's hard to say."

She put down the magazine and slipped off her tank top, then reached back and unfastened her bra, letting it fall to the cave floor. "How about now?" she asked. "Without all that stuff in the way?"

Her breasts were high and firm, smaller than the magazine model's but plenty big enough for Wade. He still wasn't sure how to answer, so instead of speaking he leaned forward and took one of them in his mouth.

She moaned in response, arching her back and pressing it against his face. He took the other breast in his hands, moving his mouth between both. The next thing he knew, she had unzipped his pants and released the erection he'd been sure would split them open. With the naked flesh of a dozen photo layouts on the ground around them, Angela kicked off her jeans, sank back onto the cave floor, and guided him into her. Having not thought to bring a condom, he hesitated for a moment, but she read his expression. "I'm on the pill," she whispered. "To control my acne."

"But what about diseases?" he asked, battling the urge to shut up and enjoy the moment. STDs were a big topic of discussion in health class.

"I'm a virgin, too, silly," Angela assured him.

A moment's wonder at how she had known that he was—had he done something wrong?—threw him, but then he lost himself in the soft moistness of her and began to move with her.

That night, alone in his bed, was like the night he had felt up Jenna Blair. His mind raced in circles and he got hard all over again just remembering how it had felt with Angela. He wondered if he loved her and if she loved him. He hoped she wouldn't be offering herself to Byrd in a couple of weeks. He finally fell asleep, and his dreams were all about her.

His mom woke him up early the next morning with tears running down her cheeks. "Honey, you're friends with that Kenner boy, aren't you?" she asked.

He sat up in bed, gripping the covers over his lap to hide his erection. "Russ Kenner? Sure, I guess so. He was on the JV team with Byrd. What's up?"

"I just heard on the radio news," she said, stifling a sob. "He's been killed."

"Killed how? What happened?"

"I don't know much. They didn't give a lot of detail. Just he's been killed, and the sheriff doesn't know who done it."

"Jeez, Mom," he said. He'd never known anyone who'd been murdered, and wasn't quite sure how to respond.

"I'm so sorry, honey," she said. She wrapped her arms around him. His erection had long since vanished, so he wasn't worried about that anymore.

It didn't take long for the details to come out, at least as rumors passed from one of Kenner's schoolmates to another. Officially, the sheriff kept pretty tight-lipped about it all, but Joe Ed Botkin's dad was a deputy, and he told Joe Ed, and pretty soon everyone had heard.

On the night that Wade was losing his virginity with Angela, Russ Kenner had been drinking with some buddies out in the desert. They'd convinced someone to buy them a couple of six-packs, and got a pretty good buzz on. But Julio Robles, who was nineteen, had driven them out there in his old Firebird, and he had to get up early the next morning to drive his pregnant sister to El Paso for a doctor's appointment. So at ten, he announced that he was heading home, and anyone who wanted a ride had better come now.

All the guys piled back into the car, complaining the whole way. Julio didn't even take them all home, but dropped them off at the intersection of Palo Duro and River—in the parking lot of the Bottle Stop, in fact—and let them walk from there.

Russ Kenner lived about three miles away. He walked on River part of the way, then cut across some fields to Burns. It was on Burns Road, according to Joe Ed, that he met someone else.

Whoever that someone was, Joe Ed claimed, he was strong. He took Russ into an irrigation ditch at the edge of a cotton field and choked the life from him, kneeling on his chest with one knee, pressing down hard enough to snap some ribs and send one of them through Russ's right lung. Then he took a sharp knife, like a hunting knife, and made a cut across Russ's forehead and two more down the sides of his face. That done, he peeled Russ's face from his head. Joe Ed's dad speculated that he did that to make it harder to identify the victim. When the sheriff's deputies found Russ, though, alerted by his parents when he didn't come home that night, they were able to confirm his identity by the wallet in his back jeans pocket. His fingerprints were intact, too. And they found the raggedly torn-off face, or most of it, hanging on top of a stake that held a bollworm trap, a quarter mile up the ditch.

The news sent a shock wave through the teenagers of Malo Duro. They'd been enjoying their summer, some working (Byrd had a job as a stock boy at the Mercantile, while Wade had picked up odd farm jobs here and there), some just hanging out, maybe experimenting with sex like Wade and Angela, or booze and dope, like Russ and his pals. Suddenly, it was as if a noxious cloud floated between them and the sun, the murder in their midst casting their summer in a new, terrible light.

What made it worse was that it was only the first.

Joey Quivira came next. He had been working on a car in his garage one night. When his parents went out to look for him, they found him on the ground with his throat slashed and screwdrivers jammed through his chest and into his lungs.

Kurt Brown had been driving home after dropping off his date (they'd gone all the way into El Paso to see *Aliens*), when he'd stopped on a quiet country lane for an unknown reason. His killer propped him up with his head in the door of the car, and slammed it enough times to pulp his skull. Brains and blood leaked onto the road and soaked the floor mat.

The county sheriff started warning people, particularly teenage boys, against being outside alone at night. Most of the guys took it to heart—Byrd and Wade started spending nights at each other's house (usually Byrd's), so if they were together in the evening, neither had to bike home alone. But some didn't get the message, or didn't heed it, and the murders continued through the rest of that summer. Jason Barnett, shot through the head three times, his eyes gouged out with a spoon. Kenny Trimble, stabbed multiple times, partially scalped. Emilio Villanova, knocked unconscious, then his body was placed on the ground with his head right in front of a tractor wheel. The tractor had passed over his skull at least twice, leaving something that looked, or so Joe Ed Botkin claimed, like strawberry applesauce.

Not all of these guys were on Byrd's football team or in Wade's class, but most of them were. They were all students at Palo Duro High.

The sheriff admitted that he didn't have any solid leads. There had been tips, hundreds of them, most of them useless. Joe Ed said a woman had called from Ely, Nevada, to confess. A Baptist preacher from Hardeeville, South Carolina, had called to say that he believed one of the men in his congregation, who he was sure was a homosexual, might be to blame. A few people around Malo Duro told of seeing a dark pickup truck about on some of the nights of the murders, but it would have been more unusual in that area for anyone not to have seen a pickup or two around town.

By the time Jason Barnett died, Wade was pretty sure he knew the truth.

When Kenny Trimble and then Emilio Villanova were murdered, he was certain.

27

᚛ᚔ᚜

"It's my dad."

"Your dad?" Byrd echoed. "What is? What are you talkin' about, dude?"

"Killing all those guys."

They were at the cave. Screwing Angela there had changed it for Wade, somehow, had stolen away some of its youthful innocence. It had been like something out of *Tom Sawyer*, but now it was more *Huck Finn*, an adult tale disguised as a kid's adventure.

"Your dad?" Molly asked. She was only twelve. Wade had not wanted to say anything in front of her, but they'd started talking about the murders and it had slipped out. She'd been sitting on the dirt floor reading an Archie comic, but now she left it spread open on her lap, forgotten, and stared at Wade with eyes so wide they must have hurt. "Your dad's the killer?"

Wade blew out a heavy sigh. "I think so, yeah."

"You're nuts," Byrd said. "You're absolutely bugfuck."

"Byrd!" Molly snapped, as she usually did these days when he employed language she considered obscene or inappropriate. Which, given that it was Byrd, was fairly often.

"Sorry," he said to her. "But you are, Wade."

"I don't think so. I wish I was wrong. I just don't see how I could be."

"Why, you catch him washing blood off his hands or something? You find the keys to the tractor he ran over Emilio with?"

"Someone got run over with a tractor?" Molly asked. They'd done their best to keep her out of the rumor loop.

"Never mind, Molly. Maybe you should go play with dolls or something."

"Forget that," she said. "I want to hear about Wade's dad."

"Fuck it, I don't care," Wade said. He balled his fists and punched the cave floor. "Look, he's been going out a lot at night lately. Ever since . . . you know . . . Byrd. He hasn't laid a hand on me or Mom since then, but he's been going out. I thought he was drinking with his friends from work, maybe. He'd come home sometimes, pretty late, acting a little buzzed, but never as drunk as he used to get."

"Sounds like our little talk had a positive impact," Byrd said.

"Maybe," Wade said. "But the first murder was Russ Kenner, right? That was the night of July 19."

"How do you know that?" Byrd asked.

"Never mind, I just do. Anyway, I remember my dad was out that night. He came home after I'd gone to bed, and I went to bed pretty late, and then couldn't sleep. I heard him come in and shuffle around in his workroom for a while before he went to bed."

"So what?"

"So then when Jason Barnett got it, he was out that night, too. I couldn't remember for sure if he'd been out the nights of the other murders, but after that I started paying attention. Kenny Trimble, he was out. Emilio Villanova, he was out. That's four of them out of, what? Six. That's a pretty bad record."

"Maybe," Byrd said. He pursed his lips. Wade had never looked at him quite the same, since he'd watched him kick the shit out of his father. He was a handsome guy, deeply tanned, well muscled, and now he took on the air of a superhero in Wade's eyes. "But it's all, whaddyacallit, circumstantial, right?"

"Yeah, I guess it is." Wade dug into the backpack he had brought to the cave with him, in which he carried an extra flashlight, batteries, cassette tapes, some reading material, and other odds and ends. He pulled out an object wrapped in a paisley bandanna and unwrapped it, revealing a large knife in a brown leather sheath with a pocket for a sharpening stone. "So I went snooping around in his workroom, and I found this." He tugged the knife from its sheath, displaying a wicked blade, serrated across the top edge.

"Shit," Byrd said.

"Yeah. Joe Ed's dad said he thinks the knife that stabbed Kenny was the same one that cut off Russ Kenner's face, and maybe the same one that sliced Joey Quivira's throat."

"Joe Ed's dad is so dumb he's practically retarded."

"Mom says that's not a nice word."

"Mom's right, Molly. But it's true." Byrd inspected the knife without touching it. "Dude, you have to take this to the cops."

"I want to," Wade said. "But like you said, it's all circumstantial. Even this—it's just a knife, and there's not a speck of blood on it that I can see. I'm finally kind of getting along okay with my dad, for the first time in my life, pretty much. If I turn him in with no real proof, what's he gonna think about that? I mean, he'll hate me all over again."

"What do you want to do, then? You can't just sit on it."

Wade put the knife back into its case, wrapped it up, and shoved it deep in the backpack. "I have an idea about that."

"What?"

"I'm going to keep an eye on him when he goes out."

"Won't he be driving?"

"Sure. But there aren't a lot of roads around here, you might have noticed. There are plenty of fields, and trails across those. I think on my bike I can cut through and mostly keep up with him. He won't be watching for anyone following him that way." He had flopped around in bed the night before, trying to get comfortable, trying to forget the lurid stories he'd heard of John Wayne Gacy and Henry Lee Lucas and their kind. His father had always had anger issues, to put it mildly. Had something tipped him over the edge, sent him into a murderous rage from which there was no coming back?

He could never whisper a word of it to Byrd, but Wade couldn't help wondering if it was the fight, getting his ass kicked, finally, by a seventeen-year-old that had done it.

A tentative smile played about Byrd's lips and eyes. Wade had seen that look on Byrd before, usually as a prelude to some sort of outrageous suggestion that might get them both in trouble. That look had accompanied a thousand *I dare you*s and *Hey, why don't we*s and *I've got an idea*s. "Okay," Byrd said. "I'm in."

"Me too!" Molly added, jumping to her feet as if she'd been invited into the fun house at the carnival.

"Wait," Wade said. He pointed at Molly. "No. Byrd, I'm not asking for volunteers. It's my dad, and I've got to do something. I have to know for sure. But—"

"Wade," Byrd said. The single word carried a flat finality, the way he spoke it, a "shut up and don't argue" certainty. "We're in this together, dude. We're all in it, for that matter." His gaze swept the room, encompassing his little sister. "I don't want anybody getting hurt. Anybody. So I'm in, and I'll look out for Molly."

Molly had clasped her hands together in front of her waist, and she stared at Byrd like he was the Second Coming. "Molly, you need to keep quiet about all this. And do exactly what I tell you. Without question, without hesitation. Can you do that?"

With all the gravity a twelve-year-old could possess, she lowered her eyelids halfway and nodded her head. "Yes, Byrd."

"Good. Okay, Wade, what's the plan?"

For the next few nights, Wade's dad stayed in. He watched TV, he drank a couple of beers, from time to time Wade even caught him engaging in civil, good-humored conversation with Mom.

Summer was drawing toward a close, the days speeding past as the beginning of school neared. Wade hung out with Byrd whenever Byrd's job at the Mercantile didn't keep him tied up. He and Angela were still dating. In the timeless tradition of teenage sweethearts, the only caution they exercised was their studious avoidance of the word "love." Possibly as a result, Wade didn't know if he was in love with her, but being away from her made his chest ache and being near her made other parts sore. He saw Angela most evenings, always breaking away (an exercise in willpower he was surprised to win) in time to be home before nine. On the nights his father had left the house, presumably to go boy-hunting, he had always taken off around ten.

Five nights after the meeting in the cave, Dad went out again. Just before ten, he tugged on a denim jacket and a ball cap with the Dallas Cowboys star logo on it—because a summer thunderstorm had opened up the skies an hour before and hadn't let up—growled a cursory "See you later," and stepped out the door.

As they had discussed, Wade rushed to the phone and dialed Byrd's number. Wade let the phone ring once, hung up, dialed the number again, and once again hung up after the first ring. Byrd would be able to hear it from wherever he was in the house, and he'd know to get outside and grab his bike. Molly, Wade hoped, was already sound asleep.

The timing worked just as they'd hoped. After making his two aborted calls, Wade ran to his bike and started pedaling for all he was worth, cutting across a field instead of taking McHenry Road. Mud sucked at his tires, trying to draw him down, but he pushed through. The route led to River Road, heading toward town. He could see the diffuse glow of taillights through the rain, probably Dad in the pickup. By the time his dad passed the McCall place, Byrd should have been outside on his bike, ready to ride.

Soaked and winded, his lungs screaming in protest and his heart jackhammering in his chest, Wade rode into Palo Duro. As he came into the glow of the streetlights, which only extended for a quarter mile or so from the crossroads at River and Palo Duro, he heard a low whistle and squeezed the brake handles, having finally traded up, a year before, from the ancient Stingray to a new mountain bike.

He came to a shuddering stop, rear wheel kicking up a small fantail of rainwater. Byrd came out of the shadows between the BBQ Shack and the Mercantile, straddling his own bike. His cheeks were red with effort and he had to suck in a deep breath before he spoke. "He went into Betty's," he said, pointing at the Night Owl Saloon building down the street. "Hasn't come out."

"Anyone see you leave the house?"

"Don't think so. I can't stay out too late, though."

"Go ahead on home, man. I can stay."

"You sure?"

"It's covered." Wade's mom had watched him leave but hadn't asked any questions. He figured her world had been turned so upside down that she wouldn't know where to start.

He might have some awkward explaining to do when he got back. Then again, maybe not.

He'd try not to worry about that until it happened. Until then, he had to keep an eye on Dad, make sure he didn't go all *Texas Chainsaw Massacre* on some other poor kid.

Byrd took off, and Wade decided his spot was a good one. From the shadows he could clearly see the pickup truck and the front door of Betty's Night Owl. Neon liquor signs glowed in the building's curtained window. He put down the bike's kickstand and sat on an unpainted wooden step leading to the BBQ Shack's big screened patio. The driving rain against the building's tin roof made a noise like a never-ending train clattering by. The space between the buildings smelled like piss, and broken glass strewn about made him worry about his bike's tires. But there was an overhang above the door that kept most of the rain off him, and he leaned back against the door and tried not to think at all.

After a couple of hours, his dad staggered out, climbed into the truck, slammed the door, and drove toward home. Wade followed. When he pulled into the drive, the truck was sitting there, engine ticking. A light blazed upstairs in his parents' bedroom, but the downstairs was dark.

Wade stole inside, where he crept up the stairs and into his room without being observed. Once the door was closed, the enormity of what he had tried to do, of what his father might have done, surrounded him all at once, like a giant's fist closing in on him, crushing his ribs, compressing his lungs. He broke into an icy sweat. He peeled his wet clothes away and sat on his bed in his underwear, trembling.

Can I do this? he asked himself. *Can I really* do *this? On the other hand, how can I not?*

28

It went like that for a week. Dad leaving around ten on two more
nights, going down to Betty's for an hour or so, then returning
home. Wade followed, with Byrd (and once, Molly) joining the
chase as Dad drove past their house.

Saturday came. School would start a week from Monday.
Wade felt like his last weeks of vacation had passed him by, his
worries overwhelming the sense of freedom he should have exulted in.

Angela's parents had gone to San Antonio for the weekend,
leaving Angela in charge of her little brother, fourteen-year-old
Alan. Wade spent the day with her, swimming in the river, fooling around, while Alan hung out with buddies from his class.
That evening, Angela let three of the boys stay for dinner (frozen pizzas from the Mercantile, Cokes, and celery sticks that
mostly went uneaten). Afterward, in the early twilight, she and
Wade went for a long walk in the undeveloped desert near their
place. The Mills family lived way out of town, in the direction
of Smuggler's Canyon, and their farm contained the last cultivated fields for miles. A nearly full moon rose early and hung
low in the sky, yellow as autumn grass.

"I'm sorry we fought yesterday," Angela said, twining her
fingers in his. Holding her hand never stopped being a thrill, as
if she was plugged into an electrical outlet and conducted the
current directly to his heart when she touched him. She wore
perfume that made him think of fresh peaches.

He couldn't even remember how they had started fighting—
the simple pleasures of this day had already blotted it from his
memory. It had been over the phone, and they'd each hung up
on the other once. He'd been tense for days because of the old
man, and had snapped at her when she'd said something per-

fectly innocent. "Me too," he said. "It sucks when we're mad at each other."

"It does," she agreed. "But when we're not . . . ," she turned to face him, pressing her palms against his upper chest, "then *I* suck."

"You do?"

"I could."

"What about your brother?"

"He and his friends are playing games," she said. "They'll never even miss us."

"If you're sure . . ."

She didn't speak, just lowered herself to her knees, running her hands down his body until they reached the waistband of his jeans. She had worn a tight cotton V-neck shirt and denim shorts, and all day he had stolen glances at her body—her long legs, the way her shirt exposed the upper mounds of her breasts—and he couldn't say he wasn't ready. She had gone down on him a few times, tentatively and unsure of her expertise, and though he still wasn't sure what to do with his hands while she did it (rub the top of her head? smack the bed? clutch the sheets?), he was happy to be her guinea pig. He didn't know if this was love, but it would do until the real thing came along.

This time, kneeling out in the desert, him standing with his hands on his hips, elbows out for balance, she had her technique down and finished him quickly. When it was done, he had to sit down, his knees having turned to rubber about halfway through. She stroked his dwindling erection a few times, then tucked it back into his pants.

"You liked that."

"I did. A lot. Thank you."

"My pleasure." She smiled to show that she really was pleased. "I like it, too. And I like when you do it to me."

"You want me to?" He'd be happy to reciprocate, as soon as his legs stopped quaking.

"Not right now. Maybe later. How late can you stay?"

He hadn't told her anything about the nighttime rides, or his suspicions about his father. If Dad was the killer, then the fewer people who found out, the better, at least until he had enough proof to go to the sheriff. "Oh, you know. Nine or so, I guess."

"Sure you can't stay later, Wade? Maybe tell your folks

you're spending the night at Byrd's? I told Alan one of his friends could stay over."

He had rarely heard a more tempting offer. Maybe he could skip watching the old man this one night. It might prove to be a night he would never forget.

But if it turned out to be the night that the next kid got killed, he not only wouldn't forget it, he'd never forgive himself.

He hated his father more than ever for putting him in such a stupid position. The offer of a lifetime, from an amazingly sexy girl, and he had to turn her down. Maybe he was secretly adopted; maybe his mom had been sleeping around even in those days and he was really the son of some other guy. Anyone else would be an improvement, anyone who wasn't a killer and an abuser. If she hadn't allowed it, all these years, almost welcomed it as something that was just meant to be, he might have been able to believe it.

"I can't," he said at last. "I have to be home."

"But, Wade! It's our one chance. You always say you want to go to sleep with your arms around me, and wake up with me next to you. We can do it tonight!"

"I know, Angela." Wade was arguing against everything he wanted in life at that moment, and it made him feel like an idiot. "Believe me, I know."

"Then just stay."

"I can't."

"Wade—"

"Angela, I just can't!" He was getting mad, snapping at her again, even though she wasn't doing anything wrong. "Don't ask me why, okay? It's just the way things are."

"I . . . I can't accept that, Wade. If you loved me, you'd—"

"I'd still do what I'm doing, Angela. I have to go home tonight. There's just no way around it."

She looked away from him, and he saw the beginnings of tears welling in her eyes. This was not the kind of evening he had imagined or wanted—okay, the first part had been, but not this.

"Wade, I need to be with someone who's really in it with me. Not just sometimes, not just when it's handy, but all the time."

"Angela, I am—"

Her turn to interrupt. "No you're not! Even when you're with me you're thinking about something else. I can see it. You drift away, into some other world. Sometimes I have to call your name three times before you know I'm talking to you. If I hadn't just sucked you, you probably wouldn't even know it now!"

"That's not fair, Angela," he started to say. But he stopped, because it *was* fair. He'd been only half-present, if that, since this whole thing with his dad had started.

Maybe if I tell her—

He couldn't tell her, though. Couldn't risk it. If he told anyone, and it somehow got back to his dad, he'd never get the proof he needed.

"Wade?"

God, it happened again. How many times did she have to say my name that time? "Yes, baby?"

"Wade, I like you a lot. But I can't do this with you. I just can't, okay? We're done, Wade."

"But . . ." But what? I can change? He couldn't. Not yet.

"I'm sorry, Angela." Tears, hot on his cheeks. She was crying now, too. "I'm so sorry."

"Me too."

She stood up then and walked away from him. He sat in the dirt, his jeans unzipped, and watched one of the only things in his life that was good and true and pleasant disappear into the evening.

And he watched the motion of her ass in the tight shorts, the way her red hair swayed and brushed her shoulder blades.

And he felt the happy soreness of his cock, where she had taken pleasure in pleasuring him.

And all he could think was *At least I won't have to make excuses at night anymore. . . .*

That night, his dad went out again.

Wade had been sitting around the house, feeling like someone had flung his partially detached guts around the bumper of a speeding car. After telling his mom, in the briefest possible way, that Angela had dumped him, he had retreated to his bedroom and played the Waterboys album *This Is the Sea* over and over again, as if it contained some special message he could understand if only he had the key. He considered his musical tastes far more sophisticated than most of his friends', an attitude demonstrated by the poster of a broody Morrissey fronting The Smiths that he kept on the wall as a dartboard.

A little before ten, he heard the front door close and his dad's truck's engine start up. He hurried to the phone, dialed the number his fingers could punch automatically. One ring, hang up. Call back. This time, the phone was picked up instantly, and the angry voice of Byrd's father shouted "Who the hell is this?" into it. Wade hung up.

"Wade?" His mom stood in front of the door. She spoke with all the energy of a wet tissue. "Where are you goin'?"

"Out," he said.

"It's late. It's after ten. You been out all day."

"Mom, I . . . I just have to ride around some. Angela broke up with me today, remember? I'm restless."

She gazed at him, an even, appraising gaze that assured him she wasn't fooled. *What about all those other nights?* she might have asked.

Instead, she simply said, "I'm sorry about Angela. She was a nice girl," and moved out of the way.

"Yeah," Wade said. Outside, he ran to his bike. The light was on over the garage door and bugs clouded around it like the reverse image of a nebula being drawn into a black hole. But it hadn't rained for a couple of days, and the ground was dry and packed, and his bike seemed to roll effortlessly. He made good time across the field, and when he hit River Road's paved surface he was flying, gliding on air.

When he reached the McCall place, Byrd was still waiting by the road with his bike.

"Why aren't you following him?" Wade asked.

"He hasn't come by."

"Are you sure?"

"I got out here right after you called. My dad was yelling at you and didn't even hear me leave."

"But . . . where else would he have gone?" McHenry Road was the last real road in town, and not many families with kids lived out beyond the Scheiners.

Except for the Mills family. He'd told Mom earlier that the kids would be home by themselves tonight. If she told Dad . . .

"Oh, fuck! Angela and Alan!"

"What?" Byrd asked.

"If he turned right on River instead of left, he might be heading toward Angela's!"

"No way!"

"Unless he's going to some other town," Wade said. "Come on!"

He jumped back on his bike and started to pedal. He thought he heard Byrd coming along behind, but he didn't bother to look back. Head down, he pumped his legs, and once again the bike seemed to fly along the roadway. At McHenry he made a sharp right onto the road, then a left into a field, cutting across it on an elevated path bordering an irrigation ditch. They'd be off-road much of the way now, but it was a shorter route than taking the pavement, and he knew it well from visiting Angela so often over the summer.

He checked behind him once to make sure Byrd saw the route. Byrd was maybe a quarter mile back, and in the bright moonlight he could easily see where to turn.

Behind him, another quarter mile or so, was Molly.

29

Part of him wanted to stop and send her home, but he couldn't
spare the time. Maybe Byrd would. They had agreed she could
go along on these trips, but that had been under protest. She
had been there and overheard and there was nothing they could
do about it at the time. Wade had counted on her forgetting, or
being asleep or involved in other things.

Byrd raced toward him, though, seemingly oblivious to
Molly's presence. Wade plowed on into the field, bike wheels
spinning across the dirt as if it offered almost no friction, only
gravity keeping him earthbound. He flew toward a break in the
fence, slipped through it and into another field. Past that came a
mile or so of open land, low hills and scrub.

Wade hit that and the bike started bouncing, lurching over
the uneven ground. On hills, his wheels left the dirt, sailed over
open earth, landed hard and rolled on. His teeth clacked together and he tasted blood. He kept riding, eating up the distance to Angela's house.

Finally he reached River Road again, where it curved
around toward the Mills' driveway. It seemed like hours had
passed, but really it couldn't have been more than twenty-five
minutes since he'd left home, thirty at the outside. He could get
to Angela's place in fifteen minutes when he pushed it, but he
had detoured to Byrd's first. And he had never pushed it like he
had now.

Somewhere behind him were Byrd and Molly—Molly
probably way behind, which was for the best.

Wade started up Angela's driveway, then came to a screeching halt that kicked dirt up around his legs.

His dad's pickup truck was parked in the long dirt drive, its lights out. He couldn't tell if anyone was inside. The house, blocked by a low, scrub-covered hill, was barely visible from where the truck sat. Lights glowed from that direction.

Wade hadn't figured out just what he would do in this scenario. He didn't have any weapons, and he wasn't as strong as Byrd. Plus, if his father had really killed all those people, he didn't know if he could match the man's ferocity, his sheer ruthlessness.

But if the man threatened Angela, he would sure try.

He had wasted too much time already. He stood up on the pedals, pressed down, started the bike in motion. He decided just to confront his dad and see what happened. His route took him past the truck, and he was almost even with it when he realized his father was sitting behind the wheel, staring at the house.

With his legs straddling the bike, Wade bent down and scooped up the biggest rock he could reach. Shaking with rage, eyes so wet he could hardly see, he hurled it at the truck. Missing the windshield, it hit the roof, bounced, and landed in the open bed with a loud clatter.

His father saw him then. He snapped his head around, hard eyes glowing white in the shadowy cab, and stared at Wade with an emotion that could only be described as pure hatred. A line of drool on his chin shone silvery in the moonlight.

"Get out of here!" Wade screamed. "Leave them alone!"

His dad moved in the truck, and his window started to lower. "Or what?" he asked, his voice level.

"I know what you've been doing!" Wade shouted. "I'm going to the sheriff!"

"You'll do nothing of the kind, boy. You go home and I'll deal with you when I get there."

"Fuck that. Fuck you! You're a monster! By the time you get home, we'll be gone. Mom and me, we'll be at the sheriff's office turning you in."

His blood was roaring so loud in his ears he almost didn't hear the truck's engine catch. Then the lights flared on, and the vehicle started to move. Not toward the house, but backward— backing up so that he could come out of the driveway, out toward Wade.

* * *

There was a dream Wade had sometimes—not a specific recurring dream, but a type of dream, that came around disturbingly often. He'd had one last night, and forgotten all about it until just now. They usually came during the late night or early morning hours, and once he got past the immediate terror, he was able to get back to sleep. By morning, they had usually faded away.

In the one last night, he had been down by the river, at a place he had actually visited in real life several years before. It was a little pond, a place to which the river had overflowed during a heavy storm. By the time he found it, the river had receded, leaving behind a boggy stew with thick grass poking up past the water's surface. It was a broiling summer day, sticky hot, and the water was cool, so he plopped down into it. As he sat on the bottom, his legs were completely immersed, but the pond was only about waist high. Refreshing. Until, that was, he realized that insects were crawling up his shorts, their tiny legs tickling his thighs. He leapt up and smacked them away, and that's when he saw them, pale wriggling things about an inch long, like big whitish cockroaches. Seeing those, he jumped onto the bank, peeled his wet shorts off to make sure he'd found them all, and then hurried home to take a hot shower.

That had been real life. In the dream, he was back at the little pond, not inside it, just standing on the bank looking into the shallow water. The disgusting insects milled about on the bottom, a writhing mass of pale, soft exoskeletons, like flesh that had never seen the sun. As he watched, the water began to bubble. Wade realized that the ground under the water had opened up—a fissure formed, and air leaking from it caused the bubbling. It seemed to agitate the insects, too. They moved faster, spreading away from the fissure in every direction with jerky, anxious motions.

He stood on the bank as they emerged from the pond, streaming out in limitless numbers. When they swarmed around his sneakers, he tried to step away, but his feet might as well have been glued to the ground. They skittered up his legs, tickling the curly hairs on his ankles. He wanted to stomp, to run, but he was frozen in place.

The water had started to churn, and he could see something pushing up through the crack in the bottom. An insect leg, white like the rest, but easily as big around as his own legs, and as long. Now he really wanted to get away, didn't have any desire to see the rest of that thing (the ground beneath the roiling surface splitting lengthwise, the once-minute fissure now several feet long and still growing). The water level dropped as water flooded into the open crack. And still the thing came, more legs shoving through.

Wade tried to look away, tried not to see the thing's face as it rose up through the earth, because from his first glimpse it seemed to have a human face.

That was when he realized that he was in bed, dreaming. That realization didn't help, though. He was in his bed at home, but he was absolutely paralyzed, as surely as if ropes had been wrapped around his arms and legs and tied off. But the thing was coming anyway, in bed, on the banks of the stream, and the small ones were climbing up his legs, up his pajamas, their legs like hot wires slicing his flesh. He couldn't shake them off or run away, and when he tried to scream all that came out was a strangled gasp, caught in his throat. He was dreaming, he knew he was dreaming, and it made no difference at all.

The long, thick, pale legs of the huge insect touched him just below the knee, searing his flesh where they landed. That was the impetus it took to roust him from his paralysis. He twisted and lurched in the bed, covers furling around him; his eyes popped open, and he slapped his legs, knowing that the bugs weren't there, never had been there, but unable to stop himself.

Released from a paralysis every bit as complete as during the previous night's dream, Wade jumped on the pedals again. He raced down the drive, the way suddenly illuminated from behind. His shadow stretched crazily out before him.

The end of the drive neared. Bracing for the shock when his wheels hit pavement, Wade leaned over the handlebars and bore down. He passed from the headlights' glow for a moment, as the truck came over a low, curving rise, its beams spiking into the sky. Then they fixed him again, and before him, instead of just his shadow, were Byrd and Molly.

"Move!" Wade screamed.

Byrd moved.

Molly stood there with her bike in her hands, frozen, probably exhausted. Her face was red and blotchy in the headlights, her eyes the size of softballs.

Wade skidded past her, onto the road, over it, off into the ditch on the far side. He gained his feet and scrabbled up.

The headlights stabbed at Molly. The truck bore down on her.

Wade couldn't reach her in time, and she wasn't budging.

The truck looked huge compared to her, its grille fearsome as a predator's maw, its engine roaring like a prehistoric beast.

"Molly!" Wade cried, reaching uselessly into the road.

The truck charged.

And Byrd flew from the shadows, in full tackle mode, arms outspread. He swept into Molly and her bike, then Wade lost them both, blinded by the oncoming headlights. The truck raced over the spot where she had been and kept coming, across the road, scraping its undercarriage and sending sparks into the darkness, into the ditch on the other side. Dust choked the air.

But when Wade blinked his eyes clear, Byrd and Molly were mounted again, their bikes steady on the paved road. "Come on, dude!" Byrd shouted.

Wade's father's truck had gone into the ditch past its front wheels. He had it in reverse now, but those wheels were spinning, and though the back wheels tried to drag them out, the front ones found no purchase. Smoke belched from the exhaust, and under the growl of the motor Wade could hear a stream of curses spewing from his father's lips.

He found his bike, heaved it up onto the roadway. "Is Molly okay?" he asked.

"She's fine," Byrd said. "Where to?"

"We can't go home," Wade said. "That way!" He nodded away from the town, toward the open desert beyond the Mills place. He was a little surprised Angela and Alan hadn't come out to see what all the racket was, but maybe it hadn't gone on for as long as it seemed.

They rode along the pavement, following the curve around past the Mills farm. They had only been riding for a few minutes, however, when there was a change in the sound of the truck's engine.

"He's coming!" Wade shouted, once again taking the lead. Edging past the others, he waved them onto a dirt road that cut across the Mills place, separating two of their fields. Usually Mr. Mills drove it in an ATV, but sometimes he took a truck on it. Wade's hope was that his dad would stay on the pavement and miss it altogether.

The road climbed a gentle slope that would get steeper, then drop quickly into a valley on the other side. Moonlight etched the way.

As they neared the high point of the rise, Wade slowed his bike and looked back.

His dad's truck raced past the dirt road. A shiver of joy coursed through Wade's body; it took all he had not to throw his arms in the air and whoop. He did turn to Byrd and swap grins that, under any other circumstances, would have been absurdly enormous. Even Molly, puffing like mad, reached the hilltop and gave the boys high fives.

The screech of brakes snapped their attention back to the road and broke the mood like a brittle rubber band.

"Oh, shit on a stick!" Byrd said.

Molly glared at him but didn't say anything.

Below, the truck backed up to the road, made the turn. Wade realized they were standing at the top of the hill, illuminated by the bright moon. "Go!" he shouted, waving the others down the other side. "Go go go!"

Byrd and Molly kicked off and hurtled down the hill with Wade following right behind. He couldn't see the truck anymore, but its familiar engine sound grew louder as it swallowed up the dirt track. His mind reeled as he tried to think of a way off this road, someplace that bikes could go that the truck could not.

When he saw the tall rocks looming ahead, he could hardly believe he hadn't thought of it already.

Smuggler's Canyon.

30

The rocks of Smuggler's Canyon were still almost a mile away.
Wade could see them, when the dirt road wasn't bouncing his
eyeballs out of his head, but the road would end soon and they'd
have to cover the rest of the way cross-country. He was pretty
sure he could do it, and Byrd could do damn near anything. But
Molly? She was twelve. It was probably midnight. She'd been
riding for miles. Sometimes she seemed to have limitless energy—usually when Wade and Byrd wanted to go someplace
without her—but other times she wore out quickly.

He was astonished that she hadn't given up yet. She aped
her brother, hunched over the handlebars, butt in the air, feet
churning the pedals like a robot.

Their best hope was that the cross-country route would be
even harder for the truck than for the bikes. That wasn't much
to pin three lives on, but it was all they had.

The road turned rutted and rocky on the down slope, ending
altogether at a T intersection with a track that was little more
than a horse trail. Byrd skidded to a stop and looked to Wade
for directions.

"Just keep going!" Wade shouted. He waved toward the
rocks jutting up from the riverbank. "To the cave!"

Byrd nodded his understanding and struck off across the
hard-packed earth. Wade caught up to Molly. "You doing okay,
Molly? Can you make it?"

She spared him the briefest of glances. Her lower lip had
been tugged almost completely inside her mouth. She gave
him a single nod and kept pedaling.

"Good girl," he said. He slowed his own pace a little to stay
close to her. If Dad caught them, he caught them, but Wade refused to allow the possibility that he might catch only Molly.

The truck roared to the top of the hill behind them, scraping its belly as it humped over, and started down toward them. Wade figured they'd be harder to spot now, since they were on a fairly level plain, weaving and dodging through desert scrub. It wouldn't take Dad long to realize they hadn't taken the little trail, though, if he slowed enough to look for their tire tracks.

A mesquite bush nearly knocked Wade off his bike. He swerved around it at the last second but its branches snagged his clothes and jabbed between his spokes, and he barely kept his balance, the bike wobbling perilously in his hands. He had to stay focused, worry less about where the old man was and more about his surroundings. By the time he'd righted himself and continued, Molly was well ahead of him.

Then, almost before he expected it, he burst out of the desert and onto the track connecting Smuggler's Canyon with River Road. Byrd had already hit it and made the hard right turn toward their cave. Molly was just doing the same. Wade's rear wheel fishtailed when he took the turn too fast, but he held on to the handlebars, touched down with his feet briefly, and followed.

The parking area was just ahead, covered in gray gravel. At the edge of the lot were a plastic Porta potti and a trash can, and beyond those, nothing but the big rocks, the caves, and the river.

They ditched their bikes by the outhouse. They could hear the truck coming fast, see its headlights spearing into the sky, but it couldn't go beyond the parking area. And they knew the rocks and caves. Without experience, a map, and a flashlight, he'd never find them in the canyon.

He might be able to wait them out—they hadn't kept the "supplies" as current as they had when they were younger, and even then they'd consisted mostly of candy bars and warm Cokes. But Wade would worry about that later. Right now all he wanted was to get everyone safely hidden.

They dashed into the big rocks, climbing some, circling around others. They all knew the route. Pebbles rolled under Wade's shoes, threatening to spill him against the stones, but he kept his balance. Familiar pictograph masks gazed down at him from their aerie. With each step, his confidence grew.

They were going to make it.

They were within sight of the opening—a slab that had fallen from above, leaning against the base of its mother rock at a slant—when they heard the truck engine stop and the door slam. "You little shits can't hide from me!" Dad screamed.

Next they heard a sound they had never experienced at the canyon: the thunderous crack of a gunshot. It echoed off the rock walls on both sides of the river. Wings beat in the night; birds or bats startled by the noise. "Fuckin' shit!" Byrd said. "He's got a gun!"

"He has several," Wade reminded him. With the sound fading, Wade dashed the rest of the way to the opening.

When they'd first discovered the spot, ducking under it had been easy. These days, he and Byrd had to turn sideways and ease themselves through the narrow space.

He reached it first, dropped to his hands and knees, and scuttled in. Once past the slab, he had to climb a low shelf and go through an actual cave opening. It was just high enough off the ground that water never got inside, no matter how much rain fell. The shelf also hid the opening, so that if anyone bothered to look beyond the slab they wouldn't see the cave itself. In all their years here, only twice had they found signs of other human visitors.

Inside, Wade went straight to one of the old ammo boxes. The clip stuck. He smacked it a couple of times, knocking dirt from it, and was able to tug it open. Yanking out a flashlight, he thumbed the switch. Nothing. He beat it against his other palm a couple of times and it flickered into faint life. Hoping it would last, he beamed it through the opening for Byrd and Molly to follow.

Molly's small hands came into view, then her dark head, her thick hair blown and tangled by their wild ride. "You okay, Molly?"

"I guess so," she said. "Scared is all."

"Scared is fine."

"It better be," Byrd said, shoving in behind her, "because my drawers are totally brown by now."

"Byrd!" Molly said reproachfully. "That's so gross!"

"Shh," Wade said. "I don't want him to hear us."

"How long do you think we can stay in here?" Byrd asked in whispered tones.

"As long as we have to," Wade answered. "He can't stay out there forever. Border Patrol will come around, or a park ranger or something."

"How many park rangers have you seen here over the years, dude? One, maybe?"

"I'm not sure I've ever seen one," Wade admitted. "I was just hoping. Someone has to empty that outhouse, right?"

"Yeah," Byrd said with a smirk. "And the guy driving the shit truck is going to want to go up against a crazy man with a gun." He studied Wade for a minute in the faint glow of the flashlight. "Sorry. I know he's your dad, man."

"It's okay. He's completely nuts. I wish I knew what happened to him."

"He's always been an asshole, Wade."

"Yeah, but there are degrees of assholishness. He wasn't a murderer before."

"Shh!" Molly put her finger across her lips in the universal symbol for *shut up, you bozos*.

From outside, Wade could hear the crunch of shoes on dirt and rocks. Dad walked slowly, taking his time, like he was in no hurry at all. "I always knew you were stupid," he called. Wade didn't have to wonder who he was addressing. "Y'all think you wouldn't leave footprints?"

Wade clicked off the light. "Crap," Byrd whispered. "You think . . . ?"

Wade listened for another few seconds. He was still walking around out there, hadn't found the entrance yet. But he would.

And the old man didn't just keep a gun in his truck, he kept a flashlight. To have tracked them this quickly, he had to be using it.

"We need to keep going," he said, jerking his thumb over his shoulder, even though the others couldn't see him in the dark. Their cave had an opening at the back, a low-ceilinged slot you had to crawl through for about eight feet before it opened into a much bigger passage. They had explored it a couple of times, but never very far. The passage led to a few fairly large rooms, some the size you'd find in commercially developed caverns, but without the impressive geological formations of those. After a while, in the darkness and the sameness, they had been afraid they would become hopelessly lost and had always turned back.

The same frightening maze-like quality would make it easy for them to lose the old man inside, Wade hoped. Let him get lost in the warren of caves and tunnels, and they could escape and head for town.

"Are you sure?" Molly asked. She sounded terrified. Wade was glad of the darkness, so he didn't have to see her eyes.

"He'll find us here, for sure," Byrd said. "He's got a flashlight, probably, and a gun. In here he'll pick us off easy."

"That's what I was thinking," Wade said. "If we go back into the deeper caves, we'll be able to find someplace to hide."

"I hate it in there." Molly had only gone in once, and they'd had to bring her out almost immediately. She'd been crying, nearly panicked. Wade worried that she might flip out partway through the crawl space. If she screeched and carried on like she had before, Dad would be able to find them in no time.

"I know, Molly," Byrd said. "But it's our best chance."

Wade could tell she was sucking in a sob. "Okay," she said. "I'm ready."

"Wade goes first," Byrd suggested. "Then I'll help you in, Molly. Soon as you're through, I'll come after."

"O-okay."

Wade knew about where the opening was, and as he approached it in pitch blackness he felt the faintest draft brush his face. He risked flicking on the dying flashlight for just a second, to make sure the way was clear, and then, in utter darkness made deeper by the momentary light, he lowered himself to his belly and began the terrifying, painful crawl. When he hunched his shoulders to move his arms forward, his back scraped the ceiling. The air smelled vaguely sour, with an undertone of ammonia that he supposed came from bat shit. Guano, it was called, a word that could cause Byrd to explode in paroxysms of laughter.

He tried to imagine Byrd doubled over laughing, his strong arms folded across his gut, because it was better than thinking about the fact that it had been a couple of years since he'd tried this, and he'd filled out in those years. So had Byrd. Molly might be scared, but she was the only one guaranteed to fit through—unless, of course, Wade got stuck and blocked her way.

Wade was not normally claustrophobic, but the idea that he might get trapped began to haunt him. Did the passageway narrow toward the end? What if something shifted above him and the ceiling dropped suddenly?

Before the panic could get too severe, though, he reached into a wider space. He was nearly through. Grabbing the sides of the passageway's mouth, he hauled himself out. With one hand above his head to make sure he didn't bean himself on the ceiling, he stood, stretched. Plenty of space. He turned back to the opening and flashed the light though briefly. Molly waited on the far end.

"Nothing to it, Molly. Just crawl forward, and watch your head."

"She's cool," Byrd said.

"Yeah, I'm c-cool."

For about the millionth time, Wade regretted that she had been there for that first discussion of his suspicions, and especially regretted that she had trailed along. Risking Byrd's life was bad enough, but at least Byrd was old enough to make that decision for himself. Molly had been driven by hero worship of her older brother (and, Wade had to admit, maybe a little of him as well).

He followed her progress by the scuffling sounds she made through the passageway and by her labored, sniffly breathing. Soon her flailing hand swatted his leg, and he reached inside to help her out. "You're through, Molly, that's awesome!"

"Thanks," she said softly, getting to her feet, balancing with the help of a hand on the rock wall. "Byrd's turn now."

Wade flashed the light down the passage again. "Byrd," he said quietly. "Move it or lose it!"

"On the way," Byrd said. He ducked into the opening as Wade thumbed the light off. He made a lot more noise crawling through than Molly had, and he swore a few times when he barked his knuckles or knees against the rock, but in a couple of minutes, he emerged.

"I feel like he's right behind me," Byrd said when he gained his feet. "Like he was breathing on my neck in there."

"He's not that close," Wade countered. "But we should get a move on."

"Roger that, good buddy."

Wade beamed the faint light ahead of them, lighting the way down a tunnel almost wide enough for the three of them side by side. It was probably eight feet high, the ceiling lost in shadow. It tapered again soon, and the first side tunnel veered off from the left shortly after that.

They had barely entered the first tunnel when they heard a scraping noise from just outside the cave opening. They froze.

"Okay, then," Dad said. "At least y'all are making this interesting. But it's gettin' late, so it's time to wrap it up, children. You and me, we're going to have us a good time now."

31

"Come on," Wade said. He played the pathetic flashlight around the tunnel so they'd all have a sense of its dimensions. "We've got to find a place to hide."

"You think he can crawl through there?" Byrd asked.

"He's a human cockroach, man. I wouldn't want to bet against him."

They rushed through the tunnel as fast as they dared. Where it curved slightly to the left, Wade risked a glance over his shoulder. He saw light flashing around on the far side of the passageway, some of it even spilling through. The old man had already made it into their special cave.

"Faster," Wade urged.

"Won't do us any good if we clock ourselves on one of these walls or a low ceiling," Byrd said.

"Maybe not, but I'd rather take my chances with that than get a bullet in the back."

"Good point."

Molly grabbed Byrd's hand, and they picked up the pace. The flashlight flickered and died just after they rounded the bend. Wade smacked it and it illuminated again, fainter than before. Just a glowing bulb now, its beam hardly cut the blackness ahead.

"I hear you!" Dad shouted. "I'm right behind you!"

His voice bounced around the cavern walls, making it sound like he was all around them. Wade shivered. They couldn't speed up any more—running in here *would* be suicidal. If his father started firing that gun, and the bullets ricocheted around like his voice did, they'd all be dead meat.

"We've got to hide Molly someplace safe," he said. Urgency made his voice tight.

"I want to stay with you guys!"

"It's too dangerous," Byrd said. "Wade's right. We need to find someplace we can tuck you in, somewhere small so he won't see you."

"But, Byrd—"

"No buts," Byrd snapped, sounding like every parent who had ever lived.

"Down here," Wade said, drawing the other two into the side tunnel. It was narrower than the main one, tight enough that his shoulders bumped the sides. He tried to remember where it went, but couldn't. It either intersected another, slightly larger tunnel . . . or it didn't. He drew a blank.

If it didn't, if it dead-ended, they were screwed.

A turn. Another turn, to the right this time.

And then a solid wall, slightly slick with moisture seeping from above. Wade shone the weak light around, felt the walls with his hands in case there was a gap he couldn't see.

Nothing.

Dead end.

"Byrd—"

Byrd had already sized things up. "Fuckin' A, dude."

"Now what?"

Byrd's response was so immediate, his plan must already have been formulated. "Tell you what," he said. "You keep Molly safe in here, and I'll lead him on a wild goose chase. He'll never even see this passage."

"But, Byrd—" Molly began.

He cut her off. "It's the best way, Molly. One person can make better time than three, and he'll never get near me."

Wade put his right hand on the girl's shoulder. She was trembling, but she managed to keep the fear mostly out of her voice. "Okay," she said.

Because Byrd said so, Wade thought. *This girl will do anything her big brother tells her to.*

"That's a good girl, Molly." He sounded like he was addressing a dog, but Molly's tremors calmed slightly.

"I gotta go," Byrd said. "Before he gets too far in."

Wade had already been concerned about that. He wanted to argue, didn't want to see Byrd play hero, but arguing would take time they didn't have. Instead, he handed Byrd the flashlight.

Anyway, Byrd wasn't playing hero. He *was* a hero. It was as much a part of him as his brown hair or his crooked teeth or his raw vocabulary. Without another word, he slipped back out into the main tunnel—an action Wade would have found terrifying beyond belief.

Byrd probably did, too. But he did it anyway. To Wade, that was the definition of the word "hero."

Wade stood in the dark, his right hand remaining on Molly's shoulder in a way he hoped was comforting. The blackness surrounding them felt greasy and alive somehow, as if it contained a billion infinitesimal fingers and all of them brushed across Wade's bare arms, neck, and face.

Beyond the narrow walls of this passage he heard Byrd's voice. "Hey, you old fucker! You want a rematch? That what you're lookin' for?"

Wade tensed, expecting his father to answer with his gun. Instead, the old man said, "You'll find out what I'm after when I take it out of your useless, dead hide."

"Sounds kinky!" Byrd shot back.

Wade's dad gave a low, unintelligible growl. From the sound of his footsteps, he was just passing their hiding place.

The rest of it, Wade only found out later.

Byrd was willing to talk about it—desperate, in fact, to discuss it at length—for a few days. After that, he clammed up. No amount of prodding or prompting could get him to discuss the events of the next twenty minutes or so. Wade knew the story by then, so he didn't need to hear it again, but there had been times over the years that he had thought about some aspect of it and wanted to talk it over. Byrd was adamant, though.

Wade tried not to push him on it. Byrd proved himself, that day. He had earned the right to reveal as much or as little as he wanted.

He had gone back into the main tunnel and waited near the next bend until he heard Wade's father getting close. That was when he'd shouted out the taunt and started to run. Dad had sped his pace, too, dashing right past the side tunnel, flashlight bobbing as he ran, casting mad shadows all down the tunnel.

Byrd used what remained of his light's juice to keep from smashing face-first into one of the walls. He stuck to the big corridor at first, counting on its twists and bends to protect him from Dad's gun. He could hear the old man's labored breathing, hear the grunts he made as he raced through the unfamiliar tunnel, banging into the occasional wall.

Finally, Byrd came to a stretch he remembered being long and straight, with another extremely tight passage at the end of it. He didn't want to be wedged in there trying to get through and have Wade's father taking easy, carefully aimed shots at him. So when he reached the last side tunnel, he veered down that. It wouldn't be hard, Byrd guessed, for his pursuer to figure out, when he wasn't in the straightaway, where he had gone. Just in case, he shouted a curse as he made the turn, letting it trail off slowly.

He heard the old man pass the side tunnel, then quickly double back.

Now Byrd knew he was in a potentially tricky spot. He had no idea where he was going, or how long this side tunnel would continue. He had no weapon except a piece-of-shit flashlight that kept blinking out on him.

And behind him, coming up fast, was an insane armed man who he was convinced had already murdered several boys around his age.

It was, all in all, a pretty crappy situation.

He did what he could do, which was to keep going. The tunnel hardly had any straight parts at all, just one bend after another, dizzying from the speed at which he was trying to move, with bad light. He kept throwing out his left arm to fend off the walls.

Bouncing like a pinball, he discovered that this passage went on longer than he had dared hope, always sloping down, down beneath the earth, and angling toward the river. For all he knew, he had already passed under the river, and was beneath Mexico now. He had definitely crossed a boundary, entered a frontier, although not the kind found on maps. Wade's dad kept coming, but Byrd thought he had put a little more space between them on the tight turns. He started to feel better about his chances of evading the man. Sooner or later, the guy would tire of the chase, right? He'd turn around, wanting to get out of the caves before he was completely lost. He would decide that Wade would come home sometime, and he could take care of him then. He knew where Byrd and Molly lived, too.

It was, no doubt, wishful thinking.

Because the guy just kept on coming, and Byrd was starting to feel winded, worn out, not all that sure he could go much longer.

And then the light finally went out altogether.

Byrd slapped it against his palm. When that didn't work, he slapped it against the nearest rock wall. That resulted in shards of plastic and bits of lightbulb spraying all over the floor, crunching loudly when he stepped on them. For what purpose he couldn't quite fathom, he hung on to what remained of the shaft, and continued on into the dark.

Except, he realized, the darkness wasn't as total as he'd thought.

The last thing he'd seen before the light died was a wall blocking his path, a wall that would probably put an end to the whole chase. He hoped that Molly and Wade had already left the caves and were on their way—ideally, in Wade's father's truck—to get help.

Because he was up against it, for real and for good.

But after the light died and he smashed it into the wall, he discovered that he could see a little. There was something, some kind of glow, illuminating the tunnel ever so faintly.

Byrd hoped it wasn't the gleam of Brent Scheiner's light, filtering down to him.

He didn't think so. Looking around for the source, he found a slender gap in what he had thought was a solid wall. The glow came from that, or more precisely *through* that.

He peered in, but couldn't see anything through the narrow slice.

He didn't know if he could make it through. There was light there, though, and he had run out of options on this side. He turned sideways, facing front, so that if Wade's dad caught up to him he wouldn't have to see the bullet coming, and started in.

The walls scraped his temples, his cheeks. He left skin behind as he went. But the gap was slightly wider at the bottom than at the top, so he had room to move his legs, room to slide his hips and his chest and shoulders through. It was a grind, somewhat literally, but not impossible.

The farther he went, the brighter the glow became. Still faint, at least it was enough to illuminate the rocks that were about to lacerate him.

He could hear Wade's father getting closer. He tried to hurry, to force himself through the crack, but it was going to take as long as it took, and rushing it would only get him stuck.

Which would get him dead.

Imagining himself as a slice of toast buttered on both sides, he kept easing through the gap, into the slowly brightening glow. His sweat smelled sour, rank, but the farther he went the more it was overwhelmed by some new stink from the other side.

And then he was out, the toast metaphor continuing because he seemed to pop through when he reached the far side.

He felt like he had died and gone to heaven, or maybe hit his head harder than he'd thought and begun to hallucinate.

He had entered a kind of chamber. The ceiling and far walls were lost in shadow. What he could see, and in considerable detail, was dozens of stalactites and stalagmites, although he couldn't remember which was which, some of which joined to form solid columns from the floor up beyond where the glow reached. There were also much skinnier tubes, hundreds of them, and other formations, big flattened surfaces and swirls and a bewildering array of colors.

All of it was illuminated by a pool of water, maybe ten or twelve feet in diameter, almost perfectly circular, that glowed with some freakish internal light. The stench—something like ammonia mixed with methane and sulfur; it burned his nose when he breathed it in too deeply—came from the water.

Water might not have been the right term. It was white, milky, if milk had been irradiated and become its own light source. But it was pooled inside a cave, close to the Rio Grande—for all Byrd knew, *under* the Rio Grande—and no one had been milking cows down here. So water it would be, if he had anything to say about it.

Staring in amazement at the chamber, he almost forgot why he had reenacted his own birth and forced himself through that tiny crevice. The racket of old man Scheiner duplicating his feat, with more swearing and grumbling, reminded him.

He could hardly believe the man could do it. *He* had just barely made it, and he was thinner than Wade's father. But as he watched, a foot swung into view, reaching out, probing for its next step. Then a hand showed, gripping a flashlight. Byrd had to hide before Scheiner saw him.

He had started casting about for someplace he could duck down, when another thought dashed that one to bits. *Hide? Why bother?* When Brent Scheiner emerged, he would be just as spellbound as Byrd had been. He wouldn't be human if he didn't gawk for a few seconds.

Instead of hiding, Byrd flattened himself against the wall the gap opened out of. He waited, keeping his breathing shallow and silent, still clutching the stupid, busted flashlight.

When Wade's father came out of the squeeze and into the chamber, carrying a small revolver in his other hammy fist, Byrd thought the man would hear Byrd's heart slamming around in his chest like a tennis ball in a dryer. Scheiner stared, however, at the pool and the rock formations, just as Byrd had, his gaze drawn by the glow of the pale liquid. Finally, as if he remembering his quest, he started swiveling toward Byrd.

Byrd drove the flashlight's shaft into his face. Jagged plastic sliced flesh, and leftover shards of bulb filled the man's right eye socket. Wade's father screeched in pain and reeled back, throwing his hands into the air. His flashlight fell to the ground and the gun slammed into Byrd's face, tearing a gash in his left eyebrow, before hitting the rocks and bouncing into the pool. Old man Scheiner grunted wordlessly and stumbled after it, splashing into glowing water up to his knees. Byrd had a second or two of thinking he was safe.

That was before Wade's dad lunged for Byrd, reached out, snagged his T-shirt, and yanked him toward the pool.

32

The water Brent Scheiner splashed onto Byrd's chest burned his flesh. Byrd tried to wrench free, but Wade's father had a fistful of T-shirt and wasn't letting go. His mouth opened in a soundless howl, his bloody face twisted in pain and rage, and with his other hand, instead of hitting Byrd or using it to pull him in, he made a fist and punched at empty air.

But Scheiner had splashed milky water onto the rock floor, and Byrd's feet slid, unable to get enough traction to resist the man's pull. He grabbed the man's wrist and hand, trying to break his grip, but it was like trying to smash concrete with a cotton ball. In another few seconds he would be in the pool, too, and judging from Wade's dad's reaction, it wasn't exactly a spa.

The once-still pool churned and spat as if simply stepping into it had pissed it off in some way. Worse, where it landed on the man's flesh, it bubbled and adhered, resembling nothing more than the skin on cocoa. Smoke or steam rose from those spots, and Byrd figured that was why Scheiner seemed to be feeling such agony.

He'd still only felt secondhand water, transferred to his shirt by the man's fist, and that was bad enough, as if he had leaned on a hot burner. He didn't want the full-on dunking.

It looked, however, like he didn't have much choice.

Then Wade's father let out a shrill scream and his back arched abruptly. For a brief instant, Byrd thought he would let go. Instead, he held on all the tighter and jerked Byrd several inches closer to the pool. Struggling for balance, Byrd caught a glimpse of the man's skin where the liquid—it wasn't water after all, no water could do this—had started to eat away his flesh. Byrd saw exposed fat and muscle, splotchy red and white and pink stuff he couldn't identify. Wade's dad's flesh started to fall off his body in chunks, splashing into the roiling pool. Byrd's gut heaved, but if he puked, old man Scheiner would haul him in for sure.

Instead, he took what he thought would be his last shot.

The man's face, purple with fury and pain, had started to disintegrate. Touching it seemed like a bad idea, but it was close enough to reach and he still couldn't break the grip Scheiner had on him, or get out of his shirt.

He slammed his fist into the man's bleeding eye.

Wade's dad shrieked again and released Byrd's T-shirt, clapping his hand over his injured eye. He reeled backward, losing his own balance and landing on his ass in the pool. There he twitched and writhed and batted at himself as if wasps were swarming him.

Byrd didn't hesitate. He snatched Scheiner's still-working flashlight off the ground and squeezed back into the tiny gap through which he had entered this chamber of horrors. He had to fight to control his own panic, knowing it would only make things worse to try to rush it. A few desperate minutes passed, and then he was out. With the light, finding his way back to the main tunnel was easy, and from there it was just a matter of covering the distance to the entrance, with one brief detour to make sure Wade and Molly had left.

Byrd burst from beneath the slab that overhung their cave's en-trance like he'd been shot by a cannon. In another context, it would have been comical—his frantic emergence, hands pawing at the ground, mouth open, eyes blazing like a crazy person's. To Wade, though, watching from behind a large boulder close by, it was terrifying. Byrd was the bravest person he had ever known, so anything that had scared him that much had to be beyond awful.

He held Molly back for a few seconds, until he was sure that Byrd had come out alone. Then he released her, and rushed with her to Byrd's side. "Byrd!" he called as he ran. "We're over here!"

Byrd looked at them—through them, it seemed, like he couldn't focus on anything directly in front of his eyes, and his mouth worked silently. Wade reached Byrd first, and he threw his arms around his friend, helping him to his feet. By then Molly had joined them. Tears ran down her pudgy cheeks, tracking the dirt that caked them. Byrd's shirt was soaked, making Wade and Molly damp when they hugged him, and blood dripped from an ugly gash above his eye.

"You okay, Byrd?" Wade asked.

Byrd nodded a few times, and finally spoke. "I guess."

"What happened in there? Where's my dad?"

"He—the pool . . ." He started to speak again, swallowed, couldn't get anything out.

"It's okay now," Wade said. "Whatever you did, it's okay."

"Not me," Byrd managed. "The pool . . . it glows. Burns."

Wade didn't understand what he was talking about. Pool? They had never seen any kind of pool in there. "Slow down, man," he said. "One step at a time. What pool? Where's my dad?"

Byrd looked right into Wade's eyes, finally, and Wade could tell that his friend had been through something horrible, something that would leave scars for the rest of his life. "I don't think he's coming out, Wade."

"What do you mean?" Wade asked. He was getting the picture already, though. Byrd had killed him, somehow. That explained Byrd's awful, haunted stare—he had not only become a killer, but the person he had killed was Wade's father. "It's okay, Byrd," he said again. "You just did what you had to."

Byrd shook his head impatiently, like he did when Molly failed to grasp something that should have been obvious. The action flung blood from his cut. "No, no, no. Wade, it was—"

He didn't finish his sentence because they heard a low snarl, like a rabid dog, coming from the direction of their cave. "Oh fuck me fuck me no no no!" Byrd said. Panicked, he tried to run, but Wade held him. He didn't know what was coming out of the cave, but he would want Byrd's help to deal with it.

Although Wade didn't think it was possible, whatever was emerging from the cave actually budged the stone slab that had leaned there as long as anyone knew, maybe for thousands of years. Not a lot, but enough to be visible, shifting it just enough to change its angle of lean by a degree or two. What had been in that cave with them? Wade wondered. A bear? A big cat? What had that kind of strength?

The growl came again, at the same time that his dad crawled out from under the leaning rock. The man pawed at the ground, his fingers cutting deep furrows in the hard-packed earth there. When he shook his head, foam and spittle flew in every direction. He stared at them with one eye—the other had been brutalized, liquefied somehow, a hellish soup of blood and eye goop and sweat mixing on what remained of his cheek—and although Wade could tell it was his father, he looked more like a wild thing, a monster, than anything human. The clothing that had been perfectly fine an hour ago had turned into rags and ribbons, barely concealing his skin.

And he was strong. He had not only moved the big leaning rock, but his fists closed around smaller stones and pulverized them. He crept toward them on all fours, as if he had forgotten how to walk upright.

Finally, for the first time, he spoke words that Wade could understand. "Wade," he said. "Help . . ."

He might have said more, but his lower jaw fell away from his face, dangled there by a few strings of flesh, and then he swatted it angrily with his left hand and it tore off altogether, flying into the rocks. Blood drained from his head, pattering to the dirt and making a trail as he kept crawling toward them.

Next to give way was his right arm, which had begun to buckle under his weight when he lifted his left hand. When he shifted onto it again, it collapsed beneath him, snapping off at the shoulder. He gave a grunt and dropped, blood from his face and now his shoulder soaking the dirt. A nauseating odor, as if he'd accidentally wandered into a dysentery ward with backed-up plumbing, flooded over Wade like a wave.

"Dad . . . ," Wade said, horrified in spite of his anger and hatred. "Dad, are you . . . ?"

His father tried to rise again, but his left wrist snapped. He pushed himself up on the stump for a moment, bone shards digging into the soaked earth. He might have been trying to say something, but his ruined face made it impossible. With defeat dulling his remaining eye, he slumped back onto the blood-pooled dirt.

It happened fast after that. His skin bubbled and disappeared, like foam breaking up on the side of a beer glass. Wade wasn't sure what he was looking at beneath it—muscles and fatty tissue and bones, he guessed, like the models he'd seen in biology class, but before he could really grasp that, they dissolved, too.

Molly started to scream, long, keening wails that hurt Wade's ears. Byrd had fallen to his hands and knees, puking on the dirt. Wade's guts were doing backflips, but emotionally he was numb, worn out and wrung out, and watching his father turn from a powerful, evil man to a puddle of softly burbling goo and soaking into the desert floor didn't do much to change that. He had already given up on the man. Now there was no man left to worry about.

Molly had often described memory as resembling a river, sometimes calm on top while beneath the surface it could be roiling and churning madly. You couldn't tell unless you ducked underneath and checked.

Submerged in memory's depths, Wade barely realized that they had walked through the rocks to the river's edge. The Rio Grande ran there as it always had, but its flow was less than in years past. It ran in a stream inside its channel, almost chocolate brown, reeds and grasses hemming it in. Since the old days it had been set off, on this side of the border, by a tall wire fence with razored coils on top.

What struck Wade was that the river was always there, but not the same water—each drop that passed by was gone forever, replaced immediately by another one.

Wade took a deep breath, inhaling the musty aroma of riverside vegetation, letting it overcome the remembered stink of his father's sudden decomposition. That had never left him, that smell, or any of the rest of it. You could tie concrete blocks to the ankles of something like that and throw it way out in the middle of memory's river, but you couldn't make it stay under. Sooner or later, usually when you least wanted or expected it, it floated back to the surface and horrified you all over again.

"I always thought it would affect me, in some way," Byrd said. He unconsciously touched the scar that bisected his brow like a pale worm. "Spent my whole life waitin' for it. Now I think I know. I think it's what caused my leukemia."

"What the hell are you talking about?" Molly asked.

But Wade thought he knew. "The pool?" His own thoughts had been full of that night since they got here. Why not Byrd's?

"Yeah, the pool. That water, or whatever it was. The way it . . . it just ate your dad up. I didn't get nearly as much on me, and thank God y'all just got a little bit, whatever you got off of me, I guess. I was sure it couldn't do that to him without having an effect on me, too. Now that I know what it is, it's kind of a relief. I mean, I'm fuckin' pissed, too. But at least I'm not waitin' for it anymore."

"Do you really think that, Byrd?" Molly asked. "That after all these years, it just hit you now?"

"We don't know how long it's been simmering inside me," Byrd said. "Maybe years. Decades. It only became noticeable recently, but that doesn't mean it wasn't lurking somewhere. Then it progressed way faster than any of the doctors had ever seen, right? Like something unnatural."

"We probably should have been checked out at the time," Wade suggested.

"We were dumb kids. We were immortal. What did we know? Anyway, that would have meant tellin' someone what had happened."

They had made a solemn vow, there on the spot, never to do that. As far as Wade knew, they had all kept that promise. That night, after Wade's father was nothing more than a puddle seeping into the ground, they threw their bikes into the back of the truck, and after dropping Molly and Byrd at their place, Wade drove it out into the brushy west Texas back country and abandoned it.

When his dad didn't come home, his mother called the sheriff. The truck was found a few days later. His father, of course, never turned up. It was assumed that he had run out on his family (almost everyone in town, as it happened, had figured out about his abusive nature, and most people thought Gloria and Wade Scheiner were far better off without him around).

Wade pretended to be concerned, then sorrowful, but in truth, he had to agree with popular opinion. He thought that he should have felt the ache of genuine sorrow, even grief. The fact that he didn't disturbed him, and he waited a long time for it to set in. One morning he woke up from a sound sleep and realized it never would. His mother remarried six years later, after his father was declared legally dead, and moved to Beaumont. Wade was in Philadelphia at the time, working for a newspaper. Her second husband died a few years ago, and Hurricane Rita demolished her house. She lived alone in a FEMA trailer park now, having turned down all of Wade's insincere invitations to move in with him. He spoke to her twice a year, on her birthday and Christmas, and even that was a hardship for him.

The murders stopped. Angela and Alan Mills never found out how close they had come to becoming victims.

Wade and his friends drifted away from the river, Wade paying more attention this time. It didn't take a lot of concentration to figure out their next destination, agreed upon without a single word being spoken, and soon they stood outside their cave, on almost the same spot where Brent Scheiner had spent his last moments on earth oozing into the dirt.

Byrd angled his head toward the leaning slab of rock—still tipped at the angle to which Wade's father had shifted it with his final burst of superhuman strength. "Anyone want to go in?"

Wade hadn't been inside since that night, more than two decades earlier. He doubted if the others had. For all he knew, the ammo boxes still waited inside, the candy bars in them way beyond stale. "Hell, no," Wade said. "I doubt I could even fit anymore."

"At least you're a boy and can say 'doubt,'" Molly said, patting her behind. "With this ass? No chance."

"I really can't recommend my diet," Byrd said with a grin. "The pounds just melt away, but the side effects blow big-time."

"True, but you're the only one of us who we know could fit through the opening."

"You think I'm goin' in there, pal, you're sadly mistaken. I have zero interest in confronting that particular bit of ancient history any closer up than this."

"Sounds like it's unanimous," Molly said. "Let's get out of here."

No one argued with that.

By the time they returned to the parking area, it was late after-noon, edging toward dusk. The day had been warm, for November, but an autumn chill bit at the tip of Wade's nose and chapped his cheeks. Byrd's Xterra sat where they had left it, and the Kia Sportage hadn't moved either—but now there was a woman, tall and frizzy-haired, standing in front of it with the hood open and a sour look on her face.

Wade struck out ahead of the others, aware as he did that once upon a time, that would have been Byrd's role. "Hey there!" he called. The woman glanced up, relief washing over her face. "You need a hand?"

She gave a shrug. "I'm guessing it's a dead battery," she said. "I got here pretty early, and probably left the lights on all day."

"I bet we can help with that," Wade said. When he drew close enough, he put out his hand. She took it, her grip firm and steady. "I'm Wade Scheiner," he said. Indicating the others, he added, "That's Molly McCall, and her brother Byrd."

"Ginny Tupper," the woman said. Her face was long, partially obscured by big glasses, red curls, and smudges of dirt, but open and friendly. She wore a blue windbreaker, jeans, and hiking boots. "Thanks for being here. There's never mobile phone service around here, of course. And I haven't seen any other people all day."

"That's what we always liked about it."

"Liked?"

"We're local kids. Up in El Paso now, just checking out the old stomping grounds." He turned back to his friends. "You got jumper cables in that truck, Byrd?"

"Should have."

"I think they're in the back," Molly said. She, not Byrd, had been driving it lately.

"Local kids?" Ginny repeated. "Cool. I'm an anthropologist. My dad used to be fascinated by this site, and now I guess it runs in the family. You ever hear of him? Hollis Tupper?"

Wade dunked a net into the memory river but came up empty. "Doesn't sound familiar."

"It was a long time ago."

Molly joined them at the Kia, cables looped like red and black snakes over her hands. Wade took them from her. "I'll hook them up, if you can bring the truck closer."

"Byrd hates it when people call his baby a truck," she whispered. "It's a car, to him. Or an SUV. Or maybe a girlfriend."

"I'll try to keep that in mind." He went to Ginny's hood, removed the cover from her battery's positive terminal, and started getting the clips in place.

"Thank you for this," Ginny said. "Really, I thought I was pretty far up the creek. If there hadn't been that one truck—car, I mean—in the lot, I'd already be making the long trek back to Palo Duro."

"That's where you're staying?"

"That's right."

"The beautiful downtown Palo Duro Motel? Freeway noise no extra charge?"

"Sounds like you know the place."

"It's kind of a landmark."

Molly drove up in the Xterra. Byrd had already taken his seat in back, looking worn out. Molly killed the engine and popped the trunk, and Wade opened it up and hooked the cables to her battery.

"Hop in," he told Ginny. "And when she starts up Byrd's girlfriend, you start yours."

"Got it." Ginny climbed in behind the wheel, leaving her door open.

Wade gave Molly a sign and she cranked the Xterra's engine again. As soon as it started up, Ginny started hers. The Kia's motor roared, and she kept one foot on the gas.

"Okay, Wade said. "Drive it around for twenty minutes or so before you shut it off again." He pulled a business card out of his pocket and wrote his cell phone number on the back. "We'll follow you as far as the highway, but we have to get Byrd back to El Paso. If it does die, though, and you have service, call me and we'll come back."

Ginny took the card, glanced at it. "Thanks, Wade. Oh, wait, CNN?"

Wade hated this part of meeting anyone. "Yeah. You've seen me on TV, maybe?"

"Hardly ever watch it," she said. "But I thought your name sounded familiar. You were kidnapped, in Iraq? It was in the *New York Times*."

"I was, but I'm all better now."

"Glad to hear it," she said. "It's a pleasure to meet you."

"You, too, Ginny. Good luck."

She gave a wave and backed out of her parking space, made a semicircle, and headed down the road that would link to River Road in about a mile.

Wade climbed up into the Xterra's passenger seat. "She's never seen me on CNN."

"Is that unusual?"

"It seems like it sometimes. Especially when women come on to me—not that she was, I just got a little of that vibe."

"She doesn't look like your type, Wade."

He buckled his seat belt, glanced at Byrd. He had fallen asleep in the back. "I have a type?"

"I don't know. The stripper type."

"I don't date strippers."

"You did that one! I would think that double-H cups or whatever she had would be hard to forget."

"Okay, okay. One stripper, three dates. There are lots of strippers in Atlanta, as it happens. You'd be surprised."

"What was her name? Bambi?"

"Her stage name was Misty. Her real name was Helen. She was only a double-E, and she'd been to community college. Still, we didn't have a lot in common."

"Okay, I take it back. Maybe this one is your type, after all."

"She's smart. She's an anthropologist. Said her dad used to study Smuggler's Canyon, way back when. And I think it's sexy that she's never seen me on TV."

"I see you haven't lost those reporter's instincts. Always investigating."

"Some habits are hard to break," he said. He took another look in the back. "Byrd's out cold."

"I hope this wasn't a bad idea," Molly said. "I know he wanted to do this, but it really took a lot out of him."

Wade nodded. "He may not have a lot of field trips left, though. It was a strange day, but I'm glad we did it."

"Yeah, I think I am, too." Molly steered the vehicle onto River Road. The quickest way to the interstate was back through Palo Duro, right past the Palo Duro Motel. It was as if they had traveled backward through time, and had to reverse their route to reach the present again. "But you're right, Wade. It's been a strange day."

33

"Mr. Truly."

Truly regarded his boss for a moment. "Mr. Loesser?"

"You're sitting in my office, Mr. Truly. Do you know what that means?"

"It's a sign of the apocalypse?"

"No, not that."

"Good, Ron, because I don't think I can take any more omens and portents this week."

Loesser's office was twice the size of Truly's, with a decent view of the Langley campus through a large window behind his desk. A grinning George W. Bush looked down from the wall beside the window; other presidents, reaching back to Reagan, were lined up on another wall, with certificates of various sorts. "Well, that's part of the problem. Portents and omens and all that crap you deal with on a regular basis, James. It's driving you a little nuts, maybe, and it's raising eyebrows around here that I'd prefer not to see raised."

"Can you be more specific, Ron? It's like you're speaking a foreign language. What's the issue here?"

"The problem, and this is why you're sitting in my office, is that Moon Flash is a giant crock of steaming shit, and you, my friend, have it all over your suit."

Truly had seen Loesser in some foul moods, but rarely in one this bad. "You're going to have to narrow it down more than that."

"Well, Jimmy, you're going to have to help me there. All I really know is that people upstairs from me have been kicking your name around, and it's filtering down to me now. And you know how I feel about that."

"You're so bad at disguising your feelings, it's a wonder you ever became a spy."

"You'll notice I sit behind a desk. I was a field operative for about eleven days, and the fact that I didn't get killed was pure dumb luck." He picked up a pencil from his desk, tapped the eraser end on the sleek, polished wood. "Anyway, you've been stirring up some sort of shit hurricane, and it's got people agitated. I want to know what it is, and I want to know when you'll stop. By which I mean what time *today* you'll stop."

Truly tried to ignore the soft *tap tap tap* of the pencil. "It has to do with Lawrence Ingersoll, I think. And Millicent Wong."

"The Chinese woman who was murdered while under your protection in Colorado."

"That's right. And Ingersoll was the American psychic who was killed, also in Colorado."

"Sounds like a job for the Colorado police."

"Right. Only they don't know anything about the victims. Not really, not like we do. Plus, I have to believe that Millicent was killed because she was helping me. Which makes her death my problem."

"You're not a cop, James. But go on . . . I still haven't heard anything that should rattle the cages we're talking about."

Truly considered briefly, wondering just how much he should reveal. Finally he decided there was no percentage in holding back anymore. "I obtained some security video from the night Millicent was killed. I know who I think did it, and he was caught on camera entering the hotel. I also saw him sitting with Millicent, and I snagged the glass he was drinking out of, and got a partial print off it."

"You've been reading detective novels?"

Truly ignored the jibe. "With the print and the video footage, I was able to identify the man. He's Captain Vance Brewer, U.S. Army, stationed at the White Sands Missile Range."

"White Sands."

"That's right."

"That's in New Mexico."

Truly didn't understand the drift of the conversation. "Yes."

"Which—correct me if I'm wrong, geography was never my strong suit—shares a border with Colorado."

"It does indeed."

"So a military officer visited a neighboring state to attend a dance, and you think this is a problem?"

"Only if he killed Millicent while he was there."

"And what makes you think he did? Someone saw him?"

"He spent a lot of time with her there. Someone saw them go out onto a balcony together. When I followed, she was dead and he was gone."

Loesser stopped tapping and began turning the pencil around and around in his hands, like rolling a tiny log. "Sounds iffy," he said. "I hope you have more than that."

"Here's the weird thing," Truly said. "I figured out easily enough who Brewer is, but I can't get any farther. His records are practically blank. They show his last posting as White Sands, but I can't actually determine whether or not he's still there. I couldn't find any commendations or promotions, not even his date of enlistment. I really can't tell from the records whether he's alive or dead."

"I'd guess alive, if you saw him in Colorado."

"Me too. But there's a difference between being alive and being officially alive as far as the government is concerned. I just don't get why an army captain's history is so hard for an Agency operative to access. Every avenue I try to take to find out more, I run into a roadblock."

"There's army, and then there's Army," Loesser said. "They have their spooks, too, right? Maybe he's one of them."

"Maybe. You'd never know it from the file."

"Hardly surprising."

"So what, Ron? You think me digging around trying to find out more about this guy has got people agitated here?"

"I think it must be. I don't see any other reason. Your Moon Flash operation isn't making waves anywhere else, is it?"

"I don't think so. Ever since Ingersoll's death, this has been consuming all my energies."

Loesser finally put the pencil down. He'd been hanging on to it like some kind of life preserver. "Well, that's going to come to an end."

Dizziness swept Truly, like he'd been picked up and suspended upside down over Loesser's desk. "Meaning . . . ?"

Loesser's tone changed. He leaned forward, a frown creasing his forehead. "They're shutting it down."

"Shutting down . . . ?"

"Your whole operation. Moon Flash. It's history, James. Wave bye-bye."

"You're kidding." The suspended feeling vanished, replaced by the sensation of falling from the ceiling into a subbasement.

"I'm not kidding. Effective immediately. You know as well as I that it's all a bunch of horseshit, James. All that psychic crap. It's a huge waste of taxpayer dollars, all for a ridiculous holdover from the Cold War. Oh no, the Russkies have mind readers, we need them, too!"

"It's not quite like that," Truly said. He realized he'd bit the words off, snapping at his boss, and it surprised him. He had shared that basic sentiment the entire time he'd been running the program. Now that it was being taken away seemed like an odd time to develop a sentimental attachment.

"It *is* like that. Those are the roots of it, anyway. And can you honestly say the program has made a quantifiable contribution to the American intelligence effort since, I don't know . . . ever?"

Truly had held the same argument with himself a thousand times, and he always came up with the same answer. "Not really. Not quantifiable in any real way. It's always been more about potential than actual benefit, like the Missile Defense Shield."

"That's a low blow."

"But it's true. If the idea is that we might face possible threats of various sorts and we should have defenses in place to cope with them, then Moon Flash makes as much sense as anything else."

"If you happen to believe in things like ESP."

"Do you happen to believe that Al Qaeda has the capability to launch ICBMs?"

Loesser grinned and placed his palms down on his desk. "Point taken."

He was silent for a few long moments. Truly couldn't stand it anymore. "So that's it, then?"

"You'll be transferred into an analysis post. It'll be better for your career, anyway. Same for your staff. You'll all come out of this fine."

"We will," Truly said. "But what about Lawrence Ingersoll and Millicent Wong? What about the rest of the psychics?"

"They're on their own, like they've always been. What do you want, for us to give them gold watches? We can't admit we were ever in bed with them, James. You can make a few phone calls, let them know what's going on. That's about it."

Truly nodded slowly, but his mind was already racing.

A few phone calls.

That, he would definitely do.

He started with one to his father.

"I'm going to need a favor," he said after the usual formalities had been dispensed with. "Maybe several favors."

"Tell me," Willard Carsten Truly said. His tone was flat, neutral. As a United States senator, he had been asked for a lot of favors. Some he had done, others he'd turned down. Favors were the politician's stock in trade—that and campaign cash— and Truly's father understood how to play the game as well as any politician in recent American history. Truly would never believe that the man couldn't have been president, if he had decided to run. In the end, he had been happy with a long career in the Senate, during which he had wielded plenty of power.

It was that power that Truly counted on, even now, more than a decade out of office.

"The Agency is killing Moon Flash."

"In what way?"

"Defunding it, shutting it down, closing the doors. How many ways are there to kill an intelligence program?"

"More than that," his father said. "You're serious?"

"As a heart attack."

"Well. It's about time, I must say. You've been chasing those ghosts quite long enough."

Truly started to formulate an argument, something about how chasing ghosts wasn't the job, but decided not to bother. They'd had the debate plenty of times, and as when he argued with Ron Loesser, he couldn't put his full weight behind his own position because he agreed too readily with his father's.

"What is it you want from me?" Willard Truly asked. "Will you finally be needing a new job?"

"No, that's not it. The Agency's going to shuffle me to some other post."

"What, then?"

"I'm going to make some waves, I'm afraid. I'm in the middle of something, and I want to finish it before I ride off into whatever sunset they have lined up for me. But it's going to piss people off. Including people who live upstairs from Ron Loesser."

"That's a fairly elevated address, as I recall."

"That's right. They're the ones applying downward pressure, making him close my shop."

"I see." Truly detected a note of enthusiasm in his father's voice. He was intrigued by this, as he always was by the gamesmanship of government.

"So what I'll need is some major ass-covering, when things hit the fan. I don't want the plug pulled in the middle of what I'm about to launch. And I don't want to be killed."

"Son, the Agency doesn't—"

"I'm not one of your constituents, Pop. I'm me. Save it."

"You so rarely call me that anymore. I quite like hearing it."

"So you'll do it? You'll run interference for me?"

"To the best of my abilities, son. Happily. I must tell you, I'm pleased to see you showing this kind of spine. Going to give those hidebound intelligence bureaucrats fits, eh? Count me in."

"I'll try to keep you posted, Pop," Truly said. "But just in case, it wouldn't hurt to keep your ear to the ground so you can listen for trouble when it starts."

"I always do, James. I always do."

Truly hung up, pleased with his father's reaction. All these years later, he had finally done something that made the man proud—and all it took was a promise to disobey a direct order from his immediate supervisor at the CIA.

Maybe I should have done that sooner, he thought. He picked the phone up again, to reserve a flight to El Paso and a rental car. *Still, better now than never.*

34

ᗰᕮᗰ

Molly drove her own car that night, because Wade would immedi-ately recognize the Xterra after their trip to Malo Duro in it. She owned a grayish, decade-old Toyota Camry that even she didn't recognize half the time. She sat outside the Hilton Garden Inn, watching Wade's Focus as she had the other night. This time, she was determined not to lose track of him. She had downed two cups of coffee, and had a third with her. Although the trip that afternoon had exhausted her (not nearly as much as it had Byrd, whom they'd had to pile into a wheel-chair just to get from the car to the hospital door), she meant to stay awake, no matter what. Anyway, the excursion that day had reminded her how effective surveillance of a killer could be.

Wade emerged shortly after eleven. He had changed into black jeans, a dark sweater, and a denim jacket. A black Braves cap was pulled low over his brow. He didn't look around, didn't seem particularly concerned that anyone might see him. He simply walked to his car, got in, cranked it up, and switched on the lights. Molly gave him a few lengths and followed.

He headed straight down Oregon Street. For a few minutes, she wondered if he would go to the freeway and drive back to Palo Duro. He had given that woman his number, after all. And he was a TV star, at least in certain circles. The woman had claimed never to have seen him, but maybe that was just a line to lure him in. Maybe she had called, and he was headed for the Palo Duro Motel for a late night assignation.

But he drove past the on-ramp and into downtown. Here, the traffic was thicker despite the hour. She stayed a few cars back, hoping he didn't lose her at a light. He didn't seem to have a specific destination, but cruised El Paso, Santa Fe, Sixth,

Seventh—the Port of Entry area, where most of the shops would have been at home on either side of the line. Piñatas dangled from window overhangs, as did net bags of soccer balls and bright paper flowers. Garish statues of Elvis Presley and the Blues Brothers stood in front of Dave's Pawn Shop, and Molly could hear "Hound Dog" blasting from the store's speakers overtop her car stereo.

Most of the people out on the streets—and even at this hour, there were quite a few—were Hispanic. Some had obviously just crossed over the border, and were carrying shopping bags with purchases from Mexico; others were emerging from bars or heading inside them.

Wade navigated these streets slowly, deliberately, like someone looking for a particular address. *Or a particular victim,* Molly thought. She scratched the back of her left hand. In Palo Duro, her skin hadn't been dry and itchy, but it had started up almost as soon as she was back in town.

After about twenty minutes, he drove up Santa Fe toward the Convention Center. Traffic was lighter here, the dark sidewalks largely empty. Molly had to stay farther back. When Wade suddenly pulled into a parking spot, she was already committed to the block—on which she saw no other available spaces—and she had to drive past, turning her head away and down as she did.

Another block up, she found a spot near the Convention Center—not a legal parking place, but she didn't plan to leave the car. She could see Wade's Focus, illuminated by a lonely streetlight, in her rearview. He was still sitting in it, hands tight on the wheel.

It wasn't until she looked past his car that she saw what must have made him stop in the first place. Two people trudged up the sidewalk on the far side of the street, burdened with shopping bags. One of them was probably in his forties, Hispanic, short and squat. The second was younger, mid-twenties maybe. She could have been the first one's daughter. And she was soon to be a mother, her swollen belly bulging out between the flaps of her winter jacket.

Mesmerized, Molly watched them close in on Wade. They chatted wearily as they climbed the gentle slope. The young woman laughed at something the man said, teeth catching stray

light and flashing white in the darkness. Molly wanted to warn
them, to leap from her car and shout something that would send
them running in the other direction.

But she didn't.

When they were even with his car, Wade threw his door open
and jumped out. The pair gave little screeches of surprise—
startled, not truly frightened yet. When he dashed across the
street toward them, the real terror began.

The older one let out a loud cry for help. The pregnant one
dropped her bags, holding on to her purse and swinging it at
Wade by its shoulder strap as he charged them. It bounced off
his shoulder without effect. He went for the older one first,
bulling past the shopping bags. Wade drove the butt of his palm
into the man's chin. The blow snapped the man's head back
and he went down.

The pregnant woman faced Wade, legs apart for balance,
purse strap clutched in her right fist. She looked strong and determined, a lioness defending her unborn cub. Molly thought
Wade had a fight on his hands.

He didn't waste any time getting into it. He ducked down
and scooped up some of the stuff that had burst from a dropped
bag, hurling it toward her face. When she threw up an arm to
block it, he attacked.

He drove into her midsection, shoulder-first, barreling her
to the ground. There he straddled her, ignoring her blows, and
wrapped his hands around her throat. As he choked her, he
forced her head up and down, slamming it against the pavement. Molly watched, thinking it would be over in seconds, but
the woman kept struggling and Wade strangled her and bashed
her over and over and over. Finally, the woman's arms and legs
spasmed and relaxed. Wade rolled off of her.

Molly watched the attack with her fist clenched excitedly. It
was as if the night's darkness had erased everything else, with
Wade and his victims spotlit just for her voyeuristic pleasure, a
ballet of violence and terror that could only have one conclusion.

The man was up on his hands and knees now, pawing inside
his pocket. He brought out a cell phone just as Wade reached
him. Wade slapped it from his hands, grabbed his head, pressed
his knee against the man's spine and yanked it backward,

toward him. Molly couldn't hear the snap from where she sat, transfixed, but she could imagine it.

Wade didn't stand around enjoying his kills, but hurried back to his car, slammed the door, and drove away. Molly ducked when he passed her, just in case. After he was gone, she found she couldn't follow. Her legs vibrated from excitement; her back and sides were drenched with sweat. She wiped damp hair from her brow.

She sat like that, gripped by a bizarre, undeniable thrill, until she heard the first siren. As if that had released her, she started the Camry and drove off, leaving the fresh corpses alone in the night.

Wade woke up—that was the best way he could phrase it—while driving east on Interstate 10, in the right-hand lane, near the Zaragosa exit. He had no idea how long he had been driving, didn't remember even leaving his hotel room, but the rental's clock said it was 12:32. Fortunately traffic was light, and whatever had possessed him to go out sleep-driving, if there was such a thing, at least seemed to be in control of the car. It wasn't until he jolted into consciousness that he swerved out of his lane. A speeding pickup blasted its horn and Wade snapped the car back into place.

The sound of his tires on the roadway spoke to him in words he could almost understand.

Hands trembling, he pulled off the highway, onto the frontage road, and into the first parking lot he came to. There he killed the engine and sat, his body quaking as adrenaline drained from him. He felt weak, nauseous. *What the hell was that about?* he wondered, resting his forehead on his knuckles.

A bolt of unexpected pain lanced through him. He yanked his head back, reached up, flipped on the dome light.

His knuckles were raw, scraped and bruised.

He didn't remember damaging his hands in Palo Duro. Maybe if they had tried to go in the cave, he would have, but they didn't, and

pregnant

and if anything else had happened to them, he couldn't bring it to

kethili
bring it to mind.

Images flashed through his head, unfamiliar and yet somehow not. A pregnant woman, on her back, struggling for breath. A man, carrying bundles, screaming in horror.

In the light from overhead, he examined his hands more closely. Brown-red stains on the sides looked like blood, but not his. Was he

kethili-anh ra nia tapotec istryllium kethili

was he losing it, somehow? Hallucinating, or worse?

He started the car again, turned the radio on, punched the tuning buttons looking for local news. A few minutes later, he found a station and listened, his breathing shallow and strained.

"Two people were reportedly killed tonight near the Convention Center, in what a police spokesman is describing as an especially brutal double homicide. Detectives are—"

Wade snapped the radio off.

This couldn't be happening.

He had spent the day reliving memories of his father. His father, the murderer, whose killing spree had been stopped only by Byrd and that strange, glowing liquid in the cave.

His father, the madman.

Could madness be hereditary? That kind, brutal, homicidal?

Brent Scheiner had been a bastard, an abuser, a man who preyed on the weak, but until after his fight with Byrd, until he suddenly snapped, he had never been a killer.

Hallucinatory nightmare scraps swam in Wade's vision, splashes from memory's current. *Two people on a darkened sidewalk. Blood pooling under the pregnant one's head. The* crack! *of the other's spine, his body suddenly limp under Wade's knee, the stench when he voided himself.* Kethili-anh ka nakastata ne gasta. *A lipstick tube, price tag still affixed to its lid, rolling off the curb and into the street.*

He touched his shoulder, sore, maybe bruised—

Where she hit me with her purse.

Oh, fuck me, he thought, tears springing with sudden urgency to his eyes, a moaning sob escaping his lips, *where she hit me with her purse.*

35

Molly sat with a cup of coffee—cream, no sugar—and a single slice of buttered toast. The TV was on. Matt and Meredith were sparring behind their *Today* desk when her phone rang. Early morning calls were rare, and she worried that it was the hospital, that yesterday's jaunt had been too much for Byrd. With a trembling, reluctant hand, she lifted the phone. "Hello?"

"Molly, it's Wade. I've got to talk to you. Can you meet me for breakfast?"

She swallowed the bit of toast in her mouth, brushed crumbs off her lower lip. He sounded awful, like he hadn't slept and was coming down with something. "Sure. Is everything okay?"

"I'll tell you when I see you."

"Where?"

"Pick a place. Not too far away. I want to do this now."

She named a coffee shop usually frequented by university students, not far from the hospital. It might be crowded, but its chairs were gathered into cozy groupings between large pillars, offering a degree of privacy. "It's just got pastries and such," she said. "If that's okay."

"It's fine. I'll be there in ten minutes."

"I'll need twenty," she said. "But I'll be there as soon as I can."

She hung up, tossed the rest of her toast into the trash, poured her coffee down the sink. Before she left, she called Franklin Carrier and told him she would be late, and why. "Go get him, girl," he said.

"That's the plan."

Given what she had seen last night (the almost erotic charge she had experienced remembered vividly, making her tingle all over), she would have been surprised if Wade had slept at all.

Unless he was used to nights like that.

He was ensconced in a chair when she reached the coffee shop. He had managed to find the most remote table in the place, tucked back in a corner with a pillar and a rack of coffee mugs and pots blocking access to it from three sides. The table was small and round, its surface a tiled mosaic. Wade had a huge mug steaming on top of it, no food. Molly waved and ordered a coffee and a croissant at the counter. When she had them, she carried them to the table, set them down, and leaned over to kiss Wade's cheek. He didn't return the gesture. His eyes were bloodshot, his brow furrowed.

"You sounded bad on the phone, Wade," she said, settling into a plush wing chair. "What's up?"

"I . . . had a rough night," he said. He scratched the outside of his thigh through his jeans.

"I'm sorry to hear that."

"Me too. I mean, sorry it happened."

"You want to talk about it?"

"No."

She sipped her coffee, watching him over the rim of her cup. "You wanted to see me, though."

"Yeah." His gaze darted around the place, landing on the coffee shop's framed art (amateurish, vaguely Warholian watercolor portraits of writers, musicians, and artists), the other mismatched tables and chairs, the employees bustling about, but never meeting hers. She was getting used to the beard, but he hadn't even combed his hair. Dark bags weighted his eyes and his cheeks looked gaunt, as if he'd lost weight overnight.

She knew he hadn't. He had lost some in captivity, though. His natural good looks and cheerful manner had disguised it, hidden the emotional toll it must have taken on him. Today he displayed it all.

"So what's up?" Knowing his secret gave her a private pleasure, a kind of power over him.

"I . . ." He stopped, picked up the giant mug, took a loud drink. "I haven't told you what happened over there."

"In Iraq?"

"Right. Or Byrd, either. I told the story a hundred times to the authorities and to people at CNN, but that was just a version of it, you know? *Like* the truth, but not the whole truth."

"And now you want to tell it?" Franklin had called this one. Next time she would trust his instincts.

"I think something happened to me over there, Molly. Something . . . I don't know, weird. Something that's not right."

"What do you mean?" Molly dabbed at her lips with a napkin, hiding the grin she felt coming on.

"I'm not really sure. I just thought maybe if I told you about it, it would help me understand it myself."

"I'm here, Wade. I called work, so they know I'll be late. As long as you need."

He nodded, looking grateful. "Well, you know the basics already, right?"

"I know what was in the news. You were kidnapped, you got away."

"I was supposed to have a meeting with an insurgent leader. It took me days to set it up. Weeks. Working channels, talking to people who knew people who could get to him. Finally, one day, I got the call. Get to this address, right now. Sami, the Iraqi who worked as my driver and translator, was sitting in the lobby of the Palestine, my hotel, playing cards with some of the other men who did the same for other journalists. I grabbed him and we hustled out to his Mercedes, a gray, paint-peeling piece of crap that must have been thirty years old. We drove to the address where the meet was supposed to happen, through a few checkpoints, into a neighborhood where most of the houses were relatively intact. But when we parked and knocked on the door, someone answered without opening it more than an inch or two and shouted at us. Sami shouted back, then shrugged and started back to the car.

" 'What's going on?' I asked him. 'Meeting's off,' he says. 'Canceled. They will call when it can happen again.'

"Well, I was pissed. I yelled at Sami, yelled at the house, even though the guy had shut the door and there were no signs of life inside. Sami was used to things not working out— he was Iraqi, after all, so that was a way of life for him. He gave me a few shrugs and started up the Mercedes to drive me back to the hotel. Before he got out of the parking space, two black trucks drove up and blocked us in. Then these masked guys jumped out of the truck beds with guns. I ducked down in the back, but they weren't shooting at me. They killed Sami."

"You must have been terrified."

"I can't even tell you. It was the most horrible—well, okay, not the most horrible moment of my life, because we both know when that was. But it was close."

"I'm so sorry, Wade."

He shrugged. "They dragged me out of the Mercedes and threw me into one of their trucks. Tied me up, wrapped duct tape over my eyes and mouth. We drove around for a long time. I couldn't tell where we were. I know we went through some checkpoints, but either they paid off the soldiers or they had allies there, because we were never stopped, even though anyone could see there was a gift-wrapped American journalist in the back.

"Finally, we stopped and they hauled me out of the truck. We went inside somewhere, and down some stairs. A lot of stairs. I kept thinking they had to end. A few times I stumbled, but they always caught me. I kept telling them I was an American, a journalist, but that didn't bother them in the least. They knew who I was. They had set the trap for me, after all.

"I'm told I was missing for seventeen days. I tried to keep track, but I couldn't see the sun. When they took off the duct tape I was in some kind of cell, a cave with an iron door. People brought me meals, but they wouldn't answer questions. Sometimes they demanded that I renounce Christianity and accept Allah. Sometimes they asked me questions about troop movements. They claimed I was a spy for George Bush."

"I guess they didn't know you very well," Molly interrupted.

"Apparently not. After what seemed like a few days, they started occasionally torturing me."

"Oh my God, Wade."

"Nothing real terrible. Beating me with sticks. Taking my clothes and throwing cold water over me, keeping me cold and wet for hours on end. When they did these things, they would rant about Abu Ghraib, like I was personally responsible for what went on there. Of course, I didn't know anything that would help them, and the questions they asked hardly made sense anyway. When they told me it would stop if I made a propaganda video for them, I went ahead and made it. I tried to make it obvious that the things I was saying were scripted, all lies—crossing my fingers in front of the camera, winking, sometimes saying things like 'Is that good? Is that how you want me to say it?'"

"We all watched that online," Molly told him. "It was awful, seeing you in that condition, with those armed men standing behind you. But you're right, it was obvious that you didn't mean a word of it. Byrd cracked up, said it was the worst propaganda tape ever made, and you'd better not try to join the Screen Actors Guild."

Wade smiled for the first time that morning. He had been sitting in his chair, arms held close to his sides, tense, but now he relaxed a little. He took a drink from the big mug, set it back down. "Glad to hear that," he said. "I tried to be terrible. Anyway, I'm not going to bore you with all the details. It was one thing after another. I lost track of time and I was pretty sure I was going to die. Then one day when I expected someone to bring food, it didn't show up. I waited, and still, no food. Finally I shook the door and called for some dinner, and the door swung open in my hands. Who knows how long it had been unlocked? I went out, expecting to be caught or shot at any second, but the place was empty. Up and up and up, out of the cavern and into a bombed-out mosque full of garbage, and finally out into the streets. Even they were empty. It wasn't right, wasn't natural, that there should be no one anywhere.

"The first living thing I saw was a pig, trotting down the street. Eventually a U.S. patrol came around. I waved them down, they picked me up, and drove me into the Green Zone. There I was fed and debriefed at length by intelligence types. I think you know the rest—physicals, more debriefing, the trip to El Paso."

He stopped, drank deep, as if the story had parched his throat. Molly hadn't been taking notes, but she had a good memory and tried to store away every detail. She could pump him for more later, when she started writing. "It sounds horrible, Wade. But what is it you think happened there that's affecting you now? Besides the bad memories, I mean?"

"I don't really know. Maybe in that dank cave, wet and cold and naked, I caught some kind of . . . some freaky virus." His gaze bored into her, intense enough to be frightening. "Do you think that's possible?"

"There's a hospital right up the street."

"I can't go there. Not yet. I . . . I feel like I'm losing my mind, Molly. Losing my grip."

"I guess there are viruses that can affect you that way, right? Mentally."

"Probably. I think so. But . . . I know we don't ever talk about it, but we've both seen magic at work, right?"

She gave him a questioning look. "I mean, come on, if there were a rational, scientific explanation for . . . for what happened to my dad," he continued, "we'd know it. There isn't. That wasn't a naturally occurring pool full of super-potent acid or anything. Which only leaves irrational, unnatural—or supernatural—explanations. Magic. Maybe there was some kind of magic working in that cave in Iraq, too, and not necessarily the good kind. There were unexplained lights, strange dreams. Given what's happening to me now, maybe it was an evil magic, a dark magic, that I never should have been exposed to. And the way I got out, the way everyone vanished—that wasn't natural either."

"What about what's happening to you now? What's that?" she asked.

His jaw worked, but then he clamped his mouth shut. He was still for a moment, as if listening to something. Molly could only hear the gentle rush of other people's conversations, the ticking of the ventilation system as it blew warm air into the shop, the hissing of the steam machine. "I don't want to talk about it," he said finally. "Not yet, anyway."

"You can trust me, Wade. We've always trusted each other, right?"

"I know, Molly. That's why we're here. That's why I called you."

"Then—"

He cut her off. "I'm sorry, I just can't. I can't, Molly. When I can tell you, I will."

"You'd better, mister." She knew, of course. She could have pressed him harder, thought about mentioning the Convention Center, the pregnant woman, or the three migrants in the park. Even Gretchen Fuchs. A thrill coursed through her.

"Kethili-cha," she said quietly, not fully understanding why.

Wade stared at her like she had unexpectedly removed the top of her head and poured her coffee inside. *"Kethili-anh."*

Electricity flowed between them. The fine hairs on her arms and neck stood on end. Every pore in her body tingled with anticipation, with power. A point had been reached, she understood, a turning point from which there would be no going back.

Dump your coffee on the floor.

As she thought the command, she visualized him obeying. Leaning forward in the deep chair to pick up the mug, holding it out past the edge of the table, tipping it slowly, watching the dark liquid splash on the floor.

Dump your coffee on the floor, Wade.

His lips curled in a faint, uncertain smile. He caught her eye and gave the slightest shrug, raising his right eyebrow just a fraction of an inch. The body language said, *I don't know why I'm doing this.*

Then he leaned forward, took his mug in his right hand, held it out, poured the coffee. It hit the ground, splashed, puddled.

When he put the mug back, Molly rose and flagged down one of the coffee shop's employees. "Excuse me," she said. "My friend has spilled some of his coffee."

"Be right there," the young man said. "Thanks."

"God," Wade said, blushing, as she sat down again. "What a klutz, huh? Sorry. I didn't get you, did I?"

"Don't worry about it, Wade," she said. She kept her voice calm, but inside her emotions raced.

She had made him do that. Ordered him to, with her mind. And he had done it.

She *controlled* him.

It felt right, somehow. Natural. The way it should be, should always have been.

She had been waiting for this, she realized. Waiting for a very, very, very long time.

Kethili-cha . . .

36

The White Sands Missile Range was less than thirty minutes from
Las Cruces, New Mexico, out Highway 70 on the other side of
San Agustin Pass. The tiny town of Organ straddled the highway in between, and much use was made by soldiers from the
base of the Organ Mountain Café, but for serious drinking,
they tended to make the trek into Las Cruces.

One thing a CIA operative had to know for any posting was
how to find out where the right people drank and socialized, in
any country, in any language. In the States, it only took Truly a
few minutes and a couple of phone calls to identify some popular spots. He staked out the Conquistador Lounge, a place that
had probably been seedy in the early sixties—when it was
built, and the big, overdone monument sign placed on a pole
out front—and had only gone downhill since. The decor was
strictly illuminated signs provided by beer distributors, a pool
table, and scarred wood-grain tables between seats that had
been torn and repaired with duct tape. No one came for the
scenery, but soldiers liked the bar's extended happy hour, cheap
pitcher prices, and the easy availability of the working girls
who frequented the place.

Truly got there about eight and sat at a corner table, nursing
a light beer and watching the crowd. An hour later, he had
found his mark in Specialist Owen LaTour. The slender man
came in alone, sat at the bar, and slammed down two beers
within the first ten minutes, before switching to tequila. He
didn't talk to anyone, although he nodded to a couple of other
uniformed soldiers. He wore civilian clothes, but the haircut
and posture were unmistakably military. Truly gave him a half
hour to get oiled up, then moved in. The place had become

more crowded, but the stool next to the young soldier was empty, as if he was sending out a "keep away" vibe.

Truly bumped into the soldier as he approached the stool. "Excuse me," he said, slurring his words just slightly. "Seat taken?"

The soldier shook his head. Truly sat down heavily. "Is now," he said. "What are you drinking?"

The soldier shot him a wary glance, like he didn't really want company and suspected Truly was out to pick him up. "Tequila," he said, touching the rim of an empty glass.

"Barman!" Truly called out. "Get my friend another tequila. And one for me."

Another glance, and the soldier stiffened slightly. But a free drink was, after all, a free drink, so he offered a shy grin. "Thanks."

"No problem. Nothing's too good for a man in uniform, right? Thank you for your service."

The soldier shrugged, cheeks reddening. "You do what you can."

"Exactly," Truly said. "You do what you can. Perfect attitude. You, sir, are a gentleman."

The soldier blushed more. "Look," Truly said, leaning toward him and lowering his voice. "I'm not trying to hit on you or anything like that, so don't worry about that. I'm just a patriot, a man who serves in his own way, and appreciates those who wear the uniform."

"Thanks," the soldier said again.

"James Truly." He stuck out his hand. Reflexively, the soldier shook it.

"I'm Owen LaTour."

"A pleasure," Truly said. "Listen, you want to get a table? It's getting a little crowded here at the bar."

Owen agreed, and they went to Truly's corner table, which was still unoccupied. After a couple more drinks—for the soldier, Truly barely sipped his—he showed Owen his CIA credentials. The young soldier whistled, still green enough to be impressed by the presence of an intelligence agent.

Truly told war stories of the spy game, mostly ones he'd heard from other people, becoming freer with information as the evening wore on. Owen followed suit, going from close-mouthed about goings on at White Sands to dishing on the base's officers and activities.

Around ten, Truly acted like he'd had a sudden brainstorm. "Your girl broke your heart, right?" he asked, picking up on a thread Owen had dropped earlier in their conversation. Owen had explained his determined drinking as an attempt to wash away the memory of her betrayal.

"You better believe it."

"I know the feeling, man," Truly said. "Better than you can imagine. It hurts like hell."

"That it does."

"You know what would make it feel better?"

"What's that?"

"Getting laid."

Owen looked at the tabletop. "I don't know, Jim. These women in here—"

"Who's talking about these women?" Truly interrupted. In truth, the women in the bar were perfectly acceptable to most men, himself included. But he was trying to make an impression. "We're only an hour from Juárez, Owen. World-class tail."

"Juárez? Are you sure about that? I don't have a lot of scratch on me. . . ."

"My treat, soldier. You know what I say, nothing's too good for a man in uniform. My car's just outside, if you're ready to leave here and have some real fun."

The soldier remained unconvinced. "Maybe I should be getting back to base. . . ."

"Owen," Truly said, grabbing the man's arm. "It's just a little harmless fun. Just take a look at the ladies. If there's nothing you like, then I'll drive you back, no harm done. But if someone tickles your fancy, I'm buying."

Owen tried to refuse again, but by that point he'd had too much to drink to make a strong case. Truly left some cash on the table, showing Owen a big roll as he did, and steered the young, drunken soldier out to the parking lot, where his rented Crown Vic waited.

Owen dozed off on the drive from Las Cruces to El Paso. He didn't miss much. Even in the dark, Truly knew when they passed the massive stockyards at Mesquite, by the sudden rich stench of what must have been millions of pounds of manure. The road was smooth and dark; then they crossed into Texas, and the lights of El Paso and Ciudad Juárez grayed the night sky.

Not wanting to drive across the border, especially since he had alcohol on his breath—though precious little of it in his blood—Truly parked on the American side of the Santa Fe Street bridge. Owen's nap had sobered him up slightly, and the adventure ahead worked to subdue his mood even more. He went back to his taciturn ways, and his pace was brisk.

Truly paid thirty-five cents for each of them, and they began the long walk up the high, arching bridge to Mexico. Even at this hour, with a cold wind whipping across it, the bridge was crowded with cars and pedestrians. Below, lights from the U.S. side washed over the concrete riverbanks, illuminating anti-American graffiti. Young men stood below the bridge with paper funnels and drink cups, calling for the crossers to throw down coins for them to catch. Closer to the Mexican side of the bridge, vendors worked the lined-up cars, washing windshields with filthy rags, selling DVDs, cheap necklaces, yellow bobblehead chicks, and other tawdry goods.

Owen started to laugh. "Chickens?" he said when he saw a man carrying an open box of the bobble-heads. "Why would anyone want to buy a toy chicken from these people?"

Truly couldn't come up with an answer to that, and Owen chuckled nervously the rest of the way across the bridge.

Juárez always seemed to Truly to vibrate at a different frequency than anywhere else, especially at night. Darkness drew a curtain over the extreme poverty of the city, where thousands, if not tens of thousands, worked at American-owned *maquiladoras* for five dollars a day, in a place where the cost of living was 80 to 90 percent as high as on the other side of the river. At night the grunge and smog and tears and blood were hidden. In the colored lights, even the whores working the clubs and corners on Ugarte and Mariscal looked fresh and lively. Neon and incandescent lights glowed bright, music wafting from nightclubs and car windows and apartments had its own special beat, even the kids carrying baskets of churros for sale on Avenida Benito Juárez and the women clustered outside the offices of discount doctors were more colorful than in other border towns. Truly half expected to see zoot-suited *pachucos* and movie stars mingling on the sidewalks or sitting, cradling heads in their hands, along crumbling curbs with drunken *gringos* and unemployed migrants from Mexico's interior. He had never been able to determine why it was, but every trip here seemed like a journey to a strange, half-wonderful planet.

A cabdriver with four teeth, one of them covered in gold, took them to a club called the Pink Lady, on Altamirano, in a taxi that reeked of tobacco and dead animal. The driver told them that his dog had died three days before, but he hadn't figured out where to bury her yet so she was still in the trunk, wrapped in a towel. He didn't want to bury her in the deserts on the outskirts of town, he said, because that's where foreign murderers had dumped all the bodies of girls and women they had killed, at the height of Juárez's long string of murders, and it seemed disrespectful. He loved his dog and wanted her to have better company in death than a bunch of mutilated murder victims.

The Pink Lady was jammed with tourists and strippers, in what seemed like equal numbers. After a few false starts, Owen chose one he liked, a woman called Lourdes. She was on the heavy side, with smoky eyes and thick, lustrous hair and about thirty extra pounds on her frame. Her smile appeared genuine and she brushed Owen's neck with gentle hands, and he looked like he had fallen deeply in love. Truly paid for a handful of dances, then accepted her offer to take Owen to a private room and show him a good time. Truly handed her some cash, promising more when she brought the young soldier back. That occurred forty minutes later, by which time a wide smile creased Owen's slender face.

"You liked that," Truly said, after he paid Lourdes off and refused, for the second time, a turn of his own.

"What's not to like?"

"I told you," Truly said. "World class."

On the way back over the bridge—only thirty cents from this side, paid to a toll machine instead of a human being—the young soldier whistled softly, hands in his pockets. Halfway over, the international boundary line was marked, and there was a recessed area in the wire-enclosed bridge. Truly pulled Owen over. "Here's the actual border," he said. "Right below our feet, in the middle of the river. You can stand in two countries at once."

Owen did just that, still grinning happily. "That's pretty cool."

"Listen," Truly said, now that he had the soldier in the mood he wanted. "I just remembered something maybe you can help me with."

"Help you?"

"That's right. And your government."

"I guess so, then. What do you need?"

Truly drew a photo of Vance Brewer from his coat pocket. "Do you know this man? He's a captain, named Brewer."

In the faint light, Owen studied the photo carefully. He looked at Truly, then back at the picture. His allegiances were divided, which was a good sign. If they hadn't been, it would have meant he didn't recognize Brewer, and this whole excursion would have been a loss. Or at least a draw—he'd be able to use Owen to get introduced to other soldiers from the base, who might know Brewer. But it'd be easier if he struck the jackpot from the start.

"Well?" he asked after a while. Wind fluttered the photo, almost snatching it from Truly's hands.

"He looks familiar," Owen said. "I think I've seen him around?"

"Around where? Las Cruces? White Sands?"

"White Sands. The base."

"Know anything else about him?"

"Not really. I guess . . . I guess when I've seen him, it's usually been around Victorio Peak. Way in the back country there."

"What's out there?"

"Just, you know, they've got different buildings all over the range, to test different aspects of the missiles, I guess. I don't know what they do out there. I've had to drive over there a few times, and that's just where I remember seeing this guy, I think. He has one of those faces, you know? That chin, that nose. Kind of guy you don't forget."

Truly put the photo away. "Yeah, you don't forget him. Come on, Owen. We should be getting you back."

* * *

Brewer paced around the little room. The old man was testing his patience. For two days now, all he had drawn was representations of Indian pictographs. Faces, hunters, animals, warriors on horseback, even elaborate battle scenes. But mostly masks, the same ones, over and over. Big eyes, hooked noses, clown mouths. Or crosses for eyes and narrow slits for mouths. One was cross-eyed, with its mouth making a surprised O.

Often, over the years, the old man's drawings had been hard to interpret. Sometimes not so hard, sometimes as plain as if he'd taken a photograph of whatever was on his petrified little mind. But this . . . Brewer wasn't sure what it meant.

He didn't like not being sure. Uncertainty was a weakness he preferred to exploit when he found it in others.

He watched the man scratch out a couple more, just like the rest. Papers fluttered to the floor when they were full, and the pencil flew over the next page in the pad. Finally, Brewer stormed out of the room and slammed the door behind him.

Not that the old man would ever know. . . .

⊐═╫═◧

37

Wade sat in his hotel room and scratched his skin. It itched everywhere. He was sure the itching was made worse by his worry, his constant obsession over what he seemed to be turning into.

Dwelling on it wasn't helpful, but he couldn't stop himself. Every time he closed his eyes, he saw images of the murders—the pair downtown, the boys near the border, the young woman in her own backyard—like half-remembered movies projected on the insides of his eyelids. Guilt sat heavily on him, a crushing weight. Every time someone looked at him, he imagined they were seeing the blackness of his soul, judging him and finding him guilty. He had wanted to confess to Molly, but when he was face-to-face with her he couldn't do it. He was afraid to see Byrd. For the first time since arriving in El Paso, he didn't spend most of the day with his friend.

Instead, he stayed in his room at the Hilton, with daytime TV swallowing his brain cells whole. Every voice on TV declared his murderous deeds to the world, but at least it almost drowned out the nearly constant chatter of electrical currents and vehicle tires and breezes rattling autumn leaves, all of which spoke to him in that language he almost understood.

He wasn't sure which symptom of insanity was worse—the murders he had committed without conscious knowledge, the paranoid certainty that everyone else in the world knew about them, or the continuous sense that he was being whispered to.

To calm his shattered mind, he catalogued rivers. It had always worked before. Selway, Snake, Sun, San Juan, San Pedro, Sandy, Salmon, Shoshone, Salt, St. Mary, Swan . . .

The litany did relax him, and his mind drifted, like a boat eddying out after a run through some especially gnarly Class

232 Jeffrey J. Mariotte

IV whitewater. He couldn't remember how many times he and Byrd had done just that, finding a smooth eddy and letting the boat drift while their hearts slowed from the adrenaline rush of the rapids, maybe cracking open some beers and letting their clothes dry after mist and spray had soaked them to the skin.

The year after the events at Smuggler's Canyon had been a bad one for the three friends. They didn't talk much, to each other especially, but really, to anyone. Wade felt like he had died, too; each morning he woke up half-expecting to be back in his old world, but that world was gone. Months passed in a kind of waking dream, full of bad grades and worse relationships. By year's end, his hopes of an Ivy League education were gone, and he felt lucky to get into UTEP.

It wasn't until halfway through the next summer, after new friends had introduced Byrd to river running and Byrd persuaded Wade to join them on a trip to run the Rio Grande in northern New Mexico, that he felt alive again. They put in near Arroyo Hondo, and going into Powerline, his first rapid, Wade had been anxious. But by the time they ran it—as noisy and spine-shattering as riding on top of a runaway freight train—he was exhilarated, and he looked forward to the upcoming rapids wearing a grin so wide it hurt.

He and Byrd reconnected on that trip, and the river linked Wade to the rest of his life. Together they learned the world of fluid dynamics, of fast water, the vocabulary of haystacks and highsides, Sportyaks and standing waves, grease bombs and river games. Byrd took to wearing Patagonia shorts and Teva sandals and a ball cap from the State Bridge Lodge with an assortment of T-shirts he picked up around the West, most of which looked a decade old after the first run or two. Byrd dropped out of UTEP, which he'd largely been attending just to escape Palo Duro anyway, and took to the river rat life full-time.

Rivers, Wade would always believe, returned them both from the dead. The boatman who rowed them back across the River Styx was legendary river guide Norm Nevills, or maybe it was Ken Sleight or Clair Quist. Wade had met none of them, but they were the gods other boatmen worshipped and could run the Styx in high water or low. Katie Lee sang the anti-dirge that accompanied rebirth. Byrd's resurrection, in turn, saved Molly's life.

There had been a dark hole at Byrd's center after that summer, which showed itself in times when Byrd faced difficulty off the water. They'd all had one, but Byrd's had been the deepest and the coldest, a great melancholy that could only be chased away in a dory or a kayak or a rubber raft. Each of them faced it, he suspected, in those dark morning hours when everything seems the bleakest, and it interfered with every aspect of their lives, their careers, especially their relationships with other people. Of the three of them, only Byrd had even tried marriage, but from the start Wade thought that was a fake attempt, an effort to fool whatever forces ruled Byrd's life into thinking that he had moved on, left the darkness behind. His wife had seen through it, soon enough. The darkness was at his core and couldn't be covered by a phony patch of light.

When Wade's cell phone rang, it startled him so much that he jumped in his chair.

Hands shaking, he snatched it off the dresser, flipped it open. "Hello?"

"Hello, Wade?"

The woman's voice was unfamiliar. A police detective? "Yes," he said tentatively.

"Hi, this is Ginny Tupper. We met at the Smuggler's Canyon site yesterday. You jumped my car."

"Sure," he said, relaxing once she had identified herself. "How's it running now?"

"It's fine," she said. "I really appreciate the rescue."

"Not a problem."

"Listen, this is going to sound nuts, but I was wondering if I could meet you someplace, to talk. It's about something you said, about growing up in Palo Duro. It's kind of important, maybe. I'm here in El Paso."

"Sure, I guess." He'd already met with one woman today, Molly, and the whole experience, being out in public, feeling the gazes of strangers boring through his soul, had been almost too much to bear. "I don't want you to think I'm being overly forward, but would you mind coming to my hotel room? So we can talk in private?"

"That would be great. Private, I mean. Don't worry, I won't assume that you'll be overtaken by lust. Or that I will."

Wade told her where the hotel was, and his room number, and then sat down to continue trying to stave off the madness he was sure waited for him to drop his guard again. Only after he had disconnected did he wonder if unimagined rage, not lust, would overtake him, and if Ginny would be safe in his presence.

She knocked on his door fifteen minutes later.

"Come on in," he said, opening it after a quick glance through the peephole. He was surprised at how attractive she was, in an unconventional way—her blue eyes alert and hinting at intelligence, her smile genuinely friendly, her frizz of red hair like a celebration. Instead of a purse, she wore a backpack slung over one shoulder. "I'm glad the car's okay."

"I was just lame," she said. "But the battery's not that old, so it held the charge fine."

He gestured toward the room's round table, which had two chairs tucked beneath it. "Want to sit? We can order drinks or something from room service, if you want. Are you hungry?"

"Some tap water would be great."

"That I can do." He took the paper cap off one of the glasses, carried it into the bathroom, filled it up. He had already used one in there, so he poured more water into that one and carried them both back. Ginny had shed her jacket and made herself comfortable at the table. Her jacket and backpack were next to the bed, and from the backpack she had taken an old, worn manila envelope.

"Thanks, Wade," she said when he put a glass down in front of her. "I mean, thanks for everything. It seems like you keep doing me favors."

"I haven't done much yet." He sat down across from her.

"Only saved me from a long, lonely hike. And here I am, showing up on your doorstep and asking for more."

"I'm pretty much on sabbatical, so I have plenty of time. What is it about Palo Duro you're interested in?"

"Not Palo Duro so much as Smuggler's Canyon specifically."

An alarm bell went off in Wade's head. The last place on

Earth he wanted to answer questions about was Smuggler's Canyon. He had already agreed, though—if he sent her away now, he would just make her suspicious.

"What about it?"

She opened the envelope, the kind tied shut with a short length of twine, and spilled faded photographs onto the table-top. "These are pictures of my father," she said. "Taken at various fieldwork camps, over the years, mostly. Some my mom took." She tugged one away from the others with a fingertip, twirled it to face Wade. A stooped, smiling old man with gray, thinning hair and black plastic-framed glasses squatted beside a little redheaded girl who was blowing out five candles on a birthday cake. "That's me, with him."

"That's adorable," Wade said.

"Thanks. These were all taken more than twenty-one years ago, before he disappeared. I think I mentioned, he used to be fascinated—you might even say obsessed—with Smuggler's Canyon, and as far as anyone knows, that's where he vanished."

Wade held on to the edge of the table to keep the world from spinning out from under his feet. Twenty-one years ago would have been the year before his father had . . . dissolved. If Ginny's father went into that same glowing pool, his disappearance would be explained—to a point. But he couldn't tell Ginny about the pool. "It was a . . . a dangerous place in those days," he said, trying to come up with a legitimate-sounding reason why. "At least, that's what our folks always told us. There were real smugglers crossing the river there. Drug runners, criminals. We hid in caves, sometimes, if we heard people around, so I don't know if the stories were true or not. For all I know, we might have been hiding from your father."

"It's possible," Ginny agreed. "Take a closer look, Wade. Maybe you saw him there, once or twice."

Hardly able to focus, Wade thumbed through the photos. Ginny's father was tanned, slight but strong, with a ready smile. He looked like an academic, albeit one happier outside than in a classroom. There were a couple more pictures with her in them, and some included a dark-haired woman that Wade guessed was her mother.

"I don't know. Maybe, I guess, but nothing that left an impression on me. I'd swear that this is the first I've ever seen him."

She gathered her photos together and tucked them back into the envelope. "I figured it was a long shot," she said, her usual smile gone now. "I just hoped, since you said you spent a lot of time there. . . ."

"I understand, Ginny. I wish I could be more help. That was a long time ago, though, and I just can't be sure enough to say either way."

"Yeah." She retied the little string. "I appreciate you giving it a shot, Wade. I owe you. I owe you a couple."

He waved away her thanks. "I didn't do anything."

Putting the envelope back into her bag, she stopped suddenly and looked at him. "One more thing," she said. "There's a word that kept cropping up in his last several letters and notebooks. It's not in the language of any of the Native Americans who lived there, that we know of, and I've never been able to figure it out. But maybe it's just some kind of local slang. Have you ever heard of *kethili*?"

Once again, Wade felt like the room turned inside out with him in it. "Doesn't sound familiar."

"You're sure?"

"Yeah. I mean, maybe I've heard it, but I don't remember it."

That much was true, but at the same time, it was familiar. The fluorescent light in the bathroom said it behind its buzzing, the rush of traffic outside the window repeated it all day and night. The first time he remembered hearing it was that evening he had dinner with Molly, at the mall. She had said it, or he had, a nonsense word neither one understood. And then again just this morning, at the coffee shop, he had heard it again, then thought he must have imagined it. That had been right before he'd spilled coffee on the floor, and the embarrassment of that had made him forget to ask Molly about it.

Kethili?

He almost said it out loud, but realized that Ginny was staring at him. He didn't like it. She knew something.

He blinked and she lay dismembered on the hotel room floor, her head, eyes open, upright on the bed, blood leaking from the neck, her chest cavity cracked open, guts scooped out through smashed ribs like a pumpkin emptied for a jack-o-lantern. He blinked again, covered his eyes with his hand until the image passed.

"You should go," he said, his tone terse. "I'm sorry I couldn't help you, but you need to get out of here now."

"Okay," she said, eyeing him warily. She zipped her back-pack, drew on her jacket, and shrugged through the shoulder straps. He didn't like making her think he was a crazy man, but that word, *kethili*, had prompted a flood of conflicting emotions in him.

It terrified him. At the same time, he felt a growing excite-ment, anticipation of some significant, wonderful event.

And he felt something else, too . . . a festering, malevolent fury, at Ginny and everyone else, that would explode if he held it in much longer.

"You need to go." He spoke with greater urgency now, com-manding instead of suggesting. "Now."

"Yeah," she said. She appeared frankly afraid of him by this point. He didn't blame her a bit. She kept her distance and made for the door. "I hope you feel better," she added as she left.

When the door closed, the flood of barely restrained vio-lence that had welled up inside him passed as suddenly as a summer cloudburst.

What it left behind might have been worse—agonized self-doubt, combined with a hefty serving of self-loathing. He had apparently become a murderer, somehow, without knowing it. This time, he'd been fully conscious of the urge to kill, but al-most powerless to resist it. This must have been the way his fa-ther felt, that awful summer. Maybe that murderous urge had lived inside him for years, kept in check only by releasing it in increments against his wife and son, like steam escaping from a pressure cooker.

He was gripped by a sudden need to see Byrd, to find out if Byrd recognized the word Ginny had mentioned. *Kethili.* What did it mean, and why did his vision go red when he thought it, as if he looked at the world through a scrim of blood?

He found his keys and wallet and made it to his car, unsteady on his feet, afraid that at any moment he would lash out against whoever was closest. The hospital was only a couple of minutes away, but the drive seemed to take forever.

Fortunately, when he stumbled into Byrd's room, no one except Byrd was there. His friend had been drowsing, but he snapped to attention when Wade entered. "What's up, man?"

Wade hadn't planned this far ahead, didn't know what to say. "I . . . I think I'm in trouble, Byrd. I'm losing it."

"What? You look fine to me."

"I'm a long way from fine. I can't even remember what fine was."

"Wade, slow down. What's the matter?"

"I . . . I can't tell you, Byrd. I don't want to get you in trouble."

Byrd stared at him, concern evident in his eyes. "Wade, bro, your trouble is my trouble. Tell me."

Wade started to, wanted to, but he checked himself. "Just tell me. The word *kethili*. Does that mean anything to you?"

"Say again?"

"Kethili." It tasted like sweet wine on Wade's tongue, and like the bitterest poison. *"Kethili,"* he repeated.

A shrug. "Never heard it. Is it Swahili or something?"

"I have no idea. It's just a . . . Never mind, Byrd. Go back to sleep. Forget I came."

"Wade, man, if there's anything I can do for you, just say so. Anything."

"I will." Wade swung back toward the door, not wanting to look his friend in the eye any longer. "I will, Byrd."

"I'm tired, man. I'm scared, too. But mostly I'm just so tired."

"I know. I'll hit the cafeteria, grab some food, and come back. You want me to bring you anything?"

"One of the cafeteria ladies. Especially if they have any with blue hair. Like that one in eighth grade, remember her?"

"I remember, Byrd." He did, too. One with blue hair, one with bright orange, like rust on iron, both wearing hairnets, dishing up the green beans and mashed potatoes and fish sticks.

"Get out," Byrd said softly.

"What?"

"Karl Marx. 1883. He said, 'Go on, get out! Last words are for fools who haven't said enough!'"

"You've got plenty left to say," Wade said.

"Can you hand me that oar, Wade?" Byrd stifled a yawn, then let another escape. Wade got the broken oar from the corner, gave it to him. Byrd clutched it, feigned paddling for a moment.

"I just love the feel of it in my hands, you know? The promise . . . it can take you anywhere."

"Yeah," Wade agreed. "We had some good times out on the water."

He looked back at Byrd, but his friend was already asleep, head tilted back on the pillow, mouth hanging open, oar still gripped in his fists and lying across his chest.

On his way to the cafeteria, shoes squeaking on the tile floors, Wade realized that the more he said the word aloud, the more familiar it sounded. *Kethili*. Maybe it meant nothing to Byrd, but it did to him. It meant a lot.

If only he could remember why.

38

Molly wouldn't have said that visions of Pulitzers danced in her head, exactly. Maybe they did in Frank Carrier's. In truth, she was disappointed with what she had been able to get from Wade. He'd given her the basics of his capture and escape, but not a whole lot of detail about what had happened during his imprisonment. Torture, he'd said, but he had glossed over it. She still didn't know what he was fed, or where he slept, or much of anything. And when she'd tried to press him for more details, after her little thought experiment, he had put her off, seemingly desperate to return to his hotel room.

Frank wanted her to start on the story anyway, convinced that she had enough exclusive material, and that Wade could fill in the rest later.

She sat at her desk, her scribbled notes open beside her computer, and typed madly. From Wade's description, she tried to put herself on the scene, in the car as gunmen surrounded it and assassinated the driver, in the underground cell. She tried to taste the fear that he must have lived with all those days, not knowing if he'd ever see sunlight again.

This could be the biggest story of her career—Frank swore it was, anyway—but she couldn't keep her mind from drifting. Thinking of Wade and fear made her envision other things, which blurred out the monitor and made her fingers lose their place on the keyboard.

Wade's fear tasted as sweet as strawberry ice cream on a hot summer Sunday. But it wasn't enough. It was a spoonful, and she wanted buckets.

Molly saw people filling the streets of El Paso with panic in their eyes and unvoiced screams dying on their tongues. A wall of fire as tall as a mountain swept down from the hills, down toward the river, engulfing everything in its path. Homes crackled, then exploded, windows shattering outward, gas lines rupturing and shooting geysers of flame into the air. Terrified people tried to run, but as the blaze neared them it sucked the moisture from their bodies. Blood boiled in their veins, eyeballs popped in their sockets; dry, desiccated corpses clacked to the ground like dominoes thrown down in a rage.

She tried to focus on the individuals who starred in her mind-movies, hoping she could taste the terror more truly in smaller doses. A woman racing down a steep road with two children in tow, not much more than toddlers. Slavering monsters chase them, teeth gnashing, claws clicking on pavement, hot saliva splashing the street and sizzling where it struck.

Kethili

A man caught in the grip of nightmare as a truck tears through a stop sign without slowing, smashing into his car, his wife and daughter wailing as twisted steel and spraying glass split their flesh, pierce their organs, and try as he might, he can't do anything to stop it.

Kethili-cha

Another man, younger, this one barely into his twenties, swimming against the rising tide of a ferocious river. He puts his all into it, reaching out with his hands, kicking with his legs, pulling and tearing at the rushing current. Then Molly sees why—he's after a little boy he saw fall into the water from a small bridge rocked by the flow. He spots a sneaker, black and orange and white, and he thrashes through the water and gets a grip on it—but the sneaker is empty, water running from it, and the boy is gone.

Kethili-cha riai tururensti ka—

"Everything okay, Molly?"

The moment broken, Molly blinked away her visions. Frank had parked himself on the corner of her desk, arms folded over his chest, shirtsleeves rolled up and tie loosened, the very image of the hardworking newspaper editor.

"What the fuck, Frank? I mean, what the fuck? I'm concentrating and you come along and throw out your shit, right in my face?"

He took a step away from the desk, physically reacting to her verbal assault. "Whoa, Molly. I was just asking. You looked . . . I don't know, strained. I was worried about you."

"Just . . . don't. Don't you worry about a thing, Frank." Molly pushed her chair back from the desk, leaving the computer on, the story only partly written, a partial word, "captivi," on her screen with the cursor blinking at its end. "Or worry, if you want, but you're not worried about the right things. Whatever you're worried about, that's not what you have to fear."

The *Voice* newsroom had gone utterly silent. People sat with fingers frozen over keyboards, phones pressed to their ears, trying to watch without looking like they were watching, except in the case of those who frankly gawked. Molly wiggled into her coat, grabbed her purse, and stormed out. The last thing she heard was someone saying the word "rehab."

But Molly McCall was beyond thoughts of rehab. Substance abuse had nothing to do with her behavior.

It was all about power now. Power and destruction and violence—the holy trinity of her new, improved worldview.

Kethili-cha.

39

"I've done some digging, like you asked," Robb Ivey said. Truly had taken the call in his Las Cruces hotel room, sitting on the bed with his feet up. "I'm still not sure why, after what happened to Millicent."

"Maybe because you understand that wasn't my fault, and you know I'm trying to make it right, and you'd be helping me," Truly said. He'd already had a version of this conversation with Robb, as well as with everyone else in his group.

"I suppose that's one way to look at it. The other, of course, is to wonder if I'm putting my head on the chopping block just by talking to you."

"Nobody's been hurt for talking to me, Robb. I hadn't talked to Ingersoll in months. Something's happening, and it's bigger than who talks or doesn't talk to me."

A heavy sigh. "I know. It's just all got me nervous."

"You're not the only one." Truly wanted him to get to the point—hand-holding was the part of the job he liked the least, and he wasn't even on the job anymore, officially speaking. He had asked Robb to research Victorio Peak, because with his large collection of occult literature he might be able to find out things that wouldn't turn up in a Google search. "Were you able to find out anything?"

"That's a strange part of the world," Robb said. "I haven't come up with a lot, but I found enough to suggest that there's more going on there than meets the eye, as they say. More than the government probably wants to admit."

"We do keep a lot of secrets."

"I keep forgetting you're part of the government."

"Maybe not for much longer. What'd you learn?"

"For starters, there are a bunch of caves out there. Early

races in the area, the Ancestral Puebloans and Apache among them, used them long before the Europeans came along—the peak is named for an Apache war chief. They considered the mountain a special place of power—not one of their holiest sites, but an important one. After the Spaniards came in, they used the caves, too. Eventually, long after the United States took the land from Mexico, it was explored again, in the 1930s and '40s. This time, explorers found a room containing twenty-seven skeletons, lined up in a row, like dancers or warriors. Exploring further—I'm not sure I'd have been willing to—they found old Spanish silver and gold coins, weapons, armor, and so on. Beyond that, they found a huge room full of crudely formed gold bars. Left over from the Spanish occupation, they believed, and some of them may have dated back earlier than that."

"What, they think the Apache shaped gold into bars?"

"Who knows? There might have been trade between Apaches and Mayans, or Puebloans and Mayans. Or maybe Apaches just stole it from Spaniards. Either way, gold could have wound up in the hands of Apaches, who hid it there. The claim was that there was a lot of it—I'm talking tons and tons, not just a few bars here and there."

"What happened to it?"

"That's the curious thing. The discoverers kept it in the family, for the most part. They used it like a bank, drawing enough out to live comfortably, knowing that there was plenty more. But in the late thirties, trying to open up a passageway with dynamite, they accidentally brought a chunk of mountain down on top of the main entrance to the treasure room. Now the interior was full of gold and they couldn't get to it. They kept pulling out little bits and pieces that had been stashed in other rooms, but that big haul was out of reach, no matter what they tried.

"Then the army moved in. During the Second World War, they took over the whole area as a bombing range, and the original family was denied access. Some military people exploring the mountain found treasure in another, previously unexplored room, guarded by a Spanish cross on the wall. One of them took a bar to military authorities in nearby Fort Bliss, figuring that since the mountain was on army-controlled land, it would require an official government expedition to bring out any substantial amounts."

"What happened to him?" Truly asked.

"Within a few days, he was transferred to the Pentagon. Or at least that's the story his friends were told, although they never heard from him again. There are rumors that other bars surfaced now and then, but anyone who asked too many questions—or worse, tried to get in and see for themselves—had sudden health issues."

"Health issues?"

"Like, murder threats. Maybe actual murders."

"You're kidding."

"One man, an airline pilot, claimed that CIA agents threatened him and his family."

"Well," Truly said, "that part I can believe."

"Here's the kicker. According to various reports, in the 1960s, Lyndon Johnson and former Texas governor John Connally spent ten days at the peak, after which modern excavation equipment was brought in. Theoretically, many tons of gold bars were removed from the mountain and shipped aboard military aircraft to Johnson's ranch in Texas, then to Zurich, where it was sold to a Middle Eastern buyer."

"That's pretty far-fetched, Robb." He had seen some of the same information online, but only at sites of questionable authenticity.

"I'm not saying I vouch for it, just that it's out there. There's a lot of detail in some of the more esoteric journals—the kind that favor huge conspiracy theories, especially. For your purposes, I think the important thing to know is that the Native Americans considered the mountain a place of immense spiritual power, and that even today, for whatever reason, it's one of the most heavily guarded spots on the White Sands Missile Range. The public can visit a missile museum on the post, and certain people, like members of the press, can get tours of some of the other areas. Nobody gets to go to Victorio Peak, though, without high-level clearance."

Which presumably Captain Vance Brewer had, since Owen LaTour said he spent a lot of his time at the peak. "Is that it?"

"So far," Robb said. "If I turn up anything else, I'll let you know."

"Thanks, Robb. I appreciate the insight."

"Just take care of our people, Truly."

"I'm trying, man. Honestly."

"I know. Incidentally, I've been in touch with Simon Winslade and Johnny Crow. Simon tried a ritual summoning, to see if he could shed any light on what's going on, but he said it turned into a disaster that nearly killed him. And Johnny's in Las Vegas—not all that far from you, right? He says things are well and truly—no pun intended—fucked up there, occult-wise. Do me a favor, Truly. If it looks like things are going haywire, give me a heads-up, okay? Let me get out of Dodge."

"I'll do that, Robb. Thanks again."

He hung up the phone and sat there on the bed. Clearly, the army was hiding something at Victorio Peak. Was it gold? Or was it something more rare and precious—something to do with the power the region's indigenous population had sensed there?

Given Brewer's involvement in the Ingersoll matter—*presumed* involvement, Truly amended, based on the fact that he had probably murdered Millicent Wong when she came to look into it—he suspected it was more about the power than the gold. Either way, he wanted to find out.

Specialist Owen LaTour was scared, which was just the reaction Vance Brewer had been going for. The young soldier had spotted him at the gym on Picatinny Avenue, where he'd been sweating through a basketball game with a handful of soldiers younger and taller than himself. To his credit, Owen had waited around until the game was finished, with Brewer's team victorious, and then had approached the captain privately, drawing him toward empty bleachers. In hushed tones and tremulous voice, he had described his meeting with the CIA agent.

"He knew your name, sir," Owen said. "And he had your picture. I thought he knew you. Besides, he was with the CIA, and they're on our side."

"There are a lot of sides," Brewer said. "And a lot of players on each one, or crossing over between them. You know the DoD has its own intelligence service, right?"

"Yes, sir," Owen said. He swallowed anxiously, and wouldn't meet Brewer's gaze anymore.

"Do you know why? Never mind, I'll just tell you. It's because the others are run by civilians. That means we can't trust them. They have their own agenda, and it isn't necessarily ours."

"But they're not the enemy," Owen protested.

"They're not always our friends," Brewer said. "They don't always see things the way we do. They may not be the enemy, but that doesn't make them our pals."

"I didn't mean to do anything to compromise you, Captain."

He wasn't sure he had been compromised at all, since Owen LaTour couldn't have known much about him. "Precisely what did you tell him?"

"I was pretty buzzed, sir," Owen said. "I think all I said was that I'd seen you in the area of Victorio Peak. That's really all I can remember, anyway."

"When did you see me there?"

"I don't know. I drive people over there once in a while. I just saw you sometime, and remembered you because . . . I don't know. You're just a memorable guy."

Brewer couldn't argue. He had tried to minimize that, to blend into the crowd, but in the end he couldn't do much about it. He was who he was, and if people noticed his broad shoulders and wide nose and jutting jaw, he couldn't control that.

Just now he chose to emphasize his gray-blue eyes. He grabbed the younger soldier's chin and turned his head up. Owen met his gaze fearfully, which was just the response Brewer intended. "Listen to me," Brewer said, lowering his voice to a menacing whisper. "If you see that bastard again, you keep your mouth shut, and let me know immediately. And you never, ever, talk about me or anything else you see here on the base to anyone from the outside. Is that clear?"

"Yes, sir."

"That's all, then. Dismissed."

Owen snapped to attention, saluted, and hurried away. Brewer gave serious thought to trailing the soldier and killing him. He decided not to, because he doubted the man had given

away any genuinely useful information, or had it to give if he
had wanted to. Killing him would make Brewer feel better
temporarily, but in the long run it might create more problems
than it solved.

He rushed to the locker room, showered quickly, then
dressed and hurried to a Jeep. Driving through the populated
sections of the base, he controlled the impulse to floor the accelerator. As soon as he had left the collection of buff-colored
buildings behind, out in the backcountry, he pushed the Jeep
for every ounce of speed it had to give.

He parked in the small lot outside Victorio Peak's operations center, in the shade of a tall mesquite. A handful of other
vehicles had parked nearby. Most people on the base never
knew there was anything here at all, and those assigned to staff
the center were closemouthed about it. Brewer went inside,
nodded brusquely to the MP on door duty, and strode down the
long hallway that led deep into the mountain's interior. Here he
found more doors, including one that required a retinal scan to
pass through.

This door gave him access to a tunnel carved from the rock
of the mountain itself—carved thousands of years ago, and improved upon by the U.S. Army over the past several decades.
Brewer took the tunnel to another, smaller tunnel, one that—
except for the electrical conduits tacked to the walls—felt
hardly different, he imagined, from those the Indians must
have used before Columbus brought disease and promise and
civilization to the savages. His footsteps sounded dully on the
rock floor, as if they were swallowed up by the walls instead of
echoing. Halfway down this tunnel was a steel door.

He inserted his key into the lock and gave a twist. The lock
released, and he tugged on the handle. Inside the little room,
the old man sat at his table, drawing pictures. The floor around
him was littered with ones he had finished and shoved out of
his way. His pencil was a gnarled stump. The stench of him—
well, Brewer was used to that. It would have made young Mr.
LaTour run puking into the hall, he was sure.

Brewer picked up a couple of the latest pictures. *Still drawing masks?* he wondered. But when he looked at them, a chill
raced through his body. He had seen the old guy draw a lot of
things, some of them strange. But they had always made some

sort of sense, always reflected something that existed in the world, whether it was masks or locations, people or animals or objects.

These did not fall into that category at all. These were beings, creatures, but not human ones—or worse, partially human, but not entirely so. They weren't any animals he could recognize. Their facial features were humanlike, but not *right*—the proportions out of whack, mouths and eyes far too large, ears and noses minimized almost out of existence, and in the mouths, so many teeth. . . .

The bodies were even worse. They changed from picture to picture, but they were all monstrous, freakish. One had a bare belly with an extra face showing, as if pressed up against its skin from the inside. One had at least a dozen arms, all ending in thin fingers as long as the arms themselves, so that the character almost looked like she was wearing fringe. Another sat spread-eagled, clearly naked, but where its genitalia should have been was a fly's head, its many-faceted eyes rendered in incredible detail for a blind artist. Yet another was only a head, the shading of its neck turning it into liquid that flowed away from it, forming a river.

Perhaps worst of all, this one and several others bore words. In all the old man's years in this room, Brewer had never known him to write words on his drawings. Now he had, and they shook Brewer to his core.

"Too late," the man had written. The letters were shaky, but distinct.

"Too late."

Suppressing a shiver, Brewer tried to figure out what came next.

40

Molly drove through the streets of El Paso. She knew it was El Paso, because a part of her recognized the streets: Montana, Radford, Hardaway, Raynold.

But only a part.

The rest of her—most of her—saw an entirely different landscape.

She saw buildings flattened, piles of brick and stone spilling into the streets, smashed glass glinting among the rubble. Cars and trucks were abandoned everywhere, the promise of escape they offered illusory in the end. Floodwaters were receding, leaving rings of muck behind, coating everything with a film of dark goo. Power poles had fallen; uprooted trees and limbs and leaves were scattered amid the wreckage. Everywhere, *everywhere*, bodies lay: corpses bloated in the streets; bodies hanging from windows, as if trying to get out or get in; one dangling from a flagpole, rope tied around a leg that threatened to give way at any moment; another cut nearly in half, looking like it was crawling underneath a stalled delivery truck.

Among the corpses, vultures feasted, their bare gray heads slick with blood.

This was El Paso as it *could* be. The *world* as it could be. Not Molly McCall's vision of it, because she was no longer simply Molly McCall.

She was *Kethili-cha*, and devastation was her due.

She was *Kethili-cha*, and power belonged to her.

She was *Kethili-cha*, and at long last, she was *free*.

Early in her awakening, she had forced Wade to kill for her, drinking in his terror and confusion as he looked into the mirror and saw his father's face looking back. His overwhelming guilt had been delectable. Thinking of that morning in the coffee shop, while Molly tried to draw information from him and *Kethili-cha* tried to pretend she didn't know what was really troubling him, she had to laugh out loud.

That sort of pleasure-by-proxy, while she relished it, was too inefficient in the long term. She saw the killings through his eyes, tasted blood and sweat, smelled the tang of horror in his victims' sweat and piss, but finally, she yearned to kill with her own hands, letting the deaths of others fill her own senses.

Her time had come. The reign of *Kethili-cha* had begun again.

Molly's phone rang. *Kethili-cha* wanted to ignore it, but Molly took over, yanking it from the purse she had tossed on the passenger seat of her brother's SUV. *Probably Frank,* she thought, *calling to fire me.* "Hello?"

"Molly, it's Wade." His tone was somber. Something was wrong. The mood of triumph she'd exulted in just moments ago vanished.

"What is it? What's happened?"

"It's Byrd, Molly. I'm sorry. He's gone."

"Gone?"

"I was in the hospital. I told the nurses I was going to the cafeteria for a while, and they found me after it happened."

She was having a hard time tracking. "After what?"

"Byrd died, Molly. He was in his room sleeping, and then he was gone."

She scanned the street ahead, saw an open space, and shot into it. Still holding the phone at her ear, she shut off the engine with a trembling hand. The other gripped the steering wheel. "He died?"

"Peacefully, they say."

"Who was with him?"

"Nobody. He was alone."

"Oh my God, Wade, alone? Byrd died alone?" She didn't understand why that fact seemed so important, out of everything.

"That's what they told me, Molly."

"Okay, okay. I . . . Are you still at the hospital?"

"I'm here."

"I'm on my way, then. I'm in the car. I'll be there in a few."

"Drive carefully, Molly. If you need me to come and get you—"

"No!" She screamed it into the phone. "Sorry, Wade. I'm okay. I'll drive over. Just don't leave him alone anymore."

"I'll be here, Molly. Don't worry."

She folded the phone and dashed it to the floor on the passenger side, as if it alone had been responsible for the news.

How could there be a world without Byrd in it?

Nothing makes sense anymore, she thought. *Nothing at all. . . .*

⊐╫⊏

41

Truly needed to find out what was going on inside Victorio Peak, but he wasn't likely to gain access to it.

Unlike most of his fellow CIA drones, however, he had another option—one they couldn't imagine, and wouldn't believe in if they did.

Hell, he wasn't sure how much he actually believed. Having run out of other choices, however, he was willing to give it a try. So he had called Bernard Frontenac in Paris. The CIA had sunk hundreds of thousands of dollars into trying to develop the application of remote viewing to intelligence purposes. Their success had been limited at best.

Bernard was supposed to be one of the best they had. If anyone could "see" inside the mountain, it was him. A long shot, to be sure . . . but maybe Truly's best shot.

"Have you found it?" Truly asked. "Almost in the middle of the state, east to west, but not far up from the border. Above Las Cruces."

"Yes, yes, I have located it on the map," Bernard said. Truly could hear the rustle of paper over the phone. "Now, please, Mr. Truly, a moment of silence."

Truly shut up. Bernard cleared his throat. The map rustled again. Bernard hummed a little, tuneless. Mouth noises.

Truly waited as patiently as he could. These things couldn't be rushed, and he wasn't the one trying to . . . well, whatever it was Bernard was doing. Reaching across the miles, across the Atlantic and most of North America, mentally homing in on a spot that was, for him, just one of those triangles on a map indicating a mountain. He had asked for a couple of days to prepare, and Truly had given him ten minutes, then called back after seven.

He was glad the Frenchman wasn't a mind reader, because then he might have known that Truly wouldn't be able to pay him from the Agency account. If he got anything useful out of the man, he would write him a personal check.

"A big man, you say. Gray and black hair?"

"That's right. He has a prominent nose, heavy, dark eyebrows, a jaw he could break down a door with." He hadn't known how many rooms—or whatever—there were inside the mountain, or how to narrow Bernard's search, except to have him try to locate Vance Brewer inside it.

"Yes, yes, I see him. His shoulders are as wide as two of me, side by side."

"Sounds like him," Truly agreed. He didn't know if he believed what he was hearing. Bernard sounded convinced, though, so he'd play along unless it got too outlandish.

"He is alone in a small room. No . . . no, not alone, forgive me. The room is very small. It has one door and no windows. The walls are rock, like a cavern. There is a table. The other person, a man, an old man, he sits at that table. Something is on the floor. Paper, many pieces of paper. This man, your man, he looks at some of them, crushes them in his fist. He is angry, perhaps, or frightened, or both."

"What's he afraid of? The other man?"

"No, I think not. This other man, he is very old. He holds a pencil and writes—no no, draws—pictures. This is what your man holds, some of these pictures. They are the things on the floor, the papers, as well."

"Can you see what they're pictures of?"

"No . . . no, they are too faint. They are drawings, pencil drawings, but of what I cannot say."

"Anything else, Bernard? I need more to go on." Impatiently, he clicked the TV remote, pressed MUTE even as the image flickered into life. On the screen, fishermen in the North Atlantic battled giant waves. The waves looked just as real as what Bernard described—in other words, illusions, tricks of light and photons or whatever made TV images work these days.

"One thing more, I think. The old man, the one making the drawings? He is very old. From him I get no sense of vitality, of life. He only draws, like an automaton. And I believe he is blind."

"He's *blind*? He's drawing all these pictures without seeing them?"

"So it would appear, Mr. Truly."

"And you're seeing what's happening now? Right now, as we speak?"

"That's correct. The man—your man, the military officer, although he wears no uniform—he has thrown his papers down, the drawings he held. Now he goes to the old man. He is angry, I think. He knocks the pencil from the blind man's hand, takes the blind man by the elbow, pulls him from the chair. The old man's legs are weak; I think he does not walk much. His legs shake. The stronger man leads him toward the door. The old man is very weak, very pale. His hair is thin, like hair you see on a dead man. I sense he has not left this room in a long time, but your officer is taking him out of it now. A very, very long time, it is, since he has been out in the sun. He goes willingly, though, following your soldier out the door."

"What else, Bernard? Keep going."

"A strange word. I don't see it, but it is there in the room with them just the same, I can sense it, almost taste it."

"What is it? What's the word?"

"Kethili."

"What does it mean, Bernard? Can you tell anything else?"

Bernard swore. *"Rien de tout,"* he said. "It is gone, all of it. I have lost the image. Forgive me, Mr. Truly. These things happen."

"No problem, Bernard," Truly said, sounding more gracious than he felt. His dad's influence, he was sure, all those lessons in diplomacy. "Thanks for all you've done."

Bernard tried to chat further, but Truly felt a sudden urge to get out of the hotel and up to White Sands. He cut the Frenchman off with another quick thank-you and hung up the phone.

42

⊐₩⊏

Wade paced the hospital hallways. Byrd's body had been covered with a sheet, just like in the movies. By now it might well have been taken away. Surely every hospital had a morgue. When Molly got here—he checked his watch again, on his wrist along with the yellow rubber bracelet that hadn't halted Byrd's cancer after all; thirty-three minutes and counting and where the hell was she?—they would have to go down there, he supposed. Assuming it was "down." Would she have to identify the body? That made no sense—Byrd had been in their hospital for weeks, months. Surely they knew him as well as anyone by this time.

She'd have to arrive soon, he decided, and he went to the small lobby area just inside the back doors to wait. If she managed to park out front, which was unlikely—she could page him. He waited with a mother and two small children, one still in a baby carrier, staying inside out of the drizzle that had started falling from leaden skies, while the father brought their pickup truck around. His stomach and chest itched like mad, and the overhead lights kept jabbering at him.

Finally, he saw Byrd's Xterra roar into the parking lot, going much too fast for the confined space. He only caught a glimpse of Molly at the wheel, but she looked distracted. She spotted a parking place and zoomed in, miraculously missing the Mercedes next to it by inches.

He started out into the lot, wondering where the light rain had come from. The leaden sky had been cloudless earlier. She stalked briskly toward the hospital, hadn't seen him yet. "Molly!" he called.

Her head snapped up at the sound of Wade's voice. He didn't like the look in her eyes, angry and bitter. They were ringed with red, and he guessed she had been crying. They both went between the same two cars, met in a crushing embrace. "Oh, Molly, I'm so sorry."

"I know," she said. She drew away from him, met his gaze. The angry look had passed; now she just looked sad. So very very sad. "Is he . . . ?"

She didn't finish. He didn't know what she meant to ask. Certainly she didn't think there had been a mistake, or Byrd had come back to life. He shouldn't have left Byrd alone—that had been the one thing she had asked, after all—but he just couldn't stay in the room with him. "He's in there," he said, having to stop himself from adding, "he's okay." But he was. Byrd's pain was gone, his sorrows finished. He was, in fact, more okay than Wade and Molly were, or would be.

"Thank you for being here," Molly said. "I don't know why I . . . Why I was so stressed about him being alone. I guess in the end it doesn't matter much one way or the other, does it?"

"Probably not."

"I'll miss him."

"We all will. You and me most of all."

"He's . . . He was the best brother. The best friend. I can't imagine . . ."

"I know, Molly. There's no one like him. No one at all."

Wade tried to reach into his clouded, confused mind for something else to say, something comforting and pithy and smart, but before he found it, Molly—

Well, she *changed*.

Her lips tightened. Her eyes narrowed. Her jaw pulled up, setting itself, firm. Her shoulders squared. She must have been slouching, because suddenly she was nearly as tall as Wade, and she just—she just wasn't. Had never been.

There was a smokiness to her eyes that was new. She tilted her head back, ever so slightly, as if taking on an imperious air, regarding the scene before her from some new height.

Even her scent was different, more metallic than it had been, with an ashy undercurrent.

The transformation confused Wade. He had expected her to fall apart. Byrd had been her rock. When their parents died, Byrd had handled all the details, leaving Molly free to mourn without having to be practical or reasonable. Wade had just assumed that he'd have to take on that role now, that Molly would collapse into herself. Instead, she seemed to be growing, taking on strength she had never known before.

"You . . . ," she said, only the voice Wade heard didn't belong to Molly. It was more strident, and even that single word carried a tone of condescension, ". . . are weak."

"Molly?"

"Do not speak to her. She is not part of this."

So that's it, he thought. Mental breakdown. Dissociation, wasn't that what they called it? Something like that. Her grief had forced her to invent a second personality to cope with it.

He reached for her. He had to get her inside the hospital, out of the cold drizzle. "Molly, please, listen to me."

She batted his hand away. Her motion was casual, almost offhanded, just the slightest swing of her arm, but he felt like a truck had smacked him. His hand flew into the nearest car, landing with a loud bang.

"Don't touch me!" the voice that had never been Molly's snapped. "*Kethili-cha* will not be handled by the pathetic *Kethili-anh.*"

Wade cradled his hand against his stomach. "Molly, please."

She stared at him—stared *down* at him, it seemed—with fury burning in her eyes. "Shall I finish it now? While you still wear that useless suit of flesh?"

"Molly, you need to get some help. Please, come inside with me and let's—"

Her hand darted toward him, curving into a fist, and Wade knew several things at once.

He knew that hand could kill him if it touched him.

He knew he had to get out of there.

And he knew that he was Wade Scheiner, but he was also *Kethili-anh.* Until he could bring *Kethili-anh* to the fore, however, until Wade stopped holding him back, he was in terrible danger.

He dodged the fist, barely.

Then he ran.

Molly—*Kethili-cha*—didn't try to give chase.

She laughed, peals of laughter echoing off the hospital walls, rolling throughout the parking lot, probably even audible down the hill at UTEP. Laughter that could shatter bricks, that could burst brains inside skulls.

Hands clapped over his ears, Wade ran as fast as he could.

The statue of Christ the King at the peak of Mt. Cristo Rey towered over El Paso and, like the ASARCO smelter smokestacks, could be seen from vantage points all over the city. It was actually in Sunland Park, New Mexico, however, so *Kethili-cha* had to drive down Sunland Park Drive, out of Texas and into the spur of New Mexico beneath it. Here, the Rio Grande was contained within the borders of the United States. Across the river, in New Mexico, she turned off the main road onto a dirt track and climbed the steep hill toward the statue. A few weeks before, on the last Sunday of October, the hill would have been crawling with worshippers—literally in some cases, as they crawled its heights, some flagellating themselves as they went, in an annual pilgrimage to the statue's feet.

Kethili-cha hoped there would be mystical power left over from that recent event, power generated by the believers' faith in the supernatural. But that was not her primary reason for forcing Molly's brother's vehicle up the hill. No, she climbed it because from there, she had a clear view of the river snaking its way into El Paso and beyond.

She gunned the vehicle up the slope. Small rivulets from the sudden rainfall ran down the hillside, carving curlicues in the dirt road. Rocks spat out behind her wheels, but the tires held the trail and carried her up. At a parking area, she stopped and walked the rest of the way. Bandits often lurked here to rob unsuspecting tourists and pilgrims, but, as if they had known *Kethili-cha* was coming, they had fled.

When she reached the statue, she saw that vandals had chipped off some of the Christ's toes. No one would dare treat *Kethili-cha* with such disrespect.

Anyone who did would quickly regret it.

The river wound below her, muddy and slow. It had once raged, pouring from its source high in the Rocky Mountains and cutting a swath through what would, in time, become the United States.

It would do so again.

Kethili-cha thrived on destruction, on devastation, but in the service of what she considered a greater good. She was an Earth goddess, of the Earth and for the Earth. Rivers were the planet's circulatory system, as critical to its survival as blood to a human being. Earth suffered a plague, and had for millennia, but that plague had been getting worse—upon awakening this time, she had been astonished and disgusted to see how bad it had become. On this peak, looking down at the river, she could see houses, thousands upon thousands of them, spreading up the hills like fungus, like disease. In each of them, humans lived. Those humans were a disease, and they would kill precious Earth if left unchecked. Already they were choking the life from the Rio Grande.

No longer. She would not suffer them to keep spreading their blight upon the skin of the one she loved.

By returning the rivers to health—restoring Earth's circulation—she could cleanse it.

Kethili-cha held her arms to the sky, the sky that had already, at her merest thought, begun to weep. Clouds had been gathering for the past hour or so, massing overhead, their tops climbing higher, bottoms gray and ragged as old walked-on hems. She cried out to them in a language not heard on Earth for thousands of years, and the clouds responded, crashing together in their urgent desire to do her bidding. Lightning flashed in their depths and thunder rolled out from them, filling the air with its sound.

Then the rain, which had fallen only lightly so far, began in earnest.

Kethili-cha delighted in the feel of it on her face, running down her neck, between her breasts, and across her back. Her flesh split where it had been cracked, exposing new, pink flesh as the old skin spread apart. She had begun to transform the body she had been born into, Molly McCall's body, into one more suited to her—taller, stronger, faster, with beautiful red eyes and jaws that could grasp and tear. The rain soaked through what remained of Molly's clothing, cooling her from the heat of transformation.

Through firmly planted feet, *Kethili-cha* felt the vibration of millions upon millions of lives, crowding into this place where only fifteen thousand years ago no one had lived.

Through senses unknown to humankind she experienced a million voices raised in chant, in song, in hymn, in *canción*, in *corrido*. She knew the drumming of billions of feet touching earth in the sacred ritual of dance. She delighted in the knowledge that all those people were out there, unaware, believing themselves secure in their pathetic small lives.

The skies opened, the rain fell, faster and harder than anyone in the two cities below her could possibly have remembered or imagined. Lightning lanced the gray sky, everywhere at once, a jagged bolt even striking one of the statue's outthrust hands, far above her. Sparks showered down.

And in its constricted channel, the river began to rise.

PART THREE

THE RIVER

Like a ghastly rapid river,
Through the pale door
A hideous throng rush out forever,
And laugh—but smile no more.

    EDGAR ALLAN POE, "THE FALL OF THE HOUSE OF USHER"

Dark silent forms, performing
Remote solemnities in the red shallows
Of the river's mouth at the year's turn

    ROBINSON JEFFERS, "SALMON-FISHING"

I turned homeward from Colorado early in September, but I stopped for
several days at the Grand Canyon, descending alone to the depths, to sub-
merge myself in the steep silence, to be overcome by the fearful immen-
sity, and to drown everything in the deafening roar of the Colorado, watching
its snakey writhings and fire-tongued leapings until I was entranced as with
the vermilion waste of the Navajo desert and many other places.

    EVERETT RUESS, LETTER,
    IN *EVERETT RUESS: A VAGABOND FOR BEAUTY*

43

Rain drummed on the roof of the Crown Vic, danced up the wind-
shield until the wipers snagged it, splashed off the hood in a
fine spray. Truly had caught the local news the night before
and no one had predicted a major storm, but one had slipped
in from someplace. In the time it took him to reach the rented
car from his hotel room, his raincoat had been soaked, his
short hair pasted to his scalp, and he was shivering from the
cold. He kept an automatic pistol and spare ammunition in a
waterproof zippered bag, which was currently on the floor in
front of the passenger side's bucket seat, so those, at least, remained dry.

He raced up Highway 70. As soon as he cleared the pass, the
White Sands Missile Range occupied most of the land on his
right, into the Organ Mountains. Including, of course, Victorio
Peak.

He had to use whatever clout he still possessed—unless the
Agency had broadcast some kind of warning about him—to
bluff his way onto the base and into the mountain. Coming
down the far side of the pass, with nothing before him but wide-
open desert, he took the Owens Road exit and drove past an
"Oryx Crossing" sign toward the base entrance. Water sheeted
the roadway; through it he couldn't even see the double arched
entrance at the end of the road.

About halfway to the entrance, he saw headlights charging
toward him through the rain. He recognized the vehicle as a
Hummer, but a civilian one. As the vehicle roared past, spraying his windshield, Truly glimpsed the driver's face and almost
lost control of his car.

Vance Brewer drove it, fists tight on the wheel, leaning forward slightly as if that would help him see through the down-pour.

Sitting in the backseat, his face blank, was an old man.

The blind man? Truly couldn't tell. He wished he had made Bernard Frontenac describe in more detail the man who drew all the pictures. Then again, who else was it likely to be?

Truly continued toward the gate for another twenty seconds, then, hoping the rain would hide his actions, he braked, turned around, and followed.

The Hummer's taillights had already vanished.

That didn't matter. Owens Road ended at the highway. From there, Brewer could go toward Las Cruces and El Paso, or north toward the White Sands National Monument and Al-amogordo.

Truly's guess was Las Cruces and El Paso. When he reached the highway, he chose that direction, gunning the rented car's big engine. There wasn't much traffic, and unless Brewer drove like a madman, he'd catch the Hummer in no time.

Something terrible had torn through Wade's life and stolen away the two people who were most important to him, the only two whose significance had deepened over the decades instead of fading. Molly's sudden transfiguration at the hospital had, quite bluntly, scared the crap out of him—as had the inti-mation that something similar might be happening to him. The cracked and itching skin, the whispering in a half-remembered language, worst of all the certainty that he had committed murder . . . it all had to mean some terrible change was overtak-ing him.

He needed to figure out what was going on and why, and he needed to do it while he was still Wade Scheiner. For lack of anyplace better to go, he raced back to the safety of his hotel room.

Entering the room, he froze in the doorway.

The walls had been covered in half-legible scrawls. Used-up markers, their caps off, were scattered everywhere. Some of the words had been scrawled in other media than ink—in brownish red letters that looked like blood. Wade looked at his palms and saw fresh cuts there he didn't remember. He didn't recall any of this, writing all over his room, but the handwriting—while done rapidly and without concern for neatness—was clearly his.

"Kethili inth kusili tia ti niala," one line read. There was no punctuation, just spaces between what appeared to be different phrases. *"Ina talaka ni Kethili-anh kinistero Koni ni tia tilistira katala."* It went on like that, none of it making any sense to him . . . and yet distressingly familiar at the same time.

He put out the "Do Not Disturb" sign, closed and bolted the door. Standing near the bed, he turned in a slow circle, scanning the walls. The writing was everywhere. When could he have done this?

After Ginny Tupper left, obviously. She would have taken one look and run away screaming.

He wouldn't have blamed her a bit. He wanted to do the same. But he couldn't, not now.

He had come here to call her in relative privacy, not knowing that stepping into his own room would chill him to the core. He sat on the bed, trying not to look at the scribbling on the walls, and dialed her number. She answered on the second ring.

"Ginny?"

"Wade . . . I don't think—"

He cut her off mid-sentence. "I was an asshole, Ginny. I'm sorry. I can explain—well, maybe I can explain. The point is, I had a reason for what I did, for sending you away. I didn't want to hurt you."

"Hurt me?"

"Look, I can't go into it over the phone," Wade said, fighting against the desperation he heard in his own voice. "I would never hurt you of my own accord, I can promise you that. And I don't pretend to understand all of this myself, but there's a possibility that it ties in to your father's disappearance. I think maybe it's connected to Smuggler's Canyon, anyway." That part was a long shot, a wild guess with only the vaguest hunch to back it up.

But something unnatural was going on. His earliest encounter with the supernatural was the night his dad had chased them into the cave at Smuggler's Canyon. If Byrd had been right, what happened to them that night had some kind of long-term repercussions they couldn't know until they manifested.

Maybe *Kethili-cha* and *Kethili-anh* were those manifestations, for Molly and himself.

Anyway, he had nothing better to go on. If Ginny's father was an anthropologist studying Smuggler's Canyon, maybe he had turned up something helpful. "I just have a quick question. That word you asked about, *Kethili*. You said he used it in letters and notebooks. Do you know if he went into any more detail about it?"

"I have boxes and boxes of notebooks, journals, and reports," Ginny said. Wade heard traffic noise in the background. "They're all back in my motel room in Palo Duro."

"Where are you now?"

"I'm still in town, getting ready to head back down there. Turns out there are a lot of things you can't buy in Palo Duro. Like, you know, everything." She paused, as if giving consideration to an idea that had just come up. "You want to go back there with me? Maybe together we can get though them faster, see if anything more on this mystery word turns up."

He hadn't imagined she would offer such an invitation. Not that long ago he had scared her half to death in his hotel room. Now she wanted him to come to hers?

"Maybe that's not such a good idea."

"You seem to have this flawed notion that I couldn't kick your ass if I needed to," Ginny said. "Unless I'm mistaken, you've spent most of the last decade or so sitting or standing in front of a TV camera, right? I've spent it hiking to remote locations, scrambling up and down mountains, surviving the elements . . . I think I can handle a pretty newsboy."

In spite of himself, he had to smile. "Okay. If you can swing by my hotel, we can take my car, and maybe we can figure this out together."

"Your car? You don't trust mine?"

"Mine's a rental and CNN's buying the gas."

"We'll take yours," Ginny said.

He glanced up at the walls again, defaced by madness. "I'll meet you in the parking lot," he said, "so we can go right away."

* * *

"Wade?"

He snapped to attention, realizing that the car was drifting toward the highway's centerline. He shook his head to clear it, corrected course. "Sorry."

"Are you falling asleep?"

He had to think about it for a second. "No, it's not that. It's . . . hard to explain." He was afraid he knew, although he didn't want to go into it with Ginny. Wade had faded away because *Kethili-anh* had crowded out his consciousness. Ginny had brought him back. But from what he'd seen of Molly, that wouldn't always be an option.

There was an up side, he reminded himself; if he was being possessed by some ancient entity, it meant he wasn't turning into his father.

In the half-light of merged memories, he grasped at some that threatened to flicker away. *If* Kethili-anh *can mess around in my head,* he thought, *why shouldn't I dig into his?*

One overwhelming sensation buried all the rest, and it tied into something *Kethili-cha* had suggested. *Kethili-cha* and *Kethili-anh* were ancient enemies, engaged in a war that had been interrupted millennia before. He remembered towered cities razed, villages burned to the ground, swollen rivers flooding through narrow, winding streets and carrying off children, mules—everyone and everything in their path. He remembered the wails of the living and tears shed for the dead. All of it, the effects of that war between gods. Now that they were released from their mystical imprisonment deep beneath the earth, that war would begin again.

Or maybe it already had.

"I thought explaining things was what this was all about," she reminded him.

"There's only so much I know. Most of it, I need your dad's notes for."

"Tell me what you can, Wade. That'll help me know what to look for."

"It's hard to even know where to start. Something happened to me—to us, really, me and my friends, the ones you met the other day, at Smuggler's Canyon. Now Byrd is dead and Molly is changing into something else, something monstrous and murderous, and I'm afraid the same thing is happening to me." He stopped, glanced at her in the passenger seat. Outside, a curtain of rain blocked everything more than a dozen feet away. "That sound ridiculous enough?"

"Anthropologists have to learn pretty early in the game that we don't know everything. What's bizarre and implausible in our culture is everyday and commonplace in others."

"Including magic, or, I don't know . . . paranormal weirdness?"

"Especially magic."

Her ready acceptance surprised him. "Okay, here's one more thing. The thing that I said happened at the canyon? It happened twenty years ago. A year after your dad disappeared. And it also involved my dad, who . . . well, I guess you could say he disappeared. But we saw it happen, and it was horrible."

Her jaw was as tight as if it had been wired shut. She stared straight ahead, looking at something that was not in the road, but in her past. "I always knew that he might be dead. I never wanted to admit it, but I'm a practical girl."

"I'm not saying I know that anything happened to him. I only know about my own case, and what happened to my father."

"I get it, Wade. I'm just telling you I'm ready for whatever we find out. One thing, though—I've seen some strangeness at Smuggler's Canyon myself, now that you mention it. I think maybe we should split up after all."

"Split up how?"

"You can drop me at the motel and go on to the canyon. I can dig through Dad's stuff and see if I can find anything pertinent. But it sounds to me like this all begins and ends at Smuggler's Canyon, and I'd hate for us to waste a lot of time in the room."

"But if you learn anything, how will you let me know?" he asked. "There's no cell phone reception out there."

"I'll . . . I don't know. I'll hitch a ride."

He couldn't hold in a chuckle. "Because there are so many people headed that direction on a good day, much less one like this."

"You have a better idea?"

"You drop me at the canyon, then backtrack to the motel. That way you'll have wheels."

"That'll work," she said. "It's not too far back to the motel."

Through the downpour, the three signs for the Palo Duro Motel loomed like lonely roadside ghosts. Wade pulled off at the exit, passed the motel, and took Palo Duro to River Road. His life's history unspooled out the windows, painted in runny watercolors.

They couldn't make it all the way to the canyon. The irrigation ditches that diverted much of the river's current had swollen from the heavy rain. Chocolate-colored water washed across the road, carrying branches and other bits of plant matter. The bridge was underwater, almost invisible.

"This car can't make it through that," Wade said, stopping on the near side of the flood. "Or it might, but I can't be sure. It's got no ground clearance at all. And there's another ditch after this one."

"What do we do, then?"

"I think I can get across on foot," he said, hoping he sounded more confident than he felt. "I used to be pretty good at navigating rivers. You just go back to the room. Maybe by the time you come back for me this will have receded. If not, don't try to run it in this car."

"Okay."

When he opened the car door, Ginny put a hand on his arm. "You're sure about this?"

"I think you're right, Ginny. The answers are at Smuggler's Canyon, somewhere. Anyway, *Kethili-anh* wants to be there and I can't hold him back much longer. If you learn anything, hurry back."

She looked at him curiously, but didn't ask what he meant. "I will. You be careful."

Instead of answering, he slammed the car door. The time for being careful had passed long ago.

⊐╫⊏

44

Ginny backed away from the irrigation canal and turned the car around. She wiggled her fingers at Wade as she drove away.

He faced the submerged bridge with trepidation. This was a flash flood, not a river, and the rules were different. He couldn't boat across. The water was probably no more than three feet deep, but since the banks had disappeared he didn't know for certain. The water's speed was hard to gauge, but it could have been running at thirty or forty miles an hour, gaining speed and strength minute by minute. Under the surface, he might encounter anything—rats, rattlesnakes yanked from their cozy homes by its current, rocks, bigger branches. The bridge itself might be damaged, and his foot might drop through it, pinning him there while the water rose around him.

The whole point of river running was that you tried to stay in the boat and out of the wet. It didn't always work out that way, and Wade had spent more time in rivers, some fast-flowing, than he cared to remember. Some of those dunkings had been purposeful, an afternoon swim to cool off, but many had not.

He was wearing jeans and a sweatshirt, a leather coat, and casual leather shoes. A far cry from river clothes.

On the bright side, he was already soaked to the skin by the rain. No matter what happened, he couldn't get much wetter.

He stepped in, felt the sudden shock of cold water against his legs, and kept going. The water ran fast and hard, threatening to yank his feet out from under him. He leaned into it and pushed on. He kept his feet close to the bottom, taking small steps. Water splashed against his legs, trying to bowl him over. A branch slammed into him. Before it could trip him, he shoved it away with one hand.

Then he felt the relative solidity of the bridge beneath his feet and relaxed a bit. There was still the possibility that the bridge wouldn't support his weight, but he had recently crossed it in an SUV. Fast water could knock down a bridge, but he didn't think it had had enough time to work on this one yet.

A few minutes later, the first canal was behind him. One more to go. That one he approached with more confidence, and he made good time across it.

Finally, so drenched he might as well have been naked, Wade reached the rocks. Water tumbled down from the higher reaches, mini-waterfalls running everywhere. The answers were here, Ginny had suggested. *Kethili-anh* seemed to think so, too. But where?

He started up toward the inner sections, figuring that anything he would need to find wouldn't be here on the edges. The rocks were slick, treacherous, and several times he had to catch himself with his hands, rubbing them raw.

Rounding a curve, he saw something yellow glowing through the rain, like the neon lights that had once decorated Betty's Night Owl Saloon. But there should be no neon at Smuggler's Canyon, where there was no electricity. Wiping rainwater from his eyes, he pushed on.

When he found it, the source of the glow made him wish he still had water in his eyes, or mud, or anything else he could blame.

He had reached one of the areas where the pictographs were most numerous. Dozens of them decorated a rock wall. As a boy, he had wondered about the people who had made art so high up on a wall, curious about what it had meant to them and why they had been so determined to make their pictures last.

They had not, he would have been willing to bet, intended for those images to glow with their own internal light.

Now they did, however, bright and steady, like beacons through the night and the weather.

Wade approached the lowest of them, the ones he could reach, and held out his hand. Heat radiated from them. He couldn't get within six inches without burning himself.

There was no shortage of things that didn't make sense in the new reality he found himself inhabiting. As he stood there,

nearly blinded by the brightness of the ancient images, he felt
Kethili-anh's presence again, like a hallucinatory waking dream
filling his consciousness.

But Wade remained as well, and in the interface between
the two of them, he knew.

He remembered.

Kethili-anh and Kethili-cha had always been enemies, even though,
as all the gods had been in their time, they were also siblings.
There was no time in the memory of either when they had not
been foes. *Kethili-anh* couldn't remember if there had been
some initial disagreement—as far as he knew he had been born
hating her, and she him. Their births, though, were lost behind
the veils of millennia, invisible even to gods.

Their enmity had grown and grown, until finally they fell on
each other in vicious combat, using mystical attacks and claws
and teeth to hurt and tear and rend and break. The battle was
epic, lasting sixty years and ninety-three days, the way humanity reckoned time. As it progressed, they both weakened, until
finally those mortal sorcerers and shamans who lived ten thousand years ago took advantage of their weakness and cast im-
prisoning spells, hoping to rid the Earth of the last of *Kethili*'s
children.

The web of magics engulfing them worked. *Kethili-cha* and
Kethili-anh were torn away from one another's terrible embrace. *Kethili-anh* found himself entombed in an earthen prison
so small that he couldn't move. Over the centuries, his consciousness waned until only a spark remained, unaware of itself or anything else. The flesh rotted from his body, and he
grew ever weaker, unable to feed on the faith of his believers or
the consumed souls of the dead. *Kethili-cha*, for her part, had
preferred the souls of the living, which she claimed made a
tastier meal. *Kethili-anh*'s respect for the living had always
been one of the points of antagonism between them.

Finally, *Kethili-anh* had been reborn, into the body of Wade
Scheiner, inside a cave beneath Baghdad.

From this point, Wade's memories became intermingled
with *Kethili-anh*'s. The glowing images on the walls of his
cave prison, the night before his escape, the miraculous way no

one saw him or stopped him, the empty streets—all part of the magic that had freed *Kethili-anh* from entombment. Somehow, the glowing water Byrd had described, from the depths of Smuggler's Canyon, the water that had dissolved his father like the strongest of acids, must have had some property that made him and Molly vulnerable to possession by the *Kethili.*

So he had been freed from his Iraqi captors and swept into a different prison at the same time. As *Kethili-cha*, Molly was stronger than he. Maybe proximity to Smuggler's Canyon had made her manifest more quickly. However it happened, and he couldn't pretend to know, she had been able to control him. Before he was even aware of *Kethili-anh*'s burgeoning presence, *Kethili-cha* made him murder innocent people. Just for her own enjoyment? No, he decided—because she enjoyed it, and because their suffering made her stronger.

That was just the sort of foul act *Kethili-cha* would find endlessly amusing, and the reason he had so long opposed her. At least, he could assure himself, the murders hadn't been his doing, not really. His body, but someone else's consciousness, and *Kethili-cha*'s plan.

He guessed the rain was her doing, too. Celebrate her return to the world by drowning it.

That was just like her.

45

⊐╫⊏

Brewer had wanted a helicopter, but he'd been told that since the weather had turned so dramatically and violently, they were all grounded. He had taken his own vehicle instead, knowing it could cut through anything a simple storm might throw at him.

He was beginning to think this was no ordinary storm, though. He had never seen driving rain like this. It turned Interstate 10 into a soupy mess. Truckers had pulled off under the shelter of overpasses, waiting it out. Those vehicles that did press on did so slowly, wipers flicking and lights blazing.

Brewer wove between them, unwilling to let surface conditions dictate his speed. Miles back, he had realized that a car had been tailing him almost since White Sands. On the interstate, the driver had come closer than he should have, probably trying not to confuse Brewer's taillights with anyone else's, and Brewer had recognized him.

It took a few minutes to recall the name. He had seen the baby-faced man first in Colorado, with Robb Ivey and then with Millicent Wong. Then today, there had been drawings of him mixed in with all the other whacked-out shit the old man had sketched. Truly, that was it. James Livingston Truly. CIA. He should have realized when Specialist LaTour said he'd been talking to a CIA drone that it was Truly. To be honest, he hadn't given the agent that much credit.

The guy had turned into a real pest. He'd like to have stopped and dealt with him on the spot, smoked him there on the rainy shoulder of I-10. He told himself he was getting soft in his old age, and he had to guard against that. In years gone by, anyone who had gotten so close to the truth would have been feeding worms in a shallow grave long ago.

But the old man in his backseat was more agitated than

Brewer had ever seen him, rocking in the seat, his dry mouth
clicking, scribbling drawing after drawing and spreading them
all over the vehicle. Any delay would be too much at this
point.

An expert at the base had positively identified some of the
old man's drawings—from the six-hour stretch Brewer had
started thinking of as his pre-Columbian phase—as representing ancient Indian rock art found at a place called Smuggler's
Canyon. Brewer knew it well, although he hadn't had occasion
to go back there in the last twenty-one years.

In theory, if the old man was drawing Smuggler's Canyon,
that meant Brewer needed to be there. Things were coming full
circle. And if the legend the old man had been writing on some
of his pictures, "Too late," had any meaning, Brewer had to
hurry.

Which meant no stopping to cap some obnoxious spook. If
the guy survived the drive to the canyon, Brewer could take
care of it there. He tried to forget about the spy, to focus instead
on guiding the Hummer over the perilous roads.

Everywhere great rivers flowed, the rains came. In Baghdad, the
Tigris and Euphrates swelled and overran their banks. In Paris
and London, the Seine and the Thames, engorged by sudden
storms, washed into the cities, crumbling ancient buildings
where they stood, sweeping away cars with their drivers inside.
In Cairo, the Nile rose so fast that people were trapped in their
houses, drowning as they tried to break through their roofs. In
Keokuk and Cape Girardeau and Memphis, Greenville and
Ferriday and New Orleans, the Mississippi burst over its banks
and swamped streets, shops, houses, and hospitals with equal-
opportunity ferocity. In Bismarck, in Pierre, in Sioux City and
Omaha and St. Joe, the Missouri did the same.

The combined fury of both those rivers struck St. Louis,
roiling away the ground beneath the Gateway Arch and bringing that landmark tumbling down. The staff of a city jail fled
for higher ground, leaving forty-seven prisoners on the lower
tier to drown in cells they couldn't escape. A traffic jam in a
mall parking lot killed another thirty-four who couldn't flee the
wall of water that swept over them. Eighty-eight residents of

an assisted-living facility for seniors were killed when a mud flow brought their building down around them.

The president declared a state of emergency, but there was little he or FEMA, the National Guard or the Army Corps of Engineers could do about it. Rain fell in volumes never seen in recorded history, feet, not inches, every hour. Every other nation's leaders made similar grand pronouncements, but behind closed doors, all were equally helpless. The waters rose, the rivers raged, the people in their paths were obliterated.

Kethili-cha drove Molly's brother's SUV, allowing Molly's personality just enough leeway to keep the vehicle under control since driving was a skill *Kethili-cha* had never learned. She left the driver's window open to feel the rain and road spray, knowing that back in El Paso and Juárez and every city close to a major river, destruction reigned.

But as Molly drove and *Kethili-cha* sent her consciousness racing around the globe, sucking in whatever pleasure she could from the suffering and death she caused, *Kethili-cha* encountered unexpected resistance. Probing, opening all her senses, she realized it could have only one source.

Kethili-anh.

She would have liked to killed his new host before *Kethili-anh* fully inhabited the man, instead of amusing herself with him. He might simply have chosen another host, one to whom she didn't have such ready access, but she could have taken that chance. There weren't many who were suitable as hosts; Molly and Wade were not random choices, but had been selected by circumstance long ago.

But it had been Wade's imprisonment deep underground, so near where *Kethili-anh* had been entombed, that had begun the process that freed them from bondage. Until both he and *Kethili-cha* fully manifested, she couldn't chance aborting that process. Since she hadn't been able to kill Wade, she had to deal with what was, not what might have been. *Kethili-anh* had come into his powers, and he needed to be crushed.

Molly negotiated the coursing waterways and soon stopped at the place she thought of as Smuggler's Canyon. *Kethili-cha* thought of it as her prison, or at least the outward manifestation thereof, and returning to it brought her little joy.

It would, she devoutly hoped, bring her power beyond imagining.

The Rio Grande tore furiously at its banks, just beyond the big rocks of the canyon. Among the rocks, smaller rivers flowed. The parking area was hidden under inches of water. Somewhere here, *Kethili-anh* worked to thwart her desires, holding back the rain she summoned. She would find him, and she would put an end to the annoyance he had been millennia ago and remained today. Their eternal struggle would be finished after this encounter, she promised herself.

She left the vehicle she hardly fit into anymore, forcing Molly out her head altogether. She didn't need the mortal now and wanted no distractions. With the confidence due a goddess, she strode into the tall rocks. Water splashed all around her, and the rain on the stones sounded like thousands of running feet.

Finally, she found him, standing on a shelf of rock near an array of brightly glowing pictographs. He no longer looked much like Wade Scheiner; the only lasting resemblance was in the thatch of light hair on his head and the darker hair on his chin, just as she still had Molly's dark mop. Like her, he was taller than before, probably nine feet tall, although that was hard to gauge with him high above her in the rocks. His head had elongated, jaw coming to a sharp point, mouth full of jagged teeth. The back of his head also tapered to a point. His ears were triangular and jutted out like a bat's. His yellow eyes beamed with internal light, much like the rock art he stood beside. His legs and arms were long, bent twice, once in each direction, giving him a spiderlike aspect. He swayed from side to side, palms toward the sky, and chanted softly. A flash of lightning etched his shadow against the dun-colored rocks, paling the glowing pictographs into momentary insignificance.

She looked much like him, with the same elongated head and multijointed limbs. Molly's soft, pasty flesh had been replaced with hard, scaled gray-green tissue that could more easily withstand the battle ahead. Her red eyes observed with more clarity than Molly's ever had.

As she started up into the rocks, *Kethili-anh*'s head turned. He saw her, his eyes widening, their yellow heat boring into hers.

"You interfere with my designs," *Kethili-cha* said, scarcely containing her fury. "We are reborn after so long, and already you mock my authority."

"You hold no authority over me, sister," *Kethili-anh* said. "But obviously your inflated sense of self-worth has not been affected by your time in bondage."

"My authority is in my strength, brother. And I have been hampered by your weakness for too long. The time is here, at last, for our final reckoning."

He extended his spidery legs and started down the rocks, toward her.

Very well then, she told herself, *the battle will be joined.*

46

⊐ℍℂ

"In El Paso," the TV voice said, "the Rio Grande and the Franklin Canal have spilled from their channels and run together. El Paso has called for a mandatory evacuation of the downtown area, and urges all residents to get north of I-10 at the very least, and up into the Franklin Mountains would be better. Traffic is at a standstill, though, and the water continues to rise. In Ciudad Juárez, meanwhile . . ."

Ginny glanced up at a tremble in the newswoman's voice. The woman sat behind her glitzy news desk, but she held a sheaf of papers in her hand, as if the news was coming in so face they didn't have time to put it on a teleprompter. Her eyes brimmed with tears. Ginny didn't remember ever seeing that happen before, no matter how horrific the news.

She wished she could change the channel to something less disturbing, but she couldn't get many channels in the motel room, and they all had the same thing—bad news from around the world. Bizarre, unexpected storms like the one she had turned the set on to drown out in the first place, thunder and lightning and rain that wouldn't quit. So far, no water had come into her room, and that was a blessing because her father's papers were in boxes stacked on the floor, and she would hate for them to be soaked. She didn't know how she would get safely back to Smuggler's Canyon, assuming she found anything that would be helpful to Wade—at this point, she wasn't sure the little rented Ford Focus would get out of the parking lot. She wished she'd brought her SUV instead.

She had found a passing reference to *Kethili* in one of the journals. She didn't think it would help much, but its context gave her another idea. She went back to her father's letters home, leafed rapidly through them, and finally found several

paragraphs that might be useful. She spent another thirty minutes or so making sure there was nothing else—not that she
could know for sure without rereading every piece of paper—
but it looked like what she had was the best she would get.

She put on her still-damp hooded sweatshirt, which she had
hung over the shower curtain rod to dry, pulled the hood tight,
covered it with the windbreaker—also damp—and stepped into
the deluge, sloshing through inches of water to Wade's car.

She got the unfamiliar car started. The wipers were worth-
less against the watery onslaught, and the headlights barely
sliced through the downpour. She backed out of the space and
drove around the building, to the driveway onto Palo Duro
Road. Headlights emerged from the gloom to her left, coming
from the highway, so she held back and let a huge SUV barrel
past. She started out onto the road, but then spotted more headlights—this time, a large American car. When that had passed,
she pulled onto Palo Duro. Three vehicles at once were more
than she had seen there since the day she checked in.

She followed, hoping if the cars ahead of her were bound
for Smuggler's Canyon, they would clear the irrigation canals,
and reveal to her whether or not she could do the same.

Listening to the news reports blanketing the radio waves, Truly
shuddered. He could barely imagine the devastation wrought
by hurricanes Katrina and Rita, or the Asian tsunami of a few
years back. From everything he heard, the current disaster
made them all pale in comparison. The only thing he could
liken it to was the meteor activity that had, according to one
theory, driven the dinosaurs to extinction. Rain hammered his
car and lightning bolts seared themselves onto his retinas and
thunder ricocheted around like cannon fire at a free-for-all, and
he knew that everything he was experiencing was minor league
compared to what people in riverside cities were dealing with.
He'd already heard of entire towns in China submerged by the
Yangtze, of a series of villages swept away by the Congo's
surge, of a Brazilian city called Macapa, near the mouth of the
Amazon, where the mortality rate was said to be a hundred percent, give or take a few possible survivors who would have lost

everything they had ever known, and of devastation by the Potomac in Washington, D.C., where his neighborhood, Georgetown, was only one of the areas too dangerous to enter even by boat.

Following Captain Brewer, he had turned off the interstate and sped through a tiny town called Palo Duro. Once he saw it—what little he could see through the storm—he understood why he had never heard of it. He flipped open his mobile phone and tried to call Robb Ivey, because he seemed to be a fount of knowledge on a wide variety of topics, to see if he could find out anything about the town or the area. He couldn't get a decent signal, though, and he gave up, jamming the phone back into his pocket in frustration.

Just off the interstate, he passed a shoddy-looking motel where a car waited in the driveway. When he passed by, the car pulled out, heading in the same direction, into and through the town, instead of going toward the highway (which, frankly, he thought would be the preferred destination of anyone out tonight, away from the Rio Grande and toward higher ground).

He wondered if Brewer was drawing him into a trap. Him up ahead in the Hummer, someone else behind. If they hemmed him in on one of these little country roads, he wouldn't have anyplace to go. Hardly anyone else was on the road, so any confrontation would go unwitnessed.

The trailing vehicle stayed pretty far back, keeping a consistent but not threatening distance. Truly tried to keep an eye on it while also watching the Hummer's taillights and the treacherous, wet road. They drove a couple of miles from town, past cotton fields more sensed than seen. The wind-driven rain in his headlights looked like it was leaping up from the road, tiny glowing sprites performing a gymnastics routine.

Ahead, the Hummer splashed through deep, running water. Truly didn't think there was much that could stop the powerful Crown Vic, but if he turned out to be wrong he could be in a lot of trouble. Beyond the fast water, lightning—or something like it, anyway, although it appeared to be more long-lived than any lightning he'd ever seen—illuminated a massive jumble of light-colored stone.

He braked, wanting to gauge the water's speed and depth

before he proceeded. The Crown Vic was heavy and powerful, but so was the Hummer, and that had four-wheel drive to boot. He wasn't sure he'd be able to follow.

While he considered it, the other car, a Ford Focus, came to a sliding, unsteady halt behind him. He didn't believe it could possibly cross the flooded bridge. He was no longer convinced of a trap—Brewer had gone pretty far ahead for that, unless he was now doubling back on foot, but that would be dangerous through the swiftly flowing water.

Still, Truly didn't want to give away any advantage to Brewer, so he drew his .45 automatic Colt, loaded with 230-grain hollow-points, from its zippered bag and threw open his door. He dashed through the soup toward the little car, letting its driver see in the glow of its headlights that he had a gun pointed toward him.

Or her, as it happened.

The driver lowered her window tentatively, looking scared. A sweatshirt's hood surrounded her rawboned face. "Hey," she said, her tone more combative than her anxiety suggested, "go easy with that thing. Is there a problem?"

"I don't know. You're the one following me."

"I'm just trying to find a friend at Smuggler's Canyon." She stretched her arms out the window, showing him empty hands. She looked taller than Truly, and lean. Curls of reddish hair showed at the sides of her hood.

"Is that where we are?"

"Not many people would come all the way out here without knowing where they're going, especially on a night like this." The worry etched on her face had turned to concern, but her voice was strong and confident. "You didn't see the signs?"

"I didn't see anything except you back there and the tail-lights of the car ahead of me."

"So *you* were following someone, and thought I was following you?"

He couldn't help laughing. "Occupational hazard," he said. He flashed his ID at her. "I'm James Truly, CIA."

"Ginny Tupper," she said. "AAA."

"You're with the Auto Club?"

"American Anthropological Association."

"Okay. And you have a friend in there?" He jerked his

thumb over his shoulder, toward the rocks. "Do you know this place well?"

"As well as anyone, probably. I've been studying it for weeks, on site, and most of my life from a distance."

"I'm not sure what's going on myself," he said. "But it could be dangerous around here tonight."

"It'd be at least somewhat less dangerous if you'd put that gun away."

"Tell me what you're doing here, what your friend is doing here, and I might." The rain pounded down on him, having already soaked through his raincoat and glued his sweater and Oxford shirt and casual trousers to his skin, and he made a hasty decision. "Look, let's get into my car where we can talk without drowning."

She hesitated, then agreed. "Let me just get some papers," she said. She bent over in her seat, reaching into the passenger side foot well. He aimed the Colt at her, in case she came up with a weapon, but when she sat up again all she had were what looked like old journals and stacks of letters rubber-banded together. "Okay."

"Run," he suggested.

She emerged from her car—as he had thought, taller than him by a couple of inches, and rangy—and they dashed to the Crown Vic, flung open the doors, and scooted in. "Some storm," he said.

"You're not kidding."

"So your friend? What's he up to in there?"

"I wish I really knew. *Kethili* hunting, I guess." She looked away, toward the rain pinging off the windshield. "All I know is that it's bad."

"Bad how?"

"You'd never believe me."

"You'd be surprised at what I've come to believe." Bernard had used that same word, *Kethili*, or something like it. Anyway, Vance Brewer was involved in whatever was going on, and he had come here, too. Truly couldn't shake the feeling that Ingersoll's death, and Millicent's, and the disruption of the ley lines that had put his psychics on edge all linked together here. Vance Brewer was a connecting thread of some kind. This woman showing up and saying the same nonsense word

that Bernard had meant something, too. Truly decided he had
to give a little away to win her trust. "I head up a CIA operation focusing on psychic phenomena," he said. "The paranormal, the supernatural—that's what I do. So whatever you've
got, however out there it is, don't think it's too far out for me."

He could practically see the wheels turning in her head as
she decided to trust him. Maybe a bad decision, lying to her by
using present tense instead of the past to describe his job, but
he needed her to spill what she knew. "Okay," she said. "We
shouldn't sit around talking, though. My friend might be in
trouble."

Truly had to agree, especially with Brewer closing in. "Tell
me more about this *Kethili*," he said as he started the car again.
He drove cautiously into the stream. He was an Easterner, city-
raised and not accustomed to flash floods, but he guessed that's
what this was. His headlights picked out the side rails of a
bridge. He took care to drive between them, holding the wheel
steady, keeping enough pressure on the accelerator to make
sure the car didn't stop rolling. The force of the water, flowing
from north to south, pushed against the car and he had to correct the wheel to stay on course.

"My father was an anthropologist who studied the indigenous residents of Smuggler's Canyon, particularly through
their rock art, for years," Ginny began, speaking loud enough
to be heard over the din of the storm. "He was convinced that
this was a sacred spot in ancient times, and that the art here had
ritual significance far beyond most other rock art sites. It wasn't
until he started experimenting with mind-altering substances,
though, that he learned what it was really all about."

"So what, you're here because of some hallucination?"

"Some hallucinations reveal deeper truths. Or at least that's
what he believed. I don't know how much of this to credit, but
in an altered state he claimed to have learned things he couldn't
any other way."

Once Truly had crossed the first stream, he started to relax a
little before noticing that a second followed right after. The
Hummer had made it through without any problems, though,
so Truly applied the same principles he had to the first one. The
water was faster this time, and he had a few seconds of near-

panic when it felt like he was being shoved toward the edge of the bridge.

Then he was off it, on solid ground once more. Water was everywhere, but not flowing as fast as in the streams. The Hummer had parked, its lights off. It looked empty from here. "Keep going," he said, pulling as close to the rocks as he could. Logs intended to mark parking spaces looked like islands floating in a vast sea. "And quicker would be better than slower. The *Reader's Digest* condensed version, please."

"The seven original *Kethili*, my father wrote, were the beings, or gods, who created the world. Each one dug his or her hands into the ribs of two others, tugging their bones and flesh out, bone building upon bone in a great sphere to form the Earth's skeleton, flesh upon flesh to form the land around it. As they drew away from each other, reaching the diameter of the Earth, the flesh gathered and folded to make the valleys and mountains and meadows, while the tears they cried from the incredible pain filled the oceans and rivers. Animals and people sprang up from drops of blood they spilled.

"Having made the Earth and watched the population grow, however, the seven *Kethili* disagreed on what they should do next. They went to war with one another, fighting over the course of eons until only two were left, *Kethili-anh*, who wanted to let the world continue on the course that was begun, and *Kethili-cha*, who wanted to wipe it clean and start over."

Truly didn't know what to make of her fantastical story. "We going into the rocks?" he asked, nodding his head toward the pale, rain-soaked stones ahead. Brewer must have gone that way.

"Looks like we should."

"It's going to be wet."

"Is there anyplace that isn't?" She checked the strings on her hood, and he wished he had one, too. Even a hat would help. Or a force field. He reached into his zippered bag again, removed two spare magazines for his weapon, then zipped it shut. He dropped the magazines into the side pockets of his raincoat and opened his door. "I don't remember reading about all that in the Bible," he said as they sloshed through standing water toward the first of the huge rocks.

"There are far older writings than those contained in the Christian Bible, Mr. Truly," she replied. "And older stories still, which have only been written on stone, which no one has ever dared to put down on paper."

"So you believe this tale?" He slipped on wet stone, and she caught his arm, held him until he regained his balance. Forty days and forty nights of rain had been in the Bible, and he hoped that wasn't about to repeat itself.

"I don't know what to believe. But I refuse to not believe in it. And if you have any special relationship with God, I expect that praying would be a good idea right now."

Truly ignored the suggestion. "And your friend? What's he doing here?"

"That's hard to say. I need to look for him, and maybe we'll both find out."

Ginny Tupper had calmed considerably since he had stopped pointing a gun at her, but she was still anxious for her friend. Truly thought he sensed an undercurrent of excitement, too, as if she believed herself on the verge of a major discovery. Perhaps they both were.

She was smart and she had a fierce wit even under pressure. Unlike most of the women he dated, she wasn't too young for him, or too married, judging from the lack of a ring on her left hand.

He wanted to kick himself. In the midst of the worst storm in history, heading into a rock formation he had never heard of, chasing a murderer who was traveling with an old blind man, listening to tales of homicidal gods, he couldn't help thinking that the woman beside him—whom he had met all of ten minutes before—was strangely attractive.

Keep your mind on business, he told himself. *Try not to be a dope for once.*

But people couldn't change their true natures, and he doubted he'd be able to take his own best advice.

47

"It's not a great night for rock-climbing," Truly pointed out.

"It's not a great night for anything," Ginny said. "Except maybe a stiff drink and a movie on TV. I'm not even sure where we should go. Besides up, there are also caves in there, whole networks of them. But given the river's height, I'd rather go up than underground."

"Works for me." She obviously knew the place better than he did, so he let her lead. He tried to emulate where she put her hands and feet, knowing the rocks could be treacherous in this heavy rain. His leather street shoes weren't meant for serious hiking or climbing.

Amid the rocks, the lightning and thunder seemed louder, closer, more violent than they had en route from the city. It didn't make sense—not that "sense" meant what it once had— but it almost seemed that the blinding flashes and crashing thunder originated within the tumble of rock instead of outside it.

Ginny led him up a trail of sorts, winding up a series of ever-higher outcroppings. Along the way they passed images painted directly on the rock: a sunburst, some parallel wavy lines, creatures that might have been deer, and a shield, all glowing as if white-hot. "What the hell? That's definitely not normal," Ginny said. It seemed like a vast understatement, but Truly didn't offer any comment.

Strange as the glowing images were, his attention was fixed on something else. The storm made its own crashing, banging racket, its particular light show in the sky, but there was definitely something going on within the rock formations as well. Cracks of thunder echoed off the stone surfaces, drowning out that coming from the clouds. Other sounds were interspersed with that thunder, rattling booms like an army of convicts breaking rocks with sledgehammers. Occasional whining sounds sliced through the rest of it like devilish buzz saws.

"What do you think that is?" he asked, not really expecting an answer.

"We'll find out soon, I expect," Ginny offered. They had almost reached a pinnacle from which they would be able to look down onto whatever transpired below. The rocks were steeper here; the fall, should they lose their footing, potentially lethal. Wind and weather had smoothed the stone, leaving handholds that were little more than bumps on its surface. Realizing he could see better the higher he climbed, Truly determined that what he had first thought was thunder and lightning glowed bright enough to cast its illumination all the way up here.

When she reached the top and stared down the other side, Ginny let out a gasp. Her body went stiff. Truly hurried the last few feet, joining her at a jagged edge from which he could see all the way to the river more than a hundred feet below. Blinking rain from his eyes, he gazed at a scene he couldn't quite bring himself to believe.

Two . . . *creatures* was the best word he could summon, not human, although they had human attributes . . . faced each other in some sort of mystical battle. Both were naked and their genders were clear—one, with longer, dark hair, had visible breasts and a slightly softer, rounder form, while the other had shorter, blond hair and beard, and genitalia swaying between freakish, spidery legs. They stood across from each other on a wide rock shelf that had stone spurs shooting up all the way around it, forming a natural amphitheater, the walls of which were covered in glowing pictographs. They conversed, Truly guessed, as they circled each other—a series of squeaking hisses interspersed with whoops and barked comments in a language that didn't sound like anything he had ever heard, or heard of.

The male's oddly jointed arms worked together in a motion that looked like he was scooping up empty air—except that the air bent and wrinkled where he held it, as if he'd formed a huge soap bubble—and then he hurled his ball of seeming nothingness at the female.

She bobbed on legs that made Truly's teeth hurt to look at, ducking under the male's attack. While Truly couldn't see the projectile in flight, except for a vague wrinkling of the air where it flew, it hit the wall behind her and exploded, sending shards of stone flying everywhere. The blast unleashed a stink, like burning rubber but with an unexpectedly sweet undercurrent that reminded Truly of fennel.

The female hissed something unintelligible at the male and blasted him with her own unseen missile. It glanced off his left shoulder, spinning him around, then crashed into the wall and sprayed him with bits of stone. He dropped to one knee, or whatever those inverted joints were called, and clapped a hand over his shoulder. Purplish blood seeped between fingers as long as Truly's forearm—seven of them on each hand, he noted, ending in inches-long claws.

Ginny's expression was rapt, awestruck. She stared in what Truly could only describe as wonder at a scene that no anthropologist—no human—had witnessed since the dawn of recorded history.

Truly's belief system had undergone serious changes since he had taken the job running Moon Flash. But it hadn't altered enough to accommodate whatever he was seeing. Looking at them made his stomach churn and he had to swallow back bile. He wished it was a nightmare so he could wake up, or that in the brief time Ginny had been in his car, crossing the flooded bridges, she had dosed him with LSD. "What are those things?" he demanded.

"I can only take a guess," Ginny said, her voice much calmer now than his. "The guy used to be my friend Wade. I'm thinking the other one looks like—and I use that phrase loosely—his friend Molly. But now? Now I'd have to say they're *Kethili*."

Truly didn't bother arguing. No other explanation was any more plausible than hers, and at least she'd ventured one. "So one of them wants to—how did you put it? Wipe the world clean and start over? Which one?"

"From what Wade told me, that's Molly. *Kethili-cha*."

"Then we'd better damn well hope she loses."

He tore his gaze away from the struggling creatures, or gods, and looked toward the river. Lightning and the illumination from the explosion of their mystical weapons lit it momentarily, like a camera's strobe, and he saw figures floating in it, whisked downstream by its ferocious current. A cow, he thought, and maybe some deer. Leaner shapes might have been human beings.

Movement across the way caught his attention, and he tried to focus through the rain. On the far side of the rock amphitheater, mostly tucked away behind some large boulders, Vance Brewer watched the battle. The blind man, standing slightly behind him, appeared oblivious to it all. The rain had pasted the old man's few tendrils of hair to his scalp, giving him a cadaverous appearance.

Truly still owed Brewer for killing Millicent, not to mention wanting some answers about his involvement in this whole mess. "Wait here," he told Ginny, fully aware that he held no authority over her whatsoever. "There's something I have to do."

She touched his shoulder as he started away. "Be careful."

"Don't worry," he said. "I'm good at that."

More confident than when he had first climbed up, Truly descended and worked his way around the natural clearing where the two *Kethili* fought. The flares and flashes of their conflict lit his way, lightning providing secondary illumination. Every now and again the clouds parted enough to reveal the moon, a flat, pale pewter disk that offered no light. When his balance threatened to falter, he grabbed at the yucca or mesquite breaking the stony surface here and there—all of it sharp, slicing his bare hands, but better than a fifty- or sixty-foot drop.

Fifteen minutes later he had circled all the way around, coming up behind and slightly above Brewer and the old man. Brewer still watched from hiding, but the old man had sat down behind him in a puddle, inscribing images on the rocks with his fingertips. His mouth moved, but no sounds came from it.

Truly could shoot Brewer from here. One in the back of the head should do it. That might avenge Millicent but it wouldn't help with his other goals. Anyway, the man was a captain in the United States Army. Although it hadn't seemed like it, they were, ostensibly, on the same team. Better to give Brewer a chance to explain himself.

He maneuvered toward a narrow bench from which he could drop down behind Brewer, taking him by surprise. Dodging the old man would be the only hard part, since he had moved to the center of the small hidey-hole Brewer had found.

As Truly slid around, trying to position himself for the drop, though, he slipped, his hands gliding out from under him on the rain-slick stone. Instead of a dramatic landing, he plopped six feet to the ground, splashing into the puddle, one outflung arm smacking against the old man's leg. The old man didn't react, but Brewer did.

He spun around and aimed a sudden kick at Truly's head. Truly saw it coming, but off balance, hands and feet in the puddle, he could only jerk his head to the side. The kick glanced off his shoulder instead, knocking him sprawling.

"I should have taken you out of this a long time ago," Brewer said, his voice a menacing growl. He started toward Truly, who was still shaking off the effects of the fall and the kick. Truly scrabbled to regain his feet before Brewer reached him, and almost made it. At the last second, still trying to rise, he scooped up a fist-sized rock from the ground, and just before Brewer slammed into him, he hurled it at the captain's head. The rock caught the side of Brewer's temple, staggering him for a moment.

"I thought attacking women was your thing," Truly said. Taking advantage of Brewer's temporary instability, Truly charged through the puddle and drove the officer back against the boulder behind him. They landed with a bone-breaking crunch. Brewer groaned.

He was at least twenty years older than Truly. Maybe thirty. But he outweighed Truly, outmuscled him, and he was probably a more skillful hand-to-hand fighter. Even smashed up against a rock, he managed to bring a knee up into Truly's thigh and a fist down against Truly's ear. Truly's hold relaxed. He fell away, and Brewer followed up with two more quick jabs, a left and a right, blinding Truly with flashing lights and driving him back through the puddle. There the old man's outstretched legs tangled with his and he went down again.

Brewer came at him once more. A kick to the jaw snapped Truly's head around. A second landed short, catching Truly's leg with a glancing blow. On the third, Truly caught Brewer's foot in both hands. He yanked, twisted, and Brewer fell hard.

Truly scrambled over him, pummeling with both fists as he did. Brewer, on his back, rained blows up at Truly. His right fist caught Truly's cheekbone, tearing flesh. Truly tasted blood. He jabbed a thumb toward Brewer's eye but Brewer whipped his head to the side. Truly's thumb mashed against the side of his face, then Brewer turned his head again, snapping at the thumb. He nipped it before Truly could yank it away.

Truly favoring his damaged thumb gave Brewer another moment, and he used it. He bucked Truly off him, got to his knees, and lunged into him, shoving him down in the puddle once again. Truly landed on his back with Brewer swarming over him, punching and kneeing his ribs and chest. Truly was weakening, barely able to take the punishment and still give anything back. Brewer was a killer, and he didn't show any sign that he would stop until Truly had joined his list of victims.

Truly got the break he needed when the old man suddenly lurched to his feet, tried to take a step, and tripped, coming down across Brewer's back. Brewer half-turned to shove him off. Truly shot out his left fist, catching Brewer squarely in the throat. Gagging, Brewer reared back and Truly squeezed out from beneath him. He gained his feet and shoved a hand in his coat pocket, drawing out the Colt.

"I don't want to do it this way, Brewer," he said. "But if you make a move toward me, I will."

Brewer held out his hands in a show of truce. "Don't worry. One thing I'm not is suicidal."

The old man had fallen back into the puddle, and drew himself to a sitting position, as if forgetting he had ever tried to stand. "All right, then." Truly relaxed a little, but kept the gun pointed at Brewer's midsection. If the officer charged, he couldn't kill him outright but he'd put a hurting on him, giving himself time to take a second, more fatal shot. "Why did you kill Millicent Wong?"

Brewer's mouth opened in surprise. "That's what you care about? You didn't notice we have some far more urgent concerns right now?" He ticked his head toward the battle that, from the evidence of noise and light, continued below.

Truly shrugged. "Okay, point taken. You obviously know something about what's going on here."

"About the *Kethili*? Yeah, something."

"Tell me what," Truly said. "Why are they here? Why have they come back from wherever they've been? Where do you fit in, and what's the army's interest?'

"Hold up," Brewer said, raising his hands again. "That's a lot of questions."

"Then you better talk fast, because I still have the gun."

Brewer clenched his right fist, then loosened it again. "We brought them back," he said. "You're CIA, right?"

"That's right."

"You've got your occult research section. Army Intelligence has ours, too. And we're way out ahead of you on that. Maybe we're a little less hidebound, less bureaucratic, I don't know, but we were willing to make some intuitive leaps, consult some sources you guys didn't seem interested in. You know how intelligence sharing is—not really a priority for either of us.

"Anyhow, way back, I don't know, thirty years ago or so, we turned up information on the *Kethili*. Someone in our group thought if they could be restored, controlled, they might be useful weapons. Those were the waning days of the Cold War, remember—we needed any edge we could find in case the Commies decided to launch any nukes at us."

Truly had a hard time accepting what he heard. He spat blood. His tongue probed a spot where a tooth he had probably swallowed had been. He was sure the gash over his cheekbone still bled, but the cold, stinging rain had numbed it and washed away any blood as soon as it surfaced. "You thought you could bring gods back to life and control them?"

"Someone did. I'm not naming names. I was a junior member of the team back then. An errand boy. Somebody told me who to hit or where to go, and I followed orders."

"Where have I heard that excuse?"

Brewer ignored him. "Eventually they determined who knew the most about the *Kethili*—at least, in the world of English-speaking white men—and they pointed me in his direction. I went and found him, snatched him up, and . . . let's say, persuaded him to perform a ritual that would restore their physical bodies. This is still ages ago, twenty, twenty-one years, something like that."

"Sounds like it wasn't the most successful ritual ever."

"Not at first. We thought it was a total flop. The old guy swore it would work, but it might take time. Twenty years, fifty, a hundred, five hundred, he didn't know. Naturally, that pissed me off royally—flying missiles could be here in a matter of hours, not years. I bitched, but he said there was nothing to be done about it."

"Where did all this happen? Victorio Peak?"

"Yeah, back inside the mountain," Brewer said. He dabbed at his mouth with the back of his hand. "The old guy said the correct vessels—that's the word he used, 'vessels,' had to be in the right place at the right time. He said his spell sank down into the water table, where it would join the rest of the Earth's waters, flowing through rivers and streams and across oceans, until it found the vessels it needed."

"And the nearest flowing water to White Sands is the Rio Grande," Truly observed. "So it flowed down the river and wound up here, and that's why this is their new battleground."

"At a guess, something like that. Plus this is where I found him in the first place, and he said it was a place that had special significance to them. We figured the old guy could control them whenever they were reborn, or reemerged, whatever, because he was the one who brought them back. What we didn't count on was that the ritual itself sapped the life out of him. He lived for thirty-three more hours, give or take, and then he died."

Truly had been expecting the blind man to be the old guy Brewer was talking about. He spared a glance for that old man, sitting in the puddle drawing designs on the air.

"That's right," Brewer said, answering the question Truly hadn't asked. "He died, but he wouldn't lie down. He remained animate. He couldn't see or hear or talk; his brain function was at zero and holding; he didn't need food or sleep or anything else. Once the doctors had put him through every test they could think of, we locked him into a room inside the peak. When it became obvious—because he was doing what you see here—that he was trying to draw something, we stuck a pencil in his hand and some paper in front of him, and he started making drawings. We kept the pencil and paper coming. He kept drawing. A lot of it was meaningless, but every now and then he seemed to tap into something, and we tried to follow up on what we could. He drew the Berlin Wall in rubble weeks before it happened. Before 9/11 he drew airplanes and buildings, but that didn't give us enough to go on, and we couldn't predict the attacks.

"Because I was the one who brought him in and convinced him to perform the ritual, I became his keeper. I've killed to protect his secret, including your friend Millicent. You'd probably like me to say I'm sorry, but there's not a chance in hell of that. If this thing worked, if it became real, it was too big to let some psychic bitch get in the way of it. She was starting to clue in on me, despite my blocking her, and she had to go."

Truly swallowed his rage. Given the circumstances, it would be counterproductive. "Well, it's real now. Where's the control?"

"We didn't expect him to die," Brewer said, indicating the old man. "Or that, having died, he'd stick around this long. When I realized the *Kethili* really had come back, I had to bring him out in case there was anything he could do."

The old man sat in the puddle, drawing in the air with his fingers.

"Not looking that way."

Given the timing—and the connection to the Rio Grande—Truly had to guess that the disturbance in the ley lines that had caught Lawrence Ingersoll in what must have been some kind of psychic feedback was related to the reemergence of the *Kethili* into the world. Certainly an occult event of such magnitude would be beyond the experience of any of the people in his network.

"He said he knew spells," Brewer went on. "He could rein them in. But he hasn't spoken a word since he died, and his drawings don't communicate anything as substantial as specific spells. I don't think we can control them now. I think we're just fucked." He paused, then added, "Unless you want to try shooting them."

48

⊐╫⊏

"Shoot them?" Truly asked. "You think?"

"I'll do it," Brewer said. "If you're okay with that."

Truly twitched his Colt in a kind of shoulderless shrug.

"Reaching for my weapon," Brewer said. His movements were slow, exaggerated. He drew an automatic from a holster concealed beneath his winter coat, holding it between his thumb and index finger until it was pointed safely away from Truly. There was something comforting, Truly thought, about dealing with professionals.

Truly moved closer to the vantage point from which Brewer had been watching the *Kethili*. The battle raged on. Both gods were hurt now, purple blood flowing freely from numerous wounds. *Kethili-anh*, the one who had been Ginny's friend Wade, seemed to have taken the worst of it. They had also done significant damage to the rock around them, exposing enough fresh, pale stone to make the place resemble a small-scale strip-mining operation.

The weird, disconcerting chatter between them continued, too, a combination of screeching, whining, and hissing noises, clicks and pops and low, almost subsonic moans.

Truly had been fighting his nerves, struggling to hold his weapon steady, but Brewer seemed to have no such problems. He aimed his pistol at *Kethili-cha*, his arm still and relaxed. He squeezed the trigger. The report echoed off the surrounding rocks and the bullet slammed into the back of *Kethili-cha*'s right shoulder. She spun around, clapping one of those long freaky hands over the wound, and glared up at them. Brewer fired again.

This time the bullet hit her squarely in the chest. Purple

blood bloomed there for a moment, but ceased to flow almost instantly.

With a furious scowl, *Kethili-cha* made a throwing motion directly toward Brewer. The army officer ducked behind the boulder he had been leaning on. The top of it exploded, spraying sharp-edged stone all over the three people hiding behind it.

Brewer turned back toward Truly, wiping blood off his face. "Guess that just pissed her off."

"It looks that way," Truly agreed.

"Maybe if we both try—"

"Maybe you should put that thing away," Truly said. Shooting a goddess with regular bullets wouldn't do the job. She had felt their impact, but hadn't been terribly disturbed by them, and if the mystical bolt she'd hurled had hit Brewer it would have taken his head off. "Before someone gets hurt."

Brewer tucked the gun back into its holster under his coat. "You got any better ideas? The only other weapon I brought is an old blind man. A *dead* old blind man. And that's about how useful he turned out to be."

Truly looked at the old man again, and a thought flickered through his mind. "Maybe . . . ," he said. "I'll be right back. Don't go anywhere, and don't try to engage them again."

He didn't have any control over Brewer except when he had a gun pointed at him, but he hoped the man would see reason and do as he was told. Following the same route he had taken before, more confident than ever, Truly made it back to Ginny in just a few minutes.

"Did you shoot at her?" she asked when he climbed into view. She helped him up the last bit, her grip powerful.

"Not me. Another guy, an army intelligence officer."

"Military intelligence. Greatest oxymoron ever. He a friend of yours?"

"Not in the least. In fact, he killed a friend of mine. But right now he's the only ally we have, and he's got someone with him I think you should meet."

"Are you sure?" She looked over the side again, as if she didn't want to be torn away from the spectacle.

"It's important," he said. "Trust me."

"I don't even know you."

"We all want the same thing here, Ginny." He waved a hand at the stormy sky. From everything he had heard, insane amounts of rain were falling on rivers all over the world and they were all rising, like the Rio Grande, to potentially murderous levels. Most of the world's population lived in relatively close proximity to rivers. "Unless we want to build some arks, we have to try to stop this."

She chewed her lower lip, shaking her head, obviously wanting to disagree. "A warm bed? Temporary amnesia?" she said. "We all want the same things. You're right. Let's go, before I change my mind again."

Truly led her along the now-familiar route, up and down the rocks, past water cascading from the upper reaches, showing her the hand- and footholds he had discovered—a reversal of their first journey up into the rocks.

Together they completed the return trip in no time. Brewer and the old man hadn't budged, except that Brewer was back in his position looking down at the *Kethili*.

Truly hopped down into the rocky depression with more grace than he had the first time. "Ginny Tupper, this is Captain Brewer," he said as he helped her down—help she clearly didn't require. His father had always stressed good manners, even when—as now—they seemed wildly unnecessary. He pointed at the old man. "And that's . . ."

"Daddy?" Ginny said.

The old man didn't respond. Ginny dropped to her knees in the puddle, took his hands in hers. "Daddy, it's me, Ginny."

"He can't hear you, miss," Brewer said.

"Is he . . . Daddy? What's the matter?" She looked into his face, his lifeless eyes.

"He's dead, Ginny," Truly said. "I'm sorry. He has been for a long time."

Tears bubbled from her clear green eyes. "But he's . . . he's right here. He's sitting up."

"And that's more impossible than anything else around us? I thought maybe this was your father, when Brewer told me about him being an expert on the *Kethili*, especially given the timing of when you said he disappeared. He's the one who summoned them in the first place, but he didn't survive the ritual. I hoped you'd be able to get through to him, even if no one else can."

"He looks just like I remember him."

Truly didn't bother pointing out that the man hadn't aged a whole lot since she'd last seen him. She threw her arms around the dead man, her back shaking with sobs. He could hardly imagine the grief she must be feeling, the pain of looking for him for years, not knowing, assuming he must have died but keeping the flame of hope burning for his survival, and now finding him at last only to realize that he really had been dead all along.

Then the ground shifted under his feet.

"What was *that*?" he asked.

"The *Kethili*?" Brewer said. He didn't sound certain, and he peered over the side. "No, they're still at it, but they're not . . . Oh, shit."

The ground moved again, like an earthquake, but slow, rocking once, then resettling. "What?" Truly asked. He hurried to Brewer's side.

Brewer pointed down past the battleground of the gods. The river had overrun its banks and kept rising, to the point that fast water—water that looked like it was being shot out of a high-pressure water cannon—was ramming against the base of the rocks that made up Smuggler's Canyon, tearing away the earth beneath them and even chewing up chunks of the rock itself. It carried trees, cars, and rocks in its current, and smashed those against the rocks, too, helping to break them down. It was erosion at high speed, and it was shaking what had seemed, only moments ago, a stable platform.

"The river," Brewer said. "We really are fucked."

"That's not good."

"What is it?" Ginny asked.

Truly explained briefly. "We need to get down from here."

"What about my father? What about the *Kethili*?"

"Unless we can come up with a way to stop them, it's only going to get worse up here. And everywhere else there's a river. *Kethili-cha* seems to be having her way, and it doesn't look like *Kethili-anh* can stop her. He needs . . . I don't know, reinforcements."

Ginny released her father and stood up, taking another look down at the *Kethili*. "James, I might know a way to reach my father."

"How?"

"It'll mean interrupting them."

"The *Kethili*? That's crazy."

"It's suicide," Brewer said. "I tried to shoot one of them and she nearly took my head off."

"I know the risks," she said. "But he's my father. If there's any chance at all, I've got to try it."

She told the others her idea. Truly listened, impressed at its audacity if nothing else.

It didn't stand much chance of working, he was sure. But she wasn't going to be dissuaded, and the sooner she tried it the sooner they'd be able to put some distance between themselves and that river.

A few minutes later, they had worked their way down to the level on which the *Kethili* were locked in combat, hiding behind some of the tall boulders ringing the natural amphitheater. *Kethili-cha* still had the upper hand. *Kethili-anh* looked weakened, injured, favoring his left leg and right arm. The ground at his feet was slick with blood, black in the light cast by the spells they hurled and the still-frequent lightning bolts.

Ginny gave her father's hand a squeeze and then walked out from behind the rocks alone, into the arena.

Kethili-anh was doing something with his hands, weaving a spell of some kind, but he stopped and stared at her. *Kethili-cha* did the same.

Ginny stopped, a dozen feet before *Kethili-anh*, looking directly at him, hands at her sides. "Wade," she said. "I need your help, Wade."

There was a shift in *Kethili-anh*'s posture, a loosening of the shoulders.

"It's me, Wade. Ginny. I know you recognize me."

"She's nuts," Brewer whispered. "He'll tear her to pieces."

Truly didn't answer. Ginny's courage was inspiring, even if her plan had little hope of success.

"Wade, I need you to look inside yourself. I need you to help my father, okay? He summoned you here, and he needs your help."

"That's our cue," Brewer said. He took the old man—Hollis Tupper—by the arm and started walking him around the boulder. "If they come for me, kill me."

"No problem," Truly said. He hoped it wouldn't come to that, but he kept the Colt in his hand.

Brewer and Hollis Tupper stepped into full view of the *Kethili*. Both inhuman gods turned to stare at them, *Kethili-cha*'s posture threatening and aggressive.

"Wade," Ginny said, gesturing toward Hollis. "This is my father. He brought you here. But doing that killed him." *Kethili-anh* gazed at her, then him. He might have been listening to her.

He might just as easily have been sizing her up, debating whether to eat her whole or take two bites.

"Wade, if there's anything you can do for him, please do it now. He can help him. He knows all about you."

Kethili-anh took an ungainly step toward her. Brewer brought Hollis beside her, released his arm, and left him there. She took her father's hand and held it tightly in hers. "His name is Hollis Tupper, Wade. He's studied the *Kethili* for a long time."

Kethili-cha screeched something to which *Kethili-anh* apparently took exception. She began the gathering motions that preceded throwing a spell. Before she could do so, *Kethili-anh* closed the gap between him and Hollis, and reached out, laying one many-fingered hand on Hollis's head.

Truly hoped he didn't snap it off.

Wade Scheiner felt like he was lost in an impenetrable maze. Some small part of him had been conscious through the whole encounter with *Kethili-cha*—Molly—so far, but only just. He hadn't been able to affect the outcome, and that was more terrifying, he suspected, than being entirely oblivious to the whole situation. Each blow *Kethili-anh* took hurt him, too, but he couldn't respond, couldn't react.

Then Ginny had come out from hiding, saying words that *Kethili-anh* didn't understand. *Kethili-anh*'s first impulse was to strike her down, to rid himself of the distraction with a quick blast. Wade had wanted to cry out, to plead for her life, but he didn't know how to reach the god-being that had grown inside him, taken him over, then utterly transfigured him.

He had settled for *feeling*, for trying to convey emotionally what he couldn't express verbally. *Don't hurt her. She's a friend. She can help.*

Wade heard her words—muffled, indistinct, as if he was several feet underwater listening to someone speaking to him from a boat. He saw only through *Kethili-anh*'s eyes, which reacted more to subtle differences in heat and texture than light. But he understood her, understood that the old man who was led out by another man was her father. *Kethili-anh* reacted to the old man's presence in a way that Wade didn't grasp, with a kind of almost familial warmth.

Then he got it—the old man, Hollis Tupper, had summoned the *Kethili*. Even though he had died long before his ritual took full effect, his psychic fingerprints were all over it. *Kethili-anh* and *Kethili-cha* would both look on him as something like a father figure.

Kethili-cha, apparently, was a big fan of patricide.

She prepared to strike at the old man, to blast him out of their arena and out of existence. *Kethili-anh* moved between them, shielding the old man with his body. As if in response to Wade's silent, desperate, emotional urging, *Kethili-anh* reached for the old man, cupping his head in one hand, and speaking quiet words that Wade could only get the rawest sense of.

But they worked.

The old man became aware. The patterns of his skin changed as heat flowed into his body, especially at his chest and head, as his heart and brain began to function for the first time in decades.

"Virginia," he said. "Is it really you? All grown up?"

"It's me, Daddy!"

"Hide, Virginia," he said. "It's not safe here!"

"But—"

"*Now*, child!"

She dashed off the battlefield. The old man stayed behind. *Kethili-anh* turned away from him, his attention diverted away from his foe for too long.

Kethili-cha had taken advantage of the opportunity to gather a powerful blast, drawing *kesineth*—mystical energy—from the air, the rocks, the plants, and the forgotten ones who had worshipped here, coiling it all in her hands like wool. As *Kethili-anh* turned to face her again, still somewhat off balance, she released it. It screamed through the air and landed hard, bursting into a thousand shards of power that sliced him like glass. *Kethili-anh* fell to one knee, a nauseating wave of pain washing through him—and Wade.

Behind him, the old man started to speak.

No, not speaking. He was *reading*.

With blind eyes, he read what was written on the walls in glowing pictographs. A ritual had been written in the stone, millennia ago, that not even *Kethili-anh* had been able to translate. Hollis Tupper, dead until just now, spoke the unfamiliar words in a clear, ringing tone.

Kethili-anh wasn't sure what it all meant, but he thought it would help stop *Kethili-cha*. The old man had to be protected. *Kethili-cha* threw another blast of power, intended to bypass *Kethili-anh* and strike the old man, but *Kethili-anh* threw himself into its path, taking its full brunt. This one burned; Wade thought it must be like taking a napalm bomb full-force.

Kethili-anh screamed in agony. Wade would have screamed, too, if he'd had a voice of his own to scream with.

The old man kept speaking the words on the walls, his voice rising in power.

Wade only hoped he wasn't too late.

49

ᗄﬃᘮ

Hollis Tupper shouted out words that sounded to Truly like more
of the same unintelligible language the *Kethili* spoke, except
filtered through a human throat. As he did, something about the
battleground changed. The air became thicker somehow, harder
to see through. The rain hadn't stopped, but for reasons Truly
couldn't fathom, it no longer reached the ground inside the amphitheater of rock. Some force or substance that Truly could
only think of as mystical energy filled the space around Hollis
and the *Kethili*, roiling and churning, like someone had poured
molasses in from above and it oozed all around them. This energy affected Truly's visual perception of the battle in another
way—suddenly the *Kethilis'* motions looked choppy, as if taking place under strobe lights, although the renewed fury of
their assaults kept the light steadier than it had been before.
Through the heavy air, *Kethili-cha* kept up a furious attack. She
threw three or four blasts for each of *Kethili-anh*'s. *Kethili-anh*
took the full force of them, shielding Hollis from their impact.
He was clearly weakening, her assault wearing him down little
by little.

"Truly!" Brewer shouted. "The old man needs help! Whatever he's trying to do, either he's not strong enough or it's not
good enough!"

Truly wasn't sure what he was expected to do. Hadn't he
been the one who reunited Ginny and her father? How much
had Brewer contributed to fixing the problem he and his kind
were responsible for in the first place?

He was right, though. The fight was getting more difficult to
watch, because of the increasingly strange light show effects
taking place, but also because *Kethili-anh*—who just might

have been humanity's last chance—was getting his head handed to him.

"Isn't there someone else who can help?" Ginny asked, grabbing his arm.

"We're pretty isolated here," he pointed out. Even if he'd been able to think of someone else who might be able to help, he had already discovered that he had no cell phone service here, and Ginny had told him the same thing.

He watched Hollis shouting out his ritual now, his voice booming through the blasts and rock falling and rain and thunder and the roar of the river and the shifting of many tons of stone, and Truly realized that maybe there was something he could do after all. *An impossibly long shot,* he thought, *but the impossible, like that old gray mare, ain't what she used to be.*

He flipped open his phone. The signal was clear and strong. How could that have changed so dramatically?

Shaking his head, he dialed Robb Ivey. Trying to understand magic was pointless. Better to just go with it.

"Truly?"

"Listen, Robb, there's something going on here. Don't make me explain it more than once. Just get everyone in our group on the phone."

"Everyone? Like a conference call? Do you know what's going on, Truly? We're just about to evacuate. The San Francisco Bay is rising faster than—"

"I know, Robb. It's important, okay? Just get them on the phone. Johnny and Bernard and Maha and Simon and . . . get them all. Anyone you can reach."

Robb seemed to grasp his urgency. "Okay, hang on a minute."

Truly hung on. Ginny watched the battle with her fists clenched just below her chin. At some point Brewer had drawn his gun again. Truly had no idea what he intended to use it for, unless he thought that if things turned worse he could kill Hollis Tupper again.

Truly didn't think that would help. Hollis was, he believed, still dead. The fact that he stood there reciting a ritual inscribed on stone by shamans or magicians thousands of years before his birth didn't change a thing.

"Truly?" Robb's voice came over the phone he had already almost forgotten about. "We're all here."

"Who have we got?"

"Maha, Simon, Johnny, Yannick, Eduardo, Annalise, Sergei." The whole network, if you didn't count Lawrence and Millicent, including some Truly hadn't spoken to or thought about in ages. "Now, what's going on?"

"We're trying to put things right," Truly said. "I can't go into a lot of detail." The moment came that he'd been dreading since this idea had occurred to him. He stepped out of the protective shelter of the boulders and back into the natural amphitheater. Ginny snatched at him but he shook off her grip and kept going. "You're going to hear a voice that's not mine. He's reciting a ritual. He's been repeating a lot of the same phrases, over and over, so I think you'll be able to pick up on it pretty quickly. He needs help, and I thought maybe if you all participated, from your various locations around the world, it would strengthen his efforts."

"Who is it?" Eduardo asked.

"Never mind that, you're just going to have to trust me. It's more important than anything you've ever done. Any of you." Walking onto the battleground took unexpected effort. The air was as dense as it looked. The only thing he had to compare it to was trying to move through deep water, but water that weighed several times more than usual. It offered resistance, slowed him down. He was almost surprised to find that he could breathe.

"That's—"

"It's presumptuous as all hell. Shut up and listen." He held the phone near Hollis Tupper's mouth. Hollis continued reading the glowing images with unseeing eyes and reciting his meaningless phrases with a voice he hadn't used in more than twenty years.

Kethili-anh and *Kethili-cha* struggled. They had closed on each other and fought hand-to-hand now, hitting and clawing with those big hands, biting and kicking. *Kethili-cha* got her hands around *Kethili-anh*'s throat, her claws digging into the flesh, drawing blood. Mystical energies swirled around them. Truly sweated; it was oven-hot now; raindrops sizzled when they hit the magically charged air.

He tried to listen to the phone, but up close the screeching and hooting and clicking of the *Kethili* language was nearly deafening, and the other noises hadn't abated. He thought, after Hollis had worked through the ritual phrasings a couple more times, that other voices joined in.

Kethili-cha **was surprised that** *Kethili-anh* **had held out against** her this long. She had always been the stronger of them, more powerful than any of her six siblings, ever since they had been born from nothingness and created the world from their bodies and blood.

The world had been a failed experiment, one that had outlived its usefulness. The next world, she would create by herself, with no help from her deceased, unlamented family.

All she had to do first was finish off *Kethili-anh*.

But that noise . . .

Words, the same ones that had imprisoned her and *Kethili-anh* the first time, rolled off the walls, bounced from stone to stone, filled her head. They made it hard to concentrate on what needed to be done. She held *Kethili-anh*'s throat in her hands. She smelled the rich tang of his blood. She squeezed. His fists pounded against her scales, weakening with every minute. He tried to gather *kesineth*, to strike her with another magical missile, but he couldn't bring his hands together in the right manner.

The world shifted beneath her feet.

Not from the river battering the rocks; she had been aware of that as soon as it had begun. Part of her was aware of every river, all running strong, running fast, taking lives, running red with the blood of hated humanity.

This was something different—something *within* her. She had faded for a moment, blinked out of existence and then returned.

The ritual? Were the old human's words having their intended effect?

Voices, not just the old one's but others, from faraway places, rose and repeated the words, and with their increased volume and energy and effort, she felt the world shift, blink, and vanish again, and this time she knew it was her; she had gone away and returned, and if she didn't bring a close to this fast, it would be too late.

The first step was to destroy her brother, and she intended to do that now. She increased the pressure on his throat, changed her position so she could get more of her arm around it. A twist, a tear, and his head would separate from his jerking, gushing, lifeless corpse. She began the twisting motion, telling *Kethili-anh* what she was about as she did it.

"Have at it," he told her with a pathetically weak voice, "because I am unable to stop you. Just know, sister, that there is no good in your cause, no worth in your effort."

She almost laughed as she began the final killing move.

Other voices had joined with Ginny's father's. Together they drowned out the thunder, the river, the rain. They clattered and roared through Smuggler's Canyon as if they issued from the rocks themselves, or were shouted out by the images drawn there. She chewed on her lower lip, stamped her feet. This *had* to work.

But *Kethili-cha* had the advantage, that was clear, and *Kethili-anh*—*Wade*, she told herself, *that's Wade inside there somewhere*—appeared to be breathing his last. *Kethili-cha* had him down, on his knees, and she remained strong while he was clearly struggling just to stay partially upright. She corkscrewed his neck in a way that looked painful, and quite likely fatal.

Ginny had done what she could. Truly had done his best. Even the army officer, Brewer, had tried. Her father kept trying, kept repeating the ritual phrases, and for a few moments she had thought they would do the trick. Both *Kethili* had flickered in and out of visibility, like one of those power failures when the lights blink out and back on so fast you're not really even sure they went away, but then you look and your digital clock is blinking 12:00.

They were out of ideas. Out of options. If Wade and *Kethili-anh* couldn't save themselves now, then all was lost. The rain would keep falling; the rivers would continue to rise. Humanity would be blotted out.

But a new player appeared on the battleground, someone

she had never expected to lay eyes on. For a moment, she didn't understand what she was seeing. She blinked, wiped rain and tears from her eyes, looked again. Yes, there was a man, slight, pale, bald. Then she recognized him.

"That's Byrd!" she shouted.

"Who?"

"Byrd McCall! Wade's friend. Molly's brother." She had explained to Truly who Wade, Molly, and Byrd were as they climbed into the canyon.

"Isn't he . . . ?"

"Wade said he died. Today, I guess, or yesterday . . . I have no idea what time it is."

"So there's a dead man getting involved now. *Another* dead man."

"That's how it looks."

"Fucking great," Brewer said. "That's just what we need."

50

Vance Brewer had had enough of dead guys to last him a lifetime.
For that matter, during his life, he had recently realized, he had
spent more hours with Hollis Tupper—postmortem—than
with any other single individual. No wife, ever. No kids.
Mother dead, father playing canasta or casino or Texas hold
'em with the other codgers and grab-ass with the widows at an
old folks' home in Indianapolis. He hadn't been able to let anyone get really close to him, because any close friends might
wonder what he did with his days and way too many of his
nights, and that old cliché was ever so true, after all: if I told
you, I'd have to kill you.

So he had passed his adult life with Hollis Tupper and a suc-
cession of acquaintances, drinking buddies, football buddies,
whores, and strangers.

Now, finally, Hollis Tupper had succeeded in bringing back
the *Kethili*, as he had promised so many years ago, and when it
turned out to be a clusterfuck of genuinely legendary proportions, he was trying—still postmortem—to put things right.
With, apparently, the assistance of everyone in Truly's calling
circle.

And it wasn't good enough.

But look, Ginny Tupper had cried, enthusiastically enough
to stomp all over Brewer's last tiny shred of nerve, there's another fucking dead guy!

Byrd McCall—his ghost, anyway, his form possessing
about as much substance as a politician's promise—appeared
from nowhere and stormed up to the grunting, struggling *Kethili* and stopped with his little fists on his semi-opaque hips. He
glared like a pissed-off televangelist about to rip into the flock
for not emptying their wallets fast enough. Then he spoke.

"You took my sister!" he shouted.

For a ghost, the guy had a hell of a voice. It boomed from him like a cannonball, bounced up one side of the stones, echoed back from the other.

Kethili-cha stopped what she was doing, which Brewer believed was ripping off *Kethili-anh*'s head, a little at a time.

"Nobody hurts my sister!" Byrd screamed. "Give her back!"

Kethili-cha gave *Kethili-anh*'s head a last, sudden jerk and hurled him aside, neck still more or less intact but with the flesh torn and bleeding heavily. She did that thing with her ugly hands, scooping up something from the air, and Brewer had seen that happen enough times to know whoever was on the receiving end when she hurled it was going to be hurting.

On the receiving end this time was Byrd McCall. His ghost, anyway.

An enormous blast sent rock flying thirty or forty feet into the air and coming down again, rain of a different, harder kind. A cloud of dust.

At the end of it, the ghost hadn't budged. "You let her go!" he insisted again.

There was something different about him now, though. Brewer could still see through him, at least a little. On the other side of Byrd, *Kethili-anh* tried to get back onto his feet, but he was weak, barely able to support himself.

But now Byrd glowed, like the images painted on the walls. A pure white light seemed to emanate from somewhere inside him.

It wasn't just him, either. It came from the old man now, from Hollis. Even Truly's cell phone glowed. Light beamed from Hollis and the phone over to Byrd, and across open space to the dozens of petroglyphs, linking them all in an insubstantial chain that brightened the killing field to near-daylight levels.

Kethili-cha blasted Byrd again. This time, the magical bomb didn't even reach him; his glow rebuffed it.

The voices chanting the ritual grew louder, and as they did, Hollis and Byrd glowed brighter. The pictographs almost seemed to have burst from the walls, floating free inches from their former locations.

Trying to read *Kethili-cha*'s expressions and body language

was like trying to communicate with a praying mantis or a
cockroach, but Brewer would have sworn that she was—for
the first time—afraid.

Then Byrd did something that changed everything, that
made it clear why she might fear him.

He raised his hands, moving them around each other rapidly, and his glow grew, extended, burst toward her. She flew
back from the blow as if it had solidity and weight. If not for
the overbearing chanting, Brewer thought he might have heard
the impact when it hit her.

She regained her feet, wiping the back of her hand across
her lips in disturbingly human fashion and glaring at Byrd with
undisguised—if alien—hatred.

"I told you to give her back," Byrd said. "And I meant it."

She stared at him, took a swing at him with one of those
huge, clawed hands. He blocked it with a hand encased in armor made of light so white it hurt Brewer's eyes, returned it
with a jab of his own. This one slammed home, made her squeal
in pain.

Watching Hollis, Brewer noticed that he moved, ever so
slightly, when Byrd did, his arms swinging a little when Byrd
threw a punch, his feet shuffling when Byrd took a step. The
glow within him echoed Byrd's, or vice versa. The two were
clearly linked in some significant fashion.

Then he saw *Kethili-cha* notice it, too. He could tell by the
cock of her head toward Hollis as she feinted at Byrd. Maybe
Brewer was learning to read her, after all.

The import of her noticing struck him almost physically.

He shoved past Ginny and ran out onto the stone floor. He'd
seen the difficulty Truly had moving through the almost vis-
cous air, but something—maybe the glow shared by Byrd and
Hollis, or the ever-louder chant from Hollis and the phone and
the drawings on the walls—had lightened it, and he barely felt
a difference when he entered the miasma of light and heat that
was the battlefield. The air smelled like scorched copper.

As he ran, *Kethili-cha* turned her attention away from Byrd,
who continued to rock her with one glowing bolt of light after
another. Brewer saw her gathering for another assault, saw her
raise the sparking, amorphous energy mass, and he put on a final burst of speed.

He had spent his adult life with Hollis Tupper. Using the man, many would have said. But also protecting him. That was his job, his mission, his duty. Protect the old man, he had been told, and he had done so without question or complaint.

Kethili-cha threw her missile.

Brewer lunged.

Protect.

"Brewer!"

The soldier hurtled between Hollis Tupper and *Kethili-cha*, blocking the mystical blast just before it hit the old man. It crashed into Brewer instead, full on. The shock wave blew Truly onto his ass. The phone jumped from his hand and skidded across the rock, and Truly tried to reach for it, but it was beyond his grasp, and Brewer was . . .

Brewer was *coming apart*, flesh and muscle and organ and bone and cartilage and tissue and blood all driven to the stone floor, coating the phone, coating the floor, coating Truly on the periphery of the spray. Brewer was like a water balloon hitting the sidewalk, except that a water balloon had fewer parts.

And Truly realized it didn't matter if he held the phone close to Hollis's mouth, because the chanting had taken on its own life, and it had to be helping because . . .

It *had* to be helping because Byrd's ghost was four feet off the ground now, pummeling *Kethili-cha* with one glowing fisted blow after another, and *Kethili-anh* was back in it. *Kethili-anh* was on his feet again, and he was bigger than he had been before, bigger than *Kethili-cha* now, and he snatched magic right out of the air and smashed it down on her, using mystical energy like so many whips or clubs or maces. The chant roiled through the amphitheater and Byrd and *Kethili-anh* beat *Kethili-cha* mercilessly, and even though Truly couldn't understand what she said, there was no hiding the fact that she was afraid, terrified, and she was . . .

She was *shrinking*, that's what it was. *Kethili-anh* had grown but she was smaller, not much bigger than Byrd now, and getting smaller all the time.

And one other thing.

The images from the pictographs, designs someone had

painted on rock walls ten thousand years ago or more, had come off those walls. Glowing with the same white heat as Byrd and Hollis, warriors on horseback and others wearing masks frightening or comical or spiritual or all three at once; a tall, elongated man with his face painted half-white and half-black, headless men holding spears and bows and shields—all had stepped out of the walls and surrounded *Kethili-cha*, tearing at her, stabbing her, pummeling her, and her wails of pain and terror reached to the heavens.

Byrd was screaming, too, something that Truly couldn't make out. *Kethili-anh* screamed. Ginny was probably screaming. Only Truly was silent, sitting there on the wet ground, soaked in rain and Vance Brewer's bodily fluids, bits of skin and brain and bone stuck to him like sand at the beach.

Kethili-cha blinked out once, twice, and then was gone.

Kethili-anh raised his voice in what sounded like a roar of triumph. Then he flickered, too.

The rain fell again, no longer blocked by magic or heat or whatever had kept it from reaching the ground within the little clear space. In the sudden downpour, Truly couldn't see anyone or anything for several seconds. He stood, extended his arms, let the rain wash him clean.

Then it tapered off.

A few drops.

Nothing.

The rain had stopped.

Wade Scheiner sat up on the puddled rock floor, naked and trem-bling from the cold and wet. The motion made his head screech in pained protest, his stomach lurch. He managed to raise a fist to his mouth, belched into it, fought to keep from vomiting.

Slowly, he turned his agonized head. A man he didn't know stood watching him, water running off his raincoat. Another man—Hollis Tupper—stood near him, hands limp at his sides, eyes blank, mouth hanging open. Ginny Tupper crossed the floor toward her father. All of them were blessedly silent. The silence was healing, church silence, Sunday afternoon in the park silence, the silence of a quiet street on a hot summer day.

Molly was beside Wade, lying on the ground, also naked.

Still. Dead. He didn't have to check her to know that, which was good because that much effort might finish him off, too. He could see that there was no breath in her, no heartbeat, that her eyes, eyes that had seen so much of what he had seen during their lives, stared up at nothing, just as blind as Ginny's father's.

He remembered some of what had happened, although it had all been filtered through *Kethili-anh*'s senses. He remembered the long battle against *Kethili-cha*. He remembered that he had been losing. He remembered Byrd's ghost joining the fray, and making the difference. *As usual,* he thought. That was Byrd, protector to the end. Past the end.

He laughed when he remembered Byrd's last words. After all the books, all the lines he had tried out on his nurses and friends, his last words—uttered well after his death—had been "Nobody fucks with my sister!"

That was Byrd.

Ginny reached her father and threw her arms around his lifeless form, and as if the contact finished the job that nothing else could, he collapsed. She lowered him gently to the ground, sat down with him, softly weeping. And yet, when she caught Wade's eye, she was smiling, at the same time.

He returned her smile. Gave the slightest nod of his head—as much as he could bear.

"Yeah," he said, answering a question no one had asked. "I think it's over."

EPILOGUE

⊐╫⊏

James Livingston Truly didn't fly straight back to Washington.
Instead, he went to Mission Viejo with Ginny. She wanted to
tell her mother in person what had become of her father—why
he had vanished all those years ago, why he hadn't been in
touch, and what he had accomplished, heroically, two decades
after his death. Marguerite Tupper turned out to be a remarkable woman, lively and quick-witted, with an intellect as fierce
as her daughter's and a lack of patience for stupidity that made
Truly smile when he saw it in action. They spent a week in
California, during which Ginny took him to Disneyland—entertaining, but somehow not as magical as he might once have
found it, given recent events—and Hollywood, the beach, cold
and windy on a November afternoon, and what seemed an endless landscape of malls and cars and businesses, many adver-
tising "after-flood sales." The part he liked best was sitting in
their old Orange County home, talking about who Hollis had
been while he lived.

During that week, which culminated in a slightly early
Thanksgiving dinner that left Truly genuinely satiated, he
didn't call Ron Loesser. He didn't know if he still had a job.
The one time he called his father, he changed the subject when
the topic came up, and ended the call before it cycled around
again.

He would confront Ron face-to-face, and work out a re-
newal of Moon Flash. If Willard Carsten Truly still had the pull
he seemed to, there wouldn't be any problem. If there was a
problem? Well, he was a young man, and the world had other
challenges to offer. Maybe none as dramatic as the last, but
he'd done all right with that one. He had accomplished something that not many people ever could—or would ever know

about. But he knew. He would meet whatever came up on his own terms, out of his father's shadow at last, casting a shadow of his own.

A long one.

And maybe not a solo one, since Ginny would accompany him to Washington.

"He's kind of a strange fellow," Marguerite Tupper whispered. They stood in the upstairs hallway of the Tupper house. Truly had stepped outside to enjoy the morning air before a taxi came to whisk them to John Wayne Airport, but they kept their voices low in case he came back in unexpectedly. "Are you sure about this?"

"As sure as I'm going to be, Mom," Ginny said. "I guess he's a little odd. In case you hadn't noticed it, so's the Tupper family. At this point I think normal would bore me to tears."

"But Washington is a long way off."

"No place is that far by air anymore. It's not like you'd have to drive out to see me, or vice versa. We'll probably see each other more than when I was in school or doing my fieldwork. You'll be sick of me in no time." Ginny was stretching the truth a bit—during college she had tried to get home for every holiday and many weekends, and she couldn't see making the trip from D.C. that often.

"But what are you going to do there?"

"Whatever I can. I'm sure there are opportunities at the Smithsonian. Maybe I'll get something there, or one of the other museums. There are a ton of them there. It's all just to help pay bills while I work on the book, anyway."

Her mother closed her eyes, rubbing her forehead as if she had suddenly developed a headache. "You're still determined to go ahead with that?"

"Don't you think he would have wanted me to?"

"Why didn't you just ask him?" Ginny had told her mother that she planned to edit her father's papers, letters, and notes into a book. She wouldn't tell everything about the *Kethili*— she, Truly, and Wade had agreed to keep those deatils to themselves—but she would tell some. Enough to let the world know that Hollis Tupper had been a remarkable man who had made important anthropological discoveries, even if they had gone uncelebrated all this time.

Ginny ignored the question. "It'll be a great book. It'll restore his reputation, and maybe start making one for me."

"You running off to Washington with a spy boyfriend will take care of that, I'm sure."

Ginny sighed. "Mom, I don't know if anything romantic is going to happen there. It hasn't yet. Maybe it will, maybe not."

"It seems like you should be able to tell by now," her mother said. "How men feel is usually not a big mystery."

Ginny stepped closer and enveloped her mother in a firm hug, breathing in the familiar scents of White Shoulders and Prell. Sometimes there was just no talking to the woman. Ginny had already solved the central mystery of her life. If a few smaller mysteries cropped up now and then, what was the harm in letting them play themselves out?

She was as curious as her mother or anyone else to find out the answer to that question, and any others her future might bring.

But she had been patient before. She could be again. She had precious few virtues to fall back on, but that one she had in spades.

Truly banged the front door open, clomped to the foot of the stairs. "Cab's here!" he called. "You ready, Gin?" He had taken to calling her that sometimes, although she hated it, just to tweak her.

She squeezed her mom again, then released her. Tears showed in the older woman's eyes. "I'll be right down, Jim!" she called, turnabout being, as they said, fair play.

"I'll get the bags."

With her mother following, Ginny went down the stairs, into the block of sunlight streaming through the front door, into a tomorrow that was just like everybody else's: unknown, uncertain, filled with light and darkness and hope and wonder. Maybe especially that last.

Whatever happened or didn't happen between her and Truly, Ginny knew one thing for sure. She and Truly had both touched wonder, on a scale that set them apart from most people. A scale that might, she reasoned, leave them lonely if they couldn't share it with each other.

On the flip side, what if they could top it?

At the foot of the stairs, she met Truly, just emerging from the guest room with a suitcase in his right hand. She slipped her right hand into his left, gave it a squeeze, and walked with him, hand in hand, into the light.

He walked with a cane now. The doctors couldn't say how long he would need one, and they couldn't figure out what had done the damage that required it. Wade didn't try to explain it to them. They had enough on their hands anyway, treating the thousands of people injured by the Rio Grande's flooding. Hundreds of others had died. Property damage, in El Paso alone, was reportedly in the billions of dollars. On the other side of the line, in Juárez, because of the substandard housing throughout much of the city, the death toll was far worse.

Whatever his physical problems, Wade considered them minor compared to what others were suffering. A slight limp, pain in his joints, sometimes a ringing in his ears. Various lacerations and abrasions. He was the lucky one.

Franklin Carrier had invited him to the office of the *Voice of the Borderlands*—the temporary office in a big stone house on Yandell, up the hill from downtown. The old one on Montana had been flooded out, the building condemned. It was due to be torn down, Frank said, and they had salvaged whatever equipment and furniture they could and brought it to the place on Yandell.

He walked into the downstairs parlor that served as Frank's office. Frank indicated a chair, and Wade happily sat down.

"Thanks for coming, Wade," Frank began. His collar button was open, tie yanked away from it, shirtsleeves rolled up over forearms corded with muscle. Just the way Molly had described him, Wade thought with a quick grin.

"Not a problem. I seem to have a lot of time on my hands these days."

Frank tapped a small stack of paper on top of his desk. "I've read your story. It's fine. Fine work. Not that I'd expect any less—I've been an admirer of your work for a long time, your broadcast work as well as the all too rare print pieces. You know I wanted Molly to do this story."

"I know." Frank had told him that the first time they had spoken, several days after the flood. That was how people measured time these days—before the flood, or after the flood. "I wish she had."

"Me too. But you know, people will be interested in your take on it. And it's a fascinating story—almost unbelievable in spots, but I think the standard of believability changes during wartime. Nobody who hasn't been there knows what it's really like, and anybody who has been knows that the former version of reality doesn't quite cut it."

"Something like that," Wade said.

"Here's the thing, Wade. I appreciate you writing this for us. Appreciate it more than I can say. We were struggling financially before the flood, but after, with the expense of replacing lost equipment, Molly's death, a couple of other staffers having had to relocate . . . well, I wasn't sure how we'd be able to continue, even with our insurance. But we did some damn good coverage during the flood and its aftermath. Sure, it was online, but it came from the *Voice* and people knew it, and the first issue we printed afterward sold out in an hour. We went back to press, and sold out again the next day. That kind of response, and having your exclusive story—those are the things that'll get us back on our feet. We'll miss Molly like hell, but she would have wanted us to do whatever it took, right?"

"I know she would."

"That's what we're trying to do. Whatever it takes. I know this is a huge thing to ask, and I'm fully prepared for you to say no. But would you consider a staff job?" Frank held up one hand. "Don't answer yet. Here's the deal. You'll cover environmental issues. You'll get to write opinion pieces—a regular column, if you want. I know you and Byrd used to be big-time river rats, so if you want to do something like travel around to a bunch of rivers, look at what's happened to them since the flood, what condition they were in before, report on what might be done to alleviate any negative impacts caused by man or rain . . . All I'm saying is that I want you to cover the beat that you're interested in, whatever it might be. It's free-range journalism. You don't get that in TV."

"You sure don't," Wade agreed.

Frank wrote something on a slip of paper, shoved it across

the desk. "There's a salary offer. Probably a tenth of what CNN paid you, if that. But Oscar's looking to shift his priorities a bit, and if you stay for a few years we can work out some kind of profit sharing or shared ownership deal for you."

Wade left the piece of paper on the desktop.

"CNN's paying me full retirement," he said. "And I have a lot set aside. So money isn't a big issue for me."

"One more thing, then," Frank said. "When we got stuff out of the old building, one of the pieces of furniture we were able to salvage was Molly's desk. It was fine, completely intact. If you'd like to use it . . ."

"That would be good." Wade would miss Molly and Byrd every day of his life. He wished they hadn't had to destroy *Kethili-cha* to stop her, or that destroying her hadn't meant killing Molly. He would always regret that, although he couldn't regret helping defeat the bitch-goddess who had possessed her.

Maybe sitting at her desk, practicing real journalism for a change, would be the therapy he needed. He was sick of TV anyway, tired of fame, bored with flying in and standing in front of a camera and flying out. He needed to do some real reporting.

Frank watched him expectantly.

Wade smiled, took the piece of paper, opened it up.

"Cut it in half," he said, "and you've got a deal."

They shook hands to seal it. Wade rose, bringing a hand in front of his mouth to disguise the fact that he was unexpectedly choked up. That happened a lot, these days. It would probably continue to.

Frank offered to show him around the office, but Wade declined. "Just show me where Molly's desk is," he said. "That'll be enough for now."

Frank showed him. Wade put his scarred hands on the wooden surface and tried to feel her presence. At Byrd's house, he had found the blade end of the broken oar Byrd had kept in his hospital room. He had carved Byrd's and Molly's names into it, and planted it at the edge of the natural amphitheater at Smuggler's Canyon. They would have headstones in an El Paso cemetery, once the stonemasons caught up with the backlog, but to Wade, the oar was the real monument, the one that most honestly marked the passing of his two best friends.

The next monument—writing stories that mattered—that would be the hard one.

His friends, however, would have expected nothing less.

After sitting at Molly's desk for a while, he left the house on Yandell and drove higher up the hill, high enough to get a view of the river channel. Soon the sun would go down, beyond New Mexico and California, past the continent's edge, and the river would flow through the darkness, through the night and the day and all the nights and days that followed, more eternal and everlasting than the mountains it carved or the deserts it fed. The span of any human life was a single drop of water in the river's depths, and mattered as much to the river as that single drop, and no more.

Byrd and Molly had been the exceptions to that rule—and, Wade supposed, so was he. Once, for a brief instant, the river had known them. It would not forget them.

And Wade? Wade would remember Molly, and Byrd, and of course the river, always and forever.